The
MX Book
of
New
Sherlock
Holmes
Stories

Part IX – 2018 Annual
(1879-1895)

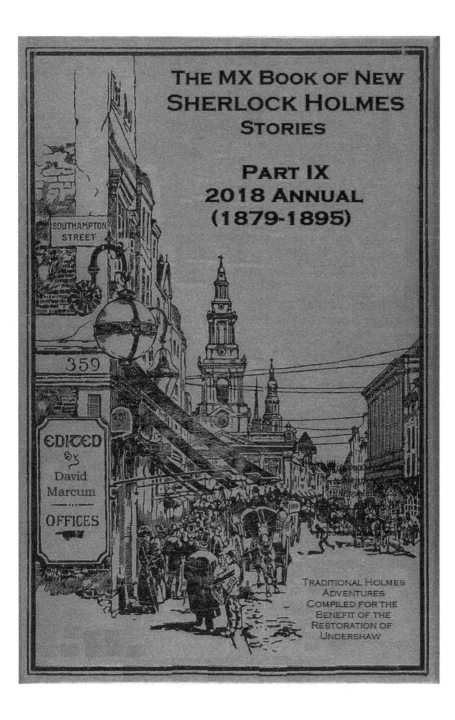

THE MX BOOK OF NEW
SHERLOCK HOLMES
STORIES

PART IX
2018 ANNUAL
(1879-1895)

SOUTHAMPTON
STREET

359

EDITED
BY
David
Marcum

OFFICES

TRADITIONAL HOLMES
ADVENTURES
COMPILED FOR THE
BENEFIT OF THE
RESTORATION OF
UNDERSHAW

ISBN Hardback 978-1-78705-281-9
ISBN Paperback 978-1-78705-280-2
ePub ISBN 978-1-78705-282-6
PDF ISBN 978-1-78705-283-3

Published in the UK by
MX Publishing
335 Princess Park Manor, Royal Drive,
London, N11 3GX
www.mxpublishing.co.uk

David Marcum can be reached at:
thepapersofsherlockholmes@gmail.com

Cover design by Brian Belanger
www.belangerbooks.com and *www.redbubble.com/people/zhahadun*

CONTENTS

Introductions

Adventures

(Continued on the next page . . . .)

(Continued on the next page . . . .)

The following can be found in the companion volume
The MX Book of New Sherlock Holmes Stories
Part X – 2018 Annual (1896-2016)

These additional Sherlock Holmes adventures
can be found in the previous volumes of
The MX Book of New Sherlock Holmes Stories

(Continued on the next page . . . .)

PART III: 1896-1929

PART IV – 2016 Annual

(Continued on the next page . . . .)

(Continued on the next page . . . .)

PART VI – 2017 Annual

(Continued on the next page . . . .)

PART VII – Eliminate the Impossible: 1880-1891

PART VIII – Eliminate the Impossible: 1892-1905

(Continued on the next page . . . .)

COPYRIGHT INFORMATION

Pastiches: The Third Leg
of the Sherlockian Stool
by David Marcum

In his introduction to *The Return of Solar Pons* (1958), Edgar W. Smith, a legendary member of the Baker Street Irregulars, wrote:

> There is no Sherlockian worthy of his salt who has not, at least once in his life, taken Dr. Watson's pen in hand and given himself to the production of a veritable Adventure. I wrote my own first pastiche at the age of fourteen, about a stolen gem that turned up, by some unaccountable coincidence, in the innards of a fish which Sherlock Holmes was serving to his client in the privacy of his rooms; and I wrote my second when I was fifty-odd, about the definitive and never-more-to-be-seen-in-this-world disappearance of Mr. James Phillimore in a matrix of newly-poured cement.

I would love to read these stories, composed by this man whose undisputed efforts to promote the admiration of Sherlock Holmes helped to make the world's first consulting detective one of the most recognized figures on the planet. The essay "How I First Met Edgar W. Smith" by one of the BSI founders, William S. Hall, *(Baker Street Journal*, June 1961) describes an occasion in which Hall, Christopher Morley, and Smith met in 1939 for lunch. After a period of Morley asking several tough Canonical questions, *"[Smith] was accordingly dubbed, with the help of an additional whiskey-and-soda, a full-fledged member on the spot. Since then I have always rated the meeting of Morley and Smith second in importance only to that of Stanley and Livingstone. The rest we all know about. Almost from that moment on, Edgar* was *The Baker Street Irregulars, and that includes most of the Scion Societies as well."*

Smith was a tireless advocate for the promotion of Holmes, and there are many who know much more about him than I who can provide specific examples. It's commonly known that he was the founder and first editor of *The Baker Street Journal*, and is still listed to this day on the title page of every issue. He edited the first "definitive" text of The Canon – if such a thing can actually exist – and that version, which was published in three amazingly handsome volumes in the early 1950's, is still being used today by the Easton Press for their beautiful leather-

1

bound editions. He had an open-door policy that allowed and encouraged others to join the fun and take the spotlight, such as when he had noted Sherlockian Vincent Starrett write the foreword to the aforementioned definitive Canon, instead of doing so himself. He had the same inclusive spirit in his cornerstone volume *Profiles by Gaslight* (1944), an amazing collection of Holmesian essays. (An amusing side-note to those who have one of the 1944 hardcover editions: The page numbers proceed normally and sequentially, until one is in the middle of the Vincent Starrett contribution, "The Singular Adventures of Martha Hudson". This essay runs from pages 202 through 229. As one proceeds, the pages are numbered as one would expect: *218, 219, 220.* And then, where one would expect to simply see page *221*, Smith adds a letter, making it *221B.* Then the next page is *222.* That single added letter shows just how dedicated Mr. Smith was to the World of Holmes.)

Smith's contributions are innumerable. Yet, with all of his support of both The Canon and Sherlockian Scholarship, the first two legs of the Sherlockian stool, he didn't forget the third: *Pastiche.*

As shown above, when referring to *pastiche*, Smith says *"There is no Sherlockian worthy of his salt who has not, at least once in his life, taken Dr. Watson's pen in hand and given himself to the production of a veritable Adventure."* Strong words from the man who shaped the Baker Street Irregulars. And words that should not be forgotten or swept aside or spoke of, save with a gibe and a sneer, in the pursuit of the scholarly side of things.

In that same paragraph from that same introduction, Smith goes on to write:

> The point that does concern me – and it is a point that all of us who are tempted to emulation should bear in mind – is that the writing of a pastiche is compulsive and inevitable: it is, the psychologists would say, a wholesome manifestation of the urge that is in us all to return again to the times and places we have loved and lost; an evidence, specifically, of our happily unrepressed desire to make ourselves at one with the Master of Baker Street and all his works – and to do this not only receptively, but creatively as well.

There are several important points to be noted from these short passages. To be "worth one's salt" is historically assumed to refer to the practice of paying Roman soldiers enough wages that they could buy salt, necessary for both survival itself, as well as for tasks such as curing meat. If a soldier wasn't effective in his job, he wasn't paid. The phrase has come down through the years to mean more generally that one must be competent, adept, and efficient to be "worth one's salt". And it was no accident that Smith began his essay in this way, for he understood, from those early days, the importance of pastiche. *"No Sherlockian worth his salt . . . ."*

Additionally, he wrote that this should be done *receptively*. For if one is truly a Sherlockian *worth his [or her] salt,* then there should be no resistance against this need to create or read additional adventures of Mr. Sherlock Holmes. It must be true. Edgar W. Smith said so.

I've long maintained, and written extensively in a number of forums, that pastiches are of supreme importance, and should receive as much credit as possible for promoting the continued and growing popularity of Sherlock Holmes. Sherlockian scholarship and speculation is a cornerstone of some people's interest in The Canon, but it can be somewhat esoteric. It is pastiche that fires the imagination of many people and serves to initially lure them to The Canon. Sherlock Holmes is recognized around the world, but how many people who admire and adore him read The Canon as their absolute first contact with him? Many, certainly, but not all. Instead, a sizeable number also encounter Holmes first in the form of pastiches – stories, films, radio and television episodes, comic books, fan-fiction – and then seek to know more about that actual Holmes Bible made up of the original (and pitifully few) sixty adventures, as brought to us by that first – but *not the only!* – Literary Agent, Sir Arthur Conan Doyle.

It's always been my contention that The Canon is the wire core of a rope, but pastiches are the strands that overlay it, giving it both thickness and strength. In other places, I've called the entire body of work, both Canon *and* pastiche, *The Great Holmes Tapestry.* It all weaves together to present a picture of the complete lives of Holmes and Watson, immensely complex and interesting. And that tapestry, with its threads of pastiches woven in and around and through the main supporting Canonical fibers, has been forming since nearly the same time when the first Canonical stories were being published.

In those earliest of days, the tendency was to parody Holmes, rather than produce true pastiches – possibly because Holmes was still new, and many of the tropes that have since become set in stone were then still in flux. However, some of those early parodies came very close indeed to having the feel of the real thing, and only a few changed words would be enough to nudge them into acceptable adventures.

In his introduction to *The Memoirs of Solar Pons* (1951), Ellery Queen presents an amazing comprehensive list that enumerates the various variations on Holmes from earlier decades, up to that time. (Richard Dannay, son of Frederic Dannay, who was half of the Literary Agent-team representing Ellery Queen, recently told me that his father's list "is truly a virtuoso, one that can't be duplicated or imitated.") It's amazing, from this distance of so many years since Queen's list was constructed, to realize just how widespread Holmes's influence was, even in those days.

I cannot say what the earliest Holmes parody or pastiche was – there is some debate on that point. It's clear from some that are on Queen's list, such as *Detective Stories Gone Wrong: The Adventures of Sherlaw Kombs* by Luke Sharp (1892), *The Adventure of the Table Foot* by "Zero" (Allan Ramsay, 1894, featuring Thinlock Bones), and the eight "Picklock Holes" stories which first appeared in *Punch* in 1893 and 1894, that the Master's influence appeared quite early.

There are numerous other Holmes-influenced stories from those early days, and more are being mined all the time. Many collections over the years have included these very valuable "lost" tales:

- *The Misadventures of Sherlock Holmes* (1944) – edited by Ellery Queen. (A most important book for any collection, with a publication history of its own that's as interesting as the contents of the book itself);
- *Sherlock Holmes in America* (1981) – edited by Bill Blackbeard. (A beautiful coffee table book of all sorts of obscure items);
- *The Game is Afoot* (1994) – edited by Marvin Kaye. (An incredible volume, with a great representation of both old and new stories);
- *As It Might Have Been* (1998) – edited by Robert C.S. Adey. (One of the first to be specifically devoted to rare old pastiches and parodies);
- *I Believe in Sherlock Holmes* (2015) – edited by Douglas O. Greene; (Truly a labor of love, with some great obscure ephemera.)
- *A Bedside Book of Early Sherlockian Parodies and Pastiches* (2015) – edited by Charles Press. (Definitely worth examining to find hidden treasures); *and*
- *The Missing Misadventures of Sherlock Holmes* (2016) – edited by Julie McKuras, Timothy Johnson, Ray Reithmeier, and Phillip Bergem. (This is a unique title,

which takes on the task of including the stories first mentioned – but not included – in Ellery Queen's *Misadventures*. I was honored to be able to bring this volume to Richard Dannay's attention, as he was previously unaware of it.)

Also, the Herculean efforts of Bill Peschel must be lauded. He has assembled six (as of this writing) massive (and very handsome) volumes of early Holmes parodies and pastiches – and I hope that he keeps going:

- *The Early* Punch *Parodies of Sherlock Holmes*
- *Sherlock Holmes Victorian Parodies and Pastiches: 1888-1899*
- *Sherlock Holmes Edwardian Parodies and Pastiches: 1900-1904*
- *Sherlock Holmes Edwardian Parodies and Pastiches: 1905-1909*
- *Sherlock Holmes Great War Parodies and Pastiches: 1910-1914*
- *Sherlock Holmes Great War Parodies and Pastiches: 1915-1919*

Initially, those early stories were created for simple amusement, with countless variations on Holmes and Watson's names that possibly seemed clever or funny in those long ago days – *Purlock Hone* and *Fetlock Bones, Dr. Poston* and *Whatsoname* – but now seem painfully like a first-grader's attempt at humor. Gradually, however, stories in the true traditional Canonical style began to appear. Vincent Starrett's "The Unique Hamlet" from 1920 is often referenced as a good early traditional pastiche. It certainly established that Holmes adventures did not have to be parodies, and that they could be presented to the public without first passing across the desk of the *first* Literary Agent, Sir Arthur Conan Doyle. In the late 1920's, a new kind of Sherlockian tale arrived, when August Derleth became Dr. Parker's Literary Agent, arranging for the publication of the first Solar Pons stories. While not actually about Holmes and Watson, these occur within Holmes's world, and are so precise in reproducing the style and substance of Holmes's adventures that they very much paved the way for additional stories using the correct format to follow.

In 1930, Edith Meiser advanced the cause of pastiche significantly. She was convinced that the Holmes adventures would be perfect for radio broadcasts. She worked out a deal with the contentious Conan

Doyle brothers, Adrian and Denis, and began to write scripts. Her efforts were rewarded when Holmes was first portrayed on NBC radio on October 20th, 1930, in a script adapted by Meiser from "The Speckled Band". In that first broadcast, Holmes was played by William Gillette, the legendary stage actor who had defined Holmes for Americans for a generation or more. The show continued after that with Richard Gordon as Holmes, and Meiser kept adapting the original stories throughout the early 1930's. Then she did a remarkable thing: She began to write pastiches of *new* cases, in the manner of the originals, and set in the original correct time period – and all of this with the approval of the Conan Doyle family. (At one point, she later sued the Conan Doyle heirs, asserting correctly that it was through her efforts that the entire perception of Holmes, by way of elevating Watson's role in the narrative, had been changed. But that's another essay for another time.) The first original story, "The Hindoo in the Wicker Basket", appeared on January 7th, 1932. Sadly, it's lost, but luckily a few of the pastiche broadcasts from that period still survive, either in their original form, or when they were re-done a few years later starring Basil Rathbone as Holmes.

Meiser deserves immense credit for setting these new stories in the correct time period, and not updating them to the 1930's. There had been several Holmes films made by that time, first silent pictures, and then with sound, such as *The Return of Sherlock Holmes* (1929) and *A Study in Scarlet* (1933). All of those were produced with contemporary settings as a matter of course – automobiles and modern clothing and all the rest. Sir Arthur would have been proud of Ms. Meiser for keeping things true. After all, he had written in his autobiography *Memories and Adventures* (1924) about his thoughts on modern aspects shown in the silent Eille Norwood films produced from 1921 to 1923, stating, *"My only criticism of the films is that they introduce telephones, motor cars, and other luxuries of which the Victorian Holmes never dreamed."* (If Sir Arthur could see what's been to damage Holmes on screen in the present day, character assassination that goes far beyond simple modernization or the use of automobiles, he'd roll over in his grave. But perhaps, spiritualist that he was, he's already seen *and* observed it. I can hear him spinning now . . . .)

The run of the show under Edith Meier's guidance ended in 1936, but it resumed without her in 1939, due to the popularity of the Basil Rathbone film, *The Hound of the Baskervilles.* By that point, the radio show was being scripted by Leslie Charteris (under the sobriquet *Bruce Taylor*) and Denis Green. However, these two continued to use the exact same format created by Meiser during her run – something that still extends its influence even to the present day.

Traditional pastiches appeared through the years – books and short stories and films and broadcasts – all serving to bring new generations to 221b Baker Street. In 1954, *The Exploits of Sherlock Holmes*, containing twelve very traditional adventures, was published. Originally appearing in *Life* and *Collier's*, these stories were presented by agents Adrian Conan Doyle and John Dickson Carr. The creative process wasn't always smooth between the two authors, but the adventures themselves are excellent.

Traditional pastiches appeared sporadically throughout the following decades, often few and far between, and difficult to find. Radio continued to present original Holmes stories into the 1950's. The Holmes television show from 1954-1955, starring Ronald Howard, was made up of mostly original stories. The film *A Study in Terror* and the related book by Ellery Queen (1965) helped to represent Holmes in the 1960's – "*Here comes the original caped crusader!*" proclaimed the posters – but pickings were slim.

Then, in 1974, an amazing thing happened. Nicholas Meyer reminded us that Watson's manuscripts were still out there, waiting to be found. Meyer had discovered some of Watson's original notes, which were published as *The Seven-Per-Cent Solution*. A film quickly followed. An amazing Holmes Golden Age began that extends to this very day.

I was fortunate to jump on this Holmes Train around the time that it was leaving the station. I discovered Holmes in 1975, when I was ten years old, with an abridged copy of the Whitman edition of *The Adventures*. I was only prompted to start reading it after seeing a piece of *A Study in Terror* on television. (It's hard to believe that the film was only ten years old then, like me.) Before I'd even tracked down or read all of The Canon, I began to absorb pastiches as well. Very soon after reading my abridged copy of *The Adventures*, I received a paperback copy of *The Seven-Per-Cent Solution*. (This was through the Reading Is Fundamental [RIF] Program. I well remember being led into the school gymnasium, where one side was set up with countless long tables covered in books – a sight that thrilled me even then, as I was always a sensible lad. I was allowed to pick two books, and I chose *The Seven-Per-Cent Solution*, with Holmes on the cover, and another that looked like a boy's adventure, something called *Lord of the Flies*. I thought from the description on the back that it might be rather like one of my favorite series, The Hardy Boys. It wasn't. But I digress.)

I must admit that, even then, with my limited Canonical awareness, (and with apologies to Nicholas Meyer), I didn't agree with all that was proposed in *The Seven-Per-Cent Solution*. A benign mistreated Professor Moriarty? Hints that The Great Hiatus didn't actually occur? No, sir. I believed The Canon, wherein the Professor was the Napoleon of crime, and the organizer of half that was evil and of nearly all that was undetected in the great city of London. And I believed that Holmes had truly fought him at Reichenbach, as reported, instead of going off to recover from his cocaine addiction in the guise of Sigerson the violinist while in pursuit of a redheaded woman.

But that whole alternative set-up between the established Canon and this new adventure forced me to start thinking, even then, in a critical Sherlockian manner – though I didn't realize it at the time. *What did I believe? And why?* This was reinforced by other seemingly contradictory adventures that I also began to encounter. I discovered William S. Baring-Gould's amazing biography, *Sherlock Holmes of Baker Street* (1962), at nearly the same time I started reading about Holmes. I also read it before I'd even found all of the actual adventures, so many of Baring-Gould's theories are hard-wired into my brain right along with The Canon – such as certain aspects of Baring-Gould's chronology, and all about brother Sherrinford, and the *first* Mrs. Watson named Constance, and a love child (Nero Wolfe) with Irene Adler. Baring-Gould related a specific version of Holmes's defeat of Jack the Ripper. But Holmes also fought a *different* Ripper to a different conclusion in *A Study in Terror*. And then it happened again just a few years later in the amazing film and book *Murder by Decree* (1979) – which, by the way, is another incredible pastiche that helped to bring people to The Canon, and also personally showed to me the Holmes that Watson describes in "The Three Garridebs" as a man with both a great brain *and* a great heart.

I began to understand that these various accounts of Holmes versus The Ripper didn't contradict one another – rather, they were simply different threads of a larger story, with each pulled out and tied off so as to present a complete picture of this-or-that particular case (or piece of a case) without causing confusion by referencing other side issues. This became very useful later as I began to discover more and more versions of some of the famous "Untold Cases", such as the Giant Rat of Sumatra. Some readers might pick one or the other of these as the only "definitive" version of this case, but I believe that, as long as the different narratives are set within the correct time period, and don't stray into some Alternate Universe or modern or science-fiction or Lovecraftian or supernatural world, then each is true. Thus, there were lots of times – each of them unique – when Holmes and Watson encountered Giant Rats. There were many Hurets that Holmes fought in 1894 – a whole nest of them, a regular *Al Qaeda* of Boulevard Assassins – instead of just one. There were a number of tobacco millionaires in London during 1895, and Holmes helped them all, while Watson lumped each of them into his notes under the protective pseudonym of "John Vincent Harden".

Back in the mid-1970's, however, before the Golden Age really began to bloom, it was still a bit hard to find good traditional Holmes stories. Nicholas Meyer's second Holmes discovery, *The West End Horror* (1976) is just about perfect – I thought so then, and still do. A few years later, I discovered *Enter the Lion* (1979) by Michael P. Hodel and Sean M. Wright, and realized that a view of Holmes's world didn't always have to be through Watson's perspective. This was reinforced when I found John Gardner's Moriarty books and Carole Nelson Douglas's histories of Irene Adler.

The 1980's and 1990's brought more and more new Holmes stories – although "more and more" is a relative term because, while there were certainly more than there used to be, they were still hard to find and hard to acquire. There were some great anthologies, including *The Further Adventures of Sherlock Holmes* (1985), *The New Adventures of Sherlock Holmes* (1987), and *The Mammoth Book of New Sherlock Holmes Stories* (1997). Master pasticheurs such as Barrie Roberts and June Thomson brought us multiple volumes of truly high quality narratives. Publishers like Ian Henry and Breese Books provided excellent stories which – with a little digging – were much more easily obtained than before. These books could now conveniently be ordered through chain bookstores and also Otto Penzler's remarkable Mysterious Bookshop. Then things became even easier with The Rise of the Internet. The world of pastiches changed forever.

I began to use the internet when I went back to school for a second degree in engineering in the mid-1990's. My tuition gave me access to the school's computer lab, where I spent a great deal of time between classes. More importantly, it allowed me to have free printing. I didn't feel any shame in printing whatever I could, literally thousands and thousands of pages, as I was being charged exorbitant fees for things like Intramural Sports, an activity in which I, as a grown-up part-time student, would never participate.

My time in the computer lab was spent searching for on-line Holmes pastiches – and there were many. I started by working my way through the links on Christopher Redmond's original mind-blowing *sherlockian.net* website, and moved on from there, printing as I went. I'm glad that I archived these stories, because many of them have long since vanished, evaporated in an ephemeral e-puff of vapor. But I have them, along with all the others I've continued to collect since then, in over one-hundred-seventy-five big fat white binders lining the floor in front of the bookshelves containing of my Holmes collection.

As I progressed in my quest to acquire more traditional Holmes stories, I was able to refine my research techniques, aided by hints provided by my incredible wife, who is a research librarian – and very tolerant of my Holmes vice. These same techniques helped me to discover and track down a previously unknown myriad of additional traditional Holmes adventures, most of which I had never before encountered. I was already an addict, but this sudden tapping-in to the mother-lode of High-Grade Holmes only fed upon itself, and I began to collect more and more. I started reading and re-reading all of it, and along the way, making notes in a binder that I took with me everywhere, containing maps, useful information, and anything that would increase my understanding and pleasure in the stories. When I finished that first pass through everything I had at that point, I found that I had constructed a rough Holmes Chronology of both Canon *and* pastiche. Since then, it's been through multiple ongoing revisions, and now it's over seven-hundred-and-fifty densely printed pages, showing the *complete* lives of Holmes and Watson, and not just what is presented in those very few five-dozen stories funneled our way by the Literary Agent. And yet, even with all of that information about the lives of Our Heroes, *it isn't enough. More! Give me more!*

In the years since the mid-1990's, the opportunity to find, read, collect, and dive into more and more Holmes adventures has only increased. Holmes has been well represented on radio. Bert Coules, who first supervised and helped write one of the best adaptations of the entire Canon for radio ever, then continued with his own set of original pastiches. Jim French, along with his able right-hand Larry Albert as Watson and John Patrick Lowrie as Holmes, guided Imagination Theatre through one-hundred-thirty original adventures (so far), as well as the only version of the complete Canon featuring the same actors as Holmes and Watson, along with each script being by written by one person, Matthew Elliott.

Over the years, pastiches on screen have included *A Study in Scarlet* (1933) with Reginald Owen, the Arthur Wontner films of the 1930's, and the Basil Rathbone films from before, during, and after World War II. The 1959 version of *The Hound* with Peter Cushing had pastiche aspects.

It was followed by the previously mentioned *A Study in Terror* and *Murder by Decree*. A new generation of movie-goers encountered *Young Sherlock Holmes* (1985). After a long wait came *Sherlock Holmes* (2009) and *Sherlock Holmes: A Game of Shadows* (2011), each with a more action-packed Holmes, and then *Mr. Holmes* in 2014. (Some were unsettled at seeing Holmes in the aforementioned action-oriented films, showing such things as bare-knuckle boxing on screen, when those had previously only been presented off-stage. Likewise, others were uncomfortable viewing an elderly Holmes in his nineties – but if one has read about the *entire* lifespan of the man, then it's only natural to see him at any age.)

On television, the 1954-1955 series with Ronald Howard – mostly pastiches – was followed by a 1979-1980 series from the same production group, this time starring Geoffrey Whitehead. Douglas Wilmer starred as an amazingly Canonical Holmes on the BBC from 1964 to 1965, and Peter Cushing followed in his footsteps in 1968. *The Hound* was televised with Steward Granger as Holmes in 1972, and again with Tom Baker in 1982 and Richard Roxburgh in 2002. The early 1980's had *Young Sherlock* (1982), two Canonical films by Ian Richardson in 1983, and *The Baker Street Boys* (1983).

Holmes's popularity was greatly increased by way of the Granada films, which ran from 1984 to 1994, featuring Jeremy Brett as Holmes, and both David Burke and Edward Hardwicke as very sensible and intelligent Watsons. As the show progressed, some of these Granada versions tended to stray into most definite pastiche territory.

Holmes's other television appearances, both Canonical and stand-alone pastiche, have included *Sherlock Holmes in New York* (1976), *Sherlock Holmes and the Masks of Death* (1984), *Hands of a Murderer* (1991), *Sherlock Holmes and the Leading Lady* (1991), *Sherlock Holmes: Incident at Victoria Falls* (1992), *The Hound of London* (1993), four films starring Matt Frewer (2000-2002), *Sherlock Holmes and the Case of the Silk Stocking* (2004) and *Sherlock Holmes and the Baker Street Irregulars* (2007).

Except for these, there has sadly been nothing about Sherlock Holmes on television since, except for a couple of shows that shamelessly trade on the use of Holmes's name but only damage his reputation. A few others, such as *House, MD*, successfully incorporated Holmesian characteristics while forgoing any attempt to replace the originals with subversive and objectionable versions. (In this current bleak period when there has been nothing about Holmes and Watson on television for ever ten years, one would be well advised to contact master dramatist Bert Coules, who has a set of scripts – complete and ready for filming – that depict Holmes and Watson in the early 1880's, the correct time period. I can't convince Bert to give me a peek, so someone is going to have to film them so I, and everyone else, will be able to know the stories!)

The discovery of new cases by Holmes and Watson only continues to increase – and that's a great thing. And it must be an indicator that people like me crave more and more adventures featuring Our Heroes. Still, I sometimes refer to myself as a missionary for The Church of Holmes, and my greatest task seems to be trying to make people respect these extra-Canonical Holmes adventures.

With ever-changing paradigms in communication and publishing, the discovery of new Holmes adventures seemingly accelerates every day. In addition to a few story collections or the rare novel presented by "mainstream" publishers, companies such as MX Publishing, Belanger Books, Wildside Press, Wessex Press, and others continue to make it possible for new "editors" of Watson's works to reach a public starving for additional narratives.

Sadly, there is sometimes an attitude from some quarters that pastiches are somehow less worthy than pure scholarly examinations of The Canon. Often pastiches are dismissed – except when a friend or celebrity has written one, in which case exceptions and are made and special dispensations granted. At other times, these new stories can only be considered "acceptable" if they are in a very pretty book from an approved list of publishers. In cases like this, where other adventures are rejected without a second glance simply because they don't have the right pedigree, the potential reader is left immensely cheated. There are some amazing Holmes tales out there – online as fan fiction, or appearing in print-on-demand books – that are as good as anything one can find *anywhere*, and with of them are better than the original Canonical stories!

In the Nero Wolfe book *The Mother Hunt* (1963), Wolfe's client asks, "But you're the best detective in the world, aren't you?"

"Probably not," he replies. "The best detective in the world may be some rude tribesman with a limited vocabulary."

Pastiches are the same way – some of the best aren't always to be found in a polished cleaned-up setting, like Wolfe in his Manhattan brownstone. Anyone who thinks so is limiting themselves and doesn't even realize it.

Thankfully, the opportunity to produce these volumes allows new adventures to be presented from all over the world, written *by* people who love the true Sherlock Holmes *for* people who love the true Sherlock Holmes. I'm incredibly thankful to be a part of it.

Pastiches are worth reading, and they're worth writing. Where do you and the Sherlockians with whom you're acquainted stand in regards to pastiches? Do you support them? Do you write them? Consider the question by way of foundational Sherlockian Edgar W. Smith's statement: As a Sherlockian, *are you worth your salt?*

As always, I want to thank with all my heart my patient and wonderful wife Rebecca, and our son, Dan. I love you both, and you are everything to me! I met my wife in 1986, when I was already settled into my habit of wearing a deerstalker everywhere as my only hat. She ended up being my friend anyway. By 1987 she was my girlfriend, and then she married me in 1988. She's put up with the deerstalker since then, and also my Holmes book collection, which has grown from a modest two or three linear feet when we met to around to around one-hundred-seventy linear feet, (based on the measurements I just made). She still goes places with me while I'm wearing the deerstalker, she keeps me company while I read and edit the stories for these books, and she's very tolerant as the Holmes books slowly devour our house, with only an occasional frantic eye-roll as the books creep ever closer . . . . My son was born into this – some kids enter a family of sports fanatics, but he joined a Holmesian Household. He's simply the best, and it turns out that he's amazing storyteller and writer. He watches and enjoys Holmes too, although with a bit less enthusiasm than his father.

I can never express enough gratitude for all of the contributors who have donated their time and royalties to this ongoing project. I'm so glad to have gotten to know all of you through this process. It's an undeniable fact that Sherlock Holmes authors are the *best* people!

The royalties for this project go to support the Stepping Stones School for special needs children, located at Undershaw, one of Sir Arthur Conan Doyle's former homes. These books are making a real difference to the school, having currently raised over $25,000, and the participation of both contributors and purchasers is most appreciated.

Next, I'd like to thank that impressive crew of people who offer support, encouragement, and friendship, sometimes patiently waiting on me to reply as my time is directed in many other directions. Many many thanks to (in alphabetical order): Bob Byrne, Mark Mower, Denis Smith, Tom Turley, Dan Victor, and Marcia Wilson.

Additionally, I'd also like to thank:

- Nicholas Meyer – As mentioned above, you started this Golden Age of Holmes. As if that wasn't enough, you also both saved *Star Trek* and nudged it in the right direction, allowing it to go – and keep going – correctly for many years to come. While it may seem as if I'm totally focused on Sherlock Holmes, I have many other interests, and one of them is *Star Trek*, which I first saw in approximately 1968, when I was three years old and a babysitter was watching an original series episode. *The Wrath of Khan* arrived in 1982, and I was blown away. I've seen it more than any other film in my life. What you brought to the *Trek* universe is reflected in every film, show, novel, and comic since then. I was thrilled to meet you at *From Gillette to Brett III* in 2011, and – even though there's no reason for you to remember it – you were very gracious when autographing all three of your Holmes books for me and answering my questions about when I could expect a fourth. Thank you very much for contributing to these volumes. Your importance to the World of Sherlockian Pastiche cannot be overstated.
- Roger Johnson – Thank you once again for showing incredible support for all of these books, and also all of the other projects. You are a scholar and a gentleman, and I'm very glad to know you. I'm looking forward to seeing you and Jean again, whenever I can arrange Holmes Pilgrimage No. 4.
- Steve Emecz – Many thanks for all that you do that helps so many people, and for the constant support for my various ideas designed to promote Mr. Holmes. It's amazing to see how far this has come in just a few years. (As of this writing, it was just about three years ago when I wrote to you about an idea that came to me in an early morning dream of editing a collection of Holmes stories. Wow.) It's always a pleasure, and I can't wait to see what we do next!
- Brian Belanger – Thanks once again for such wonderful work. I think these covers were the easiest we've assembled yet. I always enjoy when it's time for me to pick more Grimshaw paintings – luckily he painted a lot of them! – and to see how you prepare them. Excellent work, as usual!

- Derrick Belanger – I've enjoyed being your friend from the first time we ever "met" in this modern electronic sense. First came great Sherlockian discussions, and then great support as we both found our way into all of these projects. I've enjoyed every one of them, and I know that what we already have planned for the future will be wonderful as well. Many thanks!

- Ian Dickerson – In his introduction to "The Adventure of the Doomed Sextette" by Leslie Charteris and Denis Green, included in *Part IX (1879-1895)*, Ian explains how he came to be responsible for this and other long-lost scripts from the 1944 season of the Holmes radio show. Ian, I'm very grateful to you for allowing this one to appear in these volumes before it's reprinted in one of your own upcoming volumes. When I first discovered Holmes, I quickly found a number of Rathbone and Bruce broadcasts on records at the public library, and that was where I first "heard" Holmes. I can't express the thrill of getting to read these rediscovered lost treasures, having been tantalized by their titles for so long. Thank you so much!

- Larry Albert – From the enjoyment you've given me playing Watson the RIGHT way, to the time we started corresponding about my first Holmes book, and on to the incredibly helpful advice you gave as I started writing scripts, and then the efforts you've made to gather materials for use in these books: Cheers to you, sir!

- Melissa Grigsby – Thank you for the incredible work that you do at the Stepping Stones School in at Undershaw Hindhead, which I was thrilled to visit in 2016. You are doing amazing things, and it's my honor, as well that of all the contributors to this project, to be able to help.

- Michael Rhoten – Although it's likely that he'll never know that he's being thanked here, I want to express appreciation to Michael, one of my co-workers. He's a true Renaissance man, and when one of the contributors of this book asked me about early twentieth century photography, I knew that Michael could help. I presented the question to him, and within minutes he provided a wealth of information, including illustrating

15

his points by producing an actual physical camera from that era that the keeps in his office. I passed on his comments to the author with great success, and I appreciate his time and enthusiasm.

Finally, last but certainly *not* least, **Sir Arthur Conan Doyle**: Author, doctor, adventurer, and the Founder of the Sherlockian Feast. Present in spirit, and honored by all of us here.

As always, this collection has been a labor of love by both the participants and myself. As I've explained before, once again everyone did their sincerest best to produce an anthology that truly represents why Holmes and Watson have been so popular for so long. These are just more tiny threads woven into the ongoing Great Holmes Tapestry, continuing to grow and grow, for there can *never* be enough stories about the man whom Watson described as *"the best and wisest . . . whom I have ever known."*

David Marcum
January 6th, 2018
The 164th Birthday of Mr. Sherlock Holmes

Questions, comments, and story submissions
may be addressed to David Marcum at
thepapersofsherlockholmes@gmail.com

Foreword
by Nicholas Meyer

There's a cartoon, known, I suspect, to all Sherlockians. It depicts a small boy in bed, staring with consternation and dismay at the last Sherlock Holmes story in the book he holds before him. *What now?* His expression seems to signify.

I was – and am – certainly not alone in identifying with the expression on the boy's face in the cartoon, as well as the feelings to be inferred behind it. When newcomers to the Holmes Canon reach the end of the sixtieth Doyle story, feelings of bereavement typically predominate. None of this is new. It is said that when Doyle killed off Holmes – (apparently!) – in "The Final Problem", young men in London went to work wearing black mourning armbands.

Just as surely, I am neither the first nor the last to have slid into the next phase of grief: Denial. The impulse to write my own Holmes story, to continue the adventures of that unique personage and of his Boswell. Fan fiction. Whether executed as straight-faced pastiche or broad parody, there are far more Holmes adventures penned by "divers hands" than the mere sixty penned by Arthur Conan Doyle, who remained oddly obtuse about the appeal of his creation and his own relations with The Great Detective.

Yet the unconscious plays strange tricks. Doyle, who kept trying to kill off Holmes, nonetheless seems to have expressed a knowing kinship with him. Holmes tells Watson he is descended from the sister of the French artist, Vernet. Being fictional, he is descended from no one. It is Doyle himself whose ancestor was Vernet's sister. One could thus term them cousins. Further, both Doyle and his alter ego bank at the same bank. Even more suggestively – as Holmes would observe – both are offered knighthoods in the same year. Doyle's impulse was to turn his down – he felt it would identify him as an establishment patsy. He relented at the insistence of his mother, under whose thumb he spent much time. By revealing contrast, Holmes disdains his knighthood without a second thought. And we never hear a word about Holmes's mother – only his skittish distrust of women in general.

Finally, and perhaps most tellingly, when Doyle did kill off Holmes, in the memorable struggle with his nemesis, Professor Moriarty, at the picturesque Reichenbach Falls, he conveniently failed to produce the detective's corpse, thus opening the floodgates for . . . the rest of us?

All of which leaves much from for speculation, embroidery, and additional Holmesiana.

In any event, even Doyle couldn't kill off Holmes, who, as we all know, rose from the dead, not on the third day, it may be, but still, there was a resurrection that has been going on ever since – first at Doyle's hands, but later, at ours.

Although cynical folk have argued that these "ripoffs" of Holmes and Watson are conceived with mercenary motives, speaking for myself, I don't think this is either fair or true. The small boy, despairing in his bed, doesn't dream of adding to The Canon as a way of enlarging his purse. Certainly I didn't. Writing my own Holmes story was simply an itch I had to scratch. Sixty stories are not enough! That my books went into profit surprised no one more than their author.

I hazard the guess that the stories that follow were all written out of affection and enthusiasm, not with any thought of piggy-backing on the genius of Doyle for pecuniary gratification. I could be wrong. You be the judge.

Nicholas Meyer
December 2017

We Can Make the World
a Better Place
by Roger Johnson

Sherlock Holmes, as we all know, is the great English detective. Except that he was part French, his grandmother being "the sister of Vernet, the French artist". (But which Vernet? There were four generations of notable painters in the family: Antoine, Joseph, Carle and Horace. The last, born in 1789, was probably Holmes's great-uncle.)

It's little wonder, then, that the French have claimed the detective as their own, especially since his author, Sir Arthur Conan Doyle, freely admitted that an important influence on the creation of Sherlock Holmes was the great French amateur reasoner, the Chevalier C August Dupin – but Dupin was himself a fictional character, created by an American, Edgar Allan Poe. Holmes himself dismissed Dupin as "a very inferior fellow", but Conan Doyle made his position clear in "To an Undiscerning Critic":

> *As the creator I've praised to satiety*
> *Poe's Monsieur Dupin, his skill and variety,*
> *And have admitted that in my detective work,*
> *I owe to my model a deal of selective work.*
> *But is it not on the verge of inanity*
> *To put down to me my creation's crude vanity?*
> *He, the created, the puppet of fiction,*
> *Would not brook rivals nor stand contradiction,*
> *He, the created, would scoff and would sneer,*
> *Where I, the Creator, would bow and revere.*

And what of Arthur Conan Doyle himself? He seems always to have thought of himself as an Englishman, for all that he was born in Edinburgh, of an Irish mother and an Anglo-Irish father. Arthur's childhood was divided between his Scottish home town and his English boarding school, Stonyhurst College in Lancashire. He went back to Edinburgh to study medicine at the University, and after graduating in 1882, he moved to the south-west of England. He never lived in Scotland again, but, as you can hear in the interview filmed in 1927, he retained a distinct Scottish accent throughout his life. (The film is easily accessible on YouTube. The statement that it was made in 1930 is erroneous.)

19

Besides, he was happy to acknowledge another, even more important influence on Sherlock Holmes: Dr Joseph Bell, one-time President of the Royal College of Surgeons of Edinburgh and lecturer at the Medical School at Edinburgh University. In his memoirs, Conan Doyle wrote: *"I thought of my old teacher Joe Bell, of his eagle face, of his curious ways, of his eerie trick of spotting details. If he were a detective he would surely reduce this fascinating but unorganized business to something nearer an exact science."*

The Scots – and the Irish too – know that England has no exclusive ownership of the great detective, or of his creator.

The Americans have also asserted their right: *Elementary*, with its updated Holmes living and working in New York, is evidence of that. In fact, what Robert Keith Leavitt felicitously dubbed "221b Worship" has from the start been stronger in the United States than almost anywhere else. The first authorised dramatisation was the work of an American, William Gillette – there had been numerous unofficial adaptations and spoofs before Gillette's 1899 play *Sherlock Holmes* – and it was in America that the detective was first portrayed on film, on radio, and on television.

In 1944, President Franklin D. Roosevelt, not then widely known to have accepted honorary membership in the Baker Street Irregulars, rather dubiously declared that the detective was actually American, and that "his attributes were primarily American, not English".

Mostly, however, admirers around the world have been content with the idea that Sherlock Holmes is as English as, well, as most Englishmen – which is to say, not entirely. Nicholas Utechin, my predecessor as co-editor of *The Sherlock Holmes Journal*, has proud Russian ancestry; I, like Holmes, am part French. In all probability, there's no such thing as "pure English blood".

The authentic chronicles of Sherlock Holmes comprise sixty tales, long and short, nearly all narrated by the faithful Dr. John H. Watson. Only a few of those cases took the detective himself away from England, but in at least thirty-five of them, an essential part of the puzzle – not necessarily criminal – originated abroad. On occasion, Holmes acted as a spy or a counter-spy, as in the affair of "The Bruce-Partington Plans", which he investigated at the urgent request of his brother Mycroft – who sometimes, as Watson was astonished to learn, *was* the British government. The man behind the theft of the top-secret plans was one Hugo Oberstein, identified by Holmes as "the leading international agent".

We may mourn the days when hand-written letters were the norm, but Holmes himself, remember, preferred the telegram, and in later years had a telephone installed at 221b. He would surely approve of the amazing technology that helps strengthen the ties between the widely scattered groups of his devotees and enables us to keep in touch around the world almost instantaneously.

There are literally hundreds of such groups, large and small. Peter Blau, Secretary of the senior American society, *The Baker Street Irregulars*, maintains an invaluable list, accessible at *www.sherlocktron.com*, which shows that most of them are in the United States, though *The Sherlock Holmes Society of London* and the Japan *Sherlock Holmes Club* probably have the largest membership, with well over a thousand members each.

It isn't only clubs and societies. There are restaurants, bars, hotels, and shops throughout the world, all celebrating Sherlock Holmes, Dr. Watson, and their creator. Two of the finest screen adaptations of the stories are lavish television series made in Russia. The most important book on the Holmes phenomenon — certainly the most important of this century — is *Från Holmes till Sherlock* by the Swedish scholar Mattias Boström, published in the UK under the misleading title *The Life and Death of Sherlock Holmes*. (The American edition, printed from the same plates, is correctly entitled *From Holmes to Sherlock*.)

In these divisive times, with nationalism, racism, and xenophobia prominent in the news, the devotees of Sherlock Holmes form that elusive ideal, a genuine international community, and our divisions are guided by taste and informed opinion.

Never mind Hugo Oberstein! The *true* leading international agents are Sherlock Holmes and his creator, Sir Arthur Conan Doyle.

Roger Johnson, *BSI, ASH*
February 2018

Undershaw:
An Ongoing Legacy
for Sherlock Holmes
by Steve Emecz

Undershaw
Circa 1900

When the first three volumes of *The MX Book of New Sherlock Holmes Stories* came out less than three years ago, I could not have imagined that in May 2018 we would have reached volumes IX and X, and over two-hundred-and-thirty stories. It has been a fascinating journey, led by our editor David Marcum. We have raised over $25,000 to date for Stepping Stones School – the majority of which from the generous donation of the royalties from all the authors, but also from some interesting licensing deals in Japan and India.

MX Publishing is a social enterprise, and getting introduced to dozens of new authors has also helped our other major program – the Happy Life Children's Home in Kenya. My wife Sharon and I have spent the last five Christmases in Nairobi, and now lots of the Sherlock

Holmes authors are helping out with Kenya too. Long may the collection continue! It's brought us many new friends, and is something that all involved can be very proud of.

You can find out more information about the Stepping Stones School at *www.steppingstones.org.uk*

Steve Emecz
February 2018

A Word From the
Head Teacher of Stepping Stones
by Melissa Grigsby

Undershaw
September 9, 2016
Grand Opening of the Stepping Stones School
(Photograph courtesy of Roger Johnson)

Undershaw proudly grows with over eighty young people, with hidden disabilities and barriers to society flourishing and growing. Holmes states, "It may be that you are not yourself luminous, but you are a conductor of light." Whilst his comment is about dear Watson, I feel that my staff are also deserving of such comments: Calm and intelligent, they support and guide those under their watch to become the best they can be and embrace life ahead.

Undershaw offers us a home and place to support each of these young people to shine, with its beautiful demeanour providing the perfect place for the staff to ignite the light of learning in each young person's mind.

Melissa Grigsby
Executive Head Teacher, *Stepping Stones,* Undershaw
February 2018

Parts IX and X of The MX Book of New Sherlock Holmes Stories *are respectfully dedicated to* **Jim French***, who passed away at the age of eighty-nine on December 20th, 2017, the same date that this script was being edited for these books. He was very supportive of this and other related projects from the first time that he was approached, and what he accomplished over his lifetime in the fields of radio and entertainment and imagination is immensely respected by all of those who knew him or were entertained by his efforts. He will be missed.*

Sherlock Holmes (1854-1957) was born in Yorkshire, England, on 6 January, 1854. In the mid-1870's, he moved to 24 Montague Street, London, where he established himself as the world's first Consulting Detective. After meeting Dr. John H. Watson in early 1881, he and Watson moved to rooms at 221b Baker Street, where his reputation as the world's greatest detective grew for several decades. He was presumed to have died battling noted criminal Professor James Moriarty on 4 May, 1891, but he returned to London on 5 April, 1894, resuming his consulting practice in Baker Street. Retiring to the Sussex coast near Beachy Head in October 1903, he continued to be involved in various private and government investigations while giving the impression of being a reclusive apiarist. He was very involved in the events encompassing World War I, and to a lesser degree those of World War II. He passed away peacefully upon the cliffs above his Sussex home on his 103rd birthday, 6 January, 1957.

Dr. John Hamish Watson (1852-1929) was born in Stranraer, Scotland on 7 August, 1852. In 1878, he took his Doctor of Medicine Degree from the University of London, and later joined the army as a surgeon. Wounded at the Battle of Maiwand in Afghanistan (27 July, 1880), he returned to London late that same year. On New Year's Day, 1881, he was introduced to Sherlock Holmes in the chemical laboratory at Barts. Agreeing to share rooms with Holmes in Baker Street, Watson became invaluable to Holmes's consulting detective practice. Watson was married and widowed three times, and from the late 1880's onward, in addition to his participation in Holmes's investigations and his medical practice, he chronicled Holmes's adventures, with the assistance of his literary agent, Sir Arthur Conan Doyle, in a series of popular narratives, most of which were first published in *The Strand* magazine. Watson's later years were spent preparing a vast number of his notes of Holmes's cases for future publication. Following a final important investigation with Holmes, Watson contracted pneumonia and passed away on 24 July, 1929.

Photos of Sherlock Holmes and Dr. John H. Watson courtesy of Roger Johnson

The MX Book
Of
New Sherlock Holmes Stories

PART IX – 2018 Annual
(1879-1895)

Violet Smith
by Amy Thomas

I know the hand of judgment quick
To condemn with incisive, sharp
Strokes woman alone, dissecting
Her every point, analyzing
All she saw, all she is. Reduced
To a single moment of fear.

I ring the bell, subsume my fear.
My heart beats a tattoo too quick,
Afraid to be again reduced
By eyes, by voice, by pen so sharp
It denounces by analyzing,
Each word, expression, dissecting.

Open door, commence dissecting,
Extracting every ounce of fear.
My hand shakes for his analyzing;
I speak too low, too soft, too quick,
Feeling his gaze upon me sharp.
I refuse to be reduced.

Become my specimen reduced.
Commence, my own dissecting.
He finds my gaze to be as sharp
As any man's, I fancy. Fear
Has no place in his movements, quick,
clean. He endures analyzing.

I speak sweetly, analyzing.
Each item in his room reduced
By my magnified wit, placed quick
Under my glass for dissecting.
I pull focus from my fear.
Tables turn; examination sharp.

I miss nothing; I am too sharp.
I see him cease his analyzing,
Devoid of judgment as of fear.

I am augmented and reduced
By his suspended dissecting.
Client. Classification quick.

Extinguished fear; my mind is sharp.
We're both too quick with analyzing.
Sherlock Holmes is not a man reduced by shared dissecting.

The Adventure of the Temperance Society
by Deanna Baran

It was autumn when I returned to our lodgings to find Holmes working diligently upon his mementos past. A dozen piles of newspaper clippings were spread over the table, sideboard, and floor, and six or seven scrap-books lay spread about in a rough crescent before him. It was the first time I had seen him in three days.

"I take it you found a happy conclusion?" I inquired.

"Indeed I have," he replied. "It was one of the assistant sommeliers, of course. The rough shape of the matter was obvious from the first, but it required a little effort to determine which one, because it would have been unjust to indiscriminately punish them all. Once I realized that I was seeking a colour-blind Belgian, things fell into place."

"Now, surely, you're being sarcastic," I said. "A colour-blind Belgian, indeed!"

"I do not jest," said Holmes placidly. "You would agree that the English spoken or written by a Londoner, a Scotsman, and an American is not the same, whether in accent or word choice or, perhaps, spelling? That there are regional differences, depending on one's upbringing, that influence the way one conveys ideas? Just the same, there are differences between a Parisian, a Belgian, and a Québécois. They are not freely interchangeable. They may be told apart. Although, as it turned out, it had been his grandmother who was the Belgian; he himself was from Hornsey. But it was a timely reminder to me about the impact previous generations may have upon their offspring, and even after they are buried tidily in the churchyard, their habits may still be observed preserved within their posterity. It is an interesting thought. I must cultivate it."

"I'm afraid you've quite lost me, Holmes," I said.

"Take this man, for example. He is not French; he has never been to France or any other French-speaking country. Yet he learned his French at his grandmother's knee. So he does not learn French of to-day; he learnt the French that his grandmother knew, and expresses his grandmother's idioms of his grandmother's day and his grandmother's region. You may see a similar occurrence in the descendants of a left-handed woman, whose handedness has never been corrected. Perhaps she performs a common task, such as sewing or spinning or ironing, left-handed. She teaches her daughter how to sew or spin or iron, and her

35

daughter teaches her own daughter how to sew or spin or iron. That characteristic of left-handed sewing or spinning or ironing may be preserved through infinite generations of right-handed women, if they never take the time to analyze the motions that have been taught to them.

"You may observe it in handwriting as well. One's character brings certain distinguishing traits to a hand and will always make it unique unless pains are taken to suppress that character expressing itself upon the page, and making the shape of the letters conform to the dictates of the model. However, there are still those characteristics of the hand itself that change with time and fashion, and various hands become the handwriting of one's forebears and are not normally seen upon modern correspondence. Suppose a man was taught the hand that was popular when he was a boy – say, perhaps, a fine Italian hand. That youth grows up, and acquires a job as a tutor. He teaches the hand he knew in his youth, even though thirty years may have passed and it is no longer in vogue. One of the girls of the household grows up, having acquired that fine Italian hand in her childhood, and proceeds to teach her own children to write in that hand, yet another twenty or thirty years in the future. And her children may continue to preserve that hand, even into their own old age. The hand is thereby promulgated, even though it may be a century out of fashion long before he ceases to write."

"I almost fear to ask you how you hit upon the colour-blindness."

"A person who is unable to properly perceive colour is more likely to stumble over certain mistakes that would never have been committed by someone who could properly observe the full spectrum. In this instance, it made no sense at all, because of the red jacket. But then it occurred to me – what if he mistook the red jacket for a green one? And then it all made sense."

"Sometime, you will have to put down all the facts for me. I cannot possibly comprehend a story told in fits and starts and mild hints," I said.

"Perhaps. It was so pedestrian, I fear to bore you with it any more than I already have. The other case might be more to your taste for the sensational, and would require significantly less embroidery to inject the romantic element. Before I left, I was able to clear up a small matter for an Indian maharajah who happened to be staying at the hotel. It had to do with a very fine turban ornament in pearls and emeralds. You would have liked it."

"Was it stolen, Holmes?"

"Substituted in paste by a son who had come to England to study, and had fallen into gambling debt," said Holmes absently, placing a clipping upon a page. "The boy's mother had fallen out of favor, and the maharajah was happy for the excuse to disinherit him. I got a very fine

36

Mughal ornament for my trouble, out of gratitude for clearing up a sticky family situation, and the Langham's master sommelier, not to be outdone by a foreigner, arranged to send along a few of bottles of wine in addition to my fee from the hotel management. I was rather hoping you would share one with me this evening as we dined."

"Which should be imminent," I remarked. "Do you suppose now is a good time to tidy up and allow them to lay our supper?"

"Note how the stones are polished, rather than cut," said Holmes, casually reaching into his pocket and handing me a small golden object almost vulgar in the number of colorful gems it displayed. "And they are set into small golden cups, rather than the claws favored by our European jewellers. A detective runs into gemstones occasionally, and it's good to have a working knowledge of such things."

"My word, Holmes! This pendant must be worth a small fortune!"

"Undoubtedly. But the exchange rate for such things is rather poor. I suppose I shall keep it as a souvenir, as it is rather artistic in its own way, and I certainly cannot wear the thing."

"If, someday, you ever become affianced, you may well find yourself pleased that you hung on to such an expensive bauble."

Holmes paused in what passed for tidying long enough to fix me with a piercing look. "If I ever become linked with a creature who would be seen in public with that around her neck, I beg you to take the utmost pains to restore me to my senses."

It was at that moment that dinner made its arrival. Momentarily flush with income from grateful clients, the ascetic Holmes had indulged in a huge Barbezieux capon truffled to the breaking point to complement the gifted vintage. It was some time before conversation resumed, as both of us turned our concentration to the scents, flavors, and textures that assailed our senses and demanded our full attention.

"I take pride in my abilities as a housekeeper," remarked Holmes, considerably later that evening. "Would that I had the purse to properly pursue my ambition."

"You prioritize your brain, at the expense of all the rest of you, neglecting sleep and food alike when tasked with a difficult problem. At times like these, it is surprising that one who is can be so deliberately bereft of creature comforts as a matter of course is able to keep a table such as this!"

"Perhaps I shall write a monograph on the pairing of food and wine on a moderate budget for a bachelor household," said Holmes. "I shall find the research quite pleasant, but I admit that I prefer to be a connoisseur of crime than anything else, and will happily give up any number of feasts such as this for one truly masterful problem. Petty

37

sneak-thieves pay the bills, whether they are of the better class of servants or the sons of nobility, but I freely admit I find myself in a drought for that which I truly crave."

"I have never tasted a proper comet vintage before," I said, eyeing the empty bottle with some dejection and my thoughts lingering upon the word "drought". "I shall not be able to drink wine again until Christmas, for until the memory fades, it would only compare unfavorably with tonight's vintage. I remember the Great Comet of 1874, but not enough time has passed to appreciate its effects preserved within the bottle. In fact, I'd say the only thing that marred my enjoyment of this most excellent repast was this stack of papers at my side."

Holmes looked rather hurt, and I hastened to explain, not wishing him to think I had returned disparagement for his generosity.

"You see, the way the papers were shuffled in their stack on the floor by my chair, there was this handbill at the very top. It was published by the Temperance Coalition, you see. *'The brittle artery, the softened heart, the gouty kidney, and premature decay'* – and here I am on my third or fourth glass of the finest vintage I've ever consumed, yet my mind is distracted in thinking about its possible deleterious effects resulting in an irregular heart!"

His face cleared. "That! Oh, that was a memento of a case of mine back in '79 when I was living in Montague Street."

"Montague Street?"

"Very near the British Museum. I had made up my mind to become a consulting detective, you see, so I had migrated to London, the center of ever so much criminal activity, to establish myself in its combat."

"Pray tell," I said, settling into my comfortable chair, the better to digest both my dinner and his words.

"I would expect you to have been abroad at the time, but there was a gang of female thieves who were very notorious during a certain period. The modus of these ladies was to go about dressed in either full or partial mourning. Given the number of women who have lost someone dear to them – a husband, a child, a parent, a sibling – you can imagine that there is, at any given time, a number of women dressed in similar raiment, and as a matter of course, are generally treated with sensitivity."

"The finest ladies usually stay isolated from society during their full mourning, and do not amuse themselves in public," I agreed. "But women – yes. There is always life to tend to."

38

TEMPERANCE COALITION

WHAT DO THE DOCTORS SAY?

Alcohol is a poison for which there is no antidote known.

~ Prof. Miller

Alcohol is a poison ; so is strychnine ; so is arsenic ; so is opium ; it ranks with these agents.

~ Dr. Andrew Clarke

The brittle artery, the softened heart, the gouty kidney, and premature decay, which might never have occurred had it not been for the daily dose of alcohol, which induced an unnatural character of the tissues, and the circulation of an impure blood.

~ The Late Dr. Murchison

In the lungs alcohol leads to congestion and bronchitis, and favors the attacks of tuberculosis. In the heart it causes irregularity, dilatation, fatty degeneration, and sometimes valvular disease ; in the kidneys, fatty or waxy degeneration and dropsy.

~ C.R. Drysdale, M.D.

Carsten Holthouse, F.R.C.S.Eng. (London) will lecture on Twelve Months' Experience of the Treatment of Inebriates at Balham at 6.00 p. m. Saturday at the Temperance Hall on Berwick St.

"The reason, of course, was the very opaque and concealing veiling that is not amiss upon a woman in bereavement," said Holmes. "It's the most natural thing in the world for a woman, attired thusly, to preserve perfect anonymity. This gang of women took advantage of the etiquette that accompanies mourning to obscure their features. At some prearranged place, at some prearranged signal, fifteen or twenty of them would suddenly descend upon a shop, which, more often than not, was a jeweller's. They would wreak destruction and havoc upon that shop for less than a minute, but what a minute it was! Their garments even were sewn to have special pockets to help facilitate their absconding with as much small, portable, valuable plunder as possible. Then they would melt away into the crowds of London in sundry different directions before the authorities could be alerted or sharp wits could delay them. This happened throughout the West End and Holborn. They might descend twice in a week, or go a fortnight without making a move. Needless to say, the shopkeepers of ever so many high-end stores lived in terror for the safety of their shop-windows and display-cases. Glass is not much of a deterrent for those who lack scruples in their dealings."

"One can only imagine the cost of such loss!" I said.

"Insurance bore the brunt of it, but we all know who pays for such costs in the end," said Holmes. "I may have acquired some small fame in certain circles these days, but at that time, I was fresh to London and quite unknown. I had visions of earning a reputation by solving this string of robberies and putting a stop to them."

"What was your first step?"

"First, I ventured to the assay office to consult their registers. All goldsmiths, jewellers, and other allied traders are kept listed in a tidy little directory. From thence, it was easy to put together a map of London marked with pins with colored heads that allowed me to trace the gang's work, both chronologically and geographically. I trod the streets and looked for common characteristics of the shops that had already been robbed. You understand that even when humans are trying to be random, they are very unsuccessful at it, and there is even a pattern to their randomness. I created a list of three jewellers that, if the gang of women proved true to their habits, were very likely future targets. Having determined this, I thereby found myself temporarily engaged by one shop, so as to have a better chance of catching the gang at work."

"Gracious. Did you confess your identity to the jewellers? Were you employed as a guard of sorts?"

"No, my motives were my secret. While I had every confidence in my eventual results, I was still young in my career, and I did not care to cultivate the expectations of others regarding a project I had assumed upon my own volition. With expectations come time-lines and impatience and other feelings of entitlement that, when not accompanied by adequate remuneration, are tedious at best. But playing the part of a low-ranking shop assistant was excellent experience, and I learned quite a bit about the trade that came in useful in the future, especially concerning such things as paste duplicates. For example, with my maharajah this weekend, my solution would not have been nearly so neat had I not had those few weeks' education behind me."

"I take it not much time passed before the gang struck?"

"They were quiet for two weeks. I always paid careful attention to any women who arrived clad in any display of mourning, although, being so low in the hierarchy, I generally was not in a position to personally serve and interact with them. One morning, shortly after opening, I did notice a matron being fitted for some rings. Working-class and local, by her accent, but subdued and polite in her manner. She had some mitts made of a very thin, open-worked lace, and through them, I observed smudges of ink upon the top of her knuckles as she considered various mourning rings in pearl, amethyst, jet, and black onyx. Then one of the other clerks then sent me into the safe to retrieve some small objects for a young gentleman, and I went off to do so. In the time it took for me to go to the safe in the workroom, find the box, and return to the floor, the gang of women had descended, struck, and fled. It took them less than thirty seconds to abscond with nearly fifteen hundred pounds' worth of jewellery."

"The woman with the lace mitts – had she been part of the gang?"

"Certainly so, for it seems the moment her confederates entered the premises, she swept the entire contents of the ring tray into her handbag and swiftly departed amidst the confusion. In addition to my verbal cues indicating her economic status and geographic residence, I had two other clues to her identity: The ink-stains upon her hand, and the odor of mineral spirits clinging rather strongly about her. What would you have made of those observations?"

"An artist?" I hazarded. "Mineral spirits are used to thin paint, are they not?"

"Close, friend Watson," said Holmes. "Rather, I was looking for a middle-aged working-class woman who worked in a printer's shop, but very possibly was involved in its management. I was a little less certain on that point, as you see, having the extra income from a series of robberies does tend to allow one to dress above one's station, but one cannot dress too conspicuously, lest someone start to wonder. Her absence from the premises could either be accounted for by not having to seek permission to absent herself for an hour or so, or possibly she could

41

have been performing some regular errand, and took the opportunity for a detour. Yet would such a woman run errands, or would not those tasks be delegated more naturally to a boy? She had the signs of the form upon her hands, so she was not merely loitering decoratively in the vicinity of the letterpress, but a compositor is too valuable to be allowed to be absent from his station for an extended period. So my thoughts progressed as I strove to generate a picture in my head of the individual I sought.

"A few queries in the proper quarters quickly gave me a short list of printers' shops that would bear investigating. I sought one not too far removed from the district in which the gang operated, possibly run by a female, perchance a widow – but not necessarily. Disguised as an eager young botanist with a horticultural newsletter in need of a printer, I proceeded to investigate the likely candidates.

"My primary candidate was a family operation. The father had died three or four years previously, and his widow continued with the business herself. They had eight children. The eldest girl and the three eldest boys did most of the presswork themselves. The middle two children looked after the youngest two. The mother was not present at the time I entered the premises, but the son who was in charge of the business during her absence was happy to show me examples of their work. There was a series of handbills about train expeditions; there was an internal newsletter printed for the Bacon Appreciation Society; some advertisements for things like clock repairs and dressmakers; sundry promotional posters for some local theatre productions; and there was the 'gouty kidney and softened heart' handbill that you see preserved before you, which the Temperance Society would distribute to passers-by at the local parks in their efforts to protect the working men of London from the deleterious effects of excessive drink."

"And you concluded – ?"

"I thought my observations not insignificant. I surreptitiously relieved the Temperance Society of one handbill, which you see I have preserved to this day."

"So you somehow perceived the Temperance Society to be, in fact, a gang of female robbers secretly imbuing phrases like 'gouty kidney' or 'premature decay' with felonious meaning? I fail to grasp your chain of reasoning."

"That would be an idea! But it would require a code-book, which is not nearly as neat and penetrable as a cipher, from the perspective of law and order. Indeed, by your theory, '*brittle artery*' may mean '*Mappin and Webb*' and '*gouty kidney*' may mean '*Thursday*' and '*premature decay*' may mean '*11:30 a.m.*', and '*softened heart*' may have no meaning at all, and good luck to an outsider attempting to find a correlation! But a cipher – a cipher may be more easily detected, and more easily cracked, especially when the cipherer is an amateur."

"So, out of all the papers in a printer's office, you lit upon this one as bearing a secret message?"

"Look at it yourself, Watson, especially at the first five lines. Do you not think that a compositor would, under normal circumstances, consider that to be an acceptable example of his work? It is very deliberately typeset to be so erratic, and it was my hypothesis that the irregularities would bear investigation."

"Yet no one in the Temperance Society ever remarked upon it?"

"It may look odd to the eye in isolation, but handed out to passers-by strolling in a busy park, few minds would dwell for long upon the specifics of its visual effect, as long as the message was still clearly conveyed. I, however, have made a study of typeface, and can say, with reasonable confidence, that if presented with a small newspaper cutting, I am capable of drawing certain conclusions regarding its origins. Frequently, I am capable of identifying the type face and its source foundry, and I have a working knowledge of where it may be commonly encountered in print. If it is my hobby to unthinkingly process such facts when I encounter a line of text, is it not unlikely for me to equally be aware of instances where that print may have been clearly misused? And if a client's copy has been deliberately mis-laid, when no other copy in the shop has been similarly abused, and when even the vast majority of that page has been set correctly, it must be for a purpose. What, then, would make a widow with eight children who is maintaining the family business risk a dissatisfied client with a few lines of careless composition?"

"So, you had a poorly-composed handbill," I said. "Tell me what your thoughts were."

"It was a germ of an idea that occurred to me when I was fortunate enough to see the handbill, juxtaposed next to the newsletter printed for the Bacon Appreciation Society," Holmes explained. "That particular issue had a fine article about Baconian epigrams. Sir Francis Bacon! Philosopher, scientist, essayist, statesman. Diplomat. Steganographer."

"*Steganographer*?" I asked faintly.

"The art of concealing a secret message in plain view," Holmes explained, warming to his subject. "In his writings, he discoursed upon various methods that served him well over the course of his career, but one remains more famous than the others to this day. It was my hypothesis that this printer, while perhaps involved in printing an article on the subject for the Society, had learned of a method employed by the great Bacon nearly three centuries ago, and decided to employ it herself for her own means. In this case, I suspected I had stumbled across something that can be described as a biliteral cipher."

"A 'biliteral cipher'?" I repeated blankly.

"The genius of it is in its flexibility," he continued. "Because a biliteral cipher is binary by its very nature. You need two types of one sort of thing. It can be lit and unlit candles. It can be red beads and green beads. It can be bold type and regular type, or italic type and regular type. It can be male and female. It can be forward-facing and profile-view. It can be eyes open and eyes shut. It can be any sort of thing, as long as there's one to represent '*A*' and one to represent '*B*'. The chances of a third party not only stumbling across the message, but suspecting that there's a second underlying message present at all and taking the trouble to work it out – those chances are exceedingly slim."

"Like Morse code, and telegraphs?" I hazarded. "Dots and dashes?"

"Not exactly, but somewhat," agreed Holmes. "So, for example, with the Baconian cipher, '*A*' is represented by '*AAAAA*', and '*B*' is represented by '*AAAAB*', and so on. If I wanted to write '*DANGER*', it would be '*AAABB AAAAA ABBAA AABBA AABAA BAAAA*'," he said, suiting the words to his actions, scrawling a string of letters on the back of an envelope. "Now, if I had a piece of paper such as this upon my person, how could it possibly escape arousing suspicion? The secret message is as plain as day, and invites anyone who comes across it to try their hand at cracking it. But! Suppose I have a woolen shawl with a fringe. Suppose I have a piece of fringe knotted in one way to represent '*A*' and I have a piece of fringe left un-knotted to represent '*B*'. I gift the shawl to the individual I care to warn. And he, being made aware ahead of time of the significance of the fringe, will be able to work out the warning, given sufficient time to examine the shawl in private. That's rather a clumsy example, but the means of communication could as well be a receipt for roast capon. All I would have to do is write my letters straight to represent '*A*' and give the letters a subtle tilt, or additional pressure, or whatever we had agreed upon, to represent '*B*'."

"I see," I said slowly. "So, what you're saying is that this gang was taking advantage of a regular, legitimate customer, who was known to distribute his handbills in public at a certain time and place, and thus coordinate their attack upon the next victim?"

"Exactly, Watson!" exclaimed Holmes. "It was a cunning plan, for it is the simplest thing in the world to have the women of the gang stroll through the park under some pretext and accept a handbill from the Temperance Society. And the distributor of the message itself would have no clue of the secret message, let alone whether the passers-by were members of a gang or members of the general public. The rest of the world would remain oblivious to the underlying secret message, and the nature of handbills is very ephemeral indeed, so there would be little paper trail that could be expected to last a week before they were transformed into spills to light ever so many London fireplaces.

"That was the method of communication as I envisaged it, but I get ahead of myself. So, having left the printer's shop, I went home with my confiscated handbill, and examined it in private to determine if I was correct in my hypothesis. Could I wrest a message from the irregularities in the type? And as it turned out, I could. Taking the normal type for '*A*' and the italicized type for '*B*', the message appeared. I will save you the trouble of working it out – '*LAMBERTS COVENTRY TUE TEN THIRTY*'."

"How exciting, Holmes! So, armed with advance notice of their next foray into crime – "

"It was merest child's play after that," said Holmes modestly. "A word or two in the correct ear at Scotland Yard, and come Tuesday by ten-thirty-two, we had seventeen of London's fairest criminals apprehended and in custody. Although some of the gang failed to show up at the appointed time, the remainder quickly fell apart regardless. I considered it rather a coup, for, as I said, I had accumulated little reputation at that point in my career."

"Amazing, Holmes! I hope some of the stolen articles were recovered?"

"A surprising number of the more valuable and distinguishable pieces, for in addition to being amateur cipherers, the women were also rather amateurs when it came to things like fences, although they did have a knack for organization and imagination," said Holmes. "As it turned out, a number of them were indeed widows, and had banded together in their criminal enterprise. I failed to be sympathetic to their cause, as it is rather disingenuous to steal fifteen hundred pounds' worth of stock from an honest shopkeeper, and then repeat the process five or ten times, and claim that one only did it for bread. However, the courts were rather indulgent with the criminals, and they got off with a lighter sentence than one would expect, after taking the children into account."

"I don't suppose you know if the children kept the printing business up during their mother's incarceration?" I asked. "Having any business at all puts them ahead of so many other unfortunates in this city."

"As a matter of fact, she was not at Lambert's on the fateful day," said Holmes. "The remnants of the gang were exceedingly suspicious, as I heard tell several months later. They wondered why those smaller fish happened to be caught, yet my ringleader was curiously absent on such a critical day. They jumped to the conclusion that she had been warned to stay away beforehand, and were not pleased at having been sacrificed. Although transportation had ended years before, the woman and her family found it prudent to somehow come up with the money for passage to Australia, and set up a very successful publishing business there. The family decided to supplement their earnings from printing with a little journalism, and put together a ladies' magazine which ended up a very profitable niche for them to fill honestly. If you look a few pages deeper in that stack, you may find an issue or two which ended up in my collection of mementoes past."

The Adventure of
The Fool and His Money
By Roger Riccard

Chapter I

At the end of my first year of association with the consulting detective, Mr. Sherlock Holmes, I found myself tracked down by an old comrade of mine from the Fifth Northumberland Fusiliers, a fellow officer named Alexander Sinclair.

Alex and I had grown close after spending several weeks together while I was treating him for a severely broken leg, sustained in a fall from his horse during a minor skirmish against a gang of bandits in India. I was fortunate to be able to save him from amputation, and he had felt beholden to me ever since.

His letter reached me at 221b Baker Street on Boxing Day 1881. I had gone out that morning to replenish my supply of tobacco. Upon my return, I was informed by Holmes of its arrival.

"There's a letter on the desk for you, Watson," he announced from his position in front of the fireplace. He was reading the morning paper as he lounged in his familiar mouse-coloured dressing gown.

I put away my Ship's tobacco tin and retrieved the letter. I was pleasantly surprised at the return address. Sitting down across from Holmes, I reached for my penknife to open the envelope when a thought occurred to me.

"Over the past year you have demonstrated some astounding powers, Holmes," I declared. "I confess that I am at a loss as to your thought processes which arrive at such accurate facts on apparently trivial observations. Please tell me what you can about this letter and explain your conclusions, for I am still very curious as to how you perform this trick."

I held the letter out to him. He reluctantly looked around the edge of his paper at me in an attitude of impatience, with narrowed grey eyes and furrowed brow. After a few seconds he sighed, folded up his paper, set it on the table, and picked the letter from my hand as if he were snatching a ball away from a dog.

"How many times have you heard me tell a client that I am not a magician doing mere 'tricks'? Pure observation and deduction, Watson –

47

that is the basis of my craft. It is the result of a disciplined mind and an accumulation of knowledge as to cause and effect."

He perused the envelope carefully, examining it from every angle, feeling the texture with his thumb and middle finger, holding it up to the light of the nearby lamp, even smelling it.

"Wait," I pleaded. "Slow down and let me make notes as you explain this process." I retrieved a pad and a pencil from the desk and sat back down, entreating him to talk me through each step he was taking.

He sighed heavily again and started over. "Are you quite ready now, Doctor?" he asked, like a schoolmaster with an inept pupil.

I nodded my assent and he continued once again. "A visual examination of the envelope shows it to be among the better quality stationery available on the market. Not top of the line, but hardly foolscap. This tells me the sender is fairly well off, or at least has access to someone who is. Feeling the texture confirms the quality and also allows me to determine if there are any enclosures other than the letter itself, such as a ring or a locket. None are present here, and the touch and lack of weight allow me to surmise there is but a single page inside."

"I see," I commented between my scribbling. "But why did you use your middle finger instead of your index finger to feel the paper?"

"Ah, you made an observation instead of just watching me work. That's progress at least," he answered – somewhat sarcastically, I thought. He continued, "A man's index finger has a tendency to have tougher skin because it is used more than the other fingers. Thus the middle finger has more sensitivity to feel finer variations of texture."

"Interesting," I noted on my pad. 'Please, go on."

Raising it up in the air again, he said, "Holding it to the light also adds to the judgement of the quality. It is finely woven which makes it strong, yet allows the paper to be thin. Not so thin as I could make out the letter inside, but I was able to note four capital letters at the bottom of the page which, from their placement and style, I would deduce *R.S.V.P.* Thus, an invitation.

"The postmark is from Gretna Green, just over the Scottish border. The return address of 'Falgreen' indicates some manor estate or castle, worthy enough to be known by a name rather than an address. Again, this would lend credence to the sender being someone of a moderate station. Well-off, but not necessarily nobility, as is indicated by the lack of title, since he refers to himself merely as 'Alex Sinclair'.

"The red sealing wax on the back, stamped with the Sinclair signet but no coat of arms, again points to someone of moderate wealth. The envelope bears no smudges and is not wrinkled, so it was likely posted the same day it was written. It does retain a musty smell, typical of old castles either near a river or surrounded by a moat. I believe the River Sark flows into the River Esk channel just south of the town. Kirtle Water is also close by.

"The name 'Falgreen' is also a clue, as it could be indicative of a castle surrounded by a green hedge or set upon a green mound, similar to Carlisle Castle, just a few miles south of there."

"This is fascinating, Holmes," I commented as I wrote. "Anything else?"

"I would deduce that your connection to him is from your military days by his addressing you as 'Captain, Dr. John Watson'. Referring to himself as 'Alex' rather than 'Alexander' indicates to me that you and he were close friends, likely in the same regiment. His station in life suggests he was an officer, but his reference to you as 'Captain' *and* 'Doctor' tells me he did not outrank you, for someone who did would refer to you as a one or the other, not both. Therefore, I would surmise that he was likely a Lieutenant.

"The handwriting is very revealing. He is obviously intelligent. There are also indications of strength from someone whom I would expect to be about your age, yet there is also a sense of overcompensation. A little too much flourish, attempting a conceit that really doesn't ring true. Hmm . . . ." Holmes stared thoughtfully at the inked address and even felt along the line for the depth of impression. "Was he ever wounded?"

I dropped my hands into my lap, dumbfounded. "That is amazing, Holmes!" I went on to explain Alex's injury and how our friendship grew out of my treatment of him. I included the fact that he called me "Captain Doctor" because I had to pull rank on him to get him to obey my medical orders about his recovery program.

Holmes nodded in satisfaction and spoke once more. "I would suggest then, that something has occurred in his life which he wishes to share with you. Something rather significant, I should think, judging by the excitement evident in his writing. So by all means, open it up and share your friend's good news."

He tossed the envelope back to me. I missed it, due to having the pencil in my hand, but it fell in my lap and I quickly took up my penknife again and slit it open.

It was indeed, an invitation to come celebrate the New Year with him at Falgreen, where he promised a fine feast, a cosy room, and an adventure that could prove most advantageous to both of us. His wording was rather cryptic and gave no clue as to what this adventure might be. I handed the message over to Holmes and asked his opinion.

A brief glance was all he took and declared, "I should say that this 'adventure' he speaks of involves something quite valuable, Watson. He obviously did not wish to name details, as he could not be sure this letter wouldn't fall into false hands. It is probably something of spiritual enlightenment, physical enjoyment, or material enrichment – most likely the latter, as I do not think he would be quite so secretive if it were a new religion or a meeting of a pair of eligible damsels. I would recommend that you accept and remove yourself from the dreariness of London's coal-smoked atmosphere for a time. A spirited romp in the country will do you good."

"What of you, Holmes?" I enquired. "Have you any plans?"

He puffed away at the pipe he had alighted while I was reading my invitation and announced, "I am determined to catch up on my indexes and old case files in these next few days, unless a new client comes along, of course. In any event, I shall be quite busy and not very good company."

I should note that at this time, being the first year of our living together, my accompanying Holmes on his cases was not as frequent an experience as it would later become. Thus, I felt unencumbered and took up pen and paper to write out a telegraphic reply to Alex, accepting his invitation and expecting to arrive on the 29th of December, per his request.

Chapter II

The journey by locomotive was a long one. I left Euston Station in London at nine in the morning and arrived at Carlisle, just south of the Scottish border, at four o'clock

The scenery along the way was pleasant enough, being primarily flatlands and rolling hills at first, until reaching the Peak District where the mountains began to rise alongside us. The afternoon found us forced to cut through the range between the Yorkshire Dales and the North Pennines and snow flurries accompanied us until we dropped back down to the flatlands around Carlisle. Being the middle of winter, I had naturally dressed for the climate, but the traveling rugs provided by the railway company were welcome all the same.

I had spent much of the journey reading a new work of Jules Verne, *Eight Hundred Leagues on the Amazon.* I found it to be an exciting tale and was impressed by Verne's attention to detail and ability to convey action with the written word. It was a skill I much admired and a secret desire of mine to be able to write in such a manner.

Needing to change trains, I was forced to wait until half-past-four to catch the next departure from Carlisle to Gretna Green. The train was crowded with several young couples, apparently seeking to start the New Year as newlyweds. Gretna Green was still a very popular spot for weddings, even though the laws which had made it so had changed. In the middle of the 18th century, English lords approved new laws to tighten marriage arrangements. Couples had to reach the age of twenty-one before they could marry without their parents' consent, and their marriage had to take place in a church.

Scottish law, however, was different. You could marry on the spot, in a simple "marriage by declaration", or "handfasting" ceremony, only requiring two witnesses and assurances from the couple that they were both free to marry.

With such a relaxed arrangement within reach of England, it soon led to the inevitable influx of countless thousands of young couples running away to marry over the border. Gretna Green was the first village in Scotland, and conveniently situated on the main route from London.

With Gretna Green perfectly placed to take advantage of the differences in the two countries' marriage laws, and with an angry father-of-the-bride usually in hot pursuit, the runaway couple could not waste time. Therefore, as soon as they reached Scottish soil in Gretna Green, they would find a place of security where they could marry in haste. Back then, that spot was the blacksmith shop, the first building couples reached in Gretna Green and even now, a century later it was a popular wedding location.

I finally arrived at ten-before-five, with the sun settling low in the western sky, and was met by Alex himself, who welcomed me with open arms in that gregarious fashion I remembered so well. He had put on weight since the last I saw him, yet retained an athletic build, the addition being more muscle than fat. He no longer wore his deep red hair in a close cropped military fashion, but rather long, though he retained his cavalryman's moustache, to which he had added a neat beard. His Scots burr was thick and hearty as he greeted me.

"Cap'n Doctor!" he exclaimed, upon wrapping both his hands around the one I extended in friendship. "It's so good to see ye again."

I had seen upon his approach that he still favored the leg I had set nearly three years ago. He noticed my observation and commented. "The leg stiffens up a bit on me durin' the cold winter months, but I can sit a horse with any man in the county, thanks to ye, Doctor. But I see yer walkin' with a fair limp yerself, Johnny. A war wound, I take it?"

51

I explained about my taking a bullet in the shoulder at the Battle of Maiwand and how Murray, my orderly, had gotten me to a horse, only to be struck in the leg by a second Jezail bullet during our retreat.

"Aye, a bloody business in Afghanistan. This leg o' mine kept me out of it, but at least ye saved it for me, and now it's time to repay ye."

"Whatever are you talking about?" I asked. "And how did you find me?"

"Let's get out o' the cold first," he replied. "I've got a coach to take us home just over here."

He led the way to a fine enclosed coach with a driver in full livery. We stowed my luggage and climbed inside. Once we were off he continued.

"To answer yer second question first, about a month ago I began me search by contacting a friend at the War Office to see about yer current billet. It took a bit o' time, but I finally found that ye had mustered out and were on a pension that was mailed to Baker Street.

"Now as to yer first question," he said, lowering his voice conspiratorially, "I believe I'm on the verge o' discovering an old cache o' money that could be a considerable sum. As I owe ye me life, I felt it only fair that ye should share in it."

I felt a bit overwhelmed, "Alex, I was only doing my duty. Any army doctor would have done the same."

"Aye, but ye pulled that 'Captain' rank on me and took a lot more time than a doctor jest doin' 'is duty. Besides I need a man o' yer intellect to confirm me findings and make sure I deciphered the clues correctly."

"Clues?" I asked.

He slapped my good knee with a meaty paw and announced, "We're goin' to find that secret cache, Johnny me lad!"

I peppered him with questions, but he put me off, saying he would explain all when we got to the privacy of Falgreen. We drove less than a mile south on the Glasgow Road, crossed over the River Sark, and entered into the walled courtyard of Falgreen Castle just as the final rays of the sun were fading in the west. The landscape in the area around Gretna Green is primarily flatlands which gradually taper away toward Solway Firth at the northern tip of the Irish Sea. The area is quite green and makes for excellent farming and pasture for sheep and cattle. I did note that Holmes was correct in his deduction of the etymology of the name, for surrounding the castle walls was an incline greater than forty-five degrees reaching high up the wall from the adjacent fields. It was thick with green vegetation and would have been nearly impossible for soldiers to attempt to climb and breach the thick, red, block walls.

Alex had my luggage taken to my room and offered me a brief tour. "We've about an hour 'til dinner," he suggested. "Let me show ye 'round a bit."

As we walked he gave me a bit of a history lesson. The castle itself dated back to 1140, when it was completed in response to the English castle at Carlisle across the border. Carlisle had originally been built as a stronghold against Scottish invaders. Seeing the usefulness of such a fortress, the Scots built Falgreen for both defense against Anglo forces and as a staging ground for its own southern-bound troops.

For such an ancient structure, I noted that it had been kept in remarkably good repair. The red and green tartan of this branch of the ancient Saint Clair Clan was prominent among banners and tapestries, and there were various suits of armor and weapons displayed. Each of these were designated by a plaque giving the name of the bearer.

We stopped before one of these suits and Alex could barely contain himself. "This could be the key to our upcoming adventure," he proclaimed as he ran his hand along an arm. "This suit of armour." Turning to me he asked, "Are ye familiar with the history o' the Battle of Solway Moss?"

"I also am of Scottish descent," I reminded him, "We are all aware of that prelude of events just prior to the birth of Mary, Queen of Scots. Though I'm certainly not up on details since my school days."

Alex smiled, "Aye, I was a bit rusty meself until recently. Let me read this for ye." He picked up a large book on a nearby table, the title of which was *A History of Scottish Wars*, and read as follows:

> *On 24 November, 1542, an army of fifteen-thousand Scots advanced into England from Dunfries. Lord Maxwell, though never officially designated commander of the force, declared he would lead the attack in person. A later report says that in the absence of Maxwell, Oliver Sinclair, a favourite courtier of King James V, declared himself to be James's chosen commander. According to this account of the battle, the other commanders refused to accept his leadership and the command structure disintegrated. The Scots advance into England was met near Solway Moss by Lord Wharton and his three-thousand men. The battle was uncoordinated and may be described as a rout. Sir Thomas Wharton described the battle as the overthrow of the Scots between the rivers Esk and Lyne. The Scots, after the first encounter of a cavalry chase at Akeshawsill, moved down towards Arthuret Howes. They found themselves penned in*

53

south of the Esk, on English territory between the river and the Moss, and after intense fighting surrendered themselves and their ten field guns to the English cavalry. Wharton said the Scots were halted at the Sandy Ford by Arthuret Mill Dam. Several hundred of the Scots may have drowned in the marshes and river.

James, who was not present at the battle, withdrew to Falkland Palace, humiliated and ill with fever. The news that his wife had given birth to a daughter (Mary, Queen of Scots) instead of a son, further crushed his will to live, and he is reported to have stated that the House of Stewart "came with a lass and will go with a lass." He died at Falkland two weeks later at the age of thirty. It is reported that in his delirium he lamented the capture of his banner and Oliver Sinclair at Solway Moss more than his other losses.

"Yes," I agreed. "Now I recall. So this Oliver Sinclair was one of your ancestors?"

"Aye, and this castle was his to command and retain after being ransomed from England. He charged a cousin, Roderick, to keep it staffed and ready to use as a staging ground for Scottish troops, which it would later become. Which brings us to the reason I've sent for ye.

"In order to maintain the castle and be ready to raise and supply an army, Oliver was constantly procurin' funds and sending the money here. Roderick always feared an attack from the English, and so kept that treasury well-hidden. Legend goes that he left secret instructions for his cousin should anything happen to him. But then he died in 1576, at about the same time as Oliver, and the treasury was never discovered."

Alex clapped me on the shoulder, smiled broadly and said, "That's why I've invited ye here, Johnny. It's believed that no one else knew where it was hidden, for there's no record of its use. The story has come down through my family for generations."

Here he pointed to his broad chest with his thumb and announced, "But I've found the message Roderick left Oliver with the clues to its whereabouts. On New Year's Day, we're goin' on a treasure hunt!"

Chapter III

"A treasure hunt?" I asked, skeptically. "You mean to say no one has found this cache in over three-hundred years?

"If they did, there's no record of it, and I doubt the instructions I found have been touched since they were written and hidden away."

"Where did you find them?" I asked with great curiosity, for Alex's excitement was becoming infectious.

"Come along, I'll show ye," he replied and led the way to a cosy chamber that was lined with bookshelves containing a wide variety of books of all ages. He went to a particular shelf, pulled out a voluminous leather-bound tome, and set it upon a table. I leaned over his shoulder and saw that it was an ancient Bible.

"I was re-arranging the books in here last summer and accidently dropped this old Latin Bible. When King James had the English translation published fer the public in 1611, these went out o' style, and I doubt anyone had occasion to look through it carefully anymore. But I noticed a loose page and opened it up to try and straighten it. Turns out, it weren't one o' the book pages at all. T'was a handwritten note, also in Latin."

Just then, we were interrupted by a servant who announced that "dinner was served". Alex put a finger to his lips to indicate our conversation needed privacy and ushered me to the dining room where we enjoyed a fine meal of lamb, potatoes, and assorted vegetables. We discussed army days and old comrades. I told him of my current circumstances and about my flat-mate, who was an amateur detective of sorts. I even explained how he was able to deduce so much merely from the letter I had received inviting me to Falgreen.

"Och! The man is a warlock, to be sure! Two centuries ago, he'd a been burned at the stake! Ye say he does this fer a livin'?"

"Oh yes," I assured him. "He's quite good at it and makes a decent living with helping private clients. Even the police occasionally call upon him for assistance."

"Tis a marvel indeed. If I'd known of him, he might have been able to help decipher the clues to me quest a lot faster than the weeks it took me."

"I'm sure your confidence in yourself will be rewarded, old friend. I'll certainly help in any way I can."

"I knew I could count on ye, Johnny. Let's take our brandy and cigars into the study and I'll show ye me discovery and me interpretation."

He led me to a roll-top desk, where he unlocked the top and retrieved an envelope with some papers. Then we sat at a round oak table under a bright chandelier. He carefully unfolded an ancient page, yellowed with age. "What do ye make of this, with all ye'r Latin learnin'?"

He turned the page toward me and it read as follows:

Ad custodem custos fide et de mammonae
Ortu solis exortu ad finem victoriae strenae
Dum se nobis pastorem, sustentare eum qui pecuniam ovium
Ex visibilibus in ostium quod aperit caelum, ita faciet ad dextram
Arma inter valle umbrae mortis et in mensam ex adverso hostium meorum
Mitte tuam solem et oculum a note, ubi umbra cadit in capitis mei
Ad simul et convertam te et auferetur regnum ad Septentrionalis
Et cum iter fecit gradus prophetia Isaiae: umbra in horologio Ahaz
Habens cubitum sub tutela sancti Andreae in vobis quaerite et invenietis in via turn enim circulo recta medium
Rursus bello oriri pretium
Et animam tuam: Deus misereatur

I was able to make out some phrases, but was at a loss to the overall meaning and confessed as much to my friend. "I can discern some of this, but since my school days, my Latin has been pretty confined to medical terms. I hope you weren't counting on me to translate this for you."

He smiled brightly through his whiskers and slid another paper across to me. "Not to fear, Johnny lad. Me pastor translated it and I swore him to secrecy," he winked. "Figured that'd be safer than some busybody scholar. Now does *that* make any sense to ye?" he said, handing me another piece of paper. I took it and read in much plainer English:

To the keeper of the faith and the guardian of mammon
The full risen sun of a new year dawns on the means to victory
While the Lord is our Shepherd, the treasure sustains the sheep
From the door that opens to the sights of the heavens, make way to the right
Between the battlements shadow of the valley of death and the table in the presence of mine enemies

56

*Cast thine eye away from the sun and note where my
      helmet's shadow falls*

*Go at once and turn thyself away toward the kingdom of the
      North*

*And march as did Isaiah's shadow on the steps of the
      stairway of Ahaz*

*A cubit beneath St. Andrew's protection ye shall find the way
      turn a circle half right*

To arise again with the wages of war

And may God have mercy upon your soul

"Well, it's certainly readable now," I commented. "But do you understand what it means?"

"I believe so, but I need someone I can trust to help me. That's where *you* come in."

His full pronunciation of "you" told me how serious he was, so I answered in kind. "Anything I can do to help, Alex. You can count on me."

"I knew it. Cap'n Doctor," he said, slapping his hand on the table and holding it out. "And ere's me hand on it. We'll share whatever we find, fifty-fifty."

I took his hand and replied, "That's terribly generous of you. Are you sure?"

He grew serious momentarily and said in solemn tones, "Ye saved me life, Johnny. If not fer that, the treasure may have gone undiscovered for another hundred years, or maybe never. T'is only fair, I say." Then his smile broadened again, "Now let me tell ye what I think this means, and ye can give me yer thoughts."

He went through his reasoning, first of all stating that he found the page inserted at Psalm 23 in the Old Testament, which he felt was significant. He went on to explain that he believed the *keeper of the faith and the guardian of mammon* was Roderick, and that his suit of armour in the castle indicated the key. The *treasure sustains the sheep* and *the wages of war* both referred to the money collected to raise up an army against the British. He was sure the *door* and the *battlements* referred to the high tower, which was the closest point in the castle with *sights to the heavens.* Standing Roderick's armour in the proper place at dawn on New Year's Day would cast a shadow pointing to the starting point of the directions which followed.

Finally stopping his explanation to take a fresh sip of brandy, my old comrade asked, "Well, Johnny what do ye think?"

57

I removed the cigar from my lips, collected my thoughts briefly, then answered, "You certainly seemed to have reasoned it out logically and I don't wish to dampen your enthusiasm, but it has been three-hundred years and there are likely changes in terrain, the heights of trees or even new trees altogether could affect shadows and steps. The land is also fairly flat, with just a slight rising towards the east, away from the river. A shadow cast at sunrise would be long indeed, likely outside the castle walls. Would this ancestor of yours risk burying the money out in the open like that?"

Alex raised his open palm, his own cigar sending smoke upwards from between his long fingers. "Aye, I know there be objections, but I've explored the area where I expect the shadow to fall on New Year's morning. I think we've got a chance here, Johnny, and certainly nothing to lose. What say ye?"

I grinned, "I'm at your disposal, Alex. If nothing else it will be a fine adventure to remember for this gloomy winter."

We clinked our glasses and toasted to a successful quest.

Chapter IV

Friday, the thirtieth, dawned cold and cloudy. I wandered downstairs and found that breakfast was being prepared but wouldn't be ready for half-an-hour yet. The cook, Mrs. Sheffield, offered me a hot cup of coffee which I took gratefully. With no sign of Alex about, I decided to do some exploring. I threw on my overcoat, muffler, and flat cap and ascended the stairwell of the castle's tower. Stepping out onto the rooftop surrounded by battlements, I found my friend leaning between two of them and looking out across the fields to the west.

I wrapped both my hands around the warm cup of coffee and took a sip, and then asked, "What will you do if it's overcast and there no sun shining at dawn on the first?"

"I've thought o' that," he answered. "I've been coming up here the last few mornings to get an idea of where the helmet's shadow will fall. It shouldn't make more than a few inches difference this close to the actual date, so we should be close to a starting point."

He leaned back and I saw that behind him, leaning against the wall, was a staff with one of the ancient helmets on it.

"I take it this is the height of Roderick," I commented. "Clever to do it this way and not have to lug his entire set of armour up here. So where do you think the shadow will fall?"

He responded by pointing to some ruins that lay between Falgreen and the River Sark. "Yesterday, the shadow fell just north of the foundation of the old kirk there. It's where the cemetery was. It's quite possible the treasure is buried among the old tombs."

"Won't that present a problem with your local pastor?" I asked.

"We'll have to see where the clues take us," he replied. "If it be an actual gravesite we'll bring in the me pastor and see what can be done. But I doubt that someone with Roderick's bible knowledge would desecrate a grave by burying his war chest in it. We'll find out come Sunday morning."

We left the cold of that thought and tower perch and retreated downstairs to a welcoming hot breakfast.

The freezing temperature and intermittent hail kept us inside the rest of the day. Alex had some business to take care of, handling the estate and the local folk who rented lands from him for raising crops and livestock. The impression I received coincided with Holmes's assessment. Falgreen allowed him to be moderately well-off but not extremely wealthy. Expenses were often threatening to overcome income, and Alex had mentioned that he may be forced to sell off some his holdings.

I was left to fend for myself in his well-stocked library, where I made myself comfortable in front of the fire with the Jules Verne book I had brought along. After a brief respite for lunch, we each returned to our activities. This time however, I chose to experiment with some writing of my own. I took up pencil and paper and began making notes for a tale of my current circumstances. I allowed my imagination to run with the situation as it existed in the late fourteenth century with the cousins Sinclair attempting to do their patriotic duty for Scotland. I imagined scenes of intrigue, clandestine meetings, and passionate debates. It was all speculation, of course, and I would certainly seek my host's permission to use his family for a fictional account. By dinner time, I had put down several ideas which gave me confidence that there was enough to start writing a story, and I resolved to begin doing so at the next opportunity.

Over our evening meal, Alex asked what I had found to read in the library. I recommended to him the Jules Verne adventure which I had brought along. The mood was congenial, and so I broached the possibility of writing a fictional account of his ancestors and their adventures during those ancient days in Scotland's history, as background to our modern day treasure hunt.

He contemplated that as he sipped his wine, a fine vintage of the Graham clan. Finally he responded, "T'would make a grand tale, I'll admit, especially if we find the treasury. But me cousins, those descendants of Oliver, are very protective of the clan's history. T'is doubtful they'd approve." He hesitated a bit and I sensed there was something else bothering him.

"What is it, Alex?" I asked, "If you have an objection please tell me. I'll not take offense, I assure you."

He leaned forward and spoke in a low voice, "It's just that, *if* we find a treasure that makes us rich, I'd just as soon not have the news bandied about. Ye know how differently people treat ye when you're wealthy. Everybody lookin' fer an investor. Every charity, tax collector, and long lost relative will come out o' the woodwork lookin' fer a touch."

I confess that this thought had never occurred to me and the look on my face must have revealed my disappointment, for my comrade spoke up again.

"Not that it's a bad idea, Johnny. Perhaps if ye changed the names and location?"

"That's a thought," I conceded, grateful for the suggestion. "Thank you."

"That's better then. Now, how's yer leg up for a horseback ride tomorrow, weather permittin'? T'is Hogmanay [1] after all and I'd like to show ye the Sinclair lands as we visit the tenants and neighbours. Might even give ye some ideas fer yer story."

"The leg kicks up with the cold," I answered, "but if the rain and hail subside, I could use a good stretching out."

"Very well, then. I've got a couple o' fine stallions that are plenty gentle but can give us a good run when so inclined. We'll start out right after breakfast."

The next morning dawned cold but clear, and we packed up our panniers with various breads, sweetmeats, and bottles of Scotch whisky, and cantered off to visit Alex's tenants and neighbours. All were welcoming on this festive day, even those who were paying their monthly rents. There was one stop where we were particularly welcomed, a small shop on the outskirts of Gretna Green where a variety of souvenirs and bric-a-brac were sold to the many tourists. When we walked in, bearing our gifts, a petite young woman of about twenty years with doe-like eyes and chestnut hair that curled round her face and across her shoulders let out a cheery greeting and proceeded to fall into a prolonged hug with my companion, followed by an affectionate kiss that bespoke more than a casual friendship. Slipping his arm around the girl's waist, Alex waved in my direction and announced, "Sarah, me darlin', this would be me good friend, Cap'n Doctor John Watson, as fine a medical man as her Majesty's army has ever produced. He's the one who saved me leg and me life. Johnny, this would be Miss Sarah Lamont, me fiancée."

I bowed, doffed my cap, and reddened slightly at this praise. "Why Alex, you never told me. Congratulations, old man!" I started to offer my felicitations to Miss Lamont, but before I could utter another word, I found myself in a bear hug that was surprisingly strong for someone so small, for she could not have been more than five-feet-two inches and weighing one-hundred-ten pounds at most.

"Oh, thank you, thank you, Doctor! You saved my Alex for me!"

Finally disentangling herself, she explained, "I've loved Alex since I was a young girl, but never told him, he being so much older than I. Then he went off to war and I thought I'd never see him again. When he came back wounded, I finally made up my mind that I had to tell him how I felt. I could not risk anything happening to him without letting him know how much he was loved."

"Imagine me surprise, Johnny," Alex chimed in, "when this slip of a girl came to visit me at the castle in me convalescence and confessed her feelin's. I had only known her as one of the girls about town. I'd never dreamed she had a crush on me. The more she visited, the more I felt such a compatibility that our love became mutual. I proposed to her on her twenty-first birthday in October, and we're to be married this spring."

At this juncture, Miss Lamont held out her hand so I could see her lovely engagement ring and said, "You must promise to come to the wedding, Doctor. Please, it would mean so much to us."

"Yes, Johnny ye must come," added my friend. "Ye must stand up with me as I take me bride."

I was flabbergasted by all this news at once, but I answered in the affirmative. "Well, I can hardly deny the request of such a charming young lady, nor that of an old comrade-in-arms. Of course I'll come."

"Wonderful!" said Sarah, clapping her hands in delight. "Now, sit, sit, sit, there by the stove and take off your coats while I get you both some hot coffee."

After a delightful visit with this bubbly bride-to-be, Alex and I mounted up and returned to Falgreen. The rest of the day was spent receiving visits from others celebrating Hogmanay. When an elderly neighbour and his wife left us just before sunset, Alex turned to me and proclaimed they would be the last visitors we would receive.

"Really?" I asked. "When I was a lad, we celebrated through the night and well into the next morning."

"Aye, that's tradition," he replied. "But the local custom here is to limit visits only to daylight hours, unless ye've been invited to dinner.

I've not sent such invitations nor accepted any this year, for we've a busy day tomorrow. I've ordered breakfast for seven-thirty, and by eight-thirty we'll need to be in position."

After dinner that evening, we retired to his library once again and discussed exactly what each of our tasks would be on the morrow. We worked out a system of flag communication between me at the battlements and Alex, near the kirk where the shadow should fall. Since he had been checking this phenomenon for several days, he already knew approximately where to begin. My signals would guide him to the exact starting point. Then I would sally forth to join him. Within the hour, we hoped a fortune would lay at our feet.

Chapter V

After a restless night, being excited about what lay ahead, I arose at seven and looked out the window. To my delight, the early morning stars still shone, meaning clear skies for the task before us.

I enjoyed a hearty breakfast with my friend as scheduled, after which Alex gave all the servants the rest of the day off to go into town and enjoy the celebrations with family and friends.

In the dawn's twilight, we saddled the horses again with panniers. Hoping this time to fill them with treasure, Alex rode out to the kirk and stood near where he had determined the shadow would fall. I took my place on the tower roof between the third and fourth battlements, counting to the right from the door, for Alex had determined these were the verse numbers in the Twenty-third Psalm, to which the "*valley of the shadow of death*" and "*the table in the presence of mine enemies*" referred.

I held Roderick's helmet on its shaft and, when the full sun cleared the horizon, I signaled with a bright red flag to Alex. I moved him slightly to his left and backward a couple of steps. When he was in position I gave him the agreed upon sign and left the tower to mount my steed and gallop out to join him.

Upon arriving, I found Alex in the old kirk cemetery, compass in hand, facing due north. "Now," he said, "we're to proceed as Isaiah's shadow, which was backwards ten steps."

He slowly retreated ten steps backwards. Fortunately he was between two ancient grave markers, both of which were marked with a St. Andrew's cross, a name, what appeared to be dates, and some ancient Gaelic or Latin script, all nearly worn away after three centuries.

"There doesn't seem to be anything significant about this spot," I mused. "I suppose that's to be expected, given the secrecy behind the treasury, but I would've thought there would be something more telling about the location."

"We've still an instruction to *turn a circle half right.*"

Alex turned to his right and stuck his shovel into the ground "So I propose we start here. Perhaps Roderick meant between the protection of two St. Andrew's crosses. We've only got to dig down eighteen inches or so to find out."

"You're sure that's what a cubit is?"

"According to me pastor, a cubit is the length of a man's arm from the elbow to the fingertips, roughly sixteen to twenty inches. If we've hit nothing by then, we'll have to ask about digging up the tops of these old graves."

Thus we began our excavation, starting about four feet apart so as to allow for any variation between the length of Alex's steps and Roderick's. The ground wasn't quite frozen, but rough digging all the same. It took us nearly a half-hour to dig out a trench four feet long, three feet wide, and two feet deep. Unfortunately, no treasure loomed up to greet us.

As this was Alex's adventure, I kept digging until he made the reluctant decision to halt. Conceding that either there was no treasure, or we were in the wrong spot, my friend agreed to pack up our equipment and return to the warmth of the castle.

The next two days passed quickly. Alex's pastor agreed to his request to search the top layer of the adjoining grave site only if he were present, and that ten percent (a *tithe* as he put it) of any treasure found be donated to the church. Late Tuesday afternoon saw the three of us again in the churchyard, but once more our efforts proved fruitless.

After another couple of days' visiting, I returned to London and Baker Street, none the richer in material goods, but certainly well pleased to have connected with my old comrade and the promise of a continuing friendship.

Holmes appeared to have made some progress in his index filing, as the usual disarray of papers about our sitting room was much depleted. When I walked in, late in the afternoon of my return trip, he was not in, but Mrs. Hudson greeted me warmly and assured me that she had received my telegram and was preparing dinner for the both of us.

"He's off with that inspector fellow from Scotland Yard," she informed me. "But he assured me that he'd be home for supper."

"Lestrade or Gregson?" I enquired.

"T'was the weasel-faced fellow," she answered.

"Ah, Lestrade then. Very well, Mrs. Hudson, thank you. Could I trouble you for some tea and biscuits?"

"Be glad to, Doctor," and she bustled off to her kitchen while I unpacked, stirred up the fire, and settled onto the sofa with the afternoon edition of *The Observer* I had picked up at the station.

About an hour later, the world's first consulting detective burst through the door, flung his overcoat and homburg at the coat stand, and greeted me in high spirits.

"Ah, good old Watson! Welcome back," he said, plopping down in the chair opposite me and warming his hands by the fire as he took in my presence with that sweeping glance of his, while I returned his salutation with a bemused, "Hello, Holmes."

He continued, "How is your friend? Not too disappointed, I hope."

I was rather taken aback by that remark and replied tersely, "On the contrary, Holmes, Alex was quite pleased to see me, and we enjoyed our time very much."

"Of which I've no doubt, Doctor, for you are excellent company," he said, smiling. "I was referring to the disappointing results of your little adventure."

I set aside the paper which I had lowered upon his arrival and leaned forward, my hands upon my knees. "How could you possibly know that?" I demanded.

He picked up his pipe from the end table, filled it methodically as he gazed at me, then began his narration.

"Being a civilian again for over a year now has softened your hands, and I see not one, but no less than *four* blisters. The placement of these indicates you were digging with a D-handled shovel. I also note that, despite the cold weather, your face, now that you've lost your tropical tan of army days, has slightly reddened, indicating considerable time spent outdoors.

"I presume that a friend who owes you his very life would not invite you to his castle to dig fence posts. Ergo, you've been digging outside for something valuable, no doubt the 'advantageous adventure' of which he spoke in his invitation.

"Your manner just now when I arrived was cordial, but only that. Had your enterprise been a success, your countenance would have revealed a more joyful expression. In fact, I would have expected you to be bursting with good news to share."

"What if I'd been sworn to secrecy?" I countered.

He shook his head as he puffed away at his clay, "It won't do, Watson. In this past year of our association, I have learned to read you as easily as you read your paper. You are not a deceitful man, a most noble quality, but one which severely hampers your abilities as an actor. Should you ever wish to take up the stage, I could instruct you, for I have some theatrical background. But in your natural state, you are the bane of my existence – an honest man.

"No, my friend. While you no doubt enjoyed your visit, there is an underlying disappointment within you."

I pushed off my knees and stood, looking down at him and shaking my head, then walked over to the sideboard and poured myself a small whisky.

"I am loathe to admit you are correct, Holmes. While I was satisfied just seeing my old comrade and meeting his friends and fiancée, I am sorry for his disappointment. As unlikely as the odds were, I believe he had allowed hope to get the better of him."

"Ah, a man in love," replied Holmes in that analytical tone of his. "That would certainly add to his eagerness to believe in something against more reasoned judgement. Tell me, Doctor, what was this high hope of his, if you are able to reveal it now?"

I paused momentarily then answered, "Since it didn't materialise I suppose there can be no harm done sharing it now, although I doubt he would want his dashed dream made public."

"My word that your story shall not leave this room," replied the detective. "I am merely curious at what motivated him to his action. Motivation is always instructive to someone in my line of work."

I went to my room, retrieved my notes and rejoined Holmes at the dining table, where Mrs. Hudson was now laying out our supper. After she left us, I began my story as I was buttering bread and cutting meat. Holmes merely soaked it all in as he sipped at his wine, deigning not to interrupt his concentration with something so mundane as eating.

When I had finished, he asked to see the translation of the instructions to the treasury left by Roderick. I handed it over and he studied it carefully, then returned it to me.

"A most interesting tale, Doctor," he offered as he handed it back, then reached for the bread and butter. "I trust you will be keeping your notes to inspire your aspirations to become a writer?"

"Why, yes Holmes," I replied. "That is my intention."

"I believe you will find your little puzzle there to be a key to your story. Keep it in a safe place. By the way, when is your friend getting married?"

This abrupt change of subject caught me off guard momentarily, but then Holmes does this quite often and I recovered to answer, "The Saturday before Easter is their intention. They are to be married in the chapel of the famous Gretna Green Blacksmith Shop, since the church will not allow a wedding on that date in the sanctuary."

Holmes stood and walked over to the writing desk to gaze upon the calendar, murmuring to himself in tones I could not make out. Finally he said "That would make it April the eighth, an excellent date."

As he sat back down I asked, "Why is that such an excellent date?"

He smiled enigmatically and offered, "It is numerically pleasing, old chum. All those even numbers divisible by each other. It will also be an easy anniversary date to remember through their years of wedded bliss."

He raised his glass as he said this and gave a toast to the happy couple, "I should be honored to attend such an event if your friend wouldn't mind."

I was a bit taken aback by his attitude, which I at first thought to be sarcastic, but now seemed quite genteel. I told him I would request Alex's permission to bring him along when the date grew closer, and we left it at that as we pursued our meal and he told me of his latest assistance offered to Inspector Lestrade.

Chapter VI

The months passed slowly, winter eventually giving way to spring. I was beginning to make some headway in establishing a small list of private patients and picking up an occasional shift at St. Bartholomew's Hospital. Holmes managed to keep busy enough to refrain from stimulating his mind with narcotics. As I recall, he assisted Scotland Yard in solving two significant burglaries, helped a widow find her missing adult son, and solved the problem of the purloined Panatelas from his tobacconist's shop.

Alex and I had corresponded occasionally during this time, and in one of my letters I had requested the company of Sherlock Holmes when I came up for the wedding. My old army comrade readily agreed, saying he was anxious to meet the man who could astound others with the powers I had ascribed to him.

Thus it was we traveled to Falgreen on Monday, the third of April. As per the same train schedule which had brought me up in December, we arrived late in the afternoon, but this time were treated to a warm spring afternoon's ride, and were better able to take in the lush greenery of the landscape.

Alex greeted us with open arms and, after we were shown to our rooms and dispensed with our luggage, we reassembled in the library for cigars and drinks as we awaited dinner.

My army friend and my civilian friend seemed to hit it off quite well. Their conversation covered many topics of local interest. I was surprised and impressed by Holmes knowledge of the history of the Dumfries and Galloway region, and said as much.

"I must confess, Holmes, that I am astonished at your historical knowledge. All this time I've been under the impression that your brain was reserved for those items which related to your chosen profession."

Holmes smiled indulgently and replied, "And you would not be wrong, dear Watson. I must admit that I have spent some few hours researching this locality at the British Museum in preparation of our visit."

Alex chimed in, "I appreciate yer efforts, Mr. Holmes, for our conversation has been delightful. But what prompted ye to go to such lengths?"

Holmes leaned back in his chair, puffing contentedly on his cigar and blowing a smoke ring toward the ceiling before he spoke. "As Watson has told you, I have invented my profession as a consulting private detective. Whereas many of my cases involve the solving of crimes, my *raison d'être* is the solving of puzzles. Intellectual exercise is what stimulates me, and this treasury of your ancestor has piqued my interest. Mind, I am seeking no compensation. The work is its own reward."

He leaned forward and entreated earnestly, "With your permission, I would like to spend the day tomorrow exploring the grounds and perhaps ride into town to gather more local information. I am sure you have many plans to finalize for your wedding day, and this endeavor shall relieve you of any obligation you may feel to entertain my presence."

Alex looked at me and I merely nodded to ensure my friend's sincerity. Pointing at Holmes with his cigar he replied, "If ye can find Roderick's treasure, I would be in your debt, Mr. Holmes. I'll instruct the groom to have a horse at yer disposal, and anything else ye desire, for ye are correct, there are actions yet to take in preparation for Saturday. Watson, as one of the wedding party, will be an asset to me in that regard. But if ye are content to entertain yerself in this fashion, I shall be happy to leave ye to it."

"Just what are you planning, Holmes?" I enquired. "Have you a new interpretation of the clues left behind?"

He merely waved his cigar in an offhand fashion and stated, "I merely wish to test a few hypotheses. I also believe there is more to consider than just the document's instructions. If I am wrong, no harm done, and I will have at least exercised my brain cells."

"And if ye are right, ye wish no reward?" asked Alex. "It hardly seems fair, Mr. Holmes."

"Several days of free room and board in the fresh country air and a chance to work a pretty little puzzle are sufficient for me, sir. Any compensation you would have bestowed, you may keep as a wedding present," replied the detective.

He would say no more on the subject, and so the conversation steered toward the upcoming nuptials until dinner was announced.

The next morning, I arose around seven, dressed, and descended to the kitchen, where I was given coffee by the seemingly ever-present Mrs. Sheffield. She informed me that, "Your friend is an early riser, Doctor. He was in here at six, had coffee from the first pot of the day, and was off with nary a crumb to eat. I hope he will return in time for breakfast, for I've much to do the next few days and can't be changing my schedule to accommodate everyone's whims."

I assured her that Holmes eating habits were quite irregular and if he missed breakfast it would certainly not be the first time. "He often goes a full day without a meal when he is hot in pursuit of an intellectual problem. He says digestion takes energy away from the thought process," I said with wink and a smile.

She was mollified by that and returned to preparing breakfast, which she informed me would be served precisely at eight o'clock. I chose to visit Alex's library and peruse a book as I awaited the start of the day's activities.

Soon I was joined by Alex, and we spoke of the day's schedule, which would begin with a ride into town to see to the preparations for the wedding feast. After breakfast, for which Holmes did not return, we went to the stables. It was a lovely spring day and we chose to ride instead of taking Alex's coach. The groom informed us that Holmes had taken out a gentle old mare just after six, stating that he would be riding the countryside and then on into Gretna Green, where he would give the old girl a good feed, water, and rest before returning in the afternoon.

Having met with bakers, caterers, and the local drum major regarding music that the pipers would play during various stages before, during, and after the ceremony, we found it was nearly lunchtime, and so stopped into a local café.

To our great surprise, we found Holmes seated by himself at a table in a far corner and went over to join him. He was in an effusive mood and welcomed us warmly. We ordered, and as we awaited our food, our host posed a question to the detective. "Have you had a productive morning, Mr. Holmes, or have ye been content to enjoy our spring weather and a brisk ride?"

Holmes leaned his elbows on the table and steepled his fingers beneath his chin before answering. "I am happy to answer in the affirmative to both your questions, Mr. Sinclair," he said. "Angelus is a fine animal and well suited to my riding acumen, which has its limits. I was able to examine your estate fairly quickly, and have spent some time in your local library, and a good hour speaking with the Reverend Duncan."

"I cannot imagine he would have revealed anything to ye, Mr. Holmes," declared Alex. "He was sworn to secrecy, and I haven't had time to tell him of yer willingness to help my . . . (He looked around to be sure we weren't overheard) . . . cause."

Holmes followed suit with his voice low, "He has kept your confidence, sir. But he was of immense help when I questioned him about the old kirk near the castle. He was able to show me records that go a long way toward confirming my hypothesis."

The waitress brought the food at that point and our conversation ceased until she left. I then asked, "Just what is this hypothesis of yours, Holmes? What did we miss?"

Holmes tucked his napkin into his collar and took up his utensils. The fact that he was about to eat a square meal told me he had reached a breakthrough of some sort, but he merely said, "This is neither the time nor place to discuss the matter, gentlemen. Let me just remind you of one salient fact to ponder until we can return to the privacy of Falgreen. Are either of you aware of the origin of the term 'April Fool'?"

My old comrade shook his head, but I said, "Something about a calendar change centuries ago . . . . Oh my God! We went looking on the wrong date!"

"Precisely, Doctor," replied my friend. "At the time Roderick's instructions were written, New Year's was celebrated by a weeklong celebration that began on New Year's Day, March twenty-fifth. After King James aligned the Scottish calendar with the Pope's decree of January first, people who were unaware of the change and celebrated on April first were known as April Fools because of their ignorance."

Alex slapped his forehead in frustration, "And March twenty-fifth was last week, so we have to wait another year to try again! Tis I who am the fool!"

Holmes finished the bite of food he had just taken and washed it down with a swallow of the local ale before replying with a smile on his face.

"My dear Sinclair, I should not have waited to tell you this news were that so. There is one other bit of calendar adjustment to take into account. In 1752, by act of parliament, eleven days were omitted from the calendar year in order to make up for all the leap years which had previously been unaccounted for. When you add those eleven days back in to get the day that aligns with New Years of 1542 you get . . . ?"

I attempted to do the calculation in my head but Alex, counting them off on his fingers, was quicker and suddenly exclaimed, "April fifth . . . . *Tomorrow*!"

Holmes held up his hand to admonish our host's raised voice and replied, "Indeed, sir. There are some other factors I wish to bring to your attention later, but for now, content yourself to know that tomorrow, you will have a second chance at your adventure."

Chapter VII

The three of us rode back to Falgreen together, Alex and I in anxious anticipation of Holmes's revelations, he as calm as any gentleman out for an afternoon ride. Upon arrival, we retired to the library, where Holmes lit up his briarwood pipe and settled into a wingback chair.

Once brandies were poured all around, Holmes again took on the role of instructor and explained his thought process. Leaning back in his chair, he gestured with his pipe stem to emphasize his points.

"The first thing we must realise," said he, "is the amount of money we are talking about. Surely to raise an army would require several hundred pounds. There was no paper currency in those times, so we are talking about possibly thousands of coins, mostly groats and placks, I should think. That will amount to significant weight, so it would likely be split amongst several containers. That would require a fairly large space. Not really something you would want to bury in the ground and not have readily available should war be declared. No, your ancestor would want someplace he could get to without digging, and to be able to store the containers away from the elements so that they would neither rot nor rust."

"So instead of a gravesite, we should have found a vault or mausoleum," I stated.

"Aye, that sounds logical, Johnny," said my old comrade in arms. "But there be no vaults or mausoleums in the cemetery of the old kirk. We've a mausoleum here within the castle walls, Mr. Holmes, but I cannot see how Roderick's instructions could have led us to that."

"They would not," agreed Holmes. "Your instincts were correct in your interpretation as far as it went. But with a new date, and thus a new position of the sun at dawn, there is another area of the old kirk much more suitable to your quest."

"But there be nothing there but the old stone steps and foundation walls. There's no place to hide several containers of coins."

"I believe there is, Mr. Sinclair," said Holmes, with an air of confidence. "At any rate, I should like to propose that we arise with the dawn tomorrow and follow the directions as before. We've nothing to lose but an hour or so worth of work, and certainly much to gain if I'm right."

It was agreed, and early the next morning found Holmes and I atop the tower and Alex once again near the old kirk, but this time farther to the south. When the sun reached its appropriate spot, I signaled our host with the flags as before and then we rode out to meet him.

The shadow had fallen at the top of the old stone steps on the bannister rail nearest the castle. The bannisters were nearly a foot thick and smoothly worn by the weather of three centuries. But there were faint engravings all along them. Having backed down the steps as did Isaiah's shadow on the steps of Ahaz, we found ourselves looking at an engraving of St. Andrews cross on the bannister.

"By God, Holmes!" cried Alex, "It couldn't be much clearer that we are on the right track this time."

Holmes had waited down at ground level and pointed at the wall below the bannister. There, roughly eighteen inches below where we stood, was an ancient bronze ring, once used for tying off a horse of a parishioner, no doubt.

"I believe this ring is your circle, Mr. Sinclair. If we dig out the dirt which has piled up against the side, we may find that turning it halfway will open a passageway."

We all put our backs to digging out the windswept dirt which had been deposited by the sea breezes. When we reached what appeared to be the bottom, we set our tools down. Alex looked at each of us hesitantly and then said, "Well, here she goes then."

With both hands he grasped the ring and attempt to turn it. It refused to budge and his face reddened dangerously. I was about to order him to stop when Holmes reached out and placed a hand on his shoulder.

"I anticipated something like this. Wait just a moment." He walked to his horse and retrieved what appeared to be a railway engineer's oil can. Methodically, he squirted oil all around the shaft holding the ring, then ran his shovel handle through the ring itself, holding it in place until Alex could grasp it. With the added leverage and the advantage of the oil soaking the ancient joint, the ring slowly began to turn. At the halfway point Alex proclaimed he felt a noticeable movement of some mechanism within. Together, the three of us put our weight to what we perceived to be a door and it gave way, slowly at first, then suddenly

71

flinging itself wide. The former Lieutenant and I found ourselves upon the floor. The sun was bearing in brightly from behind us, but our own shadows made it difficult to see into the corners. Holmes brought forth torches from his pannier, and soon we found ourselves staring at six large iron chests in a room that was the same ten foot depth that the stairway was wide. The ceiling sloped at the same angle as the stairs and all of us had to stoop once inside. Each chest was bound by a heavy padlock, but my flatmate produced a set of lock picks and soon had them all open.

One was completely empty and another only half full. Obviously, these were meant for more funds to come which never arrived. The other four were filled with brass boxes weighing nearly ten pounds each and each box was filled with ancient Scottish coins.

Alex dipped his hands into one of the boxes and ran his fingers through the gold, silver, and copper coins. "Ye found it, Mr. Holmes! Yer a genius of the first water, by God!"

The question now, of course, became what to do with the money chests? The full ones each contained six of those brass boxes, so that was sixty pounds plus the weight of the chest itself. It would take two men to lift each one without risking serious back injury. Then of course where should we take them? Were they safer right here, or should we remove them to somewhere within the castle walls? Eventually they would have to be appraised to have their value redeemed. Would a bank accept such ancient coinage? Were they more valuable as artifacts than their actual monetary designation? Should a university or museum be contacted? Would the government get involved? Would the church make a claim?

Having raised so many questions within just the few minutes which the three of us pondered there, Alex finally made a decision. He took one box from the half full chest and loaded it upon his horse. We resealed the chamber and shoveled dirt back along the front. Holmes used his canteen to make up a paste of mud to rub into the crack of the door. He also wiped away the excess oil around the ring and splayed dirt around it to make it appear as if it hadn't been moved.

With everything back to its normal appearance, we returned to Falgreen. Having forgone breakfast, Mrs. Sheffield had to be convinced to provide us with tea and biscuits, with the promise that she would not need to prepare lunch, since we would be in town.

Having taken on sustenance, we changed into more suitable attire and took the coach into Gretna Green. Our first stop was the office of Alex's solicitor, where my friend laid out his situation. Next was to the local branch of the Royal Bank of Scotland, where Alex emptied the contents of his brass box into a safety deposit box, keeping out a handful of samples to use to make further inquiries.

Finally, he dropped us at the café for lunch, excusing himself to go and visit his fiancée, Miss Lamont, to tell her the exciting news.

As we enjoyed a robust meal, such as can only be found in small, family-run establishments and never duplicated by the fanciest of restaurants, I thanked Holmes profusely for his assistance to my friend.

"It was simplicity itself, Watson," he replied, waving his fork dismissively. "As soon as you told me the date of the document, I knew your friend had dug in the wrong place. Logic, of course, dictated that the money would not be buried, but rather secreted in some hideaway where it was easily accessible."

I nodded, then asked, "But if he wanted easy accessibility, why would Roderick not keep the treasury within the castle walls? Wasn't he taking a risk in secreting them outside his fortifications?"

Holmes shook his head, "It was actually quite brilliant. If the castle were ever overrun by the enemy, forcing him to escape, he could get away quickly. He could then retrieve the money from the kirk for the Scottish army that would be raised to retake the castle."

"I imagine his faith was also a factor," I posed. "He was obviously a religious man and probably felt that God would protect his funds for his righteous cause."

"No doubt," responded Holmes, quaffing his ale. "And for three centuries it has been done. Now, at last, the money will be used for a more peaceful purpose."

I raised my glass in salute and agreed, "Amen to that!"

NOTES

Since there is no future reference to Watson becoming wealthy, it is speculated that between government claims and legal fees, Alexander Sinclair was either forced to turn over the funds, or left with so little that Watson's share was insignificant.

1 – Hogmanay is the Scots word for the last day of the year and is synonymous with the celebration of the New Year in the Scottish manner. It is normally followed by further celebration on the morning of New Year's Day. There are many customs, both national and local, associated with Hogmanay. The most widespread national custom is the practice of *first-footing*, which starts immediately after midnight. This involves being the first person to cross the threshold of a friend or neighbour, and often involves the giving of symbolic gifts such as *salt* (less common today), *coal*, *shortbread*, *whisky*, and *black bun* (a rich *fruit cake*), intended to bring different kinds of luck to the householder.

Food and drink (as the gifts) are then given to the guests. This may go on throughout the early hours of the morning and well into the next day. The first-foot is supposed to set the luck for the rest of the year.

The Helverton Inheritance
by David Marcum

On that particular Saturday in October 1883, I nearly reached a crisis. Looking around those rooms that I had shared with Sherlock Holmes for over two-and-three-quarters of a year, I was hard-pressed to find either a single object of my own that wasn't covered or crowded or obscured by some criminal relic, and there wasn't a single empty space upon which to lay an additional item of my own, should I have desired to do so.

Perhaps my frustration was not wholly due to the overwhelming state of the sitting room that I had just entered upon that brassy afternoon. I had recently concluded one of several tedious consecutive days as a *locum* for a doctor on holiday from his practice near St. Pancras Station, and I was facing another bleak week of the same until his return. Every physician's office cultivates a certain *ambiance*, as the French so aptly put it, and the professional abode of Dr. Weaver was singularly constructed to weary a man's soul, consisting of plain and rather dark rooms without windows, frequent train-related rumblings – some obvious and others almost below one's awareness, except for an unsettled feeling in one's bones from arrivals and departures at the nearby station – and most of all a set of patients who were decidedly unfriendly toward this poor doctor who had agreed to treat them while their regular physician was pursuing his own likely prurient interests along the French coast.

It was with a day of this experience as my foundational basis that I returned to Baker Street in the mid-afternoon, with only the desire to put my feet up at the fire, sip a generous restorative, and lose myself in a novel of high adventure set upon the sea. Instead, I opened the door to find the sitting room especially avalanched, if that may be used as a word, under mounds of paper, stacked hither and yon across the path to my chair, which itself held a stack of books so high and skewed that I feared its imminent collapse into the fire.

Oblivious to what he had caused, for it could only have been caused by him, was my friend Sherlock Holmes, curled into his own chair opposite my own, some sort of document held close before his face, catching the last of the afternoon light from the west-facing window behind him. He looked far younger at that moment than his twenty-nine years and I, only about a year-and-a-half older then he, suddenly felt like a middle-aged parent who had returned home to find that a sheepish little

Johnny or Mary had spent the afternoon making mud pies upon the carpets.

Even as I planted my feet, afraid to try and cross that battlefield of papers before me and preparing to roar at my flatmate, he looked up with that enthusiasm of old, while waving the document this way and that.

"Morgan's palimpsest!" he cried. "I've cracked it! We only need to journey out to Hornchurch, and then a little pick-and-shovel work should set the matter right as quick as the greyhound's mouth, to borrow a bit from the Bard."

I had been prepared to list grievances, and they were still on my tongue, but they turned to ashes and, with a sigh, I let them run away. Instead, I counted to three and then stated, "That's good news for Morgan, then. Have you let him know?"

"Not yet. I only just now understood the puzzle in the moments before you arrived. I have spent the afternoon . . . ." He trailed off, looking around the room at the dunes and drifts of paper. Having been there upon previous occasions when he discovered a trail and set off where it would take him, I knew how such a mess of stacked books and scattered documents could occur. When Holmes perceived a connection, he would search and shift and sort while following the elusive fact until he found the way to the next, and so on. Only after the prey had been run to earth, so to speak, would the fever slowly dissipate, and he would peer around, as he was doing now, realizing just what his quest had wrought.

He smiled ruefully, set the palimpsest aside on his little octagonal table, uncurled from the chair, and leapt to his feet. "My dear fellow," he said, taking a few steps to my chair and effortlessly lifting a nearly three-foot stack of volumes before pivoting with them toward our dining table. "I do apologize." Setting the books down upon the table top, he ran his hands from bottom to top to align them, and then made his way to the sideboard. "A brandy, perhaps? Or no. I should think a whisky will do." He began to pour while I was left to navigate through the papers on the floor.

So after only a minor delay, I was finally ensconced in my chair, a fine old friend that I had bought from a used furniture dealer in nearby Dorset Street within a day of first moving to Baker Street. I tried not to sigh audibly with satisfaction, a reaction made more tempting as I received my curative beverage. In the meantime, Holmes turned his attention to the herding of his papers, gradually combining and collapsing the stacks until they were replaced from whence they had come, even as he explained the process that had led to his understanding of the message on the document that Morgan had brought 'round only that morning – a solution that would mean rescue from penury to the gruff old man and his two worthy granddaughters.

I only half-listened, wondering how I would get out of a planned day at Doctor Weaver's practice in order to accompany Holmes to Hornchurch, to participate in what could only be described as a treasure hunt. It was a bit awkward, asking someone else to serve as a *locum* for me, while I was already acting as *locum*, but I'd done it before. It crossed my mind, as it sometimes did, that someday, when my health was finally as good as it was going to get and I found a full-time practice of my own, I would have to discover a way to force myself to stay there every day, facing the same progression of tedious illnesses that would shuffle in and wander out of my premises with the monotonous regularity of a ticking clock. I took a sip of good whisky to chase away the thought, and that is when the doorbell rang.

Holmes glanced up from the midst of his task, a familiar gleam in his eye. We heard the sound of conversation below as Mrs. Hudson answered the door, and then steady footsteps climbing the stairs. Holmes just had time to put the substantial stack of papers in his hand upon a desk – my desk – and straighten his dressing gown. Then, following a knock at the sitting room door and, with Holmes's bid to enter, we were faced by a stranger, a young man in his mid-twenties, not much younger than Holmes or me.

I stood while Holmes spoke a greeting, directing the distraught-looking fellow to the basket chair directly facing the fire. I questioned whether he would join us in a whisky, perhaps, or something else. He declined and, with all of us seated, he began to speak.

"Thank you for the gracious welcome, gentlemen." He looked from one of us to the other. "I apologize for arriving without an appointment. I was returning to town, following the events of last night, and I fear that I allowed myself to become indiscreet upon the train, as I felt the need to discuss what happened with someone. Fortunately, I found myself sharing a compartment with a policeman returning to London from some business of his own, and he suggested that you might be able to shed a bit of light upon my dilemma."

"And this policeman was . . . ?" asked Holmes.

"I believe he said that his name was Youghal, if I'm recalling it correctly."

Holmes nodded. "Indeed. He is an inspector, and quite competent, in his own way." Turning to me, Holmes said, "He must be returning from that business in Exbourne. No doubt we'll receive a report shortly."

Holmes then gave our visitor an appraising glance, and I knew that he was seeing quite a bit that I'd likely miss. However, as I'd studied my friend's methods for a while now, I could recognize some of the more obvious things, including the fact that the man in our basket chair was a left-handed bachelor with a *penchant* for lime hair cream, someone with an office job requiring that he do a great deal of writing, perhaps in a law office, and with a nervous disposition.

Holmes said, "Watson, in addition to what you will have just observed, you might avoid making the leap to identifying his professional position as that of a law clerk, based upon the legal-looking paper peeking from his pocket. In fact, I can see that he actually works in the book publishing trade – although in the dreary business side – and that those documents you see instead relate to the matter at hand. Additionally, his nervousness is not typical, for his nails are newly chewed to the quick, and not those of someone who has an ongoing need to pursue that habit. Finally, he has had a rough night. The stains on not only your shoes, sir, but your suit from shoulders to feet indicate that you have spent some time, probably unplanned, in the woods."

The young man appeared surprised for just a moment, and then smiled. "The inspector said to expect as much," he said. He glanced at his fingertips. "You are correct about being outside and in the trees. And I am not normally nervous. But the events of last night were certainly enough to knock me off my regular perch."

"Pray, enlighten us then, Mr. . . . ?"

"Hayden. Jerrold Hayden."

Holmes nodded, and the man began his tale. "I've only just returned on the train from Exeter. I should have been back sooner, but there was a track fire along the way. I walked straight from Paddington to speak with you, Mr. Holmes, and I – "

Holmes held up a hand. "You were returning specifically from Exeter, Mr. Hayden, or one of the surrounding areas?"

"Ah. I'm sorry. From Exeter, and before that just west of Chudleigh, in Devonshire. Near the River Teign."

"Yes, I know the place," replied Holmes. "I was able to be of some service to the family at Hams Barton, back in '78. As I recall, that area you mention is just a mile or three northeast of where I visited."

"As you say, Mr. Holmes. Before I went down, I did a bit of research on the countryside, and I recall reading of that place."

"And why were you in that location?"

"I had been notified that I am the heir to a house and some land there."

"Indeed. Was this expected? I perceive that it may have been a surprise."

"Oh, I was very much surprised. I received a confidential letter on Tuesday, informing me that I had been located by a firm of West Country solicitors, seeking individuals that had been named in the will of one Clark Helverton, in order to dispose of his estate."

"Sent to your place of employment."

"That's right. How did you know?"

"From the address on the legal papers protruding from your pocket, care of the publishing firm where you are employed. You say that you had no previous knowledge of this man, Helverton?"

"You are correct. I'd never heard of him before. According to the letter, he had married my great-aunt, late in her life, and as he had no close relatives of his own, he had willed the house and land to his wife's heirs. It turns out that she also had no other remaining family but myself. I should mention that I have no personal memory of this great-aunt, as she had drifted beyond the sphere of my own family long before I was born."

"And you have no brothers, sisters, or cousins who might have also benefited from this unexpected windfall?"

"I do not. My father, who was apparently my great-aunt's only other relation, died when I was but a small child, and my late mother never remarried. I am an only child, and apparently my great-aunt – as far as I ever knew – had never married before Mr. Helverton. Thus, she had no children, and therefore my father had no cousins on that side of the family. Therefore, I am the end of that particular branch. And this was confirmed by the solicitor's representative."

Holmes leaned back. "Perhaps you need to tell me more about the circumstances."

"But don't you need to know what happened at the house last night? I can – "

Holmes smiled and shook his head. "All in good time, Mr. Hayden. Lay the proper groundwork. Surely your own experiences in the book publishing profession have taught you the importance of assembling of each element in the proper order."

Hayden nodded, took a deep breath. I again offered a tot of whisky, but he thanked me and declined.

"As I said, I received a letter early this week from the firm of Stoddard and Stoddard, of Exeter, informing me that I was the heir to the property."

"May I see the letter?"

"Certainly." Hayden retrieved the previously mentioned letter from his pocket and handed it to Holmes. "After the events of last night, I was reading it on the train, and I had also showed it to the police inspector.

79

As you can see, it rather specifically describes the nature of the inheritance, the research showing I am the only remaining heir, how I was located, and also the suggested arrangements for journeying to the West Country this weekend."

Holmes turned the sheet this way and that before reading it. "Curious," said he after a moment. "The paper and letterhead appear to be rather aged, based upon the spotting. I see that the writer, one Ethan Stoddard, had already determined that you are unmarried, and he suggested that you keep the matter secret, even from your employers."

"That is true. As he wrote, the story of the discovery of a long-lost heir might be of interest to the press, and would bring undue attention upon the matter."

"And did you keep it secret?"

"I did. I obtained leave from my employers on Friday, yesterday that is, without telling them why, and traveled down to Exeter by the late morning train, whereupon I made my way to the law offices, as suggested in the letter."

"And what of the Stoddards? I confess that, while my knowledge is not extensive upon the subject, I did have reason a few years ago to learn a bit about the legal firms of that part of the world, and I don't recall them."

"I gathered from my visit to their offices that they are a rather small concern, dealing with just a few old and established clients. I must say that I found them to be quite humble indeed. There was no clerk, and the offices are on a side street beside a haberdasher's shop. They had a feeling of neglect – an excess of dust about the place and so on, if you follow me."

"I do, indeed, Mr. Hayden. Did you have the sense that the firm had been in that location for a while, or had moved there quite recently?"

"Oh, quite a while, Mr. Holmes. I see what you are getting at, but it is a real firm, and not a quickly rented room with the intent to fool me. The sign on the wall by the front door was ancient looking and well established, and there were various certificates and photographs on the walls that testified to the long-standing presence of Stoddard and Stoddard in that area. In fact, one of the framed documents near the entryway had become crooked upon the wall, perhaps from someone brushing against it or from the vibrations of the nearby closing door, and a less-faded patch matching that object was revealed, running alongside the frame. Clearly, it had hung there for a long time. The document itself was quite faded as well."

Holmes clapped his hands. "An observant man after our own hearts, Watson!" he cried. "Clearly then, that evidence, coupled with the age of the paper, establishes their legitimacy. Do go on, Mr. Hayden. What about this Ethan Stoddard, who summoned you to Exeter?"

"He is a young fellow, about our age I would think. He apologized for the condition of the office, explaining that the original Stoddard and Stoddard had been his two uncles. One died years ago, and the other only recently became incapacitated due to apoplexy. His prognosis is not good, and Ethan, himself a lawyer, moved down from London just a few weeks earlier to take over the practice.

"We made conversation for a bit, about living in Exeter versus London and so forth, before turning to specifics, and that was when he told me that the firm had been established long ago to manage the affairs of just a few well-placed clients with interests in and around Exeter – including this Clark Helverton. A week or so ago, just after Mr. Ethan Stoddard came down to assume his new duties, he received a letter informing him of Mr. Helverton's death in New York.

"Although the old man had left England years before, he'd maintained ownership of the house near Chudleigh, out along the river, and it was this that he'd willed to any relatives of my great-aunt. In fact, in this particular case, managing the care of the old house – maintenance, taxes, and so on – was really the only thing that Stoddard and Stoddard ever did for Mr. Helverton, as the rest of his affairs were handled in America. Ethan Stoddard informed me that for a long time, the house had been rented, but sadly it has stood empty for a number of years, partly due to the decline of the elder Stoddard who ran the firm – he had been lax in finding a new tenant. As I mentioned, Ethan Stoddard's researches had revealed that I was the only heir to this particular bequest, and thus he had summoned me down to get a look at my inheritance.

"He gave me a look at both the letter from America, and the old documents from the Stoddard files – letters with instructions, previous rental records, and so on. It was confusing but seemed to be legitimate."

"Did you see the envelope for the recent letter from the United States?"

"I did. It had an American stamp and a recent post mark."

"Excellent. Pray continue."

"After making sure that I had eaten on the train, Mr. Stoddard suggested that we depart. He had a small dog-cart rented and waiting around the corner, and we set out. It was an amiable enough trip as we traveled west, the miles rolling away and the weather much like today. We wandered down ever smaller and narrower roads until we finally crossed the river and reached a ragged drive, turning and winding out of sight between two mossy pillars.

81

"As we proceeded down the overgrown lane, covered with fallen leaves and identifiable as a roadway only by its relative straightness and slight elevation from the surrounding woods, I had my first view of the house. It's a rambling structure, just two stories tall with an attic, but quite wide, with a sheltered landing that surrounded it on several sides. It looked incongruous there, like something I've seen in photographs of homes in the American South. The dark grounds, choked with black-trunked trees and wild abandoned shrubbery, slope down toward the river, and there is the suggestion that the scene should have swags of the Spanish Moss that grows in America, hanging from the trees.

"The house itself is in great disrepair. It is of a light-colored stone, but stained with mildew. Mounds of leaves and other detritus from the surrounding trees have piled along the foundation, and I could see a number of dead limbs protruding from over the edge of the roof high above us, remaining where they had fallen, possibly years earlier. We approached the front side of the house, as indicated by the imposing door centered there and the nearly obscured walkway approaching it from the drive. It has a heavy black door, quite wide. All of the window shutters were closed, but some were hanging loose from their hinges, and one was knocking against the wall in the slight breeze from the river. There are a number of dormer windows lined across the attic, and they are just high enough to catch some of the rare sunlight that penetrates the thick canopy of the trees, which themselves seemed fancifully to me as if they were somehow angry at having been disturbed from their long and ponderous isolation."

I glanced at Holmes, and I saw his mouth purse slightly. If I had been relating these events, he would have long before snapped something to the effect of sticking to the facts, or "Cut the poetry, Watson." However, he was striving to remain polite, and I for one appreciated the sense of the place that Hayden was constructing.

Our visitor, however, was not unaware of Holmes's reaction, and he strove to come back to the point. "It was then, looking at the overwhelming neglect of the house and grounds, that I began to have further questions, and just a few qualms, about whether this inheritance would actually be of any benefit to me. I hadn't really thought much about what to do before that point. Mr. Stoddard had explained that there was a small cash income associated with the house for its upkeep, but otherwise there would be no additional inheritance forthcoming.

"I was aware from our conversation that there was a bit of land along with the building, and when I saw the house and its condition, I began to calculate whether any buyer might be found to take this heap off my hands, in the condition in which it stood. It was fairly certain that the funds that Mr. Stoddard had described for upkeep were probably just enough to pay the taxes, and possibly hire someone to check the place a few times per year to ascertain that it hadn't burned. There was no way that I could fund a full restoration on my own, and I have grave doubts that I could find employment in that area, allowing me to abandon my current profession, move down from London, and set myself up as some sort of country squire.

"After we stopped, we walked a bit here and there, while I obtained different views of the house. It was in the same state of neglect upon all sides, and I suppose that my despair was becoming obvious, as Mr. Stoddard tried to cheer me up, saying that he was certain things would work out. He neglected, however, to specify exactly how that might be accomplished.

"Finally we arrived at the front door, which he opened with an age-stained key. We stepped inside, and if our eyes hadn't already been accustomed to the tree-darkened approach to the house, we wouldn't have been able to see the interior at all. As it was, I could dimly make out the hallway and stairs in front of us, and various doorways on either side. However, the smell of neglect was enough to bring tears to our eyes, and any view that had been initially obtained was quickly lost.

"We lit a couple of lamps, standing conveniently beside the door and apparently left by the irregular caretaker, and began to explore. I was happy to see that the place still benefited from the quite solid construction of the previous century. The floors were sound, and amazingly, there was no sign of leakage on the upstairs ceilings or down the walls. I quickly became confused at the upstairs layout, and was glad to find my way back down to the entry hall.

"I felt that I had seen all that there was to see, when I was shocked to find Mr. Stoddard standing in the entry way, holding a basket and telling me that he must leave, as night was approaching, and that he had brought enough food to see me through until morning. I recalled then that I had seen that same basket in the dog-cart, but I had paid it no mind.

"'Whatever can you mean?' I cried, for it was plain that he meant that I should remain there while he planned to depart.

"He apologized, saying that he thought he had mentioned that – although I knew that he had not. 'A requirement of the will,' he explained. 'Mr. Helverton stated that you must take possession of the house immediately, or it will be auctioned, with the proceeds turned over to a charity. I have consulted with my uncle,' he added, 'and we felt that some leniency in the interpretation of the document allows for you to claim the house by simply spending one night here to serve as your tenancy. Afterwards, you can declare your intent to return, an event which can be delayed indefinitely.'

"He said it all so matter-of-factly that I didn't see a way to disagree. I pointed out that, in spite of his basket of food and drink, there was nowhere for me to sleep. He seemed to think that easily solved, and led me to a side room, where the furniture was covered, and pulled a dusty sheet from a deep chair. Then, with the comment that it was getting dark and that he would be back for me in the morning, he bustled outside, ignoring my ill-formed arguments against remaining there. He pressed the old key into my hand – " and with that, Hayden pulled it from his waistcoat and handed it to Holmes, who looked at it and then placed it on the table beside him – "telling me not to lose it, as it was the only one. Then, with a warning to stay indoors, he stepped outside, pulling the door shut behind him.

"I immediately followed Stoddard to the door, opening it to see him already jumping blithely back into the dog-cart. With a wave, he turned the horse smartly and was gone.

"As you can imagine, I was stunned at how quickly this had occurred. I had gone from the despair of seeing the condition of the house and grounds to being abandoned there in the space of a few short minutes. After a time, while I stood in the doorway and considered simply trying to walk back to town, pondering that I would simply have to follow each smaller road to a larger, I realized that I hadn't paid attention to the turnings. I could certainly get out to the mossy pillars that marked the edge of the estate, but after that, I might end up walking farther from Chudleigh, and as Mr. Stoddard had pointed out, night was coming. Of course, I could always throw myself on the mercy of a neighboring farmer, provided I came across a house in my wanderings, but I couldn't even be sure of that.

"In the end, I decided I must stay. I picked up the basket and set it onto a nearby table. Opening it, I saw that it was filled with a generous supply of food – various tins and jars, a cold woodcock, a few bottles of water, and another of wine. I never eat a heavy meal in the evening, and, feeling neither hungry nor thirsty, I decided to explore the house a bit more. Taking up the lantern, I began a more systematic evaluation of the place. Some of the furniture was actually quite nice, when one ignored the dust. Upstairs, I was able to work out the initially confusing arrangement of the rooms, and I even went up to the attic, which was filled with additional old furniture, as well as numerous boxes and trunks. I heard the rustle of mice, which was not surprising, but everything seemed to be salvageable, and I was curious about what might be found amongst all the abandoned items, and frankly, how much I could get for it.

"I went back downstairs and made a light snack of some of the basket's contents. There was much more than I could eat, and I confess that I didn't open the wine, as I am a teetotaler. I glanced at my watch and saw that it was actually a bit later than I had thought. I considered pulling one of the dusty books off a shelf in the room in which I'd eaten, but first I decided that I wanted to get a breath of fresh air.

"Disregarding Mr. Stoddard's warning to stay inside, I stepped out onto the porch and pulled the door shut behind me. I'd left the lantern in the side room, not wanting to spoil my night vision, and I noticed that the heavy drapes in that room, combined with the closed shutters, prevented any of that light from leaking outside.

"Although it is October, it hasn't been cool yet, and the leaves on the trees are still quite thick, and just starting to turn. The moon was shining out on the river, and I took a few steps that way, the better to get a view of that romantic aspect. I stood for a few moments, inhaling deeply, and then, realizing that my eyes had adjusted quite a bit, I moved laterally along the river, staying an even distance away from the house. I was very quiet, without really intending to be, but it was fortunate, as it may have saved my life.

"I had come past the far end of the house, the river behind me, when I saw a movement near one of the abandoned outbuildings that we'd passed earlier. I've read that in darkness, one's peripheral vision is stronger at sensing motion than if one stares directly at an object, so I paused in the shadow of a thick tree trunk and generally cast my vision in that direction without looking too hard, if you catch my meaning. I was rewarded, as I saw the movement once again. It was a man, and he was moving slowly toward the front door of the house.

"A feeling of terror swept over me as I recalled the warning that Mr. Stoddard had made before he left, advising me to stay inside. What had he known? Was there some sinister association with this house that made living here dangerous? I was willing to believe it, when the man that I watched passed through a bar of moonlight, and I realized that it was Mr. Stoddard himself.

"With a sense of relief, I was about to hail him when I saw that his hands were not empty. In one, he appeared to hold something very much resembling a gun, and in the other – and upon this point there could be no mistake – he carried a hatchet.

"I watched as he progressed, thinking at first that he was hunting whatever the danger was that permeated these woods. But then I realized that he paid no attention to anything around him. He was focused on the front door, which he approached in a most stealthy manner, as if the enemy were within instead of without. At that point, I understood with vivid clarity that he was not protecting me, but attempting to reach me.

"He stepped to the doorway and fumbled for a moment before producing what could only be a key – another key, in spite of his recent statement that the one he had left for me was the only one. I tapped my own pocket to assure myself that it was still with me. He bent to the door, but with a barely audible sound of surprise, he discovered that his efforts had been unnecessary, as I'd left it unlocked. He opened it, so very slowly, and then slipped silently inside.

"I realized with a shock that I'd come down to that part of the world without informing anyone, upon this man's instructions, and that the only person in the entire world who knew that I was there was now approaching where he thought I waited, carrying both a gun and a hatchet. I didn't understand anything about what might be in back of all of this, but it didn't matter. All I knew then was that I needed to be somewhere else.

"Creeping along the river, staying in the trees so the moonlight wouldn't show me, I made my way back to the other side of the house, and the narrow lane leading out to the road. I could imagine Stoddard, finding the lantern and the basket, and wondering where I was. He would explore the house, trying to locate me, but eventually he'd realize that I wasn't there, and then he would look elsewhere. Seeing as how he'd approached the house without a light, I suspected that he wouldn't use one when he searched the grounds, and every step I took was with the terror that he would step out in front of me, a shadow only identified by the shine of moonlight on the gun and the blade.

"I may have sobbed with relief when, about halfway up the lane, I came upon his dog-cart, tied to a small tree. I'd loosened it and hurried the horse up the road before I even had time to think what I was doing. I reached the pillars at the main road, turned the way that seemed familiar, and kept going. Here in the open, with the moon high in the sky, the route was clear. Wherever there was a road that was wider than before, and seemed to be in the direction of Exeter, I took it. Soon I was on the main road, which I recognized, and I finally reached the outskirts of Exeter, where I found an inn of middle quality. I obtained a room, and asked that they stable the horse, with the instruction that it not be left where it could be seen. No doubt they were a bit suspicious, especially as I had no bags with me. I was fearful that the innkeeper was friends with Stoddard, would recognize the dog-cart, and somehow get word to the man, leading him to show up in the middle of the night. I don't think I slept a wink, hearing every creak and settlement in the old building.

"In the morning, I silently departed, leaving the cart, and wandered in a stealthy manner until I found a cab. I was then deposited at St. David's Station. It was still a bit before the London train, so I had a bite of breakfast in the Great Western Hotel, where I watched the doorway in fear and trusted no one, not even the old man dozing at a nearby table. My face, reflected in the mirror on the nearby wall, was ghastly. Finally it was time for my train and I departed. Along the way, I relaxed enough to fall into casual conversation with the man in my compartment and, upon learning his profession, told him my story. He suggested that it was odd, and while no crime had actually been committed, it might be something upon which you could advise me. Thus, here I am." And he spread his hands as if to demonstrate that, indeed, he was actually sitting in our basket chair.

I had felt a thrill of terror as he described the events of the previous evening, the dark and sinister isolation of the abandoned house, the moonlight and the river and the looming trees, and the sudden identification of the man who had invited him there, holding instruments of murder, moving silently toward where our visitor was thought to be innocently waiting . . . .

"The wine!" I cried.

Jerrold Hayden looked surprised and confused, but Holmes nodded. "Very good, Watson. My thoughts exactly."

"I'm sorry, but . . . ." said Hayden.

"I believe that Watson has worked out that, if you had chosen to drink the wine list night, you might have soon found yourself sleepy, or at least in such a fog as to be unable to defend yourself, making your end – for that is what we will suppose was planned by Mr. Stoddard – to be that much easier."

"You mean that the wine was drugged?"

"Possibly. He could have used a hypodermic needle to add something to the contents through the cork."

"Then why not the food or the water?"

"Any number of reasons. Perhaps what he used would have been noticeable when used in that fashion. Perhaps some of the food *was* drugged. Did you sample all of it?"

"I did not. I simply opened one of the potted meat tins and ate it with crackers."

"Of course. Both items are purchased unopened. Your lack of appetite may have saved you. Was the water sealed?"

"Yes, with a metal cap. No cork." He looked uncomfortable. "So you agree that there is something sinister about this business?"

"On the face of it, how could we not?" replied Holmes. "And yet, you say the documents, and the office itself, were legitimate enough." He leaned forward. "I will investigate this matter, although today being Saturday complicates things a bit. Do you have somewhere to stay, in order to avoid going home?"

"I . . . I can get a room at a hotel, if you recommend it."

"I do. When you are established, send word around as to where you can be reached. I cannot stress enough that you should avoid your lodgings. Where are they, by the way?"

Hayden provided an address near Moxon Street. Holmes noted it on his cuff, and then stood, indicating that the interview was over. A bit puzzled at this abrupt shift, Hayden rose as well, thanking us and moving toward the door. In moments he was gone, and Holmes was consulting one of his reference books. Then, with a snap, he shut it and replaced it on the bookcase.

"Stoddard and Stoddard is indeed an actual firm."

"Was there a doubt? I thought that the description of the old office, the framed documents, and so on, was enough to convince you."

"Confirmation, especially when it is so easily obtained, should never be ignored."

I shifted, as if to stand. "Shall I make arrangements to go with you down to Exeter?"

He smiled. "This cake isn't quite baked yet, Watson. I'm afraid that you might need to plan on substituting for Dr. Weaver for just a bit longer." He shed his dressing gown, pulled on a coat, and reached for his Inverness and fore-and-aft cap, which he wore in both town and country, indifferent to convention. "I shall likely miss supper." And then he was gone.

I did not see him that night, but he returned the next evening, looking rather worn. As usual, he didn't provide any information as to his activities since his departure on Saturday. He glanced at Hayden's temporary address, delivered to our door the previous night, and wrote a message, which he handed to our page boy. Then, hungrily attacking the remains of the cold dinner provided by Mrs. Hudson, he asked if I could make myself available for a journey to Exeter the next day. I confirmed it, frankly happy to be free and rescued from my obligation to Dr. Weaver's grim practice, and set about making arrangements with a young physician of my acquaintance who had taken over my duties in the past. While I was doing so, Holmes said goodnight and retreated to his room.

And so on Monday, I found myself on the late morning Great Western Railway train out of Paddington, in the company of my friend, along with Jerrold Hayden and Inspector Youghal of Scotland Yard.

The inspector had a jovial smile, and seemed to appreciate being included. "I knew that you could make something out of this, Mr. Holmes. I knew it as soon as Mr. Hayden here told me his story."

"I'm still in the dark," said Hayden. "Am I to understand that you know the circumstances behind the events of last Friday night?"

I wished to know the details as well. Fortunately, Holmes began to explain.

"On Saturday, after you departed, Mr. Hayden, I found a location from which to observe your rooms. I soon learned that I was not alone."

"Stoddard?" asked our client with shock.

Holmes nodded. "If your Mr. Stoddard is about five feet, eight inches tall, with broad shoulders and a squarish head, blonde hair cut rather longish in back, and a habit of standing with one foot flat and the other leg bent and resting upon a pointed toe."

"Yes, that sounds like him. He did that several times while we were talking last Friday."

"He wasn't there when I arrived, but showed up soon after, finding a place in a doorway across the street. He stayed for several hours before giving up, shifting back and forth impatiently but never trying to enter the building. He kept watch up and down the street, becoming more alert whenever someone approached."

"And he didn't see you?" asked Hayden.

Youghal laughed, and Holmes smiled. "He did not, for I did not wish to be seen." Then, the smile dropped away and he continued. "Eventually, he gave up and made his way to a small nearby hotel – fortunately, not the same one where you chose to stay! When he was in for the night, I arranged to have the place watched in my absence, and made myself useful elsewhere."

I was certain that assistance had been provided by those lads, and sometimes lasses, who made up Holmes's Irregular force. They were always willing to help, and the promise of payment was only part of the attraction. Their respect for Holmes, who valued them when often no one else did, made them very loyal allies indeed.

"I caught the late train to Exeter," Holmes said. "I had wired ahead to arrange an appointment with Fenton Stoddard, the surviving partner, and Ethan Stoddard's uncle. Although it was quite late by then, I felt that the matter would progress with a greater chance of success if I was able to make my investigation while Ethan, or so I believed the man I had observed to be, was still in London. Upon arrival at St. David's Station, I made my way to the home of Fenton Stoddard, who had waited up for me. I had revealed just enough in my message to rouse his concern. I didn't want to specify too much in my wire before I had ascertained that he wasn't in on the plot."

"Holmes," I said. "You were taking a chance. If the uncle was involved in this affair, you were placing yourself in the same position that Mr. Hayden had just a day or so earlier – traveling to Exeter and walking into the lion's den without letting anyone know where you had gone!"

Holmes smiled. "I took the precaution of arranging for covering fire, so to speak. You may recall that Thad Flatcher lives in Exeter. He and his brother met me at the station, and both of them waited hidden outside of Stoddard's home to see what would happen, and if I reappeared – which I did."

My thoughts flashed instantly to the man to whom Holmes was referring. If not for my friend's assistance, young Thad would have been hanged in late '81 for a crime he didn't commit, wherein the theft of an ancient Devonshire Charter, and the hidden message it contained, had played such an unfortunate part in the brutal and unnecessary murder of old Dr. Chambers by the wicked Pennington Gang.

"After offering refreshments," continued Holmes, "the elder Stoddard clearly wished to know more of my assertions, as I had only wired that there was a matter of grave and confidential concern regarding his practice. Now, in his presence, I related your entire narrative, Mr. Hayden, along with showing him the letter you received last Tuesday. Needless to say, he was shocked, and I was convinced of his sincerity – but only to a certain degree. After all, while he might only be discovering the plot as I related it, he might still see some personal benefit to it and make a move of his own to support it. Therefore, I remained wary.

"Following his initial reaction, he shook his head sadly, as if it wasn't so great a surprise after all. 'Ethan has always been a wrong 'un,' he explained. 'He is my sister's boy. She married a man with a temper who died young. He had a way of believing that the world owed him something, and he passed it on to Ethan. When I became ill a few weeks ago, Ethan came down to help, although he was never put in any kind of permanent position, as he implied to your client. I should have known better.'

"Old Mr. Stoddard called to his servant, asking for his coat and for the carriage to be made ready. I was careful to note that at no time did he have a chance to write or pass a message, verbal or otherwise, to anyone that might be relayed to Ethan Stoddard in London. This did much to build my trust of him. Outside, he was helped into the carriage, and I joined him, surreptitiously signaling to Thad that he should follow, in case there was still some move to be made against me.

"My fears were groundless. We arrived at the Stoddard office and made a systematic search. All of the papers relating to Clark Helverton's estate were easily found on Ethan Stoddard's desk, and his uncle's examination of them revealed something both surprising and obvious." His gaze focused specifically upon our client. "Mr. Hayden, the details of the Helverton estate, and the amount apportioned to you as the only designated heir, was very much misrepresented by Ethan Stoddard. You did in fact inherit the remote house and grounds located along the River Teign, as described. But additionally, you are the sole recipient, upon providing proof of your identity in person to the Helverton legal representatives in New York, of a fortune totaling nearly a million pounds."

This startling statement was followed by silence from all parties, with only the steady thrum of our westward train, or the occasional London-bound roaring past on the adjacent track, providing any intrusive noise. Hayden opened and closed his mouth, swallowing several times, and once his eyes widened as a thought occurred to him. He started to speak, but Youghal interrupted with a prosaic summary.

"And so this Ethan Stoddard has some plan to steal the inheritance."

"It would seem so," agreed Holmes. "Fenton Stoddard removed my last doubts of his own character and possible personal interest when he unhesitatingly summoned a local policeman of his acquaintance, making the matter official. He also sent some wires to the attorneys in New York, who could provide confirmatory information, even if it was early Sunday morning.

"Leaving the old man and the policeman to await responses to Stoddard's wires, Thad Flatcher and I, using the address listed in the Helverton papers found in the file on Ethan Stoddard's desk, found our way to the abandoned house on the river. It was as described, and the door was unlocked, although I was prepared to use the key that you had provided to me, Mr. Hayden, if we found it otherwise. The food basket provided for you was still there, as the stranded Ethan Stoddard had apparently been unwilling to carry it with him as he made his way back to town without benefit of his dog-cart. I retrieved the unopened wine bottle, as well as some of the food stuffs, and was able to obtain access to a local laboratory, using Fenton Stoddard's influence. I easily verified that the food was perfectly fine, but the wine bottle contained a possibly toxic amount of chloral hydrate. Close examination revealed the mark of a hypodermic needle through the wax and the bottle's cork where it had been added."

"So he did mean to kill me," muttered Hayden, finding his voice.

"Undoubtedly," replied Holmes. "To sneak in and shoot you if you were still conscious, or to simply dispose of you if you were fully unconscious or perhaps already dead. The dosage of chloral hydrate added to the wine was quite strong, and would have been undetectable if you had imbibed. The fact that he carried a hatchet lends further terror and grim possibilities to the speculations. Your body might never have been found, as the house and grounds are as lonely and abandoned as you described."

"Then," I said, "it was Stoddard's intention to somehow replace Mr. Hayden and assume the inheritance."

"That's how I read it," said Holmes. "He spoke the truth when explaining how he recently moved to Exeter to help with his uncle's practice, which seemingly does manage the affairs of just a few well-to-do clients, mostly in England, but a few with American connections. Only a few days after his arrival, as shown by documents on his desk, the information about the extent of Mr. Helverton's estate appeared – a fact completely unknown to Fenton Stoddard, I might add. These papers explained the true amount of the assets, the identity of the heir, and the conditions for claiming the inheritance – namely, a visit in person to the New York offices handling Helverton's fortune, with substantiating proofs in hand.

"While Thad Flatcher and I had been to the house, and then the chemical laboratory, Fenton Stoddard had received replies from New York, indicating that they had been told that the heir was found, and would present himself within a few weeks, providing proper documentation of his identity. Specifically, the heir was described to them as appearing very much like Ethan Stoddard, and *not* like you, Mr. Hayden. You will have observed that you are physically quite different from one another. This description of the heir was backed and certified by the good reputation of Stoddard and Stoddard, who had handled Clark Helverton's affairs in England for decades, and therefore it would have been completely accepted by the New York lawyers, as they indicated in their wire.

"We'll know more specifics when he is interrogated, but Ethan Stoddard realized as soon as the first letter arrived from New York that the requirements were just vague enough that he, a young man of the same approximate age, could take Mr. Hayden's place. However, rather than simply stealing documents that he could use to assume the true heir's identity, he apparently decided to make sure that any stray loopholes caused by your continued existence, Mr. Hayden, would be closed. He had quickly researched you and found that you were an orphan without living kin. After you were removed – ”

“Killed,” interrupted Hayden, with a catch in his voice.

“Yes, killed,” amended Holmes, “with no one of your acquaintance knowing anything about your trip to Exeter, he would have broken into your London rooms, found what he needed to allow him to assume your identity, prepared whatever supporting legal documents that he would need to be sent or carried from England, and then made his way to New York, after convincingly winding up his affairs here. Who could challenge him? He would have sent word to your employer and landlord that you had departed in such a way that your absence would be regretted or resented, but quickly forgotten, and also provided some story to his uncle before he himself left, while preventing the old man from ever learning about the Helverton inheritance.

“He would have sent specific information to the New York offices managing the estate from Stoddard and Stoddard to make sure that nothing else was ever sent to Exeter that might undo his story. He might have even undertaken to use more of the chloral hydrate to remove his old uncle from the picture, effectively closing the Exeter practice completely. It was an opportunity that literally fell into his lap, and he saw that he could manipulate both ends of things without it ever being discovered. He is the sort of crafty person that saw his chance and cobbled his plan together within days. The simple and unpleasant fact that you didn’t drink the wine, Mr. Hayden, was the grit in the machine that saved your life and started the unraveling of his scheme.”

“So what happens now, Mr. Holmes?” asked Youghal. “When I first heard of this on the train last Saturday, there was nothing criminal in what had occurred – yet. Mr. Hayden saw a fellow with a gun and a hatchet sneaking around in the dark, but no attack had actually occurred, and proving intent is sometimes impossible, as you know. Even now, we might make a case of fraud, based on what he told the New York lawyers, but Stoddard can rightly claim that he did find the correct heir, and that he still intended to present Mr. Hayden here at the proper time. Your theories about what he intended cannot be completely proven, and he can blow up any case we might make with legal tricks about making us provide proof.”

“I believe that a bit more will come to light,” replied Holmes cryptically. “When I left for London yesterday, Fenton Stoddard was curiously going over the books at his office, and he seemed to have found something more tangible. Additionally, he’s been in touch with Ethan Stoddard’s former employers in London, and I think they have something to say as well.” Youghal waited, but Holmes didn’t elaborate.

"When we arrive in Exeter," I said, filling the silence, "we will confront him."

"Yes," agreed Holmes. "Ethan returned to Exeter last night, accompanied unknowingly by Wiggins and a few of the other lads. They, along with the Flatcher brothers, have watched him continuously since then. Long before Ethan arrived, Fenton Stoddard returned to his own home with the plan to exaggerate his illness, in the unlikely event that his nephew tries to communicate with him in the meantime. He is genuinely outraged at the breach of trust enacted by his nephew, and he will let us do what is necessary. I expect that Ethan Stoddard is in the office now. We left the Helverton documents as we found them, so that he would not be alerted."

"Isn't that a risk?" I asked. "If he does think that his plan is coming apart, he might destroy something."

"Not too risky. He certainly knows nothing for certain except that Mr. Hayden disappeared from the river house on Friday night, along with the dog-cart that he left tied on the road. To his knowledge, Mr. Hayden never returned to his London rooms, and has seemingly vanished. Ethan may panic due to the uncertainty, but I think he's made of sterner stuff than that, and will wait to see if he has another chance. After all, he's playing for a very fine prize indeed. And even if he destroys documents in his possession, the information is still available at the New York end, as well as the testimony from those attorneys as to what fraudulent information he has already relayed to them – namely, that the heir has been found, along with a false description. Finally, as I said, the Irregulars and Thad Flatcher are in place if Ethan bolts, and the last wire I had from Exeter, an hour before we departed, reported that he had returned to Exeter yesterday evening – I likely passed him on the up train during my return – and after spending the night in his own rooms, he opened up the offices at eight o'clock this morning, the usual time."

Youghal nodded. "A workmanlike job as usual, Mr. Holmes. I look forward to speaking to this young scoundrel."

The inspector's wish was granted, and the rest is soon told. Holmes had nothing further to report and, refusing to speculate without further data, he smoked his pipe the rest of the journey while Hayden, Youghal, and I discussed the case. Hayden alternated between struggling comprehension of the sudden unexpected fortune and just how close he had come to disaster.

Upon our arrival at St. David's Station in Exeter, we were met by Wiggins, who informed us that Ethan Stoddard was still at the law practice, where he had been since that morning. Holmes then led us across to the Great Western Hotel, where Hayden had eaten breakfast just two days before. Waiting inside were several people, including a local inspector named Hanks, Thad Flatcher, and a wizened glowering old man, who, as expected, turned out to be Fenton Stoddard. Although his recent illness was apparent, he hobbled toward Holmes with vigor and shook a packet of telegrams. "Just as you thought, Mr. Holmes! It is beyond the theft of the inheritance. I have been nursing a viper to my bosom!"

Holmes quickly read through the flimsy sheets, one after another, before handing them to me. Some were from New York, confirming in greater detail the misleading statements and assertions made by Ethan Stoddard regarding the Helverton heir. There was no doubt that a case of fraud could be clearly proven. Another was from Stoddard's former employer in London. Unknown to his uncle, the nephew had been let go from his previous position in Lincoln's Inn Fields for suspected theft just weeks before being summoned to Exeter. "But even worse," said the old man, holding out a second sheaf of papers, "he has been moving against me here, forging my name to documents, and apparently cleaning out my own accounts before his departure for America."

Holmes looked at the papers and nodded. "He would have only done this, Mr. Stoddard, if he knew that you would not be around to discover it. Clearly, as I theorized, your death was part of his plan. Doubtless, you would have seemingly died in your sleep, with the story spread that it was a relapse from your recent illness. He would have quietly closed your practice, with the assets already spirited away through his earlier forgeries, and then departed these shores, with no one the wiser, ready to assume Mr. Hayden's identity. What a pity he turned such a quick-thinking mind to crime."

With a scowl and a clearing of his throat, Mr. Stoddard signaled that he didn't share my friend's somewhat misplaced admiration. Holmes announced that there was no need to put off confronting Ethan Stoddard any longer, and we piled into cabs summoned from the nearby station. Then came the slow ascent up St. David's Hill, across the Iron Bridge, and eventually left into the High Street, with the Cathedral looming over us just a block away. Parking around the corner from Stoddard's office, we assembled a short distance from the legal practice, with Holmes and Wiggins providing assistance to the old man.

We approached the doorway by crowding near to the building, so as not to be seen from the windows. The old man had informed us that his nephew was likely at his desk upstairs. From nearby, Thad Flatcher and the Irregulars made themselves known.

After silently entering the ground floor, we gathered out of sight, away from the foot of the stairs, and Fenton Stoddard called out sharply, "Ethan! Come down here!"

Overhead, we heard a chair scrape, followed by a surprised, "Uncle?" Then we heard footsteps cross the room above us and start down the stairs. "I had no idea you were well enough to come into – " He was unable to continue the thought, as his appearance in the room corresponded with both arms being grabbed by the two inspectors, who quickly handcuffed him.

He fought for a moment and then, seeing Jerrold Hayden standing before him, fists clenched at his sides, he sagged in defeat. Later, under the combined questioning of Inspectors Youghal and Hanks, Ethan Stoddard would attempt a half-hearted defense, ignoring the offer of counsel and the initial warning that his statements could be used against him. He only dug himself deeper and deeper, straight into a substantial prison sentence.

The elder Mr. Stoddard, with a combination of unnecessary guilt by mere association to the affair and a lifetime of advising a few select wealthy clients, took Jerrold Hayden under his wing, and in future years, we were to hear of the exponential growth of the original Helverton inheritance, a great deal of which was used to fund charitable activities on both sides of the Atlantic, not the least of which was an orphanage of great renown in a formerly abandoned mansion on the shores of the River Teign.

More immediately satisfying to me upon our return to London was learning of the next day's arrangements to visit Hornchurch and dig up the treasure identified in Morgan's palimpsest. I wasted no time in seeking an extension of my physician friend's services at Dr. Weaver's practice. Apparently this worked out well for the both of them, as Dr. Weaver, having met a dancer in Cannes, decided to sell the practice post-haste, and for some reason the location appealed to my own temporary *locum*, who scraped up enough money to buy it.

On the following day, Holmes and I made our way northeast of London to find the treasure. Of course it wasn't that simple, and before we were finished, I'd had a dunking in an overgrown pond, one man had lost his freedom, and another his sanity. But that is another story . . . .

The Adventure of the Faithful Servant

by Tracy Revels

"I believe my employer has been bewitched, Mr. Holmes. Is it within your powers to break a spell?"

My friend Sherlock Holmes raised an eyebrow at the inquiry, which had been spoken by a thin, elderly man, clad in a somber black suit. He had given his name as Harold Tifton, the butler of Stag Hall, and had come seeking advice as to how to aid his beloved master. He lifted his head as he waited for a reply, and I was struck again not only by the painful anxiety that had distorted his lean face, but also by the grayish film that covered both eyes. He had entered our rooms with the aid of a cane, and held himself so still that I sensed he feared the awkwardness of being in unfamiliar surroundings, where he might easily trip and upset some article of furniture. As always, Holmes's response was firm but gentle.

"I do not deal in the diabolical, sir. However, if you will tell me what troubles your employer, perhaps we can unravel a less supernatural cause for his predicament."

The man seemed unconvinced by this reply. "I know I am old and foolish, but for the gentleman I have served for years to suddenly become almost a stranger to me – it seems like dark magic. Perhaps I should seek the advice of a priest instead."

"Watson, will you pour some tea for our guest?" Holmes asked. "I have great respect for the instincts of those in domestic service, Mr. Tifton. There is no keener observer of humankind. If you feel something is harming your master, it is very likely that a difficulty exists. Please, tell us your story."

With that reassurance, and a teacup that I guided to his trembling hands, the dignified servant began to speak.

"My employer is Mr. Edwin James Asher. You may be familiar with the family name."

"The Ashers, of the Manchester mills?"

"Indeed, sir. They are among the great industrialists of our nation. My master is the only son of a junior branch of the family, and he inherited a substantial estate when he was twenty years of age. It permitted him to be a scholar and traveler. He has written a small

97

monograph on his youthful journey to America." A bit of pride brought color into Tifton's hollow cheeks. "*The Mysteries of the Okefenokee*."

"I recall it well," Holmes said. "You would enjoy the book, Watson. Mr. Asher's adventures among the strange American species known as the 'Crackers', not to mention the alligators, would appeal to your love of the grotesque." He turned back to our guest. "Did you accompany your employer on this journey?"

"No, sir. He was in America long before we met. I made his acquaintance after he returned to Manchester and began to woo the daughter of Mr. Matthew Chandler. I was the head footman in the Chandler household at the time. I am not inclined to gossip, but everyone below stairs thought it was a strange romance. Mr. Asher was some two decades older than Miss Eleanor, and not a sociable man in the least. However, she adored him. They wed and moved to a fine home in London. Mr. Asher hired me to be his butler at that time."

"Was the match a happy one?" Holmes asked.

"No couple could have been more devoted, sir. Mr. Asher often said that all he wished for was a large fireside and a little wife. He had his books and artifacts to study, and my dear mistress often said she was content with studying Mr. Asher." The cup abruptly clattered as Tifton was seized with a strong emotion. I leapt up and took it from him as he fumbled for a handkerchief. "Please forgive me. I had known her since she was a baby in her cradle. Miss Eleanor was heaven's angel sent to earth, so perhaps God wished her home."

"There was an accident?" I asked.

"No, sir, an illness, and it came upon her very suddenly. One day she was laughing and flitting around the house, and a month later we were putting her to rest in Highgate Cemetery. To sharpen the pain, she had been in the family way when she passed."

I closed my eyes. Such a loss might well cost a loving man his sanity. Holmes spoke dryly.

"And how did your master respond?"

"He could no longer bear the sight of London. He sold everything in the city and purchased Stag Hall in the village of Edendore. It was, he said, as deep as he could bury himself and still be alive. None of the other staff would abide such a rustic existence, but I could not abandon him. We settled into Stag Hall six months ago. My master hired only three people – a cook who also sees to the housekeeping, a valet, and a stable boy who tends the grounds." Tifton coughed uncomfortably. "I will not speak ill of them – they are, after all, only country folk who have never been employed by a true gentleman before – but I often am forced to reprove them for neglecting their duties."

"So Mr. Asher isolated himself?" I asked.

"He did, sir. His grief was unbearable. Then, about three months ago, on a trip into the village to mail a letter, he made the acquaintance of a Mr. Remington. He told me that Mr. Remington was an American and a fellow scholar. I encouraged him to call upon this gentleman, as the chance meeting had lifted my master's spirits. He said that he would, and I heard from the others on the staff that he did, quite often, while I was away."

"You were absent?" Holmes asked.

"Yes, sir. A week after Mr. Asher met Mr. Remington, my younger brother Albert passed away in Scotland. Mr. Asher granted me a month to settle all of Albert's affairs. My brother left behind two boys and a little girl, and I needed time to find schools for them."

"Your master sounds like an ideal employer," I said.

Tifton smiled tightly. "He is, indeed, the finest gentleman any man could wish to serve. He has his own ways, but he has been kind and generous, especially as my eyesight has grown so weak. Never once has he suggested that I leave my post due to my infirmity."

"Until now?" Holmes asked. Tifton shook his head.

"No, sir. At least, he has not said it outright, but . . . perhaps I should finish my story. When I returned from Scotland, Mr. Asher told me that Mr. Remington was returning to America, and he was going to London to see him off. Jenkins, the valet, accompanied him. They were gone for three days. When they returned, Mr. Asher had contracted a terrible cold, and Jenkins put him to bed where he stayed, racked with fever and coughing, for almost a month. I wanted to summon a doctor, but he would have none of it. Finally, Mr. Asher emerged from his room thinner and bundled in his robes, his beard unkempt, his hair disarrayed, and his voice much coarsened by the ordeal."

"Did you master make any purchases during his visit to London?" Holmes interjected, with such suddenness that Tifton looked to me in surprise.

"Yes, Mr. Holmes. The day after his return, a large iron safe was delivered to Stag Hall. I had it installed in the study. I can only suppose that, living in such a remote place, my master felt he needed a safe to secure his valuables."

"And considering what you have told us of the new staff's failings, perhaps it was a wise measure to take," Holmes said, with a satisfied nod. "So, was your master's mode of behavior also altered following his confinement?"

"Yes, sir. He lost all interest in his books and artifacts. He began to drink more heavily and – this pains me to even speak of it – he is now consorting with Lillie, the cook, who is not worthy to follow Miss Eleanor in his affections. He has become much more familiar with Jenkins and Bodie – our boy – than he is with me. He barely speaks to me, but sends his orders via Jenkins. He is nothing like himself at all."

"Do the other members of the household staff have an explanation for this change?"

"Only one, sir. Jenkins told me that after bidding Mr. Remington goodbye, Mr. Asher had the cab take him to Highgate, where – I share this in confidence – Mr. Asher spent almost a day in the rain, sobbing at Miss Eleanor's tomb. That, Jenkins tells me, is how he acquired his illness. I could believe it all . . . and attribute this queer madness to his terrible illness and his overwhelming grief . . . if not for those damnable gypsies!"

I started in my chair. "Gypsies?"

"Yes. Last week an entire tribe of them came to the estate, with their campfires and strange singing and black magic. When I objected to their presence, Mr. Asher told me to keep silent or seek employment elsewhere. I believe they are the cause of the trouble – perhaps he encountered them in London and they cursed him. I have heard that gypsies do such things."

Holmes leaned back in his chair and laced his fingers together. "Do you recall the exact date of your master's trip to London?"

"He departed Stag Hall very early on October 11th, and returned late in the evening on October 13th."

Holmes rose from his chair. "Mr. Tifton, I think I may be able to put your mind to rest and break this curse. If you will return to Stag Hall today, you may expect us around eleven tomorrow morning. Will your master be at home at that time?"

"I believe so, sir. He rarely goes out."

"Capital! Do not mention your visit here and, when we arrive, I will hand you a card and you will announce us in those terms. Do you understand?"

Mr. Tifton scowled as he pulled on his coat. "Is such subterfuge necessary?"

"All magic depends on it. Now, would you like Dr. Watson to escort you to the station?"

"Thank you for the kind offer, Mr. Holmes, but I was born in London, and though my sight is nearly extinguished, I know the city by heart. Until tomorrow, sir."

With a stiff, dignified bow, he took his leave. A moment later, Holmes sprang into action with the eagerness of a hound to the hunting horn.

"I will need to run some errands before our little trip. No, Watson, it is much too dreary and your wound is aching! Save your energy for our work in the morning." It was useless for me to ask him how he knew about my pains; I had always been an open book to him. "You can, however, do one thing that would be of vast assistance to me."

"And that is?"

"Clean your pistol."

Early the next day, we were on the train for Edendore and Stag Hall. Holmes had given me just enough time to seize a cup of coffee at the station, and I confess my eyelids were still heavy when he thrust a scrap of newspaper at me. As was his wont, he had said nothing about the butler's problem upon his return the previous evening.

"Read this."

It was a clipping from the most garish of our London tabloids, and the entire article was written in such a sensational, gruesome style that I would be embarrassed to reproduce it here. The gist of it was that a body had been found in a disreputable hotel in the city. From the clothing and the contents of the dead man's pockets, which amounted to no more than three shillings, a box of matches, and a letter, the man was identified as a Mr. Chauncey Rowe. The desk clerk revealed that a man had registered under that name at the hotel the day before. A few other guests in the hotel had noted that at around two a.m. the previous evening, three men, all in a state of great inebriation, were seen going into Room 201, which had been occupied by Rowe. As the singing and roistering had quickly ended, the other guests thought no more about it. The body had been found by a housemaid. She had fainted in the doorway, for the body stretched out on the blood-soaked rug was missing its head.

"Repulsive," I muttered, passing the clipped article back to Holmes. "Your choice of morning reading is appalling."

"But surely you make the connection?"

"Between what? Were you called to investigate?"

Holmes gave a quick nod. "It occurred while you were at the bedside of a dying patient. As you were already dismayed by the sad outcome of your case, I felt no need to burden you with this, especially as it was one of my failures."

Now I was more intrigued. "Failures? How so?"

"I could find nothing to provide data. The clothing was banal and common, with no helpful laundry marks to trace it. The physical body – of a man in his middle to later years, who had never done manual labor – was unremarkable. Several guests in the hotel had seen the three men who came into the room, but could recall no details about them, because

101

they were all bundled in cloaks and mufflers. And, besides, who truly looks at that annoying specimen of London society, the dissolute reveler? One tends to turn away." Holmes closed his eyes, his lean frame swaying with the motion of the train. "But it was wrong, Watson. So very wrong."

"Well, there was a decapitation."

Holmes snorted. "The manner of his death was unimportant, though I noted that it was done cleanly, with a sharp sword. Presumably he suffered very little, if at all, for the body and clothing reeked of gin. The bed had not been slept in, and unfortunately for me neither the victim nor the felons engaged in the vice of smoking. The room was bare of any clues, except for the body and one important conundrum."

"Which was?"

"His boots did not fit."

"Many people wear boots that do not fit!" I objected.

"Perhaps – if the footwear is too large. But what man would, under any circumstances, endure a boot that is at least two sizes too small?" Holmes smirked. "He was not wearing his boots when he was executed, and I doubt our friends in the police even noted the discrepancy. But I measured and I know." Holmes slipped the clipping back into his wallet. "It proved the proverbial dead end. No relatives could be located. The letter – so vague and purposeless that I am certain it was a fraud – could not be traced, as it lacked an envelope or any address other than the salutation to the dead man. To say that I got no further along with the business than Lestrade did is, I confess, rather humiliating. Ah, here is our station. Let us hope for better things in this investigation. And, before I forget, do you feel rather intimidating this morning? Could you beat a man senseless – besides myself, of course?"

The village of Edendore, which was a ten-mile ride from the station, seemed suspended in time, a collection of tumble-down, thatched houses and one misbegotten pub and hostelry, The Blue Dragon. Holmes presented himself to the grizzled publican, who had been dozing beside the fire.

"Mr. Asher, well, we don't see him much. Taken sick over his dead lady, I've heard, but he was never one to come and share a dram with us, so what should I care?"

A sharp giggle interrupted the publican's statement. I turned and saw the flounce of a calico skirt and a long braid of blonde hair disappearing up the stairs. Holmes leaned close.

"As you will recall, old friend, the fair sex is your department. See what you can learn from that delightful lady who was so eager to eavesdrop."

It was certainly not the worst assignment Holmes had ever given me. I climbed the creaky stairs and found the young woman briskly sweeping the hallway. Her hair was thick and lustrous and her figure was superb, but when she spun around her lovely face was marred by a smile filled with crooked stumps of teeth.

"Excuse me, Miss," I said, with what I hoped was a gallant dip of the head, "but have you seen Mr. Asher recently?"

"Naw," she drawled, "but my cousin Betty has. She'll take him away from that ginger-haired tart, you watch. Mr. Asher likes the nice girls, he does! See!" She reached into her ample bosom and pulled out a shining sovereign. "His man Jenkins gave this to me last week, says there's more if I come and see Mr. Asher one evening, when the butler's asleep. I think I just might. I could take him away from Lillie, I'd wager!"

She struck a pose that suggested just how easy such a conquest might be. I decided it was safer to return downstairs, where Holmes was waiting at the door.

"It seems Mr. Asher has all the ladies in a stir," I muttered.

"Indeed it does. With Jenkins as his procurer of female attention."

I rolled my eyes, wondering why Holmes had sent me up to speak to the girl in the first place. "It is a sad thing, when you consider it. A man was once loyal to his wife, adored her more than life itself, and now consorts with women of easy virtue."

"I doubt Mr. Asher has changed."

"But all the evidence suggests that he has. It is obvious!"

"You of all people should know that I never allow myself to be guided by obvious evidence. Very well, we have about a mile's walk ahead of us, according to our friend at the bar."

It was a rough journey over a thin, rutted road, past dull sheep and bored shepherds. At last we reached the outskirts of Stag Hall. The grounds were wild and overgrown, with a narrow gravel pathway leading towards the sagging Tudor edifice. Everything had clearly seen better days. I pitied the poor Tifton, once the major domo of a fine city house, now reduced to nagging the inefficient, lazy caretakers of this pile. I was just about to express my sentiments when the thick bushes beside us rattled. We both halted, perplexed as to what was about to come through them.

To my horror, it proved to be a bear, a massive brute of a creature with long claws and thick yellow teeth. It emerged upright, lumbering forward on two legs, swaying to and fro like a drunkard while snorting and snuffing. I snatched my pistol from my coat pocket, and would have shot the deadly beast had Holmes not abruptly knocked my firearm aside.

103

"No! Wait!"

Holmes took a step forward and held his arms over his head, making himself appear even larger. He shouted a word in a strange language and thrust out his right hand, curled into a fist. As close as he was, the bear could easily have knocked him to the ground and torn him to pieces before I could recover my gun.

Instead, the creature dropped to all fours. Holmes spoke a different word and flattened out his hand. To my utter astonishment, the bear rolled onto its back and waggled its legs in the air, with the same expectant look that a pup gives when demanding a belly rub. Holmes obliged the animal, scratching its fur-coated stomach.

"Watson, surely you see the collar it wears?"

I blinked. Indeed, the bear's neck was encircled with a thick, fantastically worked leather collar. Holmes stepped back and gave another vocal command with a hand signal. The bear sat up and walked to his side, clearly ready to follow where he led.

"Holmes, how did you . . . ."

"When I was a boy, a group of gypsies camped near our home. Having just lost an argument with Mycroft – I was about seven at the time – I decided to run away with them. I spent two evenings in their company before my father reclaimed me. In that short time, I was apprenticed to the bear trainer of the tribe. Would you like to see this fellow dance?"

I shook my head vigorously. Holmes chuckled and removed an apple from his pocket. The bear devoured it greedily.

"I was saving that for a snack on the train, but you have earned it, my ursine friend. I will never forget the expression on Watson's face. That memory of it will amuse me for the remainder of my days."

I folded my arms and gave Holmes a sour look that I hoped he would also remember for the rest of his life. "So how are the gypsies involved in this?"

"Let us find out." Together with our hirsute mascot, we made our way through the brambles to the east side of the manor, where a host of colorful wagons were circled around a fire. Women in bright skirts and jangling jewelry quickly vanished into the wagons as we approached, and a ragged little urchin trotted up to take charge of the bear. A gray-bearded man came forward, his hat in hand, asking our business in broken English. He acted deferential enough, but I noted the long knife stuffed into his belt. Without seeing anyone about, I sensed dozens of eyes watching us, and I wondered how many more weapons were even now being silently unsheathed.

Holmes assumed his sternest demeanor, demanding to know by what right the gypsies had camped on the property. While the elder's words were difficult to decipher, I grasped that they had come at an invitation, to entertain the household. Holmes grabbed the man's arm and pulled him close, whispering in his ear. The man trembled and tried to free himself, shaking his head vigorously, his eyes wide, his entire face contorted in shock. He would have broken loose and fled, but my friend shouted out a word and the bear, which had been lapping at a pan of water, rose on its back legs, bellowed in rage, and waved it paws in the air. The old gypsy dropped to the ground and nodded so hard I thought his head would break from his neck. Holmes knelt and hissed a few more words to the man, then rose and tugged me away.

"That bear is our best ally," Holmes chuckled, as we approached the ancient doorway of the house. I was struck even deeper by the decay of the estate. The steps had not been swept, nor the windows cleaned, at least since the summer, based on the accumulation of dust and debris. Holmes rapped firmly and, within moments, the door opened. Tifton was now clad in his butler's livery, his polished buttons and sharp coat a strange contrast to the squalid setting.

"Here is my card," Holmes said. "Please tell Mr. Asher that our business with him is most urgent, and he would do well to admit us without delay."

Tifton gave a nervous bob of his head and scuttled off to do my friend's bidding. I studied the chamber in which we found ourselves, noting the cobwebs, the dust, and the decided lack of attention. A whisky bottle was shattered in one corner and, much to my disgust, a lady's stocking was draped carelessly across a chair. Clearly, the room was the site of revels that mocked the sacred memory of the late Mrs. Eleanor Asher. I suddenly understood why Holmes had asked me if I felt intimidating. Indeed, it would take all my control not to punch the horrible Mr. Asher on sight.

Tifton reappeared and led us through a hallway to his master's study, quickly closing the door behind us. My first thought was that Asher was still in the throes of his illness, for he was wrapped in a heavy dressing gown, his untrimmed beard poking over the woolen scarf around his throat. His hair, thick, grey, and unkempt, spilled over his collar. It would have availed him to have a fire lit in the fireplace, but it sat idle. He coughed roughly and glared at us with hateful blue eyes.

"Who the devil are you?"

"Just who we say we are, Mr. Asher," Holmes replied, in a tone of silken menace, "representatives of the firm Byrnes and Schmitz, to whom you owe the sum of five-thousand pounds. Your bill has been overdue for almost a year now. If we do not return to London with a substantial payment, things will be rather unpleasant for you."

I could not resist smacking my fist against my palm and favoring Asher with what I hoped was a thuggish stare.

"You . . . ask the impossible. My resources as not what they once were."

"It is a debt that you owe, nevertheless."

"Yes, of course, but you must be reasonable!"

Holmes drew a step closer. His voice sank. "As reasonable as you were to Peterson, in Virginia, on the shores of the Okefenokee? You do recall that incident?" Holmes tilted his head. "It is not something I think you would want made public."

"That was long ago. I was young, I did a foolish thing! And I will give my creditors their money." He was seized with a coughing fit, and I nearly gave into my medical instincts to offer to tend him. After it ceased, he gave a pained, mournful cry. "Can't you see that I am dying? No doubt of same illness to which my poor wife succumbed."

"And that explains the drinking, the indulgence, the home surrounded by the salacious lures of the gypsies?"

Asher's voice emerged as a whimper. "Yes. What else is left for me now? Please, it will all be settled in my will. I have no heirs. Leave me in peace."

Holmes gave me a glance, as if we were sharing a thought or plan. I felt myself softening a bit in my feelings. This man was more pitiful than horrendous. Perhaps his butler was correct, in that some curse had been laid upon him, depriving him not only of his life, but his dignity and morality.

"If it were up to me, I would leave you to rot," Holmes said. "But my employers are not so generous. You will need to send surety. A hundred pounds will do. I see you have a safe."

A large green safe was tucked into the corner of the room, between a suit of armor and a dusty cabinet of curiosities. Wheezing and stumbling, Mr. Asher crossed the room toward it, Holmes in his wake.

"I – I have so little cash reserves. I – I confess I have spent too much, unwisely. But perhaps, if you would take just fifty – "

It happened so fast I had not even time to shout. The half-crippled man sprang to one side, seizing the antique sword that was mounted in the gantlets of the armor. He spun around, swinging the sword with strength and agility. But my friend, who had clearly anticipated such a move, was faster. He ducked low and threw his shoulder into the man, propelling him backward into the safe. His skull cracked hard on the metal box, and the sword flew from his hand. Before Asher could recover, Holmes had him by the throat and I was covering him with my pistol. He threw out his hands, begging for mercy.

"Open the safe," Holmes said.

"There's no money in it! I can get you money! There's plenty of money upstairs in my room."

Holmes tightened his hold and slammed Asher's knees to the floor. "I don't want your money. I want to see what is inside that safe. Watson, if he doesn't get it open in ten seconds, you have my permission to shoot him."

The threat worked effectively. With quivering fingers, Asher spun the combination and the door began to open. Holmes slipped a pair of handcuffs from his pocket, and I dragged the whimpering man to one side, quickly snapping the metal restraints on him. Holmes stood looking inside the safe.

"Watson."

I returned to his side and shared his view. My hand slapped to my mouth. A rigid, thin, green-gray face with a neat beard, and open, glazed eyes stared up at us.

"Holmes," I whispered, "the rest of them – "

" – Are clearly confederates. They know what became of their master."

"Then we are in danger! If they find us here – "

"They'll kill you!" the villain on the floor shrieked. "You won't leave this place alive! It will be your heads in there, along with his! No one will know!"

Holmes smiled at the man as he ripped away the heavy muffler and freed him of his wig of long hair. "Oh, but we have friends as well. Come and see."

I pulled Asher to his feet and herded him toward the door. Holmes flung it open. There, in the passageway, was an astonishing tableau. A burly, dark-haired man, a woman in a black dress, her fiery red hair in disarray, and a lad of about twenty, in a greasy jacket and rough trousers, were kneeling on the floor, each one securely bound and gagged, with a pair of gypsy guards hovering behind each prisoner. Their eyes screamed their anger and outrage. When they saw that their leader was our captive, the woman and the boy began to weep. Tifton hovered across from them, trembling in alarm. At the far end of the hall, the bear was blocking the exit. Tifton stepped forward, staring at the man I held.

"Who – who is this?"

"He goes by the name of Remington," Holmes said, "and also by the name of Rowe. His true name will require further investigation."

"But what has happened to my master? Where is Mr. Asher?"

Holmes turned to me. "Watson, I must rely on you to go back to the village, and find a way to get a message to Inspector Lestrade. I would send one of our comrades, but I am afraid the local constabulary might not give them the respect or credit they will give you. Mr. Tifton . . . if you will come with me?"

The last thing I saw, before setting off on my most important errand, was Holmes gently putting his arm around the old servant's shoulder, guiding him into the study, and closing the door.

"His true name is Roach," Holmes said, weeks later, as he savored his first pipe of the evening, "so I can hardly fault him for adopting an alias. You can find him in my Index: A swindler, accomplished forger, leader of a criminal gang, and fine actor."

I nodded. "He took me in. I was persuaded that he was sick and dying."

"With no fire in the fireplace on a chilly day? Doctor!"

I waved this criticism aside. "Tell me the rest."

"His confederates were already in the village, in hiding from a previous bit of misbehavior. Grief makes a man very vulnerable, and these gang members recognized an easy mark when they accepted employment with Mr. Asher. Roach posed as an American to win Asher's confidence. He studied his victim well, but not well enough. Perhaps you noted the trap? The real Asher would have refuted the imaginary Peterson and laughed at my glaring error of placing the Okefenokee Swamp in Virginia."

"But how was Asher killed?"

"Once he was in London, and in the power of two determined villains, it was a simple thing. Jenkins and Roach plied him with drink – most likely they drugged him as well – then took him back to the hotel where his clothes were exchanged for those of Roach before he was dispatched. The men were of comparable size, which made the substitution an easy one – except for the boots. They could not jam Roach's boots onto Asher's feet, but Asher's boots were distinctive and perhaps traceable. So they left the body in his stocking feet and Roach's boots beside the bed. Then, in the wee hours, with all asleep, Jenkins and Roach escaped. It was critical that the world think Mr. Asher alive and this stranger, Mr. Rowe, dead. That is why they had to take the head away. They could not risk the proper identification of the corpse. A gunshot to the face might have been equally as effective, but it would have awakened the entire hotel."

I nodded my understanding of his logic. "Why keep the head?"

"Because heads and other body parts have a notorious habit of turning up in strange places. Look how many corpses are annually pulled from the Thames, or how often dogs unearth hastily dug graves. In the safe, Roach always knew the location of the one piece of evidence that could convict him. I am sure he planned to dispose the grisly trophy, perhaps as soon as Tifton was no longer in his service."

"So why didn't he sack Tifton immediately? Why the charade?"

"He knew Tifton was elderly and almost blind, but not stupid, and from his associates, Roach knew it would not be in Asher's nature to dismiss such a loyal retainer. It was easy enough for Roach, as an actor, to pretend that sickness had altered Asher's voice and figure. He grew a beard and donned a wig that adequately mimicked Asher's appearance to the almost sightless man. He knew that if Tifton were to be dismissed suddenly, without cause, the old servant might ask questions. Better to begin a slow campaign to drive him away – to make him feel that he could no longer please his master. Once he was gone, Roach and company would live as they pleased." Holmes shook his head. "Of course, the false Asher could have dismissed Tifton by citing his advanced infirmity, sweetening the forced retirement with a sizable severance payment, a tidy legacy for his years of service . . . but Roach was far too greedy for this simple solution."

"Roach could have murdered Tifton," I said.

"True, but the butler's sudden disappearance might have alerted authorities, since Tifton possessed young dependents who would have become alarmed if they could not reach him. Tifton could not vanish without the risk of uncomfortable questions being asked."

"And no one in Edendore would have noticed the substitution of Rowe for Asher," I marveled.

"The sad fate of a recluse. Asher was not a local man, and had been a Stag Hall for under a year. If his behavior after his trip seemed strange or uncouth, the people in the village assumed that was simply Asher's nature. They had no reason to think otherwise."

"But the gypsies – "

"Young Bodie was responsible for their entry into the picture, as he enjoyed their performances and could use Asher's money to pay for them. They, however, aroused an ugly prejudice in Tifton's breast. He attributed to them dark designs upon his beloved master's soul – and that brought him to me. How ironic that the people Tifton blamed for the crime became the heroes of the moment! I was able, as you witnessed, to enlist them in our cause. I told their leader that the gang in Stag Hall was preparing to frame his people for murder. Thus, their eagerness to cooperate and seize the villains before they could do any harm."

"And Tifton?"

"I have just received a letter from him," Holmes said, pulling an envelope from his pocket and reaching for a blade to slit it open. "Let us see what he has to tell us." His eyes darted down the lines of the stationary. "He is distraught over the brutal murder of his master, of course. But there is a happy turn of events for our client. Once Mr. Asher's death was revealed and his will read, it was discovered that the gentleman left his fortune to Tifton, the only person who had stuck by him in his great bereavement. Tifton informs me that he has retired from domestic service and will devote his life to helping his orphaned niece and nephews rise in this world." Holmes smiled. "I believe the phrase 'well done, good and faithful servant' is appropriate here. And . . . ."

"What is it?" I asked, confused by Holmes's low whistle.

"It seems that Britain's newest member of the upper class has included a reimbursement for my services! And a rather generous sum it is." He held the checque out to me, and my eyebrows flew heavenward at the amount written on it. "That should keep us in tobacco and our other vices for some time, should it not? I believe a celebration is in order. A nutritious repast at *Simpson's*, perhaps?"

I jumped up and pulled on my coat. I tossed Holmes his high hat. He gestured merrily at the door.

"Exit," he quipped, "pursued by a bear!"

The Adventure of the Parisian Butcher
By Nick Cardillo

It has always been my intention to give the public as accurate and complete account of my association with Mr. Sherlock Holmes as possible. However, there have been innumerable times in our career together that I found myself having to alter facts such as names, dates, and places in order to relate matters of a sometimes scandalous or sensitive nature. On other occasions, I've found it necessary to hold back an account in its entirety; deciding as I laid my pen aside that it would be for the best that the particulars of some of Holmes's cases never be exposed at all. Such is the manuscript which follows: One of the few times when I determined it best that the document be consigned to some obscure corner of the Cox and Co. Bank vault, never to see the light of day.

Sherlock Holmes was the very last of men to ever give credence to any sort of sixth sense, so it came as something of a surprise to me one humid, rain-bedewed morning in the late summer of 1886 when Holmes sat back in his chair and said: "I have the strongest intimation that something is wrong."

I set the paper down on my knee. "Whatever do you mean?" I asked.

Holmes passed me an open envelope. "That letter came to me last evening while we were away," he said. "It is, as you will doubtlessly notice, postmarked London. However, the writer of that letter is Monsieur Andre Dupont, a wealthy French businessman. Does the name strike your ear as familiar, Watson?"

"I cannot say with any certainty," I replied. "What does this Monsieur Dupont write to you about?"

"He does not say," Holmes replied, reaching for his cigarette case. "He was most irritatingly vague. However, he says that he will present himself at our rooms at eleven o'clock on the morrow – meaning, of course, today."

"Well, I don't see what makes you so particularly inclined to think that something is wrong."

Sherlock Holmes lit his cigarette and laid the burnt-out match into the ashtray at his side. "If you would do more than to observe the latest cricket scores in that very paper which you have currently splayed out

111

across your lap, my dear fellow, you would find an article which announces that M. Andre Dupont will be arriving by the one o'clock boat from Paris, as he is conducting some business with a few prominent English industrialists."

"Which means that Dupont has been in London for a day already."

"At the least," Holmes replied. "Either M. Dupont had some business of a more illicit nature to attend to in the city, or he is very much in fear for his life. The fact that his arrival in the city has now been documented leads me to believe that he will have to go to some extremes to conceal his earlier arrival. By my estimation, a lookalike shall be disembarking from the one o'clock boat in M. Dupont's stead."

Holmes clicked open his fob watch. "It's nearly eleven now," he said. "If you would be so kind as to stay, Doctor, you could be of invaluable assistance."

I told Holmes that there was nothing that I would rather do than aid him in any way I could. No sooner had Holmes exclaimed, "Capitol!" and clapped his hands zealously together then did we hear the bell below chime. I could hear the sound of someone at the door conversing with Mrs. Hudson in the foyer and, a moment later, when our landlady drew into the sitting room, Holmes beamed at her.

"You may show M. Dupont up at once, Mrs. Hudson. His visit is not an unexpected one."

"I beg your pardon, Mr. Holmes, but it is not M. Dupont who is at the door."

Holmes knit his brow in confusion. "Who is it then?"

Mrs. Hudson produced our visitor's card and handed it to the detective. He read it, his face clouding further. Then, without a word, he gestured for her to bring the client in.

"Well," I said, once Mrs. Hudson had gone, "who is it?"

"The card is most certainly that of M. Andre Dupont," Holmes said passing it to me. "But, as you will perceive, written upon it are the words: *Alexandre – Valet.*"

"Why should Andre Dupont send his valet to you instead of coming himself?" I asked.

Holmes shrugged his shoulders. "I hope that the man shall endeavor to answer that very question."

Our landlady returned with a tall, lanky man in his early fifties. He was well-dressed, though I figured that the dark coat and bowler hat which he carried could not have been in the slightest comfortable, especially as the late summer weather had turned the atmosphere thick and cloying.

"I would not be incorrect in assuming that you have come on behalf of your master?" Holmes asked the servant.

"That is correct, sir," the man replied. He remained stiff as a board, totally unmoving as he spoke. "M. Dupont had all intentions of calling on you himself this morning, per his letter, but he decided otherwise at the very last moment. He would, however, be most grateful if you would accompany me to my master's home. He is still most anxious to speak with you."

"This business must be one of the utmost severity," Holmes said, more to himself than anyone else in the room. "Very well. I shall come with you, provided that Dr. Watson is allowed to accompany me. He acts as my associate in all my cases."

The valet nodded his head slightly. His total lack of movement made the man appear to be some kind of statue. "That shall be quite alright, Mr. Holmes."

"Excellent! Then the Doctor and I shall join you in the foyer in precisely three minutes."

Holmes quickly set out gathering up his things and, once we had made our way downstairs, we climbed into a waiting four-wheeler and soon found ourselves hurtling through the teeming streets of the metropolis.

"Tell me, Alexandre," Holmes began, "how long have you been in M. Dupont's employ?"

"This autumn will be my fifteenth year."

"Would you describe your relationship with M. Dupont to be a close one?"

"I should think that no man knows my master better than I," the valet replied.

"And you have no idea in the slightest what could be troubling him so?"

For a moment, a look of fear came into the valet's dull, grey eyes, before he said quite emphatically: "No, sir. I cannot think of anything."

I noticed the look and flashed Holmes quick glance. He locked eyes with me and I knew that he too had perceived the valet's clumsy attempt at deception.

Our cab drew up outside of a very well-appointed house, tucked back behind a mighty oak tree which grew out of the well-manicured front lawn. The valet produced from his coat a ring of keys and, once inside, he divested us of our hats and led us into a large, open sitting room. The room was lined with expensive-looking oil paintings on three of its walls, with the fourth taken up by a stylish set of French windows which looked out onto a neat stone veranda. At the furthermost end of the room was a large fireplace, before which stood the man I took to be Andre Dupont. He was tall and lean, and not a day over forty – though he looked considerably younger – sporting an elegantly waxed mustache. He was well-dressed in an expensive black suit. He looked as if he was destined to be in that room, as though he were one of the subjects of the portraits on the wall that had come to life, just to add flair to the space.

"Ah, Mr. Sherlock Holmes," he said, with the slightest trace of a French accent permeating his words. "Thank goodness you have come."

"M. Dupont," said Holmes as he moved further into the room to shake hands with the man, "you need not be a detective to figure that you are quite distressed about something."

"I should imagine that my urgent letter and my subsequent behavior was enough to convey that to you."

"Indeed," Holmes said, "I have seldom encountered so curious a starting point to an investigation in my days as a consulting detective. Dr. Watson, my friend and colleague, can testify to that point."

I shook hands with Dupont and verified Holmes's words, which seemed to put the aristocrat to some ease.

"I am in fear for my life, Mr. Holmes," Dupont replied. "Please, gentlemen, sit. I shall tell you the story through."

Dupont took a seat in a wing back chair while Holmes and I took seats on opposite ends of a plush-looking settee. After he had offered us cigarettes, Dupont leaned back in his chair.

"I am a wealthy man," he began. "As such, I have garnered a few *enemies* in my time. Business rivals have publicly threatened me, and I have more than once in my life avoided being brained by thrown rocks. I have developed a thick skin. However, petty threats and stones pale in comparison to the threatening letters which I have received in the past few weeks."

From his inner beast pocket, Dupont withdrew two envelopes. "The first," he continued, "was delivered to my home in Paris a week ago. At first I thought that it was yet another threat from a business rival. The message itself was short and quite vague: '*Your time on earth is running short.*' It was not until I examined the note more deeply did I truly begin to fear for my life. You see, Mr. Holmes, this message was written in blood."

I sat upright in my seat suddenly. Dupont passed the letter to my friend. He took it and observed it first with the naked eye before peering at it through his convex lens.

"It is genuinely blood," my friend said length. "You will doubtlessly recall, Watson, that when first we met I was in the midst of developing a test to determine whether a substance perceived to be blood is actually

114

blood. The congealed quality of the substance is enough to tell me that it is not ink."

"Naturally, I was scared out of my wits," Dupont continued. "I made sure that all the doors and windows of my home were locked. I began to carry a gun on my person and slept with it under my pillow. My wife, Michelle, started to question me about my curious behavior, but I did not wish to disturb her.

"However, my genuine terror only increased when, shortly after the arrival of that first letter, my pet dog disappeared from outside my own home in Paris. I feared that he had run away, but after searching for little more than an hour, my staff and I discovered that it had been slain. My wife knew something was amiss and confronted me that very night. I showed her the letter which I had received and together we believed that it was for the best that we leave Paris. I did not wish to make public my intent to travel to London, but it somehow it ended up in the majority of both Parisian and British papers. It was for that reason that I plotted to arrive here in London a full two days before my public arrival this morning. We traveled with some of my most trusted staff so we should want for nothing here in London. I even managed to hire a man with a similar resemblance to me to publicly be seen leaving the ship. I was taking no chances, whatsoever.

"I thought, Mr. Holmes, that I was safe. And then, yesterday morning, I received yet another letter. It is postmarked London."

He handed the second envelope to Holmes. The threatening message was, once again, terse and to the point: *"Death is Coming For You."*

"It, too," Dupont said grimly, "is written in blood."

He drew in a deep breath, attempting to calm himself. "Whoever has sent me these letters knew of my flight to London," Dupont continued. "*He* knew that I would leave early and has dogged my heels across the Channel. Mr. Holmes, I beg of you. Please protect me."

"I am not a common bodyguard," Holmes retorted, more coldly than I believed was warranted. He handed the letter back to our client, and eased back in his chair, crossing one long leg over the other in a deceptively languid manner. "I shall, however, do my utmost to help you in unmasking your stalker. However, I must insist upon one thing M. Dupont: You must reveal to me all you know."

"I have told you everything."

"I do not think so," Holmes icily replied. "You identified your stalker as '*He*' a moment ago, almost as though you know precisely who is responsible for these acts against you. If you gave me some indication of who this man might be, I can go a long way towards clapping irons about his wrists."

115

Andre Dupont sucked in another deep breath. "I know of only one man who would have cause to wish such misfortunate on me," he murmured. "But that man is dead. I am sure of it."

"Nevertheless, tell me about him M. Dupont."

Dupont leaned back in his chair and, for an instant, the ghost of a smile crossed his mouth. "You will notice," he began, "that I am a collector. These paintings on the walls are all originals. Are you an art enthusiast yourself, Mr. Holmes?"

"I can appreciate a Bond Street art gallery as well as the next," Holmes replied. I cast my friend a quizzical glance, silently asking him what this could possibly have to do with the matter at hand. Holmes met my eyes and seemed to silently address me, saying that all would become clear in time.

"I have amassed something of a collection," Dupont continued, rising from his chair and moving to a small, elegant-looking bureau in the corner of the room. From his waistcoat pocket, he withdrew a key, and inserted it into the lock. He opened a cabinet door and removed a small case about six inches across, wrapped in a light cloth.

"I have always had a fascination with art," Dupont continued, "and from time to time, I have been captivated by the *oeuvre*. I confess, that I have always been riveted by Bosch's depiction of Hell in *The Garden of Earthly Delights*. I suppose that is what led me on the path to having an eye for the fantastic and the *unique*."

Dupont accented the last word as he removed the cloth from the case. What lay beneath was a neat, glass container. It was the contents of that container which turned my blood to ice.

Within the case sat a neatly severed human hand.

Though I have a strong stomach and am immune to much, the sight made me feel dizzy for a moment. Perhaps it was the showman-like air which Dupont had adopted in revealing to us his unique piece of art. I looked to Holmes, but his face was cold and unreadable.

"Whose hand is this?" Holmes asked at length.

"The man's name was Jacques Bonnaire," Dupont replied. "He was a close friend of mine for many years until, after my wife and I married, he attempted to make love to her. I caught him in the act and shot him on the spot. He was severely wounded and, as he lay bleeding, I told Michelle to call for the police at once. When she had gone, I must have lost my head, Mr. Holmes, for I took up a knife and cut off his hand. I just wanted to make a point to the blackguard not to cross paths with me anymore. The police arrived and dealt with the matter. Luckily in France, crimes of passion are leniently treated under the law, and Bonnaire was

116

hauled away a hospital. I have not heard of him since, but I cannot imagine that he survived his wounds."

Sherlock Holmes remained silent. For once, I could read Holmes's cold, inscrutable eyes like a book and it came as little surprise to me when he opened his mouth a moment later and said, "Frankly you disgust me, M. Dupont and I shall have nothing to do with you."

"But what about the threats to my life?"

"You seem like the type of man who is quite capable at defending himself," Holmes retorted. "And, should you be too much of a coward to face your threats, then do what cowards do best: *Run*. You have shown yourself quite adept at that as well. Run away. Perhaps, back to Paris. Surely, Jacques Bonnaire will have quite a time crossing the Channel once again minus a hand and a bullet in his chest. That is my advice and I shall do nothing else but offer that alone. Good day, sir."

So saying, Holmes spun around on his heel and started out of the room.

When I managed to catch my friend, he was already standing outside hailing a hansom back to Baker Street. Once we were ensconced in the belly of the cab, I could see Holmes silently gnashing his teeth.

"It is said that you can judge a man's character by the company he keeps," he said "and I should surely never wish to keep company with M. Andre Dupont and his penchant for hacking off the hands of his rivals."

"I do not blame you, Holmes," I said comfortingly.

Holmes drew in a deep breath and sighed. "But I cannot help but think," he murmured, "that I may have been hasty in my judgment and I have sent a man to his death. I fear that if my imitations prove to be correct once again, then M. Andre Dupont's death may very well weigh on my conscience."

Holmes refused to speak on the matter for the next few days and, it was only as I sorted through the first post of the day three days later, that the business of M. Andre Dupont re-entered our lives.

"Postmarked Paris," I said as I held a letter aloft. I read the return address. "Inspector Durand. I say, Holmes, isn't that –"

"Yes," Holmes interjected. "Inspector Durand was the most competent of investigators who we ran across during that bad business at the Paris Opera House five years back. Please, Watson, do me the service of reading the letter out."

I settled into my chair and opened the letter. It was written in an authoritative hand:

Mr. Holmes,

You will no doubt remember my name well. Though we seldom worked side-by-side so many years ago, I considered it a pleasure to have seen you in action. You have developed something of a following here on the Continent as your name has begun to appear in the press with frequent rapidity.

I wish then that it could be under better circumstances that I write to you, and I severely hope that when you receive this letter that you are able to drop whatever it is that currently occupies you and join me in Paris. To put it briefly, it is murder – the murder of Andre Dupont, the wealthy businessman. If it were only a routine investigation, I should not think on troubling you as I do. However, the savagery with which this murder was committed is unlike anything I have seen in many years of working as a police inspector. Both M. Dupont and his wife, Michelle, fell victim to the murderer. They were stabbed to death and discovered with one of their hands neatly cut off.

"Good Lord, Holmes!"

The inspector's words seemed to cut into me like a knife as well, and I felt a shiver run up and down my back. I hardly had time to register Holmes bolting from his chair and perusing the train directory.

"The boat-train to Paris leaves in two hours, Watson," he said. "If we make haste, we can still catch it."

"Don't you want to hear the rest of the letter?"

"On the train," Holmes said, as he rushed off to his room with a frenzied wave of his hand. "We must act while the game is still very much afoot."

The next hour disappeared in a flurry of packing of bags. Holmes rushed off a telegram replying to Durand, and we soon found ourselves charging across the station platform and ducking into a first-class carriage. I was only catching breath as the train became wreathed in smoke and pulled out the station. Once we found ourselves hurtling across the English countryside, I cast a glance across to my friend. He stared out of the window at the passing fields, his face betraying no discernible emotion. I wondered if the deaths of Dupont and his wife were, indeed, weighing on my friend's mind. Knowing him, he would blame himself for their violent ends. I was almost inclined to say something in an attempt to break him free from his reverie, but I decided against it.

We passed the voyage in relative silence, broken only by Holmes pressing me for more information from Durand's letter. After I had read a part through, he would sit in silence and contemplate the scant words for what masqueraded as hours before urging me to continue.

Inspector Durand had explained that the room in which M. Dupont and his wife were discovered was the locked sitting room of their well-appointed abode, located on a well-to-do road in the middle of Paris. The bodies had been discovered by the valet, Alexandre, who had contacted the police at once. Aside from a servant girl, there were no other persons in the house.

A silent passage by boat was followed by another sojourn by train. It seemed as though the foul weather which had descended on London had followed us to the Continent. Rain lashed the train compartment windows and, when we finally arrived in Paris, we found ourselves rushing to hail a cab and avoid the deluge. Holmes had done us the service of booking a last-minute set of rooms at a hotel and, after we checked in, he sent off another telegram to Inspector Durand announcing our arrival. It had been a long, exhausting day, and at the end of it I found myself famished. I ate a small repast, and was not surprised – and not pleased – that Holmes refused to take any nourishment. I had just gathered up my plates and silverware when we were arrested by a knock on our door.

Holmes answered the call and found the familiar figure of Inspector Durand in the doorway. The half-decade since last we had met had been good to the inspector. He was a tall, lean man, broad-shouldered, and rather statuesque in appearance. He had a long face with deep-set eyes, and a shock of fair hair atop his head. He furled his umbrella while my friend relieved him of his coat, gesturing for the representative of the Parisian police to draw up before the fire.

"You look as though you could use a drink, Inspector," I said as I poured him a brandy from the sideboard. He accepted the libation all too readily.

"*Merci*, Doctor," he said, draining his glass. "It has been quite a day."

Holmes took a seat opposite the inspector and lit a cigarette. "Dr. Watson did me the service of reading the details of the case," he began. "Are there any particularities which you were unable to convey to me?"

"None, M. Holmes," Durand replied. "All of the facts which are in my possession were highlighted. And, alas, very little has been gained from the investigation."

"I assume that you have conducted an examination of M. Dupont's papers and personal possessions?" Holmes asked.

"Why, of course," Durand said, appearing slightly injured by Holmes's question. Perhaps the inspector did not know Holmes well enough to understand my friend's low opinion of the official police.

"Did you happen to find any mention of a man called *Jacques Bonnaire*?"

Durand considered for a moment. "No," he said. "Why? Who is this Jacques Bonnaire?"

"At present," Holmes replied, blowing a ring of smoke about his gaunt head, "he is a suspect of particular interest. However, as it is a capitol mistake to theorize before one is in possession of all the facts, I shall do my utmost not to let the lamented M. Bonnaire enter into the investigation at this time."

"But if he could have an impact on this case," Durand said, "it would be a grave miscarriage of justice not to pursue this particular thread. Who is Jacques Bonnaire?"

"Holmes and I were contacted by M. Dupont in London three days ago," I began. "Dupont had been receiving a number of threatening letters – first, here in Paris, and again in London. He believed that they were sent by a man named Jacques Bonnaire, his one-time friend who tried to seduce Dupont's wife. In retaliation, Dupont shot Bonnaire and cut off the man's hand. Dupont lost all traces of Bonnaire after the incident, but seeing how these murders have a strong link to the incident involving Bonnaire, it is understandable how he should become a suspect."

"I should think so!" the inspector exclaimed. "I shall make it a priority to look into this Jacques Bonnaire character."

"No, Inspector," Holmes retorted rather coldly. "You should make it a priority to allow Dr. Watson and me to examine the bodies. I assume they have been taken to the mortuary? Excellent. Though the hour is rather late, I can think of no time like the present to visit the morgue."

In short order, the three of us had donned our hats and coats and had stepped into the street. The deluge had lessened and a mist was falling upon us. Inspector Durand hailed us a cab and, as we climbed inside, a palpable silence descended over us. I watched as Holmes peered out at the passing rain-soaked city. The City of Light took on a haunting yellow glow as the undulating flames of gas lamps mingled with the wall of fog and mist into which our carriage trundled.

We alighted before a small, stone building tucked on a side-street. Inspector Durand eased open the door and we stepped inside. The smell of death was overwhelming and I clapped a hand to my nose. Though I have in my time been in the presence of death and decay – as both a soldier and a doctor – I would never be able to become immune to the thick, cloying stench of loss. Holmes, however, did not seem to take notice and proceeded into the room. We approached two tables standing side-by-side, the familiar shapes of cadavers atop them, covered in shrouds.

Durand drew back the white sheets which covered the bodies, and I stared at the pale corpses. Holmes circled the table and, from his inner pocket, withdrew his convex lens. Leaning over the body of Andre Dupont, he held the lens close to the wound which had been the cause of his death. Moving swiftly to the body of Madame Dupont, he did the same. In life, Michelle Dupont would have been a lovely woman. She was tall and lean, with a head of charcoal-black hair which would have cascaded down her shoulders. Despite what I knew of Dupont's dubious past, I could not reconcile the claiming of the life of someone who I was sure was guilty of nothing.

Holmes stood and pressed the magnifying glass into my hand. "I would appreciate a doctor's opinion," he said. "The wounds – they were inflicted with the same weapon?"

Approaching the bodies, I held the lens close to my eye and examined the wounds in much the same manner as Holmes had just done.

"These wounds were undoubtedly inflicted by the same hand with the same weapon," I said. "And, from the looks of it, I should think that the knife which did this was a large kitchen knife. The wounds are deep and quite wide."

"And the hands," Holmes continued. "Would you say that the same knife was used to sever the hands?"

I examined the bodies once more. "From what I could see, a different knife was used in this operation."

"A *different knife?*" Inspector Durand echoed.

"I should imagine that the weapon was not as sharp as the one which dealt death to M. Durand and his wife. The cut is far more jagged and less clean."

I returned the lens to Holmes who pocketed it wordlessly. He tapped his long index finger against his lips for a moment.

"Why should the murderer carry two knives on his person? What kind of butcher could have done this thing" Durand asked.

"I would be most surprised if the murderer chose to carry two weapons when one would be more than sufficient," Holmes replied. "A kitchen knife of the type which Watson described is a formidable weapon indeed."

"What exactly are you insinuating, M. Holmes?" Durand asked.

Holmes smiled. "At the moment, nothing. I shouldn't wish to color your investigation more than I already have. The hour, I'm afraid, grows late, and it has been an incredibly trying day for both the Doctor and myself. First thing on the morrow, however, I must make an examination of the murder scene. That can be arranged, Inspector?"

"*Oui*, M. Holmes."

"Excellent," Sherlock Holmes replied, turning sharply on his heel. "Then, Dr. Watson and I shall bid you farewell. Or, perhaps, *au revoir*."

We parted ways with the inspector in the street. Our carriage conveyed us back to our hotel where we silently made our way to our rooms. Once inside, Holmes divested himself of his coat and took up his briar pipe as he settled in before the fire.

"You are not retiring for the night?" I asked.

"No," my friend replied. "The cogs of my brain have been set into motion and I would be doing myself a disservice should I try to halt their natural processes this night. But I am sure that you are exhausted, my dear fellow, so you needn't wait up for me."

I began to undo my tie as I moved towards my room. I looked forward to a good night's sleep more than anything but, as I neared the open door, I stopped and turned around to address Holmes.

"You have begun to develop some theory, haven't you?"

Holmes blew out a ring of smoke which encircled his head. "I have," he replied. "If it is correct, I fear that this case may only grow ever darker."

I roused myself early the following morning, only to find that Holmes was already awake. To my satisfaction, I saw that he was breaking his fast and, for a moment, I considered cajoling Mrs. Hudson into preparing French pastries at Baker Street if it meant that Holmes would take some sustenance more often. I joined him at the breakfast table and we exchanged pleasantries. I informed him that I had slept well, even after the grisly circumstances of the day, and was much relieved to hear that he too had made it to bed – albeit in the early hours of the morning. Holmes also informed me that he had sent an early morning telegram to rendezvous with Inspector Durand, who would convey us to the home of the late Andre Dupont.

After we had finished, we gathered our things and made our way into the hotel lobby, where we found the inspector standing at the ready for us. We exchanged a few words before we moved outside and into the awaiting cab. Though the rain had let up, the day was cloudy and foreboding. It did little to diminish the beauty of the city which, under the cover of darkness the night before, I had failed to truly appreciate. I have only been to Paris a handful of times in my life, but each time I have come away impressed by the splendor of such a lovely place.

Our carriage came to a stop on a picturesque road in the Sixth Arrondissement of the city. As we climbed out, I cast a glance up the street and saw the great tower of the Abbey of Saint-Germain-des-Prés peering over the rooftops of the nearby buildings. Inspector Durand led us through a small garden, the vegetation of which did go some way towards tucking the house away from the street. He withdrew a key from his inner pocket and inserted it into the lock of the front door. He eased it open and we stepped through.

"I have done the utmost to keep the space just as it was when the bodies were discovered, M. Holmes."

"Your consideration is much appreciated, Inspector," Holmes replied. "Your willingness to do so has already placed you above many of the inspectors at Scotland Yard. Now, can you show us to where the bodies were discovered?"

Durand led us through the foyer and into a well-appointed siting room. The room was small, surely not as grand as the room in which Dupont had entertained us in London, but a comfortable space nonetheless which clearly spoke to Dupont's obvious wealth. A set of French windows opened onto a small stone veranda, though I perceived that the glass had been shattered and the drapes undulated in the light breeze which circulated through the room.

"M. Dupont was found there," Durand indicated, pointing to a spot on the floor before the window. "His wife was found there by the settee. I have come to believe that the murderer forced his way in through the French windows and attacked M. Dupont. Madame Dupont was powerless to stop the murderer, as she was trapped in the room."

Holmes stepped further into the room and I watched as he swiveled his head around like a great bird of prey peering through the underbrush. His piercing grey eyes scanned each opulent surface. He turned quickly and, kneeling before the window, inspected the broken pane of glass. Holmes murmured inaudibly beneath his breath as he stood and then moved to the settee on the other side of the room. I watched him consider the space – the cogs in his brain almost visible through his eyes.

"You said that the valet, Alexandre, had discovered the bodies?"

"*Oui*. They were discovered late in the evening. M. Dupont, according to the valet, was in the habit of taking a nightcap and, calling on his master, he found the door to the sitting room locked. When M. Dupont did not respond to his knock, the valet forced the door open."

"And you said that there was no one else in the house at the time of the murder?"

"There was a maid, Jeanette."

"Did she have anything to add to Alexandre's story?"

"None whatsoever, M. Holmes," Durand replied. "She said that she was in the kitchen at the time of the murder and heard nothing."

Holmes tapped his lips once more in contemplation. "I'd like to see the kitchen if you don't mind, Inspector." He started out of the room before the officer had a chance to refuse. Durand exchanged looks with me and I shrugged my shoulders. Holmes had seemed to have lost interest entirely in the room in which the murder had taken place.

Durand drew our attention to a door at the head of a narrow staircase. Then he led us down the set of steps and into the kitchen which was furnished by an extensive series of counters.

"M. Dupont had apparently given his staff leave when he departed for London," Durand explained. "His unanticipated return meant that the number of the household staff was greatly diminished. As I understand it, the valet and the maid were the only ones in attendance, having accompanied their master to London and back again."

Holmes took a turn around the kitchen and, after he had performed what I could only imagine was the most cursory of examinations, turned to us and declared, "I should very much like to examine the veranda behind the house."

"There is a second set of stairs on the opposite end of the kitchen," Durand said, indicating the spiral staircase which sat tucked in the corner.

"Excellent," Holmes cried. "Oh, I have forgotten my hat and stick upstairs. You gentlemen need not follow me back up. I shall return presently."

Holmes climbed the steps and I heard him move about upstairs. He rejoined us a moment later and, insisting that we use the servant's stairs, we made our way to the ground floor of the house and, from there, out of the house and onto the small veranda.

Holmes took a turn around the veranda and stopped before the French windows. He examined a few shards of glass and then, standing, smiled as he clapped his arms behind his back and rocked ever so slightly from his heel to his toes.

"You seem quite pleased with yourself, M. Holmes," the inspector said.

"That is because I think that things are fitting together rather nicely," the detective replied. "However, I think the time has finally come for us to devote attention to Monsieur Jacques Bonnaire. I would very much appreciate it, Inspector, if you did a little digging. Find out all you can about the man."

"I shall start at once."

"Excellent," Holmes beamed. "As for myself, I shall take a walk. Paris is a city with which I am not too intimate and I think that a perambulation will do me some good."

"Would you like me to accompany you, Holmes?" I asked.

"You needn't bother, Watson," Holmes replied. "You will find me silent company for the next few hours. Treat yourself, my dear fellow, to some of this city's more sumptuous delicacies. I know that *le petit dejeuner* we had this morning will hardly be enough to satisfy your needs. Let us meet again in three hours' time at police headquarters. Shall be that sufficient for you, Inspector?"

Durand assured Holmes that it would be and we set off in separate directions. I figured that if Holmes was willing to lose himself in the city, then I should try to do the same. I walked aimlessly for some time until I came across a pleasant café. I stopped and enjoyed a cup of *café au lait* and a baguette which was quite to my liking. Wandering a bit farther afield, I soon decided that it was time for me to return to more familiar environs and, flagging down a cab, was conveyed back to our hotel.

As I sat alone in the carriage, I cast my mind back to the scene of the murder. Obviously Holmes had seen far more than either the inspector or myself, but I could in no way put my finger on what it was. What, I wondered, had he seen that helped him divine some more specific connection with the mysterious Jacques Bonnaire, whose name hung over this case like the grisly shadow of death? As usual, Holmes would not explain, and I wished that he would have shared with me his theory. He clearly saw some dark circumstances surrounding this already morose affair.

Deposited at the hotel, I spent the remainder of the afternoon in quiet contemplation and, I do confess, that I dozed off. I managed to rouse myself with time to spare and caught another carriage to the *Place Louis Lèpine*, home of the Paris Police Prefecture. The impressive grey stone building stared down at me as I made my way inside and, after asking for Inspector Durand, was told that I could find his office on the second floor. I ascended the staircase and walked down a corridor until I came to the inspector's small office and found him seated behind a cluttered desk; Sherlock Holmes seated across from him in the process of lighting a cigarette.

"Good of you to join us, Watson," Holmes said as I took a seat next to him. "Inspector Durand was just about to tell us what he has unearthed on Jacques Bonnaire."

I took a seat next to Holmes as the inspector opened a file which sat on his desk. "To begin," Durand said, "Bonnaire was the same age as Dupont. While Dupont was a self-made man, Bonnaire was born into his wealth. They would seem, then, to be at odds from the beginning, but from all accounts, the two were close friends.

"Bonnaire married a woman one year after Dupont married his wife. Bonnaire had two children – two girls – before the death of his wife, after only a few years of marriage. Bonnaire's children were only six and eight years old respectively at the time of his *contretemps* with Andre Dupont, nearly a decade ago.

"It appears as though the details of the incident as imparted to you, M. Holmes, by Dupont were accurate. Michelle Dupont did indeed contact the police at her husband's behest. The officer who answered the call, a man called August, has since left the force, but his report was easy enough to dig up. He says that when he arrived, Jacques Bonnaire lay on the floor of the master bedroom in a pool of blood. He clutched at his chest where he had sustained a bullet wound, his other arm at his side, minus a hand. Bonnaire was conducted immediately to a hospital. He was released after nearly two weeks and, since then, he has disappeared off of the face of the earth."

"No contact of any kind you say? None made with his solicitors or bankers?"

"*Non*, M. Holmes."

"What of his children?"

The inspector turned a page in his file. "The elder daughter severed all ties with the family and has gone to ground. I could find nothing on her whatsoever. The younger daughter – as we understand it – works at a cabaret, a well-known spot in the city called *Le Chat Noir*."

Holmes leaned forward and crushed his cigarette into the ashtray perched on the edge of the inspector's desk. "She would make a most interesting study, Inspector."

"You wish to speak to Bonnaire's daughter?"

"Of course," Holmes replied rising. "The sooner the better."

"We shall go tonight then, if it is your wish."

Holmes beamed. "Capitol, Inspector!" My friend clicked open his watch. "Ah, how the time has flown. I confess I find myself rather taken with your Parisian cuisine – and judging from the crumbs which Dr. Watson has yet to remove from his lapels, I should imagine that he is too. I think you should dine with us, Inspector. We shall think no more of M. Bonnaire for the time being. I like to think that I am well-up on Continental crime, but I cannot pass up an opportunity to discuss it with someone first-hand. I leave the choice of restaurant to you."

True to his words, Holmes refused to speak about the case for some time. Instead, we soon found ourselves seated before a sumptuous multi-course feast at an expensive Parisian restaurant. Holmes and the inspector discussed aspects of various cases which, I do confess, left me completely lost. I wondered if Holmes was purposefully distracting himself from the matter at hand. Perhaps, I reasoned as I drained a glass of fine wine, he knew all too well the trials which lay ahead of us in the unraveling of this case. This matter had already taken a toll on my friend. In his mind, he had failed his responsibility and now he was doing all in his power to bring the criminal to book, no matter how arduous the task might prove to be. I wondered just how close to the truth he actually was.

Night had descended when we quit the restaurant. The rain had continued to hold off and, still deep in conversation, Holmes insisted that we walk the rest of the way. Our perambulation was not a long way and we drew up outside of a very inauspicious-looking building. Stepping inside, I was at once struck by the loudness of the music and the cheers from the crowd. The room was wide and open, a stage situated at the furthermost end. Men and woman of all shapes, sizes, and apparent statuses were distributed at tables throughout the room, from which they looked at the stage, currently occupied by a group of women performing a dance which, I would imagine in London, would have raised a decent number of eyebrows. Holmes, of course, took no notice and pressed on further into the room.

We took an empty table which was tucked away in the back of the barroom. The inspector and I followed Holmes's example as he sat, and in short order we were approached by a waiter. The detective ordered us a bottle of wine in perfect French.

"Well, Holmes," I said trying to be heard in the loud room, "what exactly do you intend to do?"

Holmes smiled mischievously and put a long finger to his lips as the waiter returned to our table.

"*Parlez-vous anglais*?" Holmes asked the waiter.

Our man nodded politely. "*Oui, monsieur*," he replied.

"Excellent," Holmes said. He stood and drew up a chair from a nearby unoccupied table. "Then I invite you to join us for a glass of this most excellent wine."

A confused look crossed the waiter's face and I am sure he was about to protest. However, Holmes all but forced the young man into the chair and had poured him a glass. Once the waiter had tentatively lifted the glass to his lips, the detective sat back in his chair.

"What is your name?"

"Henri, monsieur," the waiter replied. "Is there something I can do for you gentlemen?"

"I rather think that there is," Holmes replied. "My friends and I would like to speak with someone – one of the dancers, I believe. She would be about sixteen, I should imagine. Her surname is *Bonnaire*. Does she sound familiar?"

Before the waiter had an opportunity to answer, a big man, dressed in a garish waistcoat, sauntered up to the table. He was middle-aged, with a head of orange hair peeping out from under the brim of a battered billycock hat. He held in between his large fingers a chewed-upon cigar. He addressed the waiter sternly in French before turning to us, cocking an eyebrow.

"I am the manager of this club, *messieurs*. Henri tells me that you want some kind of information?"

"We're looking for a young woman named Bonnaire," Holmes replied. "If you could help us find her, it would be much appreciated."

Holmes coyly removed a coin from his inner pocket and slid it along the table. The glint caught the man's eye immediately and he picked it up, stowing it away as though he feared immediate robbery.

"I know precisely of whom you speak," the manager replied.

"We would like to speak with her at once," Holmes said. "It is imperative that we do so this evening."

"I shall take you to her," the manager replied, standing.

Holmes cast the inspector and I a beaming grin as the manager led us through the labyrinth of tables and chairs. Moving past the patrons of the club, we made our way to a small door which communicated with the backstage. The dimly-lit, private portions of the theater was alive with energy as dancers rushed hither and thither, and stagehands worked to lift and lower curtains and drops. I caught sight of Holmes casting a glance over the theatrical mechanisms before we were urged along by our guide.

"The *mademoiselle* you seek has not used the name Bonnaire in some time," the manager said, "but there are few girls working here who are quite so young."

I felt a sudden feeling of reprehension for the man. Having seen the *risqué* nature of some of the routines performed in this place, I couldn't imagine a mere adolescent being involved.

We came to a door which, I concluded, led into the ladies' dressing room. The manager addressed one of the dancers about to enter and, after she disappeared, he informed us that she would fetch the young lady we sought. The dancer was true to her word and emerged from the dressing room a moment later with a petite girl in tow. She was young – Holmes's estimation of about sixteen or seventeen seemed most accurate – but she

128

had quite a pretty countenance which, enhanced with the elaborate makeup utilized in the cabaret, did give the girl something of a salacious appearance. She looked at the three of us and arched an eyebrow. Holmes asked if the girl spoke English, to which she nodded.

"*Mademoiselle*," Holmes began, "my name is Sherlock Holmes. This is friend and associate Dr. John Watson, and this is Inspector Erique Durand of the Paris Police Prefecture. You are the daughter of Jacques Bonnaire, are you not?"

The girl drew in a deep breath. "That is not a name I have heard in almost a decade, sir."

"Mademoiselle," Holmes continued, "we have reason to believe that your father is very much alive and responsible for the murder of Andre Dupont and his wife. It is most important that we speak to you at once."

Her eyes darted around the crowded backstage area. "Allow me a few moments, gentlemen," she said softly. She darted back into the dressing room and emerged again a moment later, a cloak draped about her shoulders. She then led us out of the building and into a narrow alleyway behind the theater.

"I apologize for the quality of the space," she said, "but we can speak privately here. I come here to think and, I do confess, my father is often in my thoughts."

"Naturally," I said, laying a reassuring hand on the girl's shoulder. "What is your name?"

"Emma," the girl replied. "Though, most of the girls around here just call me Em. No one has called me Mademoiselle Bonnaire in quite some time. You say that my father is implicated in the murder of M. Dupont?"

"That is correct, Mademoiselle," Durand said. "You have not heard from your father recently, have you?"

"*Non*," Emma Bonnaire replied. "I do not think that I would want to after what happened."

"Perhaps," Holmes said, "you ought to explain."

"My father and my sister were the only things in my world after my mother died," Emma said. "We were a close-knit family. My father was kind, decent man. However, he – like so many – took to drink as a way to cope with the death of his wife. He soon could only take solace in the bottom of a bottle and, in his fits, he was quite uncontrollable. He was a big man, gentleman. And strong. Once, I found him seated alone in our sitting room, clutching an empty bottle. He saw me and flew into a rage and grabbed me by the arm. He very nearly pulled my arm from its socket.

"I was too young to notice it, but I suppose my father was rather keen on Madame Dupont. She was a handsome lady, I will admit and, in one of his drunken rages, I can only imagine what went through his mind, but I cannot defend what M. Dupont did, gentlemen. It was wrong and . . . *savage*. I never thought that a man could stoop so low. It was not simply enough to shoot my father, but he went and cut off his hand too."

Emma Bonnaire held back a choked sob. I proffered my handkerchief, which she accepted as she dabbed at her eyes. "*Merci, monsieur le Docteur.*

"I can recall visiting my father in the hospital with my sister," she continued after a moment. "He was barely conscious and in a great deal of pain. I could read the look of disgust on my sister's face. She felt not pity for the prostrate figure laid out before her, but anger – an anger that he would attempt to seduce another man's wife and get caught in circumstances such as these.

"I suppose it came as little surprise to me then that she ran away shortly thereafter. It was one of the hardest things I have ever had to experience in my short life. It was made all the worse when, after I learned that my father had been released from the hospital, he did nothing to reclaim me. I was subsequently entrusted into the care of an orphanage, where I remained for some considerable time. I would often lie awake at night, simply contemplating my loneliness, gentlemen. That was until I decided to strike out on my own and join this cabaret. It has served as a home for me. Hardly an ideal one, but a shelter – and a family – nonetheless."

My heart simply broke for young Emma Bonnaire, and I laid another reassuring hand on her shoulder. She cast a glance up at me and her eyes looked like shattered mirrors. She pressed the handkerchief back into my hand and drew in another deep breath.

"Mademoiselle Bonnaire," Holmes said at length, "while you may not have heard from your sister or your father, can you think of anything unusual happening to you within the past few weeks?"

"I can think of nothing," she replied, "aside from, perhaps, the man who loiters outside the theater. But I cannot imagine how that could have any connection to this."

"Humor me if you please, mademoiselle," Holmes continued. "Who is this man?"

"I have never seen him clearly," Emma Bonnaire replied, "but he has become something of a legend amongst the girls. One of my friends, another dancer named Suzette, said that one night after a show she was exiting the theater through this very door and was making her up the alleyway when she heard someone moving about behind her. She turned and saw the outline of a man standing just over there."

Emma Bonnaire pointed to a spot beyond Holmes and the inspector at the foot of a small set of steps, leading down into the alleyway.

"Suzette said that she could not quite make out his face, but he appeared to be an old man. He was hunched over and seemed to have some difficulty in breathing. It was quiet night, Suzette said, and she heard his raspy breath as he leaned on the staircase railing. Suzette was about to go and ask him if he needed help, but she said that fear overtook her. You gentlemen have certainly heard tales of defenseless women in alleyways in the early hours of the morning. With that nightmare scenario running through her head, Suzette turned sharply and ran out of the alleyway.

"The next day, she told us about him and cautioned us to be on our guard. We heard and saw nothing of the mysterious man in the days which followed. However, one Friday evening a few weeks ago, a few of the girls and I decided to celebrate the end of the week. We all left together and were making our way of the theater when we caught sight of him, standing at the head of the alleyway. He was a tall, gangly-looking man dressed in a shabby, oversized coat. His hair was long and tumbled about his shoulders. And his beard was lengthy and dirty-looking as well. So shocked were we by his sudden materialization at the end of the alley that we all turned and raced back inside the theater.

"Since that day, gentlemen, we have heard nothing from the man. We have taken him to simply be one of the less fortunate who is forced to seek refuge on the streets. I very much fear that our minds ran away with ourselves and made a demon out of him."

The faintest ghost of a smile seemed to play upon Holmes's usually cruel, thin lips. "Mademoiselle Bonnaire," he said, "I cannot thank you enough for your invaluable assistance."

From his pocket, the detective withdrew a few francs and pressed them into the girl's hand. "If these can be of any help to you, mademoiselle, please take them."

Then turning to us, he added, "Come gentlemen, I very much suspect that – despite the lateness of the hour – the night is still young for us."

We bade Emma Bonnaire farewell and walked to the end of the alleyway and into the street.

"Well, M. Holmes," Inspector Durand said, "what do you intend to do next?"

"Part ways for the time being. I should very much like it if you could supply me with a city map, Inspector. If you could annotate it, as well, showing any spots in the city where you know there to be a large population without home or shelter, I would find it of great assistance. Let us all meet then once more at our hotel in an hours' time?"

Extending his arm, Holmes hailed a cab and I clambered inside after him, leaving Inspector Durand on the street with a look of stupefaction etched on his face.

Once we were within the cab, Holmes turned to me, and solemnly asked: "You did remember to bring your service revolver?"

"Of that you can certain," I replied.

"Excellent. I very much suspect that we shall be in need of it tonight."

True to his word, Inspector Durand met with us again at our hotel. He produced a valise, in which he carried a map of Paris. He spread out on the dining table.

"In an attempt to answer your question, M. Holmes," Durand said, "I consulted with a few of my fellow officers. They all agreed that here is the place where most of the city's poor some to congregate."

He pointed to a spot on the map along the River Seine. "The place is something of a colony," Durand replied. "They live along the river and under bridges."

"Excellent," Holmes said. "Then that is where we are headed now."

Holmes moved to the door and pulled on his hat and coat. "It has begun to rain, so take proper precautions. Now, come along."

Silently we made our way outside and into a tumultuous deluge. It was quite a feat in tracking down a cab, and I fear that I was soaked to the skin by the time that we three sat ensconced in the relative warmth and comfort of a carriage.

Chilled from the wet, as well as the anticipation and suspense in which I was being kept, I very nearly exploded once we found ourselves rattling through the deluge.

"What are we doing, Holmes? I am used to your characteristically dramatic behavior, but this is beginning to be a bit much."

Holmes replied in his usual, cool tone. "We are going to confront Jacques Bonnaire."

A shiver ran up and down my spine – a chill which I cannot fully attribute to the rain which had seeped into my clothing.

In short order, our carriage eased to a halt. Holmes gestured for Inspector Durand to lead the way and, alighting, we rushed out of the carriage, seeking shelter beneath the inspector's umbrella. We stood on a bridge overlooking both the River Seine, as well as a stone walkway below which ran parallel to the river. Durand informed us that the most likely place for us to find the homeless community was directly under the bridge. Locating a set of stone steps, Holmes pressed on undeterred.

In the darkness and rain which lashed at me, I lost sight of Holmes. I followed close at the inspector's heels, but it felt as if we were headed into some black void. The waters of the Seine looking indistinguishable from the inky darkness which surrounded us. Standing, disoriented and shivering in the pouring rain, it was something of a godsend when I felt myself bump into my friend. He pressed a finger to his lips and, from the folds of his coat, withdrew a bulls-eye lantern. I sheltered my friend's hands from the rain as he struck a match, letting the single point of yellow light pierce through the night.

"Now, follow me, gentlemen," Holmes whispered, "and, pray, keep silent. If he thinks that we are searching for him, then I'm afraid that the bird shall fly the coop."

We turned together as a small herd under the bridge and into the darkness, the pinpoint of light acting as our guide. I perceived, even in the dark, what appeared to be outlines of people shuffling in the night. Just as we had suspected, we were soon surrounded by an assortment of the city's beggars and vagabonds. I have witnessed much strife in my lifetime, but I felt additional pity to see such a concentration of sorrowful beings.

As we moved on, passing knots of people sprawled out on the cold stone, sleeping huddled under makeshift blankets or wrapped in their tattered coats, Holmes stopped suddenly and shone the lamplight on a tall, rail-thin specimen who lay before us. Even in the dark, I could make out something familiar about the man. Though I had never clapped eyes on him, I knew at once that this must be the mysterious apparition who seemed to haunt *Le Chat Noir*.

The creature was some kind of nightmarish vision. He was a tall, gangly-looking man, almost to the point of emaciation. His gaunt face was shrouded, however, by an unruly, unkempt beard, and a mangy, tousled head of long hair cascaded about his face. He was clad in a shapeless brown overcoat, done over in patches and stitched back together as though someone had tried to save it from the precipice of death itself.

Holmes whispered two, haunting words: "Jacques Bonnaire."

Movement came to the man's limbs and he opened one, bloodshot eye, wincing in the light.

"*Qui tu es?*" I heard the man rasp against the wind and rain. Despite my limited knowledge of the French language, I knew that the man was asking us who we were.

"My name will mean nothing to you," Holmes replied, "but this is Inspector Durand of the Paris Police Prefecture, and we have come to arrest you for the murder of M. Andre Dupont and his wife."

It is beyond my skills as a writer to attempt to describe the look of savagery which crossed the man's face at these words. In an instant, the pity for the poor soul who lay before us melted away as he transformed into some uncontrollable beast. I watched, helpless with horror, as he dug into his inner pocket and withdrew a long knife. I caught a glimpse of his shirtsleeve dangling about where his one hand once resided. With what I can only imagine was all of the man's limited strength, he hauled himself up from the ground and attempted an escape. So startled were we by the sudden convulsion which had overcome Bonnaire that Holmes, the inspector, and I completely failed to stop him. Time seemed to slow to a crawl before Holmes cried out, "Quickly! Cut him off on the other side!"

I took to my heels and returned the way we had come, soon finding myself sprinting along the stone causeway which ran along the river. The rain had made the stones into something as slippery as ice, and I almost lost my footing on several occasions. I could barely make out the scene which transpired beneath the bridge, but with little else place to go, I stood my ground and pulled the hammer back on my revolver. I aimed, not hesitating to shoot at whatever leapt out at from the darkness.

I heard the sound of Holmes's voice calling through the night, and I momentarily lowered my gun for fear that I might strike my friend on accident. No sooner had I done so then the figure of Jacques Bonnaire flew out at me from the void. His face contorted into some satanic visage, he screamed like a banshee as the knife flashed in the air, and I let out a gasp as its point caught my coat sleeve. I felt the cold steel against my flesh, followed by a moment of intense, searing pain, as though I'd been struck by a red hot poker. I dropped my gun and pressed a hand to my wound. The man seemed to have lost interest in me entirely, however, for he turned and started to run along the way I just come. I saw him raise the knife high over his head once again, in search of either Holmes or Durand.

In one swift movement, I had gathered up the gun from the ground and squeezed the trigger. The explosion sounded tremendous in the relative quiet of the early morning. The bullet met its mark in the back of Jacques Bonnaire, and I watched as he tumbled to the ground, his weapon falling from his hand.

A second later, I felt a hand on my shoulder and, looking up, I found myself staring at Holmes.

"Tell me that you are not hurt, Watson!" he cried.

He shined the light over me. I caught sight of a gash running along my forearm, but I was numb to the pain. The terror which had surged through my body had let to go of me.

"Jacques Bonnaire," I said breathlessly, "is dead."

That was the last I recall before total darkness overwhelmed me.

When I came to, I was seated upright in my bed in the hotel. Sherlock Holmes and Inspector Durand sat on two chairs at the foot, keeping vigil. I smiled as I came to and made to reach for my watch, only to find that my arm had been wrapped in a sling.

"It's barely five in the morning, Watson," Sherlock Holmes said.

"I haven't felt this bad since the war," I joked. My jest drew a smile from both men.

"Your wound was a superficial one," Durand said. "M. Holmes insisted that we get it dressed, and our physician at the prefecture concurred that we have it attended to . . . as you can see."

"A bloodletting was worth it, I should think," I said, "if we were able to stop Jacques Bonnaire and bring an end to this business."

"I rather think not," Holmes replied darkly.

At these words, the inspector and I both turned to face Holmes, our mouths agape.

"M. Holmes, what are you talking about? Jacques Bonnaire attacked both you and Dr. Watson in his attempt to flee from the police. He was carrying a knife which, I am told, matched the type which was used to sever the hands of M. Dupont and his wife. Are you insinuating that he was innocent all along?"

"Nothing of the kind, Inspector," Holmes replied, crossing one leg over the other. "In fact, it was Jacques Bonnaire who did sever the hands of the deceased. But it was *not* Bonnaire who killed M. Dupont and his wife."

"Well then, who is guilty?" I sputtered.

"Bonnaire's elder daughter," Holmes replied. "You, Inspector, will know her better as Jeanette the maid."

"*Mon Dieu*," Durand said. "M. Holmes, I think you ought to explain yourself."

"Gladly," the detective said, as he lit a cigarette. "From the outset of this business, I thought that there was more to the case. M. Dupont showed me two letters which were making threats against his life. The second of these was postmarked London, which meant that whoever sent it had to have been in the city and returned just as quickly when Dupont and his wife decided to flee. Now, ask yourself one question, Inspector: Would Jacques Bonnaire – a man who is minus one hand and who has been inflicted with a near fatal bullet wound – be capable of crossing the channel as quickly as he did in his condition? What's more, you and I both saw how destitute he was. The man was living on the streets, and would surely have been unable to pay the fare for two consecutive trips, let alone one.

"Knowing that there was a conspirator involved in this affair was only made all the more plausible when I was struck by the presence of two different knife wounds upon the bodies. You yourself asked the question, Inspector: *Why should the murderer carry two different knives when one would be more than efficient?* The simplest answer is that there was more than one murderer involved. And, this became even more likely after an examination of the scene. You will doubtlessly recall that I took a moment to analyze a few shards of glass which I found on the veranda. You assumed that that glass was left after the murderer gained forceful entry into the house. If that had been the case, Inspector, the glass would have been found on the *inside* of the room and not *outside*. That window was broken *after* the murders were committed.

"And, lastly, you told me, Inspector, that the maid, Jeanette, was in the kitchen and heard nothing on the night of the murder. Perhaps you would be so good as to cast your minds back to the afternoon we examined the scene. I returned to the room to fetch my hat and stick –"

"And I clearly heard you moving about upstairs," I interjected.

"As I figured that you would," Holmes replied. "Jeanette would have to have been lying when she said that she could not hear anything transpiring upstairs. The design of the house and the kitchen would have placed her almost directly underneath of the room in which her employers were killed. The weapon itself is also connected with the kitchen. It would not be too difficult a task to search the kitchen for the knife, Inspector. And, if you find one, feel free to send it my way. I have developed something of a test which will differentiate blood from a whole host of other substances. Its presence on a blade should not be too difficult a thing to ascertain, given a few hours of concentration.

"As I see it, Jeannette – if her name truly is Jeannette – felt not repulsion for her father when she saw him lying, dying in a hospital bed all those years ago, but a yearning for revenge against the man who had done this. Her disappearance gave her ample opportunity to begin seeking employment in some of the wealthiest houses in France, bringing her into the social circle of M. Andre Dupont. After some years, I rather think that Dupont would fail to recognize the little girl who had once been the daughter of his friend, and he hired Jeannette, completely unaware of the conspiracy against him. Jeannette was working with her father to avenge him and began the persecution, creating fear in the

Dupont household. Even when he attempted to flee, she would follow. Dupont told us that he brought only his most trusted staff to England, and you confirmed, Inspector, that Jeannette was in London.

"On the night of the murder, Jeannette aided her father's entry into the house. She stabbed to death both M. Dupont and his wife before her father began his bloody task. Once she had managed his escape, Jeannette broke the window to convincingly approximate a break-in – inadvertently casting suspicion solely on her father – and then returned to the kitchen. I am glad only that the police investigation has run this long, Inspector. Should Jeannette have tried to flee before now, surely she would have been easily traced. However, I suggest that you apprehend her as soon as possible. News of the action by the river shall spread fast and, with nothing else to lose, I fear that she might do anything in so desperate a situation."

Durand rose from his chair. "I shall put my best men to it immediately."

"Excellent," Holmes replied. The two shook hands. "It has been an absolute pleasure working alongside you on two separate occasions and, should the needs arise, please feel free to contact me again."

"I shall do so only too happily," Durand replied. "I shall see myself off. *Au revoir*, gentlemen."

I found myself feeling in much better sorts during the remainder of the day, and the following morning, Holmes and I found ourselves once more trundling across the French countryside by train. Holmes had remained silent about the case but, as he sat, casting a glance out of the yet again rain-streaked windows, I noticed a certain melancholia descend upon him.

"You have vindicated yourself," I said trying to coax him from his brown study. "You have seen justice served once again."

"You are right, Watson," Holmes replied, "but one cannot go unaffected by what we have witnessed here these past few days. This adventure of the Parisian Butcher has only reinforced to me what a bleak world we inhabit."

"Well," I said, "it should then reinforce what a role you must play in it, then. If the world is as bleak and dark as you make it out to be, then surely the world needs a Sherlock Holmes to maintain the light."

The Missing Empress
by Robert Stapleton

Glorious weather was not the only delight putting a skip into my step that Sunday morning in June 1887. But, on returning to Baker Street, I found my friend Sherlock Holmes in a much more sombre mood.

He was sitting in front of the unlit fire, glaring at a sheet of paper lying discarded in the grate.

"This is no time to be gloomy, Holmes," I chided him. "The Queen celebrates her Golden Jubilee on Monday, and the nation is already rejoicing."

Without turning to me, he gestured towards the sheet of paper as if it were a warrant to attend the Last Judgement.

I plucked it from the fire-grate and read it through. It turned out to be a note from Scotland Yard. From Inspector Lestrade. An invitation, nay a summons, to attend immediately. To interview a drunk.

"I consider it an insult, Watson," said Holmes, without raising his gaze. "For Lestrade to send for me in this manner is little short of an outrage."

"Look on the bright side," I told him. "It might turn out to be another case."

"To interview a drunk? The fellow probably mistook his way home."

"Or maybe not. At least we should find out what Lestrade considers so important."

"The very reason I didn't destroy the letter the moment I received it." He stood up and reached for his coat, hat, and cane. "I suppose we had better go."

I stepped outside to hail a cab.

"Mrs. Hudson!" Holmes took out his frustration by bellowing at the landlady. "We're going out."

Within ten minutes, we had arrived at Scotland Yard. The inspector was waiting for us.

"You took your time, gentlemen."

Holmes ignored him. I did my best to diffuse the tension between them. "My fault, I think, Lestrade. I was delayed by a visit to a patient this morning. A lady more in need of a friendly face than the tablets I prescribe for her."

138

"The drunk," said Holmes, turning on Lestrade. "I'd like to see the reason for our being called here this morning."

Lestrade softened his attitude. "Of course. Please follow me, gentlemen."

He took us down a flight of steps to the cells beneath Scotland Yard, secure and safe below ground-level. Our footsteps echoed in the confined passageway as the Detective Inspector led us to a door at the far end. There he opened the viewing port, and looked inside. "An ugly brute, I have to admit," observed Lestrade.

This piqued my colleague's interest. Holmes took his place at the opening and stood for a moment watching the man inside. Then he stood back abruptly. "What does this fellow have to say?"

"You'd better hear him yourself, Mr. Holmes."

"First, tell me what you know."

"His name is Bessington," said Lestrade. "He's well known to the Metropolitan Police as a layabout. He gets drunk whenever he can afford it, but generally he's a harmless cove."

"Until now," said Holmes. "Or why else would you have called upon my services?"

"More a mystery, I would say, Mr. Holmes. I thought you might be interested. You see, in the early hours of this morning, he staggered into a police station in Clerkenwell, ranting about a kidnapping."

Lestrade unlocked the cell door and we followed him inside. The smell of damp clothing and unwashed humanity hung in the air. It was rank enough to turn a tanner's stomach.

Inspector Lestrade left the door open. "Not a pleasant sight, is he, Dr. Watson?"

"I've seen worse," I told him. "But what's all this about a kidnapping?"

From the bench on which he had been lying, the drunk lifted himself into a sitting position and glared up at his visitors. "That's right," he exclaimed. "Kidnap! High Treason! Treachery!" The man seemed to double in size as he spoke, and his eyes shone with an inner passion.

Holmes sat down beside the man, and looked into his bloodshot eyes. "Tell me."

"I'd been drinking."

"Of course."

"To celebrate the Jubilee of the Queen. God bless her. I needed somewhere to sleep. I happened to find myself near the Boar's Head in Clerkenwell. So I slipped 'round the back and climbed down into the basement, like I often do when I'm up that way. It's dry, and out of the night air. It suits me well enough. See? I can be gone again the next

139

morning before anybody knows I've even been there. Nobody knows. Nobody gets hurt."

"Then something happened."

Bessington's eyes flashed again. "Something woke me up. It was late. I heard a church clock strike twelve. Then, I realised I wasn't alone. I could see a light. And people, sharing a meal."

"How many?"

"Four of them. Three men and a woman. They were sitting at a table. I didn't dare move. I knew if they'd seen me, I'd be dead."

"Dead? How did you know that?"

"Because of what they were saying."

"Tell me." Holmes was becoming intrigued.

"They were discussing plans to kidnap somebody."

"Who?"

"Her Majesty."

A tense silence filled the cell.

"The Queen?"

"That's what I heard."

"When was the kidnapping to take place?"

I found myself drawn into the discussion. "On the day of her Jubilee, perhaps?"

"Nah. Not then. The day after."

Now it began to make sense. "Of course," I exclaimed. "Tuesday. There's to be a procession through the streets of London. To Westminster Abbey, for a service of thanksgiving."

Holmes nodded. "Then back to Buckingham Palace."

"But crowds will be lining the streets," I reminded him. "Nobody could possibly kidnap her then."

"That's right, Dr. Watson," said Lestrade. "We'll all be on high alert. If anybody plans to kidnap Her Majesty, it won't be then."

"No," said Bessington. "They'll do it when she gets back to the Palace."

Lestrade leaned closer to Bessington, "Tell us more."

"I didn't hear no more. As soon as they'd gone, I got out of there. In double-quick time, I can tell you."

"You say there were four of them," Holmes reminded him. "Three men and a woman."

"That's right. I saw them."

"Lestrade," said Holmes. "Take me to the Boar's Head, if you please. The place for us to begin is the location of the crime."

"Crime? So, you think there might be something in this fellow's story?"

140

"It's too early to tell," said Holmes. "I need concrete facts upon which to work."

"I'm beginning to learn your methods, Mr. Holmes," said Lestrade. "I thought you might want to visit the place, so I told them to leave everything exactly as it was."

"Good. And please ask a member of Her Majesty's household to join us there."

The basement of the Boar's Head tavern was a dark and gloomy hole. It reeked of sawdust and stale beer, but it was spacious and private.

Holmes had insisted that we bring Bessington along with us. For the moment, he remained half-hidden in the shadows, with a constable to make sure he didn't slip away. I didn't think there was much chance that he would. He had sobered up by now, and seemed keen to help.

Sir Cuthbert Hollingham joined us a few minutes after we arrived. He seemed loath to climb down into the cellar, but his determination to do his duty outweighed his reluctance. He was a small man, with greying side-whiskers and a balding head, but his presence made up for his lack of height. He introduced himself as a representative of the Queen's household, and complained that he had better things to do at such a significant moment in history.

Holmes ignored his complaints and made his way across the cellar towards a table with four chairs around it. He examined the table. "Is this the way it was last night?"

"Nothing has been touched, Mr. Holmes," said Lestrade.

"Four people." Holmes looked towards Bessington.

The man nodded.

"Might I venture to call them a Council of Four?"

"We need more light," I said. Holmes nodded his consent as I lit the candelabrum in the centre of the table.

He sniffed the air. "They dined on lamb, with a custard dessert." He bent down, and examined each place setting in turn, beginning with the chair facing the doorway. "Hello! What have we here? The man sitting in this place has expensive tastes. A tall man, possibly with connections to Buckingham Palace. Dark haired, with a liking for expensive French wine."

"Guesswork," huffed Sir Cuthbert.

"Not at all," said Holmes. "The imprint of a boot beneath the chair suggests a man about six feet in height. The wine glass contains a small but detectable trace of good quality wine. And a single hair on the table is darkly coloured, with a hint of the sort of Macassar oil favoured by the late Prince Albert.

141

Sir Cuthbert's eyebrows shot up. Now Holmes had his attention. "It could be the new fellow. Henry Tinderman. He works at the Home Office, but lately he's been helping us prepare for the Jubilee celebrations."

Holmes shifted to the next place around the table. "Ah, here we have the woman in the group. And well dressed, judging by the small feather trapped on the back of the chair. A lady's maid, perhaps. With a perfume that lingers." He looked up at me. "Don't you think so, Watson?"

I leaned closer, and sniffed. "Indeed. Not one that catches in the throat, like so many cheaper scents."

Holmes found the third place very different. "Now, this fellow smells of horse. Undoubtedly the working man of the group, judging by the fragment of sawdust beneath his chair."

"Extraordinary," exclaimed the Palace official.

"Obviously the man to drive the kidnap vehicle."

"Sounds reasonable," muttered Sir Cuthbert.

Holmes turned his attention to the fourth place. "I have to admit, this dark man is not so easy to read." He turned to Bessington. "What can you tell me about him?"

"He had his back towards me the whole time. He wore a cloak, and a top hat he never once took off. His voice was strange, as well. Foreign."

Holmes stood upright. "Here we have the mastermind. A dangerous man. But who is he? The ashtray contains the end of a cigar. Cut, not bitten." He sniffed the tobacco. "Unusual aroma. East European, if I'm not mistaken."

Lestrade broke Holmes's concentration. "Are we to assume, then, that the threat to the kidnap the Queen is real, Mr. Holmes?"

"Oh, yes. Very real."

"Kidnap?" exclaimed Sir Cuthbert. "Then we must put a stop to it at once. I'll have Tinderman put in irons."

"Don't be so hasty, Sir Cuthbert," said Lestrade. "We don't yet know for sure if it's him, or who these other people are, or how they intend to commit the crime."

"Or with what purpose," I pointed out.

Holmes sat down in the mystery man's chair, and looked up to the ceiling. "It has to take place on Tuesday, the day of the public celebrations. We have agreed that the most likely time is after Her Majesty has returned to the palace."

"That's right, Mr. Holmes," came Bessington's voice.

Holmes turned to face Sir Cuthbert. "What will be Her Majesty's itinerary for the rest of that day, Sir Cuthbert?"

The Palace official rubbed his chin thoughtfully. "On returning from the service, she will appear on the balcony of the Palace. Then she will meet officials from around the world, before attending a celebratory banquet."

"And later?"

"A firework display will be held in the grounds of the Palace. Part of the nationwide celebration."

"Hmm. Is Her Majesty to venture out into the grounds?"

"Indeed."

"Then, I suggest that might be the most likely time for these people to make their move."

As we prepared to depart, Bessington called Holmes over and whispered something to him, casting glances toward Lestrade, who was looking elsewhere. Holmes nodded and joined me by the door.

Outside, Holmes suggested he and I should take a cab to the river. We stopped at London Bridge, and wandered along the riverside. We found The Pool of London crowded. With lighters and barges cluttering up the quayside, often several abreast.

"What do you make of this business, Holmes?" I asked.

"It seems as clear as day to me."

"Well, apart from a threat to the Queen, I'm dashed if I can make much of it," I admitted.

"As with all investigations, the successful uncovering of the crime lies in careful preparation on our part."

"What preparation?"

"Well, for example, you notice that ship a hundred yards ahead?"

I saw the vessel. A small steel-hulled steamship, about the length of two Thames barges. The black hull carried a name in rusting white letters: *Drakesian*. Above the white deck-housing rose a tall black funnel. The hold took up the forward third of the ship.

"Did Bessington direct you here?"

Holmes nodded. "He had also overheard the name of the ship, but he felt that Lestrade and the police might bungle it."

"It's like so many others along this stretch of the Thames," I said. "What's so special about this one?"

"Notice the extra-wide gangplank joining it to the quayside."

"Unusual, but is that significant?"

"Perhaps we shall find out."

The moment we reached the steamship, Holmes stepped on deck and examined the covering of the hold. "It has been significantly strengthened," he said. "But why?"

He knocked with his cane on the wheelhouse door. It opened, and a man appeared. He was large and muscular, with narrowed eyes and an aggressive manner. I stepped back in alarm. But he didn't intimidate Holmes for one moment.

"What do you want?"

Holmes returned the man's stare. "I have a proposition for you."

"Who are you?"

"My name is Sherlock Holmes. I am assisting Scotland Yard in a very serious case. And your name?"

"Alfred Dexter." The man spat into the water. "You have a proposition for me, do you, Mr. Holmes? What kind of proposition?"

"Your boss has hired you to undertake a singular task."

"Says who?"

"Don't deny it."

The man shrugged, but looked suddenly wary.

"I want you to tell your boss that you have changed your mind. You will allow him to use your vessel and crew, but not with you in command."

Dexter laughed. "He'll kill me. Nemirov doesn't like traitors."

Holmes smiled. At least we now had a name for the mystery man. "Then I suggest you make yourself scarce."

"And if I don't?"

"I will see that you are hanged for treason."

Dexter looked alarmed. "Now, look here, Mr. Holmes. I went along with this business at first, but kidnapping the Queen was never my idea."

More of the plot was confirmed. "Then pull out while you still can."

"How can I do that, and stay alive?"

"Take the next train for the West Country, and lose yourself there."

"But they'll come looking for me."

"I think not. They have only two days before they have to flee the country."

"Look, I'm no supporter of the British Establishment, but I have to admit, I never was keen on this business. I prefer Mr. Marx to Mr. Nemirov."

"Then go. But first, tell me everything you know about these people. This Council of Four."

"That's a good name for them, Mr. Holmes. Although Nemirov doesn't like titles and names. The crew are mostly Dutch, but they

144

understand English, and they were hired by Nemirov, so you'd better come down to my cabin. Then I'll tell you all I know."

We all squeezed into the captain's cabin, which was more a cubbyhole than a place to sleep. Holmes and I remained standing, as Dexter slumped onto the bunk.

"Let's begin with this man you called Nemirov," said Holmes. "What can you tell us about him?"

"He's a refugee from the Russian Tsar. I don't know what they want him for, but he seems to be on the run, so to speak. He has a passionate dislike for authority of any kind."

"Hmm. A man with a chip on his shoulder."

"He plans to build a bright new world, and he's prepared to move heaven and earth to achieve it."

Holmes nodded. "I understand a man called Henry Tinderman may involved in this business too."

"A man high up at the Home Office," Dexter agreed. "That's him, all right. But he spends a lot of time at Buckingham Palace."

"Helping prepare for the Jubilee," said Holmes.

"That's right. He used to be a loyal servant of the Queen."

"But not now?"

"No."

"Why not?"

"A certain personage at the Palace took some friends to spend a week with him. I don't know what happened, but it plunged the household into financial ruin. Tinderman is now a very angry man, Mr. Holmes."

"And a dangerous one."

Dexter nodded.

"And the woman?"

"Angelique Pellier. She comes from a humble French family, but she wanted to make something of herself. She fell out and fled to England. Now she's in service at the Palace."

"And the other man?"

"Benjamin Sligo. Like his name, he's Irish. He wants to see the liberation of his country from the British crown."

"Like so many."

"He served in the army until he was injured and was forced to make the best he could of life as a civilian. His skill with horses helped him find work as a groom. And now he's a valued member of Nemirov's conspiracy."

Holmes glared down at Dexter. "That information is extremely useful. But before we go, tell me one thing. Is there to be another meeting?"

"Yes. A full gathering of their supporters."

"Where?"

"The Boar's Head in Clerkenwell. This evening."

"Of course. And the password to get in?"

"'Jubilee'."

"Naturally. Well, thank you, Mr. Dexter. Now I suggest you leave at once. London is no longer a safe place for you. I shall send a telegram in your name, informing the meeting that you no longer wish to be a part of their scheme, and that you will not be at the gathering tonight."

"Thank you, Mr. Holmes. You'd better send it to Tinderman, at the Home Office."

"I shall do that. But, for the sake of your life, you must disappear before he receives it."

Upon our return to Baker Street, Holmes immediately set about combing through his filing system. I could detect a frenzy in his search, which meant he would resent any interruption until he had found whatever he was looking for.

I sat down beside the hearth, and waited.

After several minutes, he stood up. "A-ha!"

"What have you found, Holmes?"

He held up a newspaper cutting. "Nemirov. I thought the name rang a bell."

"Sounds East European."

"A known anarchist by the name of Anton Leonid Nemirov. Born in Kiev in 1839."

"An anarchist? You mean, he hates everyone."

"He is a man with a vision, Watson. This is a report of a public speech he gave a few months ago in Hyde Park. He blames the Russian Empire for persecuting his family and murdering his parents. He now calls upon everyone who has been treated badly by the authorities in any country to join him in forming a new state, a nation where everyone is free to live out their own lives without fear of persecution."

"A utopian dream," I replied. "But to kidnap the Queen is a capital crime."

"Then we need to know what happens at that meeting tonight. We have to find out exactly what they are planning."

"Will you go, Holmes?"

"I would like for you to go instead, Watson." He looked towards me. "Take Bessington with you. Lestrade will have finished with him by now."

"Good idea, Holmes."

"And see if you can persuade Sir Cuthbert to go with you as well. He might not like it, but his presence there could prove useful."

"Won't the landlord have warned Nemirov in advance?"

"No. Scotland Yard have sworn him to secrecy."

"And how do we gain entrance without alarming the guests?"

"That is why you are taking our friend Bessington with you."

"And what will you be doing, Holmes?"

"Making plans," he replied, as he sat back and lit his favourite briar pipe.

I arrived with Bessington at the Boar's Head early in the evening. Sir Cuthbert had agreed to accompany us. He felt it his responsibility to help deal with this threat to the Queen's safety.

The sound of voices, together with the smell of alcohol, told us the Public Bar and the lounge were busy with customers. Bessington led us to the rear of the building, and lifted a metal grille. "This is the tradesman's entrance," he told us with a chuckle. "I usually get in this way. And not just at this place, neither."

In the evening light, Sir Cuthbert's face showed his annoyance. Only his sense of duty prevented him from hurrying back to the Palace.

Following Bessington, we climbed down through the opening and into the cellar we had visited only a few hours earlier.

Again, the air in that underground room smelt musty, and I could feel the cold seeping out of the stone walls.

I lit the lantern I had brought with me, and looked around. The place appeared to be empty. We found a corner at the dirtiest end of the cellar, doused the flame, and sat hidden in the darkness.

I had dressed suitable to the occasion in a tweed suit and a flat cap. Against my advice, Sir Cuthbert had tried to maintain his dignity by wearing his usual black suit and top hat. "I hope we won't have to stay here long," he muttered.

"I think we might," I told him, "so you'd better make yourself comfortable."

At the far end of the cellar, the door at the top of the stairs opened and light flooded in, while we sat hidden among the shadows. I heard somebody climbing down the steps and, peering from the darkness, I saw a man that I didn't recognise. He hung a lighted lantern on a joist in the centre of the cellar. Only now could I see properly how the room had been set out. Several rows of chairs faced towards the front, where four seats stood facing the other way. Some event was planned to take place there that evening – the meeting we had come to observe.

Another man remained at the top of the stairs. We heard him ask the next person for the password. The fellow muttered "Jubilee", and was allowed to descend. Other people followed, until the gathering had amounted to about thirty individuals.

I noticed another man arrive who looked particularly suspicious. He was dressed like a fisherman in a navy blue jersey, corduroy trousers, and a peaked cap. The seating area filled rapidly, and soon a cloud of blue tobacco smoke hung over the gathering. Somebody slammed the entrance door shut. At the front of the gathering, the four chairs were now occupied. One of the men seated there stood up and called for order. He was tall and had an air of authority about him.

"Tinderman," hissed Sir Cuthbert into my right ear.

I nodded. The man from the Home Office.

"Ladies and gentlemen," said Tinderman, "the time is drawing near when we shall see the fulfilment of our grand design." All around the room, people nodded and whispered to one another. "We are a select few. Each of us has a unique reason for being at this gathering. The fact that you knew the password secures your right to be here this evening, and guarantees the distinction of our gathering. This pleased the crowd. Tinderman continued. "I shall now hand you over to the man who had masterminded this whole affair." He sat down, and another man stood up.

This man was less tall, but stood ram-rod straight. A shock of blond hair stood out from his head, giving him an eccentric appearance. His eyes panned around the room. Then he bowed towards the gathering. "Welcome to this meeting," he said, in an accent which placed him firmly from Eastern Europe. This had to be the Ukrainian. Nemirov. "This will be our final meeting before Tuesday, when our purpose is achieved." A rumble of conversation rolled around the gathering, but faded away again as Nemirov continued. "Thanks to the support of each one of you, everything is now ready. You each know your particular roles. But a problem has developed."

People sat upright, and many leaned forward, all intent on learning about this new threat to their plans.

"Dexter." He spat the name. "The captain of the steamer has absconded." Angry words emanated from the gathering. "He has run out on us. But we still have the ship itself, and her crew. Now we need a new pilot for the *Drakesian*."

It was at this point that the fisherman stood up and pushed his way to the front. "I'll do it," he said. "I'll skipper that ship for you."

"And who are you?"

The fisherman took off his cap respectfully. "Name's Craster. An honest seaman who has spent twenty years before the mast, and has now fallen on hard times, all because of those ship owners – faceless businessmen who want to wring out every last penny from the poor, and take no thought for the honest working man."

"And do you share our goals?"

"Freedom for all men," said Craster. "That's good enough for me."

"Then you must be ready to sail on Tuesday evening – the very moment we appear with our precious load."

Craster looked up at him. "And what or who might that be, sir?"

"If you don't know by now, then it is better you don't know at all."

"You mean Her Majesty?"

Nemirov's face broke into a mirthless smile.

"May a humble man like myself ask the purpose of this action? I can see it as a blow against authority, but what will we do with Her Majesty?"

The Ukrainian stood straight and proud. "We will hold her in comfortable seclusion. In Rotterdam. And negotiate a ransom." A rumble of approval ran around the gathering. "We will force them to take us seriously."

"May I be so bold as to ask the price of an Empress's ransom?"

Tinderman stood up again. "Simple. The complete abolition of the monarchy." Everyone cheered.

I felt Sir Cuthbert stir beside me. "The bounder!"

Faces turned towards where we were sitting. "Who's there?" demanded Nemirov.

Bessington turned towards us. "That's blown it. They'll be after us now." He pointed towards the grille where we had entered. "Go!"

I pushed Sir Cuthbert back towards the steps that had brought us down into the cellar. Behind us, I heard Bessington call out, mimicking his drunken drawl. "No need to worry, gents and ladies. It's only me."

Masked by the sounds of shouts and scuffling, I pushed Sir Cuthbert up through the grille and into the night air.

Clutching his cane and top hat, Sir Cuthbert followed me, as we ran for our lives.

The next morning, Monday, Holmes seemed more interested in the newspaper than in listening to my story.

149

"Today," he told me, "Her Majesty will travel from Frogmore, and this evening will attend a dinner to be held in her honour."

My eye was drawn to the back page of his paper, and to an article in the *Stop Press* column. "Look at this, Holmes."

He turned the paper over, and read the article.

"Early today, police pulled the body of a man from the River Thames. Inspector Lestrade of Scotland Yard identified the man as one Josiah Bessington, a vagrant of no fixed abode."

I gasped. "Bessington. Drowned."

"I very much doubt if that was how he met his end, Watson."

"I agree, Holmes. The poor man must have given his life so that Sir Cuthbert and I could escape. If it hadn't been for him, the police would be dealing with three corpses by now."

Holmes folded his newspaper, and dropped it onto the table. "Today, we must wait, Watson. Prepare. But tomorrow, we shall see what will happen."

Holmes was absent for much of that day, and when I later asked him how his day had gone, he merely smiled and said it had gone as expected.

On the following day, June twenty-first, 1887, Victoria, Queen of the United Kingdom of Great Britain and Ireland, and Empress of India, rode in an open carriage to celebrate her Golden Jubilee at Westminster Abbey. She was escorted by Indian Princes and other dignitaries. Crowds thronged the streets, and people gathered to see the pageantry and to celebrate the Queen's fifty years on the throne. The Queen later waved to the cheering crowds from the balcony of Buckingham Palace. After receiving various dignitaries, she celebrated with yet another banquet.

As I sat with Holmes over afternoon tea, he gave me my instructions. "Your part in this evening's events is crucial, Watson."

"My part?"

He explained what would happen. "Naturally," he continued, "you must liaise directly with Sir Cuthbert. He has been told exactly what to do. Officially, the Queen will be wheeled outside to enjoy a display of fireworks."

"Officially?"

"In reality, she will be travelling by closed carriage, for an evening of peace and quiet at St James's Palace."

"But where will you be?"

"Unfortunately, I have other matters to deal with. But I trust you to do the right thing."

"Which is?"

"To keep Her Majesty safe. Oh, and don't forget to take your service revolver along with you."

Dusk was falling when I reached Buckingham Palace, and joined Sir Cuthbert at one of the side entrances near a coach house. He seemed agitated. "I really do not like the idea of putting Her Majesty in any kind of danger."

I took out my revolver. "Don't worry, Sir Cuthbert. I won't let anything happen to her."

"Well, for better or worse, the time has come to put into operation Sherlock Holmes's plan." He disappeared inside.

The clopping of horses' hooves made me turn and hurry towards the inner courtyard. There I saw an enclosed four-wheeled clarence waiting. The two horses seemed anxious to be off.

I slid into a dark corner beside the building as three shadowy figures boarded the clarence. A figure I recognised as the French woman, Angelique, climbed in. The groom, Benjamin Sligo, climbed onto the box seat at the front, and took the reins. Then Henry Tinderman, dressed in his finest attire, appeared and took his place beside the driver.

Once more the door opened, and Sir Cuthbert emerged, escorting a small woman. She was dressed in black and held a veil across her face. Sir Cuthbert helped the woman climb up into the clarence and then closed the door. I recognised the figure at once. "The Queen," I murmured as Sir Cuthbert joined me.

The driver shook the reins and the horses trotted slowly out of the courtyard, heading towards one of the side gates of the Palace grounds. I began to panic. The very people who had been plotting the kidnap of the Queen had now taken her into their own hands, and away from my own care. Would our plan work? Why had we let things go this far? Was this truly what Holmes wanted? Undoubtedly, it had to be part of his scheme, but I hoped with all my heart he knew what he was doing.

As soon as the vehicle had rounded the corner of the building and was out of my sight, I felt Sir Cuthbert take me by the arm. "Quickly, Dr. Watson. We must leave at once." I calmed myself – this was what we had planned.

I followed him around the corner of the coach house and towards a hansom cab standing in the shadows. It was ready to leave at once. We climbed on board, and immediately drove off at a brisk trot.

"Make sure that you stay out of sight," Sir Cuthbert called to the cabbie. Then to me. "He's a man we can trust – the best in the whole of London." We sat back, as there was nothing more that we could do at the moment. Our fate, and the fate of our Queen, remained at that moment in the hands of our skilled and determined cab driver.

Surrounded by the sound of fireworks and the voices of exhausted and drunken members of the populace, we rattled along at a fair old lick, following the clarence through the streets of London until it reached the north bank of the river. Not far, but far enough for my fraying nerves.

I could see the clarence now, in the distance and almost out of sight. It had already reached the *Drakesian*. I could now see the purpose of the extra wide gangplank, as the horses and carriage had driven straight onto the deck of the steamer and had drawn to a halt there. Several of the ship's crew were now busy tying the clarence down, whilst others cast off the ship's mooring lines from the quayside.

I could see all this happening, but I was too late to prevent the steamer from pulling away. Sir Cuthbert leaned out of the window, and called to the driver. "Slow down."

I noticed a man stepped out from the shadows. It took a moment before I realised that it was Lestrade.

"Dr. Watson," he called, "our water transport is ready and waiting."

Sir Cuthbert and I climbed down from the hansom and followed Lestrade towards where two stream launches lay at the quayside, smoke already rising from their funnels. We boarded the nearer of the vessels. The engines rumbled and belched out smoke and sparks into the night air, and the propellers churned up the water behind us into a maelstrom of furious foam – fury which reflected my inner anxiety that the kidnappers might get away.

I gazed ahead into the darkness, looking for any sign of the steamer. Then I saw it. Already well downstream of London Bridge, it was steadily pulling ahead of us. The light air was heavy with coal smoke billowing from the vessel ahead. Their ship's lights showed them to be making rapid progress.

"Look at their speed!" I cried. "They're getting away!"

"They're certainly making a run for it," said Lestrade. "In this river, at night, such speed is utter madness."

We weren't getting any closer. It would take a miracle if we were going to catch up with that speeding vessel now.

But then, the miracle happened. The ship turned abruptly towards the north bank of the river. It struck something below the water, and came to a shuddering halt. As we drew closer, I could see the carriage we had pursued through the streets, still tied securely to the rail stanchions, and presumably still holding the person of the Queen. We heard loud and heated voices coming to us across the water as men shouted at one another and quickly turned their anger upon us.

Drawing level with the stranded steamer, I leapt on board and took out my revolver. I could see three men standing in the bows of the ship. Nemirov stood farthest away from me. Although I couldn't see his face, I could tell that he was angry at having been stopped. Benjamin Sligo, the Irishman, stood between the two horses still harnessed to the clarence. He was struggling to keep the animals calm. Henry Tinderman stood nearest to me. In the darkness, I observed that he was holding a boathook, which he held out towards me in a threatening manner. I remained where I stood, while members of the Metropolitan police swarmed onto the deck.

With his eyes fixed only upon me, Tinderman failed to notice another, smaller man who jumped up onto the deck beside him. He turned too late to avoid Sir Cuthbert's swinging fist. It caught the traitor's jaw with a sickening thump, and sent him sprawling to the deck.

"You swine!" growled Sir Cuthbert.

At the sound of confusion around them, the horses began to panic. When the second launch coming up behind us sounded its steam-whistle, both animals reared up, and one of them landed on Sligo. The Irishman screamed as the terrified horse trampled him to death.

Another man hurried forward, took hold of the reins, and calmed the animals down. I recognised this man as the replacement pilot, Craster.

I dragged Sligo's body away from the horses, but there was nothing that I could do save him. The pilot turned towards me. "I'm glad to see you are unharmed, Watson."

"Holmes? What on earth are you doing here?"

"I had to make sure these rogues didn't get away."

"You mean, you deliberately ran the ship aground."

"Indeed."

I looked around. "But where's Nemirov?"

"I saw him drop over the side of the ship," said Holmes. "Lestrade is organising a search party at this moment."

"How can I help?"

"Check on the carriage."

"Of course. The Queen."

I hurried to the clarence, opened the door and looked in at the black figure sitting in the rear seat.

"Your Majesty," I said. But then I noticed another figure. Sitting facing her was the final member of the Council of Four, Angelique Pellier. She was holding a small, single-shot pistol, and was pointing it towards the figure in black. The young woman gave me a cutting stare, saying, "Step back."

"Your conspiracy has failed," I told her, raising my revolver. "Drop your weapon."

"You can kill me," she hissed, "but first I shall kill the most powerful woman in the world."

The woman in black removed the veil from her face. "I don't think so, my dear," she said.

I recognised both the voice, and now the face. "Mrs. Hudson?"

"Hello, Dr. Watson," she said. "I've never in my life impersonated the Queen before."

Even in the darkness, Angelique Pellier looked as confused as I felt.

My landlady again turned to the Frenchwoman. "If you kill me, nobody will miss me very much. Your plans were always doomed to fail. You see, you were up against Mr. Sherlock Holmes."

In desperation, Angelique Pellier cried out for her co-conspirator. "Anton!"

When she received no reply, she pressed the gun against her own head and blew out her own brains.

It was nearly dawn by the time Holmes and I returned to Baker Street. Having made Mrs. Hudson feel like genuine royalty and then delivered her to her own rooms, we stood at the foot of the stairs leading up to the sitting room. I started to question Holmes as to how he could place our landlady in such jeopardy, but he held up a hand. "There was still too much that was uncertain, Watson," he said. "We had to give them rope to make absolutely certain they were committed to the plan, so that they couldn't wiggle out of the charges. We needed someone to take the place of the Queen. There was no one else that I trusted more than Mrs. Hudson, and she was willing. And if we had told you, you would have objected."

I could see that he didn't want to discuss it further right then, but I would have a few more things to say in the future, both about the lady's safety, and my ignorance of his plan. Leaving it at that, we finally retired to our rooms.

I opened the door and immediately stood stock still. In the thin light of the early morning sun, I could see a man sitting in a chair beside the fireplace. I recognised him at once. Nemirov. He was holding a revolver.

Holmes did not seem the least bit surprised to see him, but sat down in a chair facing the Ukrainian.

Nemirov waved the gun to indicate that I should close the door and take another chair.

Holmes broke the tense silence. "Your plot to kidnap the Queen has failed, Nemirov. Sligo and Angelique Pellier are both dead. Tinderman is under close arrest. And the crew of your steamer are in the hands of Scotland Yard. Nothing remains for you except the hangman's rope."

"Nemesis," I breathed.

"Precisely, Watson."

The Ukrainian smiled. "In reality, we did nothing more than kidnap your landlady – if you can call it kidnapping. She came with us willingly enough."

"You still have to answer for sedition and murder."

"We are all driven by our dreams, Mr. Holmes," said Nemirov. "Mine is to see a world of freedom and equality."

"But not for people like Bessington."

"Who?"

"The drunk that you murdered."

"A nobody."

"On the contrary, a man with the right to the very things that you claim to stand for."

"But his death hardly affords the publicity I seek. On the other hand, the murder of the famous Sherlock Holmes would bring the attention of the entire world to my cause."

A carriage drew to a halt in the street outside. In silence, we listened as somebody climbed the stairs, and stopped on the landing outside our rooms.

Nemirov scowled at the door, and gripped his revolver more tightly.

The door opened, and a man stood framed in the doorway. I recognized him. His waxed moustaches gave him an imperial demeanour. Dressed in black, with his left hand in his pocket, he held a gun in his right hand.

I watched as the expression on Nemirov's face transformed. He looked as if he were facing the devil himself. The Ukrainian stood up, and raised his revolver with a shaking hand. The crack of two gunshots assailed our eardrums, and shattered the early morning calm.

Nemirov collapsed onto the hearthrug, with a single bullet-hole in the centre of his forehead. I later discovered the Ukrainian's bullet buried deep within the wooden doorframe. It remains there to this day.

The man in the doorway lowered his weapon. "I am indebted to you, Mr. Holmes, for giving me the chance to deal with this scoundrel myself." The man spoke with a slight but detectable German accent. "I consider Her Majesty's honour now restored. Her Majesty would like you to accept a small gift in recognition of your services last night." He held out a small box, which Holmes took and opened. Inside lay a miniature: A small painting on mother-of-pearl of the late Prince Albert.

"Please convey my thanks to Her Majesty," said Holmes, "but I cannot possibly accept this gift."

I was shocked. "But Holmes, you cannot refuse the Queen."

"Indeed not. But the gift should go instead to our landlady, Mrs. Hudson. After all, she proved more courageous last night than any of us."

I nodded. "She will be delighted."

Now satisfied, the man in the doorway gave a sharp bow, clicked his heels, and left.

Holmes breathed a deep sigh. "I do believe that this case is now at an end." He waved vaguely towards the body of Nemirov. "Lestrade can tidy up, and take the credit, if he likes."

Later that morning, I sat in our rooms, reading the newspaper reports of the Jubilee celebrations. Holmes stood in the open window, violin in hand, playing a romantic melody. His face showed a look of sublime happiness. Summer had finally come to Baker Street.

The Resplendent Plane Tree
by Kevin P. Thornton

Note to the Publisher: *Given the relative recent infamy of one member of this case, I recommend a 100-year embargo from the date of my signature.*

John H. Watson
January the 1ˢᵗ, 1918

London, that summer of 1888, was a torrid and desultory place to be. The hot days were muggy and hazy, the rain when it fell was torrential, and the drains were either dry and fetid or overflowing and malodorous. To top it all, the Australian cricket team were touring, and for the first time in history they had won a Test Match against England at home. So far it had been a dreadful summer.

Holmes had been restless since the solution of the Vatican Cameos, and what cases he'd had since were "mere trifles", as he put it. A missing woman from Barking he solved by deducing, correctly, that she was running away with another man; a theft of family heirlooms was righted without him even leaving the rooms on Baker Street, noting only that sibling rivalry was as dangerous as several gangs of cutthroats. So too did he solve the case of a haunted house in Horsham. He sat in his chair, enervated only by the answers to telegrams he'd sent, and concluded it was an ingenious insurance fraud. He was right of course, and his mood sank with each trifling victory.

Whenever Holmes lapsed into these languid torpors, there was a danger he would revert and try to medicate his brain into numbness. Consequently, I was always hoping that some form of fascinating puzzle would walk through the doors or arrive in the mail. Sadly, when Mrs. Hudson came up with the first of the morning deliveries, the only letter was addressed to me.

It was postmarked Dover from the previous day, and the return address was The Plane Tree Sanatorium. I knew only one person at that facility, and as I read silently, my worst fears were attained.

I regret to inform you of the death of Captain James McGrory, late of the 66ᵗʰ Regiment of Foot, at this establishment yesterday. I betray no confidences to you, a fellow medical professional, when I say that while we felt we

157

had made great progress in the treatment of the Captain's afflictions, all seemed to be for naught. Just this afternoon, in front of at least five witnesses, Captain McGrory dashed to the edge of the cliffs and flung himself off, there to render himself lifeless on the beach below.

There was more to follow, but I was too dumbstruck to be able to take it in.

"Come, Watson, do sit down before you fall. Tell me what has happened to your friend, the Captain. How did he die?"

"Confound it Holmes, what manner of trickery is this?" I said, unable to hide the asperity from my tone. "I have just opened the envelope to find the most distressing news, only to have you address me as if you were reading the very letter over my shoulder. How did you know it was about my friend Jim McGrory, how did you know the news was bad, and how on this earth could you possibly know his rank? Have you been steaming open my letters to learn enough to play your little mind games on me?" The minute I said that, I wished I could take it back. I had accused my best friend of dishonour. There could be no worse thing to say to a gentleman, and Holmes would have been well within his rights to take deep offense to my words.

He didn't. He looked at me gravely and said, "I can see I will have to tell you before you crush that letter in rage." I looked down and relaxed my fist, anxious not to damage the missive, even though I would dearly love to erase its contents from history.

"You are a very patriotic man, Watson, and I have observed before that the conditioning you received while serving Queen and Country comes back to haunt you at times. The letter caused you to stiffen upright and stand to attention, something you do when you hear the National Anthem, hear mention of Royalty, or cast your mind back to your soldiering memories. Your distress was so obvious that even Mrs. Hudson would have noticed, so it became clear to me it was bad news about someone you were close to. That made it likely to have been a soldier with whom you served. Such links are, I am told, of the highest bond. It is unlikely, given the quality of the paper and envelope you hold, to be someone of the lower ranks, so it is most probably a fellow officer. As servicemen are drawn closest to those of similar rank, it seemed a reasonable leap that the person who had caused you such distress was, like you, a Captain."

"It always seems so easy once you have explained it, Holmes. I am so sorry to take offense, and even more sorry that I cast aspersions on you."

"Think nothing of it," said Holmes. "If I might trouble you to see the letter?"

I handed it to him. He read it quickly.

"You have never mentioned Captain McGrory before," he said.

"Have I not? He has never been far from my mind. We served together, and although I was for the most part tending to the lame and wounded and he was a soldier in the thick of things, we became friends in the mess and shared many special evenings. Such friendships are forged quickly and deeply, as can only happen when you live as if every day might be your last."

"I see," said Holmes.

"Jim was jovial, easy-going, yet keen of intellect. When he failed to come back one day from a sortie with his men, we feared he had died in the skirmish. His unit had been ambushed by a larger force of men, and the rout of his unit was disordered and chaotic. The sergeant reported that it had been every man for himself, and the survivors came back five men short from their company. One of them was Jim."

"What happened?" said Holmes

"It was two days before they were able to go back. They arrived in sufficient numbers and overran the Afghan camp. They found the other four men staked out in the burning sun, tied with leather that had tightened and stretched them so that their joints had dislocated in the heat. They had been tortured over many hours and they died slowly, one by one. Jim was in the middle, facing them, buried in the side of an anthill up to his neck. Not only had he been forced to watch everything, but he had been slowly driven mad. They covered him in honey, Holmes, before they buried him. That sweetness must have attracted every insect in the desert, and they all feasted on Jim as he watched his lads die. He would surely have died too had they left him much longer, and nearly did."

"And you treated him," said Holmes.

"I did what I could. I helped him heal physically, but there was no reaching into his mind to cure what he had seen and suffered. The body of Jim McGrory survived those savages, but his life was over as much as if he'd received a bullet to the head."

I found myself shaking at the injustice of it all. "And now for this to happen to my poor friend. Holmes, there is something wrong here. Despite all he went through, Jim would never have killed himself. He was Papist, and devoutly so. He would never have condemned himself to hell by committing suicide. It seems impossible."

As I said this, I knew I was lying to myself. Jim McGrory had been through so much he might not have been able to help himself. Who could understand the tortured mind, save one who had suffered some of the same maladies?

Holmes went to the door and called downstairs. "Mrs. Hudson. Please, a hansom cab for Charing Cross Station." Then he turned to me. "The train for Dover leaves soon. Gather together whatever you need. We will go and see what befell your friend."

"But Holmes," I said, "There is nothing to be done. He is already dead."

"Indeed," said Holmes, "but for you to rest easy, we must find out why. You said your friend wouldn't do this to himself. Let us go there and see what the evidence shows us."

Pausing only to send a telegram to the sanatorium to signal our intentions, we left our rooms almost immediately. We made the train with time to spare, and finding ourselves alone in our compartment as we pulled out of Charing Cross, Holmes wasted no time in pressing me for more information.

"The Plane Tree Sanatorium is a small institute just north of the town of Dover. It was the home, many years back, of one who aspired unsuccessfully to the gentry. It is large, ostentatious even, and it sits on top of the cliffs, exposed to the sea breeze and all the elements. It is so named as there is a large London Plane tree in the grounds. It is said to be well over a hundred years of age, and with the great house, it dominates the landscape."

"I am familiar with the spot," said Holmes. "It is indeed a noticeable landmark."

"When the owner died, he had spent his money as quickly as he'd earned it, so there was little enough to bequeath to the general repair of the estate. The house passed through the hands of various direct kin, family members who did not wish to live in such a place or could not afford the upkeep of such a precariously placed folly. Finally the youngest cousin, by then an elderly woman, left it to her only relative from her late husband's side, the good Doctor Bishop."

"You sound disapproving," said Holmes.

"Forgive me," I said. "If my emotions carry into my voice it has nothing to do with the doctor that runs the sanatorium. I don't know what would have happened to Jim without his help. Indeed, Doctor Bishop, in setting up such a facility to cater to soldiers with injuries of the mind, has proved what our government is too blind to see. My frustration is with the powers-that-be, who would label these brave yet cowered soldiers cowards when all they may need is a healing of their souls."

"The human mind is a mysterious place," said Holmes. "My brother, as part of his work, has had access to some of the studies coming out of Austria recently, and I feel that once the crackpot ideas are sifted, the cure of the ailments of the mind may very well be the next grand leap in medicine. How successful has Doctor Bishop been?"

"Until the time I received that letter this morning, I would have said he had been very successful. He has been following some of the ideas of the German, von Gudden, who had advocated for humane treatment of mental patients, instead of the insanity of the Bethlem way."

"I know of Bethlem hospital," said Holmes. "Its other name has come to parallel that of insanity, has it not? Bedlam?"

"It has," I said. "Bishop is anti-Bedlam. He, too, served in the Army as a doctor, and when he retired, he continued with this idea of his, to help treat the soldiers who do not wholly come back mentally. He called it *mens sana in corpore sano,* but he meant more than just a healthy mind in a healthy body. He was looking to prove that such repair was possible. By the time his Board of Governors realized he was treating soldiers that others labelled cowards, the establishment was up and running. He has managed to stay afloat because he owns the property and his work has had some striking early success. Notably, he was able to return a member of the Royal Family home to kith and kin."

"Ah yes," said Holmes, mentioning the name of the Prince in question. Once again, I was astounded by his knowledge of certain specifics known to so few. "His Royal Highness was suicidal for some years, was he not? If Bishop helped him, he must have felt the gratitude of the Realm thereafter."

"He did, but who knows how long this will last. His sanatorium has been precariously funded for some years, until he can prove his ideas were working. Sadly, Jim's death may have a deleterious effect on his financial wherewithal."

Holmes he settled back into the seat and closed his eyes. He did not stir again until the train pulled in to Dover Priory Station, and when he did, there was a renewed vigour to my friend. I was glad that, however sad our excursion had started, it was doing Holmes some good.

We took a coach from the station, up from the harbour town of Dover.

The sanatorium was not far north, perched on top of the white cliffs. It was a garishly designed house, with a presenting side to the road as well as large gable windows and a veranda on the cliff side. Not thirty yards away from these windows, the plane tree stood tall and proud some ten yards short of the cliff's edge. Its lower limbs had been trimmed over

161

the years so that the bottom branches afforded headroom for even the tallest of men. The large canopy of its foliage created a pleasing shady area. Coupled with the sea breeze, the feel of the day was vastly different to the heat and smell of the London we had left behind.

Doctor Bishop was most accommodating. He met us at the entrance himself and invited us in to his office.

The doctor's rooms were in what would have been the library of the old mansion. It had an air of genteel dilapidation, common among many such Ozymandian piles created by the *nouveau riche* of the Empire. There were, however, a few signs of homeliness and effort. Some plants in pots that had not yet died, ornaments on the mantelpiece. The desk, too, had been recently cleaned and tidied, but it all gave the air of one who was trying unsuccessfully to hold back the tides, and I was sorry for Doctor Bishop. His work was important, and to have it hurt, albeit by my friend's death, was an irony too far.

Somewhat incongruously, the latest copy of *Boy's Own Magazine* lay on one of the visitor's chairs. I placed it on the casual table so I could sit down. Holmes, enervated, could not settle and paced in front of the fireplace.

Doctor Bishop seemed almost apologetic in his manner.

"It has been a long struggle," he said waving vaguely around the room, "to find the funding to survive. We have had some small successes which have been building our reputation, but we are at the unfashionable end of medicine, I'm afraid. The tradition of the British stiff upper lip does not rest easily next to a theory, largely unproven, that a healthy mind is such a vital component of a healthy body."

"I'm sure you have done wonders here," said Holmes. "Nevertheless, Captain McGrory's death must be a setback to your work."

"It is," said Bishop.

"Then you would have no objection if my friend and I look further into the Captain's death?" said Holmes. "Perhaps you could tell us what you know."

If Doctor Bishop was taken aback at this turn of events, he didn't show it. "I'm not sure how much I can share of Captain McGrory's ailments," he said.

"Please, Doctor Bishop," I said. "Help us. I was once his battlefield physician and his friend, and Holmes has my full confidence. You may trust us."

"Very well," said Bishop. "It was through your notes in his military file that I found out what happened to Captain McGrory, and I'm sad to say it was not an unusual case. The tribes we battled in Afghanistan were brutal and hard people, with little value for life. You know how they tortured him, forcing him to watch his men die unspeakably painful deaths. If that wasn't enough, the sun and the insects destroyed what little sanity he had left. By the time I could admit him here, he had, in addition to a mind that distorted reality, a continuous scratching problem. While understandable, given what he had been through, it was imperative we treat this first. This we did with lotions and careful manicure of his hands and nails to prevent his self-harm, as well as some calming exercises I picked up in the East. I am pleased to say that we had been fortunate in this treatment, so much so that this past few weeks he was well enough to walk the grounds unattended, and his scratching had stopped. It was one small step on the road to his recovery, but it was an important one. Which is why I can't understand what happened."

Holmes, never the most patient of men, tried, asking in a soothing manner, "Please, Doctor, in your own words. Tell us how he died."

"Better yet, I will show you." He led us through to the part of the home that faced out towards the cliffs, the English Channel, and France. The entire back end of the house was a high-ceilinged room that was surrounded by stairs and balconies that led to the other rooms. It had the feel of a Georgian ballroom and, when I mentioned this, Doctor Bishop confirmed my thought. "It is used now as a common lounge for our patients," he said. "The view is soothing and the room is airy and bright, thanks to the high windows." As he led us closer to the left side of the great room and the comfortable chairs gathered round a low table, the big plane tree came into view.

"It happened yesterday afternoon. When Captain McGrory came here over a year ago, we were his last chance. He had been with his parents and his sister, and then he stayed at his cousin's farm in Ayrshire. None of them could cope with his night terrors or give him the medical treatment he so clearly needed." He paused, thinking about his next words. "I don't wish to sound a braggart, but we have had successes here. The fears within my patients' minds respond best to care and compassion, and Captain McGrory had been doing particularly well."

"And why was that?" I asked. Holmes appeared more interested in the tree, and indeed he stood at the window and stared at its canopy for some seconds before rejoining us.

"My sister has been staying with us these during that period. She was widowed recently and I asked her and her son to come and visit for a while, to take her mind off her mourning. Although she has no nursing experience, she is a kindly soul and has been helping out wherever she has been able. Captain McGrory responded well to her ministrations. He still suffered nightmares, but I had hopes that their effect on him may one day have been ameliorated as his skin lesions ceased."

"Was the Captain in the habit of taking the air under the plane tree?" said Holmes.

"In the last week." said Bishop. "We have only had it cleared underneath recently, as it was overgrown and dangerous before. It has already become popular as a shelter for patients and staff.

"How then, did he die?" said Holmes

"It is as I said in my letter," said Bishop.

"Please, Doctor. Tell us what you saw."

"He was sitting under the tree on that bench you can see. Suddenly he stood up and started scratching at himself, as if all his worst nightmares and affections had returned in one fell swoop."

"And there was no one near him."

"No one at all," said Bishop. "I almost wish there was a way to lay blame, but there is none."

"Were his actions normal for the time when he was still afflicted with the continuous scratching?" Holmes asked.

"Now that you mention it, this ultimate instance before his death was far more frantic than any other I had ever witnessed. I can check with the other staff if you wish."

"No need," said Holmes. "It is best if we discover the information ourselves. You mentioned some other witnesses?"

"The others who may be of some assistance are two members of the staff – here are their names – my sister, Emily Crowley, and her young son, though I don't believe he'll be any help. He is a flighty child. Any others who may have seen it are patients. They are here because their minds have been damaged, so you must make what you will of what little they can tell you."

"You must question the patients, Watson. Try to get as complete a picture as possible. Their impressions may be vital." We separated, arranging to meet later. I was pleased he had given me such an important job, or so I thought.

There had been three patients sitting within view at the time. Major Grimsby was unable to remember much and said even less. The scar across the top of his head, where a bullet had ploughed through, told me I wouldn't get anything from him. Neither was Captain Appleyard much help at first. He had been sitting in the lounge and had heard the commotion but had seen nothing, nor had he for some years since shrapnel had torn through his eyes on the Indian border.

"There's nothing wrong with my ears though," he said. "And from what was said later, it was surprising there wasn't more noise."

"What do you mean?" I said.

"Well, from the way the story has been told to me, he was sitting under the tree when he suddenly stood up and ran over the cliff. It's only about fifteen or twenty feet, but he never made a sound. Did you ever charge into the guns of the enemy, Doctor Watson?"

"No," I said.

"Well, let me tell you," said Appleyard. "It is not a quiet event. People scream and yell to get their blood boiling, to make them feel braver. Now obviously I didn't see what happened, but I also didn't hear anything, and it strikes me that if Captain McGrory had decided to charge over the cliff, he'd have been making a lot of noise as he did so."

The third soldier was no help either. Lieutenant Hopgood sat in his chair and looked over the cliffs and saw not a thing. His hands trembled and his eyes watered, but he said nothing, and had not done so for many years. He was one of the many reasons that Doctor Bishop's work was so important and it troubled me that he might be forced to close.

"Lieutenant Hopgood is as Captain McGrory was, a troubled victim of enemy captivity," the doctor told us by way of explanation later. "Each patient manifests their trauma uniquely. With Captain McGrory, it was the imagined skin condition and his constant scratching, a reaction to his means of torture, no doubt. We have yet to ascertain what the Lieutenant is seeing in his mind's eye. Maybe if we can learn that, we can help him. For now he sits in a state of what Kahlbaum refers to as *catatonia*."

"Why did you send me to them if you knew they couldn't help me?" I asked.

"All my patients are treated with the same value," he said. "Just because a man hasn't said anything for three years, it doesn't mean we give up on him. We never gave up on Captain McGrory either. Which is why the bitter pill of his death is so hard to swallow."

Holmes had confirmed the oddity of Jim's death through his interviews with the staff ladies. By all accounts, Jim had run over the cliff as fast as possible, scratching at his head and collar. There was no extra agent, no sense of foul play. Despite Holmes's investigations, it looked like Jim had reverted to his madness and taken his own life.

Holmes had also picked up on the soundlessness of McGrory's death when he had interviewed the assistants – how like him to note the events that did *not* occur – but I had not had a chance to ask him his views. It didn't seem to matter. All the witnesses' statements were similar. He had not been coerced into jumping, and there was no other way to have forced him into his final action.

"Come, Watson," Holmes said suddenly. "We must go and look at the plane tree. Doctor Bishop, I have not been able to speak to your sister or her son. When we return, please make them available."

"Certainly. Doctor Watson, would you care to examine the body later?"

"There is no need," said Holmes before I could answer. "I know how he was killed. I need to check two more *minutiae*, and then we will have our answer."

"How can it be a murder, Holmes? Surely he did this to himself."

"Do you remember the case I had that you so flamboyantly wrote about in your journals as 'The Speckled Band'?" This is the same kind of event, Watson. It is a locked room mystery, save in the open air. Yet someone did kill your friend, in full view of everyone. It was really quite ingenious, in a way."

As we left the sanatorium building, unanswered questions tripping over my tongue so that I must confess I may have sounded as a babbling fool to any who were in the vicinity. Fortunately, it was the time of the evening meal in the sanatorium, and all were occupied elsewhere, so my ranting was private and less embarrassing. After his astonishing pronouncement, Holmes behaved as if he had not heard me at all, and as we reached the shade of the plane tree, he commenced scrutinizing the ground. "A-ha!" he said as he picked up a seed ball. "Help me, Watson, would you? Look over on the other side and see how many of these you can find. I need a count only."

Suppressing my irritation, I did as asked.

"I have found seven, Holmes." I said some minutes later.

"And I have nine," said Holmes. "It's not enough, just as I suspected. One last thing, Watson. I need to see the clearings and cuttings the doctor said had been removed from under the tree."

I trailed after him and I found my irritation dissipating. I could put up with Holmes being obtuse and frustrating. It meant that he could see that which we mere mortals could not: A solution.

Some five-hundred yards away, a small fenced off area proved to be the gardener's domain. Shovels, rakes, forks, and wheelbarrows were neatly stored next to a pile of garden waste.

"Ah," said Holmes. "This would seem to be the debris cleared from under the tree. Observe the plane tree leaves, from the only such tree in the vicinity. Now Watson, cast your eyes over it all and tell me how many seed balls there are."

166

"They are uncountable, Holmes, there must be hundreds, maybe thousands."

"Indeed, and that is where our killer made her mistake. She knew about the seeds' properties, but she chose the wrong time of the year. It was too late for them to fall in the quantity that might make such an accident possible, at least to the trained eye. These seed balls that the gardener gathered had already fallen from the tree. Any slight possibility that what happened to Captain McGrory was a natural albeit tragic event has been proven unlikely. In the last three days, because we are at the end of the tree's seeding stage, there are virtually none of the balls on the ground, which means that what happened to the Captain was not induced by nature falling from the tree, but by malice."

When we returned to the doctor's study, there was a lady sitting in one of the visitor's chairs. She had her child with her, a boy some eleven or twelve years of age.

"Madam, if I might beg of you to leave your son outside, I would like to ask you a few questions."

She did as requested. "Come, Edward. Sit in the reception area and read your magazine."

"I told you, Mama, I don't like to be called Edward."

"Yes dear," she said, and the weight of the world was in her answer.

As she came back in, I had my first good look at her. She was a handsome yet weary-looking woman, made the more tired, no doubt, by her recent widowhood and what sounded like a son at a difficult stage of his life.

"Madam," said Holmes. "Are you aware of the particular qualities of the seeds of the London Plane tree?"

"I'm sure I am not, sir," she said.

"Yet your son's magazine, *Boy's Own*, I believe it is called, often carries articles aimed at keeping children entertained. How to make a fire by rubbing two sticks together, say, or how to find true north by the altitude of the sun in the sky."

Holmes paused. "Or how to make itching powder from the seeds of a London Plane tree?"

Doctor Bishop was as startled as I. The implication was preposterous.

Mrs. Crowley looked scared. And Holmes carried on.

"You had intimate knowledge of his afflictions. You knew what a quantity of itching powder, upended on his head, would do to him. It would return him to the beginnings of his fearful ailment. I don't yet know how you arranged for the powder to fall on him – maybe an article

167

from the same magazine on how to set up a tripwire, but it was a cruel thing you did, madam. When Captain McGrory fell over the cliff, he wasn't running to commit suicide, he was trying to get away from the agonizing itching from which he thought he had been cured. He must have felt he was back in the desert, being tortured again."

"But how did she make him run over the cliff?" I said.

"She didn't. It was just luck. Maybe if she hadn't succeeded, she would have tried again. It was a devilish way to kill a man. Now you must tell us why, madam."

Then Holmes paused, and I saw something I had never seen before. It was a momentary look of astonishment. "How wrong could I possibly be?" he said. "He wasn't supposed to run over the cliff at all, was he?"

"What do you mean?" I asked. "Then why would she do this?"

"She didn't." said Holmes. "That was my singular mistake."

"He didn't mean too," said Mrs. Crowley. "I'm sure he thought it would just be a joke."

The doctor still looked puzzled as the veils were lifted from my mind. "Oh, my word," I said as Holmes strode to the door to summon in the young boy. Before he could, the agony in his mother's voice stopped him.

"Please," said his mother. "I'll take the blame. Edward is only a boy. He told me about his prank. He thought it would be funny to get Jim to scratch again. He doesn't know anything else, doesn't know that the jape caused his death. I can't burden my child with that. I'll take the blame."

"He's been acting up since his father died," said Doctor Bishop. "There have been other issues as well. He found out his father left him a third of his fortune in the will. It has made him recalcitrant and ill-behaved, but it is just a stage. He has even been so difficult this past year as to insist on changing his name. But to do something so heinous? No, I don't believe it is possible in one so young. I won't believe it."

"Did he know you were in love with Captain McGrory?" said Holmes.

Mrs. Crowley gasped. "No, I told no one. How did you even know?"

"It's what he does," I said.

Holmes scratched his chin, comparing the data he had with a possibility no one wanted to face.

"He's too young, Holmes," I said. "He couldn't have done it on purpose."

"On balance, Watson, I want to believe you," said Holmes. "Doctor Bishop, I see no value in allowing Captain McGrory's family to suffer.

Perhaps if the notification of death were to find an unfortunate bee sting that blinded the Captain, causing this tragedy, but changing the suicide report to one that will allow the family to give him the burial they choose. Watson, do you agree?"

"Yes, Holmes, I do. This wasn't a grand outdoor mystery murder. It was a terrible misfortune. The young boy must be given the chance at a normal life, unburdened with this traumatic occurrence."

I nodded. Mrs. Crowley rushed to the door as if to make off with her son before we changed our minds. Before she was halfway there, the door opened and the boy walked in as if he had been listening at the keyhole. He looked young and impossibly English, so full of spirit and life it would take a harder heart than those present to curse this child to gaol.

He looked around the room, saw his mother, and then glanced past her to Holmes. "You're Sherlock Holmes, the famous detective," he said.

"And you are Master Edward, are you not?" said Holmes.

"No, not anymore," said the boy. "I have decided to change my name to Aleister. Aleister Crowley."

The Strange Adventure of the Doomed Sextette
by Leslie Charteris and Denis Green

Sherlock Holmes and The Saint
An Introduction by Ian Dickerson

Everyone has a story to tell about how they first met Sherlock Holmes. For me it was a Penguin paperback reprint my brother introduced me to in my pre-teen years. I read it, and went on to read all the original stories, but it didn't appeal to me in the way it appealed to others. This is probably because I discovered the adventures of The Saint long before I discovered Sherlock Holmes.

The Saint, for those readers who may need a little more education, was also known as Simon Templar and was a modern day Robin Hood who first appeared in 1928. Not unlike Holmes, he has appeared in books, films, TV shows, and comics. He was created by Leslie Charteris, a young man born in Singapore to a Chinese father and an English mother, who was just twenty years old when he wrote that first Saint adventure. He'd always wanted to be a writer – his first piece was published when he was just nine years of age – and he followed that Saint story, his third novel, with two further books, neither of which featured Simon Templar.

However, there's a notable similarity between the heroes of his early novels, and Charteris, recognising this, and being somewhat fed up of creating variations on the same theme, returned to writing adventures for The Saint. Short stories for a weekly magazine, *The Thriller*, and a change of publisher to the mainstream Hodder & Stoughton, helped him on his way to becoming a best-seller and something of a pop culture sensation in Great Britain.

But he was ambitious. Always fond of the USA, he started to spend more time over there, and it was the 1935 novel – and fifteenth Saint book – *The Saint in New York*, that made him a transatlantic success. He spent some time in Hollywood, writing for the movies and keeping an eye on The Saint films that were then in production at RKO studios. Whilst there, he struck up what would become a lifelong friendship with Denis Green, a British actor and writer, and his new wife, Mary.

Fast forward a couple of years . . . . Leslie was on the west coast of the States, still writing Saint stories to pay the bills, writing the occasional non-Saint piece for magazines, and getting increasingly frustrated with RKO who, he felt, weren't doing him, or his creation, justice. Denis Green, meanwhile, had established himself as a stage actor, and had embarked on a promising radio career both in front of and behind the microphone.

Charteris was also interested in radio. He had a belief that his creation could be adapted for every medium and was determined to try and prove it. In

1940, he commissioned a pilot programme to show how The Saint would work on radio, casting his friend Denis Green as Simon Templar. Unfortunately, it didn't sell, but just three years later, he tried again, commissioning a number of writers – including Green – to create or adapt Saint adventures for radio.

They also didn't sell, and after struggling to find a network or sponsor for The Saint on the radio, he handed the problem over to established radio show packager and producer, James L. Saphier. Charteris was able to solve one problem, however: At the behest of advertising agency Young & Rubicam, who represented the show's sponsors, Petri Wine, Denis Green had been sounded out about writing for *The New Adventures of Sherlock Holmes*, a weekly radio series that was then broadcasting on the Mutual Network.

Green confessed to his friend that, whilst he could write good radio dialogue, he simply hadn't a clue about plotting. He was, as his wife would later recall, a reluctant writer: "He didn't really like to write. He would wait until the last minute. He would put it off as long as possible by scrubbing the kitchen stove or wash the bathroom – anything before he sat down at the typewriter. I had a very clean house." Charteris offered a solution: They would go into partnership, with him creating the stories and Green writing the dialogue.

But there was another problem: *The New Adventures of Sherlock Holmes* aired on one of the radio networks that Leslie hoped might be interested in the adventures of The Saint, and it would not look good, he thought, for him to be involved with a rival production. Leslie adopted the pseudonym of *Bruce Taylor*, (as you will see at the end of the following script,) taking inspiration taking inspiration from the surname of the show's producer Glenhall Taylor and that of Rathbone's co-star, Nigel Bruce.

The Taylor/Green partnership was initiated with "The Strange Case of the Aluminum Crutch", which aired on July 24th, 1944, and would ultimately run until the following March, with *Bruce Taylor*'s final contribution to the Holmes canon being "The Secret of Stonehenge", which aired on March 19th, 1945 – thirty-five episodes in all.

Bruce Taylor's short radio career came to an end in short because Charteris shifted his focus elsewhere. Thanks to Saphier, The Saint found a home on the NBC airwaves, and aside from the constant demand for literary Saint adventures, he was exploring the possibilities of launching a Saint magazine. He was replaced by noted writer and critic Anthony Boucher, who would establish a very successful writing partnership with Denis Green.

Fast forward quite a few more years – to 1988 to be precise: A young chap called Dickerson, a long standing member of *The Saint Club*, discovers a new TV series of The Saint is going in to production. Suitably inspired, he writes to the then secretary of the Club, suggesting that it was time the world was reminded of The Saint, and The Saint Club in particular. Unbeknownst to him, the secretary passes his letter on to Leslie Charteris himself. The teenaged Dickerson and the aging author struck up a friendship which involved, amongst other things, many fine lunches, followed by lazy chats over various libations. Some of those conversations featured the words "Sherlock" and "Holmes".

171

It was when Leslie died, in 1993, that I really got to know his widow, Audrey. We often spoke at length about many things, and from time to time discussed Leslie and the Holmes scripts, as well as her own career as an actress.

When she died in 2014, Leslie's family asked me to go through their flat in Dublin. Pretty much the first thing I found was a stack of radio scripts, many of which had been written by *Bruce Taylor* and Denis Green.

I was, needless to say, rather delighted. More so when his family gave me permission to get them into print. Back in the 1940's, no one foresaw an afterlife for shows such as this, and no recordings exist of this particular Sherlock Holmes adventure. So here you have the only documentation around of "The Strange Adventure of the Doomed Sextette" . . . .

Ian Dickerson
February, 2018

The Strange Adventure of the Doomed Sextette

BILL FORMAN (Announcer): Petri Wine brings you . . . .

MUSIC: THEME. FADE ON CUE:

FORMAN: Basil Rathbone and Nigel Bruce in *The New Adventures of Sherlock Holmes.*

MUSIC: THEME . . . FULL FINISH

FORMAN: The Petri family – the family that took the time to bring you good wine – invites you to listen to Doctor Watson as he tells us about another exciting adventure he shared with his old friend, that master detective – Sherlock Holmes. You know, there's something I wish you could share with *me* one of these evenings – and that's a good spaghetti dinner – the real old-fashioned kind with lots of tomato sauce and cheese and served with big thick slices of French bread. And of course, the best part – glasses of Petri California Burgundy. Don't forget that Petri Burgundy whatever you do – because Petri Burgundy is the best friend a spaghetti dinner or *any* dinner ever had. Petri Burgundy is a hearty wine – rich and red and full-bodied. And boy, that Petri Burgundy is sure a delicious wine – there's no doubt about that. One taste and you *know* it's your favourite wine from here on out. Just try Petri Burgundy with any meat or meat dish . . . you'll find that good Petri Wine really makes your good cooking taste better.

MUSIC: "SCOTCH POEM" by Edward MacDowell

FORMAN: And now let's look in on the genial Doctor Watson. Good evening, Doctor.

WATSON: (FADING IN) Evening, Mr. Forman.

SOUND EFFECT: EXCITED BARKING OF PUPPIES

WATSON: Quite, fellas! Quiet!

FORMAN: A couple of daschund puppies . . . Are they new members of your household, Doctor?

WATSON: Yes, my boy. They were given to me last week, as a matter of fact.

SOUND EFFECT: PUPPY BEING PATTED. ECSTATIC YELPING

WATSON: I've christened this one "Monty" – after Sir Bernard Montgomery.

SOUND EFFECT: FURTHER PATTING AND YELPING

WATSON: And this little fella's "Winnie".

FORMAN: After Winston Churchill, I suppose?

WATSON: That's right, Mr. Forman.

FORMAN: Very distinguished guests, I must say, Doctor.

WATSON: Yes, although they're not as dignified as their names imply. Winnie's favourite occupation is chewing at Monty's tail! However, scoop them off that chair and settle yourself down, and I'll get on with my story.

FORMAN: Last week you told us you called it "The Doomed Sextette".

WATSON: That's right, young fella-me-lad.

FORMAN: I suppose it began in Baker Street, as usual, Doctor?

WATSON: No. it began in my own house in Paddington. I had been married some months before and in consequence had seen very little of my old friend, Sherlock Holmes.

FORMAN: He and your wife never did quite hit it off, did they?

WATSON: No, Mr. Forman – a fact that caused me no little unhappiness, I may say. But to get back to my story . . . . My wife was away staying with some relatives, and I was alone. It was on a Sunday morning, I remember, that I was reading in front of my fire, when to my delight the door opened and my old friend strode into the room.

174

HOLMES: (OFF) Watson, my dear fellow, how are you?

WATSON: I'm delighted to see you, Holmes!

HOLMES: (FADING IN) And how is Mrs. Watson? I trust that the little excitements connected with our adventure of *The Sign of Four* have not been too much for her?

WATSON: What d'you mean, Holmes?

HOLMES: I understand that she's in the country, staying with relatives.

WATSON: (CHUCKLING) How on earth did you know that?

HOLMES: My Mrs. Hudson and your cook are close friends. You'd be surprised at the amount of second or even third-hand information I get about you.

WATSON: (LAUGHING) Just the same as ever, Holmes. Sit down. You can stay for a while, I hope?

HOLMES: Certainly, old fellow.

WATSON: It's a funny thing you should drop round here this morning. I was coming to see you later on . . . and bring a friend with me. A friend who sounds as if he's a potential client for you.

HOLMES: Splendid. I'm glad to see that marriage and the cares of your medical practice have not entirely obliterated your interest in our little deductive problems. Who is the friend – and what is his problem?

WATSON: His name is Taylor. Major Taylor . . . . We used to be in the same regiment together in India. He's a stockbroker now and seems to be in some kind of trouble. I received a telegram from him this morning saying that he was calling on me . . . and that he needed your help. He should be here any moment.

175

HOLMES: I shall be glad to help any friend of yours, old chap.

WATSON: That's probably him now. Couldn't have timed it better. (CALLING) Come in!

WATSON: Taylor, my dear chap. How are you?

TAYLOR: (FADING IN) (ABOUT FORTY FIVE) Hello, Watson. It's very good to see you again.

WATSON: This is my old friend, Sherlock Holmes.

HOLMES: How d'you do, Major Taylor.

TAYLOR: (SURPRISED) Sherlock Holmes! Just the man I want to see. This is splendid.

WATSON: Let me take your coat . . . that's it. And now settle down and make yourself comfortable. Hear anything of the old crowd?

TAYLOR: A few of them.

WATSON: Taylor and I were in the same regiment, you know, Holmes.

HOLMES: (DRYLY) Yes, you told me that just now, Watson.

WATSON: What happened to "Grumpy" Jackson?

TAYLOR: He's down at Bournemouth – grumpier than ever.

WATSON: And Geoffrey Hill? Ever hear of him?

TAYLOR: Married. Very unhappily, I'm told.

WATSON: How about Ronnie Russell?

176

TAYLOR: He broke his neck last year – hunting.

WATSON: I'm sorry to hear that – though I never did like the fella. Ever see "Pinky Little"?

TAYLOR: No. (CHANGING HIS TONE) Watson, old chap, I don't want to seem rude, but d'you mind if we postpone the reminiscences until later?

HOLMES: Just what I was about to suggest myself, sir.

WATSON: (MUMBLING) Only natural that when a couple of old army men get together they should . . . .

HOLMES: (INTERRUPTING) Just what is your problem, Major Taylor?

TAYLOR: I'm afraid for my life, Mr. Holmes.

HOLMES: Why?

TAYLOR: Perhaps I'd better tell you the story from the beginning.

HOLMES: That would be the most logical starting place, sir.

TAYLOR: Well . . . . Twenty years ago – or more – half-a-dozen of us were stationed on a pretty dangerous Indian outpost. We were discussing the chances of us all getting out of the place alive. Somebody – I forget who – produced an insurance advertisement, and suggested we all take out a policy. The proceeds of each policy were to go in to a trust fund which would eventually be paid to the last survivor. I suppose it was rather a schoolboy-ish idea. In fact we called ourselves, as I remember, "The Doomed Sextette" or something equally melodramatic.

HOLMES: How many of the original half-dozen of you are still alive?

TAYLOR: Only four. I'd practically forgotten the whole thing – until one of our members dropped dead of heart failure on a Scottish golf course last year. I was reminded of the agreement when I received a notification from the lawyers handling the trust fund that the insurance money had been duly credited.

HOLMES: Hmm. Who was the other member who died?

TAYLOR: Jerry Marshall. He was murdered in his flat six months ago here in London.

HOLMES: Jerry Marshall? Yes, I remember the case. The police discovered nothing. So there are four of you left, eh? Who are the other three?

TAYLOR: Oddly enough, they're all comparative neighbours of mine. I live in Virginia Water, you know. Bob Allen, the lawyer, has a house nearby. And Doctor Glendinning, another member of the "Doomed Sextette", has a practice at Egham, which is only an hour's drive from my place.

HOLMES: That accounts for three of you. How about the fourth?

TAYLOR: Colonel Robinson. And as it happens, he's staying with Doctor Glendinning for the summer. Yesterday he was out shooting and narrowly escaped death when his gun exploded. It had been tampered with. Mr. Holmes, I feel that it's liable to be my turn next. I was hoping, perhaps, that you and Watson would come down and stay a few days with me in Virginia Water, and keep an eye on things?

HOLMES: What d'you say, Watson? A few days in the country might do you the world of good, you know.

WATSON: Yes. I'd like to go down there very much.

HOLMES: Good. This is quite like old times. Pack an overnight bag, old chap. Oh – perhaps you had better scribble a line to your wife, and then we'll be on our way to Virginia Water.

MUSIC: BRIDGE

SOUND EFFECT: CARRIAGE ON GRAVEL

WATSON: 'Pon my soul, Taylor, you don't give us much chance to look at your place. We just have time to unpack our bags and then you whisk us off in your carriage to call on Doctor Glendinning.

TAYLOR: It was your friend's idea, Watson.

HOLMES: Why waste time, old fellow? Major Taylor feels that his life is in danger . . . and I think that he has every reason to believe it. Two other people concerned – Doctor Glendinning and his guest, Colonel Robinson, are practically neighbors . . . and remember that the Colonel narrowly escaped death yesterday when his gun exploded. It seems obvious that we should waste no time in calling on them.

SOUND EFFECT: CARRIAGE STARTING TO SLOW DOWN

TAYLOR: Here's Glendinning's house now.

WATSON: Charming. His practice must be a lot more remunerative than mine. I couldn't afford a place like this.

TAYLOR: He has a private income. Ah, there he is now. (RAISING HIS VOICE) Hello, Glendinning!

SOUND EFFECT: CARRIAGE DRAWING TO STOP

GLENDINNING: (OFF) Taylor! Good to see you. (FADING IN) (ABOUT FIFY, PLEASANT) And you've brought visitors. Fine. Perhaps we can have a four at bridge.

SOUND EFFECT: CARRIAGE DOOR OPEN. CRUNCH OF FEET ON GRAVEL

TAYLOR: Glendinning . . . I want to introduce Mr. Sherlock Holmes and Doctor Watson.

AD LIB: HOW D'YOU DO'S

SOUND EFFECT: DOOR CLOSE

TAYLOR: They came down with me from London today.

GLENDINNING: Sherlock Holmes? The great detective?

HOLMES: The adjective is yours, Doctor Glendinning.

179

GLENDINNING: Well, Taylor, you threatened to call in a detective, but I didn't know you'd aim as high as this. Come on. Let's go into the house.

SOUND EFFECT: FOOTSTEPS ON GRAVEL

TAYLOR: By the way Glendinning, Watson's an old army medico too.

GLENDINNING: Really? What regiment?

WATSON: Fifth Northumberland Fusiliers.

GLENDINNING: Is that so. Were you with 'em in India?

WATSON: Yes, I was wounded in the Battle of Maiwand.

GLENDINNING: Bad luck. Seriously?

WATSON: Shattered the clavicle and grazed the sub-clavian artery.

GLENDINNING: You're lucky to be alive. Well, here we are . . . .

SOUND EFFECT: DOOR OPEN AND CLOSE

GLENDINNING: Let's go in to the library . . . . I suppose you know the story of the "Doomed Sextette", Mr. Holmes?

SOUND EFFECT: DOOR CLOSE

HOLMES: Yes, and the more recent developments to the story. That's why I'm down here.

WATSON: What d'you think about it yourself, Glendinning?

GLEDINNING: (CHUCKLING) As I told Taylor yesterday, I think he's becoming an old woman. Two of us dead, and one has an accident, and he thinks we're all marked men!

TAYLOR: How d'you account for Robinson's gun exploding yesterday?

180

GLENDINNING: I don't. But even if it has been tampered with – that doesn't mean to say it's anything to do with our agreement years ago.

HOLMES: I wonder if I might examine that gun?

GLENDINNING: Certainly. It's over there in that corner.

HOLMES: (FADING) Thank you.

WATSON: By the way, where is Colonel Robinson now?

GLENDINNING: Out rabbit shooting. He should be back any minute.

TAYLOR: Seems to me that after yesterday's experience, he ought to be very careful. Something might happen again.

GLENDINNING: Rubbish, Taylor. He is carrying a .22. What could happen to him with that?

HOLMES: (OFF A LITTLE) Interesting. Very interesting.

WATSON: What have you found out, Holmes?

HOLMES: (FADING IN) Doctor Glendinning . . . is Colonel Robinson a keen sportsman? Someone that would cherish a fine weapon like this?

GLENDINNING: He's a good shot, but I don't know that he's too particular about his guns.

TAYLOR: Come now, Glendinning. You know he worships them. Why, Mr. Holmes?

HOLMES: The barrel of this gun is badly scarred. No one that had any love of guns could let it get this way. Look at it.

WATSON: (AFTER A MOMENT) By Jove, yes. What could have caused those marks?

HOLMES: From a cursory examination, I should say that someone has tampered with the cartridges and substituted a steel plug for the

181

charge of bird shot. The plug jammed in the choke barrel, causing the gun to explode.

TAYLOR: You see, Glendinning? What did I tell you?

HOLMES: Where did these cartridges come from, Doctor Glendinning?

GLENDINNING: I imagine Robinson bought 'em in the village.

HOLMES: I wonder if there are any more of the left.

GLENDINNING: I'll soon find out. (FADING) He keeps his tackle in the hall cupboard.

WATSON: Holmes, if there was a steel plug in the barrel – why isn't it there now?

HOLMES: It must have been extracted, subsequently.

TAYLOR: But who would have had an opportunity to do that?

HOLMES: That, Mr. Taylor, is what we have to find out. (RAISING HIS VOICE) Any luck, Doctor Glendinning?

GLENDINNING: (FADING IN) Here's the box . . . . It's empty. Robison must have filled his pockets yesterday with the last of 'em.

HOLMES: Hmm. How did Colonel Robinson arrive back here yesterday, after the accident?

GLENDINNING: Taylor found him wandering along the road – with a slight case of shock – and drove him back here.

TAYLOR: That's right, Mr. Holmes. And when we got here, he put the gun in that corner where you just found it.

WATSON: Could anyone else have had access to it since?

GLENDINNING: A dozen people. (LAUGHING) I never lock doors – even when my housekeeper goes down to the village to market. Patients and friends simply walk in and wait for me to come back if I'm out.

HOLMES: So that anyone could have had an opportunity of reaching the gun and removing the incriminating evidence?

GLENDINNING: Certainly.

WATSON: And yet, why didn't Colonel Robinson notice the steel plug himself – before it was removed?

HOLMES: A very pertinent question, old chap. Why, indeed?

GLENDINNING: Remember, he was suffering from mild shock.

SOUND EFFECT: SUDDEN POUNDING ON DOOR, OFF

GLENDINNING: (FADING) Now who the devil's that?

SOUND EFFECT: DOOR OPEN, OFF

GLENDINNING: (OFF A LITTLE) Yes, O'Flaherty, what is it?

O'FLAHERTY: (ELDERLY IRISHMAN. EXCITED) It's Colonel Robinson, sorr. I just found him down by the brook. He's dead!

GLENDINNING: Dead?

O'FLAHERTY: That he is, sorr. You'd better all come with me right away. Shot through the head, he is . . . and if you ask me, sorr, it looks as if he committed suicide!

MUSIC: BRIDGE

HOLMES: Suicide, eh? I think not. You'll notice that the .22 bullet hole in his head entered above the right ear and came out under the left eye.

WATSON: I don't see what that proves.

HOLMES: He's still clutching the rifle, Watson. If it had been suicide, how could he have shot himself from that angle?

TAYLOR: Why not, Mr. Holmes?

183

HOLMES: Mr. Taylor, the usual gun suicide pulls the trigger with his thumb.

GLENDINNING: Surely it's perfectly possible to fire a gun into your own head with a normal trigger grip, Mr. Holmes.

HOLMES: It is, Doctor Glendinning – from certain positions – but it would be next to impossible to aim and fire a shot slightly downwards and from the rear.

WATSON: In any case, why would a suicide choose such an awkward position?

HOLMES: Precisely, Watson. Also you'll observe there are no powder burns on the scalp, and it would not be possible to hold a gun far enough away to avoid that.

GLENDINNING: Then what do you think, Mr. Holmes?

HOLMES: (OFF A LITTLE) That we should examine the surrounding underbrush . . . Ahh . . . (FADING IN) Look here, gentlemen.

WATSON: It's only a piece of string.

HOLMES: But let us follow it . . . across the gully here . . . up the bank . . . and where does it leads us to?

WATSON: A tree! (EXCITEDLY) Good Lord! A .22 rifle – lashed to the branches – and aimed at where poor Robinson fell.

HOLMES: Exactly. And this end of the string is still attached to the trigger.

TAYLOR: You mean it was a deliberate trap, Mr. Holmes?

HOLMES: Yes – and a more than usually subtle one. You see, the string was stretched across the path over there. It was thin enough to be broken by anyone walking into it. As the string broke, it would dislodge the weight here, which would in turn pull the trigger on this rifle. A much superior method to the rather obvious trip-wire attached directly to the trigger. A fine string such as this would

184

recoil like a whip when snapped, and might easily remain undiscovered.

WATSON: Good Lord, Holmes! You mean it's . . . .

HOLMES: I mean, old chap, that it's a clear case of murder!

<u>MUSIC: UP STRONG TO MIDDLE CURTAIN</u>

FORMAN: Doctor Watson's story will continue in just a few seconds – which gives me time to ask you if you've ever tasted Petri California Sauterne. You know, Petri Sauterne is a white wine – a very famous white wine with a very rare delicate flavour . . . a flavour that comes right from the heart of luscious, hand-picked grapes. The next time you try to stretch your ration points by serving chicken or fish . . . don't forget to get a bottle of Petri Sauterne. Boy, that Petri Sauterne was just made to go with chicken and all kinds of seafood. Like all Petri wines . . . Petri Sauterne can make even the simplest war time meal taste like a feast. It's a fact – you can't go wrong with a Petri wine!

<u>MUSIC: "SCOTCH POEM"</u>

FORMAN: And now, back to tonight's new Sherlock Holmes adventure. The great detective and his friend Doctor Watson have been called in to investigate the strange adventure of "The Doomed Sextette" – a secret society of English army officers. Two members have already died when Sherlock Holmes and Doctor Watson are brought onto the scene. A few hours later, a third member is murdered. As we rejoin our story, the famous pair are discussing the strange affair with Doctor Glendinning and Major Taylor, (FADING) two of the three remaining survivors . . . .

WATSON: You know, Holmes, I still don't understand why the murderer didn't remove all the evidence of his crime – the string, the fixed rifle, and so on.

TAYLOR: Just what I was going to say, Mr. Holmes.

HOLMES: He had no opportunity. Anyway, it might easily have remained undetected for a long time if I hadn't become suspicious and looked for it. A man-trap of this kind could easily have been set

185

up several hours – or even days – in advance, and of course alibis won't mean much in this case. By the way, you and Doctor Glendinning examined Colonel Robinson's body – in your opinion, how long had he been dead?

WATSON: About three hours, eh, Glendinning?

GLENDINNING: Between three or four.

WATSON: What I don't understand gentlemen, is how the murderer knew that Colonel Robinson would pass along that particular path.

HOLMES: A question I was just about to ask myself, Watson. Can either of you gentlemen answer it?

TAYLOR: I think I can answer that. We all had dinner with the Squire last night. He owns the woods where Robinson was shot.

GLENDINNING: That's right, Taylor. I remember now. Robinson asked his permission to go rabbit shooting today, and the Squire told him the best spot was down by the brook – the place where we found his body.

HOLMES: I see. Who was present at the dinner?

TAYLOR: Apart from myself and Glendinning here, there was Robinson, of course . . . And Bob Allen, and . . . .

WATSON: Bob Allen? He's the lawyer, isn't he – the other remaining member of your "Doomed Sextette"?

GLENDINNING: That's right, Watson.

HOLMES: So that the three remaining members of the pact were all present when Colonel Robinson was told the best place to go rabbit shooting today. Was anyone else present at the dinner?

TAYLOR: Yes. Half-a-dozen other people. It was quite a large party.

SOUND EFFECT: KNOCKING ON DOOR, OFF

GLENDINNING: (CALLING) Come in! The door's open.

186

TAYLOR: (SOTTO VOCE) Talk of the devil! Here's Bob Allen now.

ALLEN: (FADING IN) (AGITATEDLY) I just heard the news about poor Robinson and rushed right over here. What happened?

GLENDINNING: He was murdered, Allen.

ALLEN: Murdered?

TAYLOR: Yes. These two gentlemen are Sherlock Holmes and Doctor Watson . . . Bob Allen.

AD LIB: HOW D'YOU DO'S

ALLEN: Robinson murdered, you say? How?

HOLMES: He was shot with a .22 rifle fired by means of a trap. By the way, Mr. Allen, where were you about four hours ago?

ALLEN: I went out for a long walk through the woods this afternoon. Why?

HOLMES: I was just curious. (TO HIMSELF) Through the woods, eh?

GLENDINNING: What do you think we ought to do now, Holmes? I've already sent for the police.

WATSON: Seems to me that with the three remaining survivors of this pact all together like this, we should take advantage of the occasion and discuss the whole thing.

TAYLOR: I quite agree. (SUDDENLY) How about all having dinner at my house tonight? I'll organise one of those red hot curries we used to have in the old days . . . and Sherlock Holmes and Watson can solve the case for us. What d'you say?

HOLMES: An excellent idea, Major Taylor . . . though I hope you're not over-estimating our abilities.

SOUND EFFECT: CLICK OF TABLEWARE

WATSON: Magnificent curry! Nearly burnt my tongue off – but that's the way I like it!

TAYLOR: Good. You scarcely touched yours, Holmes.

HOLMES: I'm afraid that curry has never been one of my favourite dishes, Taylor.

WATSON: (EXPANSIVELY) I remember when I was stationed at Madras, my "*bobberchi*", a fellow by the name of Saila, used to cook a wonderful fish curry. The secret of it, he told me, was sliced apples and raisins in with onions. Tied it myself once but can't say I was very successful.

HOLMES: And now might I suggest we consider the real purpose of our gathering – an analysis of this problem.

GLENDINNING: An excellent idea Holmes.

HOLMES: You see, I'm trying to find the pattern. The first death was a natural one, and when the five survivors were notified that the dead man's insurance had been paid into the trust fund – It probably gave one of them the idea of killing the others.

WATSON: Yes, Holmes, if there is any connection between the deaths, it must be concerned with the trust fund.

TAYLOR: Only one of the club members could benefit, and all the survivors are here now.

GLENDINNING: Therefore it must be one of the three of us. By the way Holmes, during dinner you mentioned that engineering knowledge must have played a part in Robinson's murder. It might interest you to know that our host, Taylor, was in the Royal Engineers when he was in the army.

TAYLOR: (BLANDLY) True, Glendinning, but though you yourself are a doctor – you're also quite an amateur mechanic. It's a very nice

188

workshop you have in your house. You've probably got just the right tools for making a steel plug that would jam in a gun barrel – and other tools that would extract it afterwards.

GLENDINNING: (DANGEROUSLY) Taylor . . . if you don't take that back I'll . . . .

HOLMES: Gentlemen, gentlemen. I had no idea that my simple remark would stir up a hornet's nest.

ALLEN: Yes, it's ridiculous. If it comes to that, I wanted to be an engineer myself when I was young. But I'm a lawyer and I don't see any evidence to justify our accusing each other.

WATSON: Of course there isn't. My friend was only theorizing, weren't you, Holmes?

HOLMES: Certainly. There were no personal implications.

TAYLOR: I'm sorry, Glendinning. (FADING A LITTLE) Look, let's have some smokes and talk this thing over dispassionately. (COMING BACK ON) Tobacco and cigars. I can strongly recommend the 'baccy. It's a new blend I got in London today. Care for some, Mr. Holmes?

HOLMES: Thank you, I think I'll stick to my ship's plug.

TAYLOR: How about you, Watson?

WATSON: I'll have a cigar, thanks.

ALLEN: I'll try some of your baccy . . . . Thanks.

TAYLOR: How about you, Glendinning? Oh, I was forgetting. You ever touch anything but cigarettes, do you?

GLENDINNING: Never. Don't bother . . . . I've got some in my case here.

TAYLOR: I'll stick to my pipe. Pass the tobacco, will you, Allen?

ALLEN: Here you are.

189

TAYLOR: Thanks. Help yourself to liquor, fellows. There on the sideboard. By the way, Holmes, before we go into this matter any further, it's just occurred to me . . . . Robinson left his raincoat in the back of my trap when I dropped him off at Glendinning's yesterday. It's possible there might still be some cartridges in the pockets.

HOLMES: Where is that raincoat now?

TAYLOR: I think it's hanging in the hall. Want to come and look with me?

HOLMES: (FADING) Very well.

TAYLOR: (FADING) We'll be back in a moment.

SOUND EFFECT: DOOR OPEN AND CLOSE

WATSON: While they're out of the room, I've got a story I know you fellows'll like. You've both been stationed in Agra, of course?

GLENDINNING: Oh yes. Know it well.

ALLEN: I've been there, too.

WATSON: Well, you'll love this. There was a charming little nurse over at the Chowrusta Hospital. Little red-headed thing . . . Elsie something-or-other. We started off one night to look at the Taj Mahal by moonlight, and we were spinning along in our rickshaw when one of the wheels broke. As we tipped over at an angle of . . . (SUDDENLY) Allen! What's the matter, man?

ALLEN: (GROANS, THEN SPEAKS THICKLY) I don't feel . . . I don't feel . . . .

GLENDINNING: Great Scott! He looks absolutely green in the face!

ALLEN: (GROANS, THEN) You're . . . both doctors . . . can't you . . . (GASP OF AGONY) . . . do something for me . . . ?

190

WATSON: (CALLING) Holmes! Holmes!! Come back here!

GLENDINNING: He's been poisoned! A hundred-to-one that curry was poisoned!

WATSON: Yes, it was strong enough to disguise the flavour of anything.

GLENDINNING: And yet you and I haven't felt any ill effects.

SOUND EFFECT: DOOR WRENCHED OPEN

HOLMES: (FAST FADE IN) What's wrong, Watson?

WATSON: It's Allen! He's been poisoned!

GLENDINNING: No wonder your curry was so hot tonight, Taylor.

TAYLOR: You're being ridiculous. I ate two helpings of it myself.

HOLMES: Hand me that tobacco jar, Watson.

WATSON: What's tobacco got to do with it? Here you are.

HOLMES: (SNIFFS DEEPLY) There's your answer. Belladonna has been mixed with this tobacco.

WATSON: Belladonna? There's only one antidote for that – injections of pilocarpine. D'you have any, Glendinning?

GLENDINNING: No, but I'll drive over to my house and get some.

TAYLOR: (EXCITEDLY) You mustn't let him get away! He's the killer! Who else but a doctor could have made the first death look like heart failure? And he's the mechanical genius who fixed the trap that killed Robinson today.

GLENDINNING: You're mad, Taylor!

191

TAYLOR: Am I? And you're the one who never smokes a pipe – and yet knows that you can generate a deadly gas by burning belladonna.

HOLMES: You seem to know that yourself, sir . . . and yet the fact isn't common knowledge. And may I point out that you had just as many opportunities as the man you are accusing. You knew that Doctor Glendinning's door was never locked. You knew about this workshop.

WATSON: Yes . . . and his dispensary. You could easily have stolen some belladonna and mixed it with the tobacco.

TAYLOR: But I feel ill myself. I was smoking a pipe, too, you know.

WATSON: But you put your pipe down after a few puffs – I saw you!

HOLMES: Exactly – and then found an excuse to take me out of the room. You were the man who suggested the curry dinner, which would have made it impossible for your victim – or victims – to detect the smell, or taste, of belladonna in the tobacco. Unfortunately for you – I don't like curry! (SUDDENLY) Grab him Watson!

SOUND EFFECT: SCUFFLE

WATSON: No you don't, Taylor!

HOLMES: I'm going to take the liberty of searching you, Taylor.

TAYLOR: You fools! You've got the wrong man!

HOLMES: I think not . . . Ahh . . . How very stupid of you to have left the bottle of belladonna in your pocket. I was right!

GLENDINNING: I'll drive over as fast as I can (FADING) and get that pilocarpine.

HOLMES: Splendid. And Doctor Watson and I will entertain our host until the police relieve us of the responsibility.

MUSIC: BRIDGE

192

HOLMES: What are you scribbling in that book, Watson?

WATSON: Just making a few notes on "The Doomed Sextette".

HOLMES: An unpleasant case – and it if hadn't been for your timely injection of pilocarpine, Bob Allen might have died too.

WATSON: Don't underestimate Doctor Glendinning's share in that. But there are one or two things I still don't understand, Holmes.

HOLMES: What, for instance, old chap?

WATSON: How did Taylor expect to get away with such a train of crimes?

HOLMES: He realised that a succession of deaths couldn't be made to look natural – and so he selected a scapegoat.

WATSON: You mean Doctor Glendinning?

HOLMES: Exactly. He was going to make it appear as if Glendinning was responsible for everything. Then Glendinning would be tried and executed, and Taylor would be the last survivor and inherit the trust fund. But you see, someone had to suspect foul play.

WATSON: And so he came to you for help?

HOLMES: Yes. He was afraid that the local police might not be smart enough to find the clues he was deliberately leaving.

WATSON: But supposing you had liked curry – and had taken a fill of his tobacco and been killed?

HOLMES: Then he would still have accused Doctor Glendinning. He would have said that Glendinning was afraid I would detected him and so had poisoned me as well. And I'm afraid, old fellow, that he wouldn't had had much difficulty convincing you. (LAUGHING) In fact, you'd have ended up as his best witness!

WATSON: I don't see anything funny about that.

HOLMES: Don't you? It rather appeals to my warped sense of humor. But one thing I beg of you, Watson.

WATSON: And what's that, Holmes?

HOLMES: I deplore your rather overdeveloped sense of the melodramatic. If you should have occasion to make this little case a basis for one of your stories . . . promise me one thing.

WATSON: What is it?

HOLMES: Please don't title it "The Strange Adventure of the Doomed Sextette".

MUSIC: UP STRONG TO CURTAIN

FORMAN: Well, Doctor, I guess it was a bit of a shock to learn that an intelligent, respected man like Major Taylor was a killer.

WATSON: Yes . . . I can't understand it. Guess he just had a screw loose somewhere in his mental machinery. It was at times like that, I wished I'd never worked with Holmes.

FOMAN: Yes, I know what you mean.

WATSON: Mister Forman . . . don't ever be a detective.

FORMAN: Don't worry . . . the only detecting I'll ever do is to find out which one of the Petri Wines is my favourite . . . and believe me, twelve bottles of Petri Wine make a very interesting case.

WATSON: Incidentally, which Petri wine *is* your favourite?

FORMAN: Well, I like Petri California Sherry before dinner . . . and then with dinner I like Petri Burgundy or – well, I (LAUGHS) I guess I like 'em all! They're all good because the Petri family sure knows how to turn luscious, hand-picked grapes into fragrant delicious wine. They ought to know how, they've had enough experience. Why, the Petri family has been making wine for generations . . . ever since they first started the Petri business back in the eighteen-hundreds. And, since the making of Petri Wine *is* a family affair – well, everything they've ever learned they've been

194

able to hand on down from father to son, from father to son. So believe me, no matter what type of wine you prefer . . . for any occasion . . . you've got to go awful far to beat a Petri Wine . . . because Petri took time to bring you good wine. And now, Doctor Watson, what adventure d'you have in store for us next week?

WATSON: Next week, Mr. Forman, I have a very weird and unusual story that takes place high on a cliff-top overlooking the English Channel. It concerns an actor, a dead politician, and a . . . haunted windmill!

FORMAN: Thanks Doctor. And now I'd just like to say a word about the Red Cross. Did you know for instance, that right now the Red Cross is operating over seven-hundred clubs for our fighting men overseas. Each one of these clubs is a bit of America on foreign soil . . . a place where our boys can get a meal . . . can listen to music, or read the latest magazines or books. The Red Cross doesn't forget the boys at isolated posts either. Clubmobiles . . . little clubs on wheels . . . go right up to the front with movies and coffee and doughnuts and the little things the boys miss so much. All this is just a part of the work of the Red Cross . . . work which can only continue if you help the Red Cross meet its 1945 War Fund. Two-hundred-million dollars must be raised . . . so give a day's pay and help, won't you? Your money does *so* much.

MUSIC: "SCOTCH POEM"

FORMAN: Tonight's Sherlock Holmes adventure is written by Denis Green and Bruce Taylor and is based on an incident in the Sir Arthur Conan Doyle story "The Stockbroker's Clerk". Mr. Rathbone appears through the courtesy of Metro-Goldwyn-Mayer. Nigel Bruce, who is usually heard as Doctor Watson, was unable to be on tonight's program owing to illness. His place was taken by Mr. Joe Kearns. Mr. Bruce will be back on the program next Monday night.

MUSIC: THEME UP AND DOWN UNDER

FORMAN: (OUT) The Petri Wine Company of San Francisco, California invites you to tune in again next week, same time, same station.

195

MUSIC: HIT JINGLE

SINGERS: *The Petri Family took the time*
                    To bring you such good wine
                    So when you eat and when you cook
                    Remember Petri Wine!

FORMAN: To make good food taste better, remember –

SINGERS: *Pet – Pet - Petri Wine.*

FORMAN: This is Bill Forman saying goodnight for the Petri family. Sherlock Holmes comes to you from the Don Lee Studios in Hollywood. (CUE) THIS IS MUTUAL.

196

The Adventure of the Old Boys' Club
by Shane Simmons

"The Diogenes Club. Do you know it?"

Word had come to me, as it often did, from one mouth on the street to the next. Smithy the Beggar, who worked one corner of Baker Street, told Jammer the Cripple, who held out his cup on another. Jammer passed word to Mick the Ratcatcher, who told Henrietta the Chicken-Plucker. And so on down the line, through a dozen different points of disinterest and twice as many working-class cast-offs that the greater London machine never looked at twice, until it arrived in my ear, the intended target. Sherlock Holmes wanted to see me at 221b immediately. The entire relay, from the moment his landlady had first passed on the summons to a neighbour, took less than ten minutes. I was standing at attention, hat in hand, in his rooms in twelve.

"Wiggins," he said, "you are precisely thirty seconds late."

"Sorry, Mr. Holmes," I relied. "Perry was deep in a bottle last night and he's having a slow morning."

"Inform Perry the Rugbeater that if he delays my communication network again, he'll have to buy his whisky without the aid of my weekly stipend."

The breakdown in the relay was forgotten a moment later. That's when Mr. Holmes brought up the Diogenes Club.

"Know it?" I echoed. "Well, sir, I know of it. Can't say I'm a member in good standing, or that I've ever crossed the threshold in my life."

"My brother, Mycroft, practically lives there," said Mr. Holmes. "He's slept in the reading-room armchairs more often than his own bed."

"I didn't know you had a brother."

"I hardly know it myself, I see so little of him. That is how we prefer to maintain our familial ties. Nevertheless, our paths cross at certain junctures, and such a one has arrived today."

He finished writing a note at his desk and folded the sheet over on itself several times.

"Give him this message," he said, handing me the unsealed letter. "It is a call for his attention, most urgently required, on a matter of pressing importance."

I took it and stuffed it down my deepest pocket so as it wouldn't get lost.

"When he refuses – and he shall – give him this message," added Mr. Holmes, and gave me a second folded note.

I found another pocket to carry this vital backup plan.

"We'll see if that doesn't compel him to crawl out of his cocoon of books and brandy and let the sun touch his flesh for the first time in weeks!"

"Once I collect him, where will we find you?" I asked.

"Mycroft will know. He will calculate it in an instant. To actually spell out the destination for him might be perceived as an insult, and an insulted Mycroft will not serve our cause well at all. Off you go!"

As fast as my feet could carry me – and fast it was – I beat a path through the back alleys and side streets. Away from the bustle and traffic of the main roads, I was quicker than any cart or cab. A few walls that needed climbing, or cellars that could be cut through, shaved valuable minutes off my time. At last I found myself outside one of the least known and least talked about clubs in all of England. Even the members didn't talk about it. Not to each other, not to anybody. All I'd ever heard about the place was that it was like some sort of monastery, with a bunch of old geezers not saying a word as they went about their drinking and smoking and reading. Mostly drinking.

Unless you knew London like the back of your hand, there was no chance you'd pick out the right door on the right street in right block. The Diogenes Club was exclusive in a way that tried to exclude itself from the minds of even its closest neighbours. I only knew it existed because there's hardly a nook or cranny in the whole city I haven't made it my business to know about.

With no one to greet me or stop me from poking my head in, I tugged at the heavy door and let myself into the towering lobby just inside. I didn't get more than two steps in when I was beset by some gigantic bloke in in a spiffy uniform who didn't even ask me my business.

"No beggar-boys or wee bastards in here! Off with you before I give you a tanning!"

I don't claim to dress so fine, nor bathe so often, but it was a rude how-do-you-do, even by the low standards I'd come to expect. Common courtesy should have demanded he at least ask me what I was after, but no! He grabbed me by the ear like he meant to use it to drag me back outside and throw me into the gutter. A stomp on his foot and a fist to his bullocks made him think better of it, and he let me go in favour of cupping the royal jewels.

"I have an appointment," I explained, simply enough, as the watchdog tipped over and treated himself to a closer look at the fine tiled floor. Without waiting for further objection, I took the stairs three at a time. A single floor up, I found a great hall full of books and the sort of stodgy old buggers what might be interested in reading them. It was as good a place as any to start.

"Mr. Mycroft Holmes!" I shouted, holding the pressing note high. "Message for Mr. Mycroft Holmes!"

The looks I got as I paraded through those hallowed halls were fierce. All sorts of scorn and anger were directed my way, but no one said "*Boo!*" about my intrusion. Probably following their own rule, I expect. The unspoken one about not speaking.

One set of greying mutton chops looked the same as the next white moustache or full beard to me. Which one was Mycroft Holmes was anybody's guess, if he was there at all. I kept at it, down the length of the long room, my eye on the opposite door, anticipating the next set of cross faces I'd have to brave beyond it. That's when one of the dusty old statues spoke up from the permanent dent he'd made in a deep leather chair. He set aside the day's *Times* and spoke the first words I'd heard in the place since the gent in the main hall had grunted something foul at me from his position on the floor.

"You must be one of Sherlock's creatures," said the man, like there was a bad taste in his mouth. It could only be Mycroft Holmes. There was a passing resemblance to his brother, but Mycroft was easily twice the man – at least in girth.

"Right you are!" I said, pleased to know deductions ran in the family. "And how did you figure that?"

"Because whenever there is some dirt swept into my life, I invariably find my brother holding the broom handle."

"I have an urgent message," I said.

"Aren't they all?" he sighed, as much from the effort of getting to his feet as from the imposition.

I tried to hand him the letter, but he refused to take it.

"Come, boy," he said, waving a couple of fingers at me. "There is a room for visitors where we may speak more freely."

One of Mycroft Holmes's fellow statues had taken to giving him a look just as dirty as they one he'd been giving me, holding a finger to his lips and softly shushing him. Mr. Mycroft stopped a moment and stared him down. The man dropped his finger and his eyes right quick, and stuck his nose back in his paper like he'd just discovered a headline that mentioned him by name. A shameful one.

Without any more words to foul up the silence, Mycroft Holmes led me through three more rooms and a barren hallway to a smaller chamber far from all the other club members. He had brought a big stack of documents with him, and seemed relieved when there was a table he could set them down on again.

He turned and held out his hand. At first I thought he wanted to shake mine and make proper introductions, but the gesture was nothing of the sort. He expected me to make delivery, not acquaintance, so I presented him with the first letter. Mr. Mycroft unfolded it, glanced at it for a single instance, and snorted once. He set the page down on the table next to his stack and flattened it with both hands. Once he was satisfied with how the folds were pressed out, he picked up the stack and set it down again on his brother's letter, filing it dead last in the pile.

"Is that all?" I was asked.

"I think the other Mr. Holmes was expecting you two might have a word about the problem he's working on."

That held less than no sway at all.

"Problems, problems, and more problems, ever brewing and threatening to boil over! And who is left minding the stove, I ask you?"

Mycroft Holmes tapped on his chest, as though he were pointing at his own heart. He then rifled through the stack of papers collected before him – official documents and clippings from the news mostly – and began an itemized list purely for his own benefit. I hardly understood a word.

"A double suicide in Austria involving a Crown Prince and his young mistress. Mundane on its surface, but a suspicious eye has been cast upon the Freemasons, and I fear if we keep letting these secret societies assassinate their way through the Austrian-Hungarian royal family, we may see very serious consequences within a generation. Then there's the constitution under Meiji that has come into effect. What are we to make of what was once a safely backwards feudal nation, now rapidly modernizing and establishing itself as an empire? I do not care for new players taking to the field so late in the game. Likewise, the Americans continue to collect states to unite under their republic. Four more now, including not one but two Dakotas, whatever a Dakota is. I shall have to investigate further. We've already been to war with them twice in the last century, and they may be amassing for a third go as far as we know! And, of course, there's the French. Always the French! They've gone and completed that metal monstrosity in Paris. The highest man-made structure in the world and, perhaps, its greatest eyesore. Now I am left explaining to certain imbecilic cabinet members that no, they haven't built it to spy upon us from across the Channel, curvature of the earth being what it is. One would think they should sleep more soundly at night with so little brain activity, but they are a terrible lot of worriers."

"You sound worried about the state of things yourself, Mr. Holmes," I commented.

"No, boy, not the state of things as they stand, but what is yet to come. We have elected officials to deal with the here and now. What England needs is men of vision to anticipate the threats that loom, plots that have yet to be conceived, let alone hatched."

"Like a fortune teller?" I asked.

"Not at all like a fortune teller. I seek predictions based in facts and evidence, not feelings and fanciful intuition."

"You sound busy enough, but your brother is going to want an answer. What should I tell him?"

"You may inform Sherlock that I will give his concern in this matter all due attention. He may expect a response no later than the second week of August, 1898."

I didn't fancy Sherlock Holmes would be keen to wait the better part of a decade for his brother's first impressions. He tended to not be the most patient man when it came to gathering particulars for whatever case he was working on,

"He thought you might say that," I replied. "Which is why he gave me another note to show you."

I dug into my second pocket and came up with the other slip of paper. The elder Holmes brother took it from me without a word, unfolded it for a look, and turned up his lip at what he saw. He stared in silence for a few long moments and then held the note so I could read it for myself. There was only a single word written on the page.

"Is he serious?" Mr. Mycroft asked me.

The single word, the whole of the message, was "*Kitty*".

Mr. Mycroft and I were in a hansom cab in a matter of minutes. The doorman, nicely recovering, was eager to flag one down for us if it meant serving a founding member and being rid of me.

"You know where the other Mr. Holmes is, then? He said you would."

"I know where my brother is, where he'll be next, what case he's working on, what his interest in it is, what he will discover, and how it will play out. Most pressingly, I know what he wants from me."

"You know all that from a single word on a piece of paper?"

"All that and more."

"Pardon me being blunt and all, but 'Kitty' ain't no cat is she? And it's not much of a proper name, neither. Sometimes it's a nickname, and oftentimes it's a rude one."

"You are quite correct."

I didn't dare say for what in front of so fine a gentleman, but I was sure he knew as well as me.

"Mr. Holmes weren't directing that insult at you, was he?"

"He wouldn't dare."

"So it's about something else then?"

"He didn't tell you," he said, not a question.

"All he said is he needed your help."

"He needs nothing of the sort! What he wants is my blessing. He knows this line of inquiry crosses boundaries with my own current interests. And he's afraid."

"Sherlock Holmes scared?" It sounded unlikely to me, the idea of the great detective being scared of anything.

"Petrified," confirmed Mr. Mycroft. "Of me. He's afraid he'll step on my toes as he bumbles after his clues and boot prints and cigar ashes. And if he makes things difficult for me, I'll see to it that I make things impossible for him."

"To look at you, I wouldn't have thought you two was brothers. Hearing you, though, you sure do sound like brothers. Quarrelling ones."

"Sibling rivalry is beneath me, boy. To be rivals, we would have to operate on the same level. We do not."

"Maybe if you applied yourself more, you could be in his league one day."

Mycroft Holmes looked at me for a moment, and I thought he might be angry. And then, for the first of a scarce few times, I saw him laugh.

"Why are we stopping here?" I asked, outside the building that was only ever paid any heed by visitors to the city intent on gawking. Them and, obviously, the tosh pillocks who worked there.

"Because this is our destination."

We had pulled up to the curb outside the Houses of Parliament. The gothic yellow stones stretched high above us. A palace of over a thousand rooms, Mycroft Holmes led me into those corridors of power like he knew exactly where he was going. Like he owned the place. I understood there were all sorts of rules and protocols about who was supposed to use which entrance or what door, but none of them seemed to apply to Mr. Mycroft. He went straight to the precise man behind the exact desk in the correct room, and was formally acknowledged.

"Name and purpose of visit?" asked the clerk, pen poised over his ledger book.

"I have scarce time for formalities," said Mr. Mycroft impatiently. "You know who I am and why I am here."

"Yes, sir," was the reply, and the clerk set down his pen and closed the ledger.

"Is the House still in session?"

"They're wrapping up question period now, sir. They should be out in a matter of minutes."

Mr. Mycroft looked towards the nearby stairs.

"Is he waiting?"

"Yes, sir, he's . . . ."

Mycroft Holmes was on his way up before the clerk could finish.

"I know the way," he said.

"Children aren't permitted . . . ." the clerk began when he saw me at his heel.

"He's an official envoy and he is with me," said Mr. Mycroft without so much as turning back to address the man properly. I shrugged at the clerk and ran to keep up. There was no need for a bollocks-boxing here. Apparently, whatever Mycroft Holmes said was golden.

"I'm a what now?" I asked him as we reached the first steps.

"Do you know what a go-between is?"

"Yes."

"Same thing," he puffed. Five stairs up and Mr. Mycroft was already winded. He explained anyway as he took the flight like he was climbing a mountain. "Communication between my brother and I can be strained. Having a third party present allows us to speak to each other through an intermediary. Sherlock's pet physician has served the purpose quite handily but, as he's honeymooning on the Continent, you will have to do."

"How do I envoy this go-between, then?"

We stopped at the first landing so he could catch his breath.

"Ask foolish questions, say little else, pay obsequious compliments when presented with astounding feats of intellect. The latter is not for my benefit, of course, but Sherlock seems to enjoy it and it puts him on a less defensive footing."

With that, he braved another flight. The waiting room was on the second level. I had every confidence he could make it.

"Mycroft," I heard a familiar voice say in greeting a few minutes later, before we were even at the threshold.

"Quite right," said Mycroft Holmes, as he stepped inside and into the line of sight of his brother. "Doubtless you heard the distinct squeak

203

of the Italian leather stitched together by the cobbler who custom makes my shoes. Or was it the ring of the sterling-silver tip of my cane against marble floors that gave me away?"

"Your wheezing," replied Sherlock Holmes. "It is as unmistakable as your voice."

Mr. Mycroft sat down heavily in a chair opposite the one where his brother waited patiently for an audience – either with a sitting member of parliament or the relation who had come to see him. Maybe both.

"Kitty?" said Mr. Mycroft, disdain for the term in his voice.

"Kitty," agreed the detective.

Mycroft Holmes grumbled and stewed in his seat.

"Shall I list for you the better things I have to occupy my days?"

"Doubtless poor Wiggins has already received an earful. I shall ask him for a summary at a later date."

"To that list you may add events in East Africa that have only just come to my attention. Even as we speak, Yohannes the Fourth is having his head paraded through the streets of Omdurman on a pike, as though it were the Middle Ages all over again!"

"Your doing?"

"I may have had a hand in negotiating the retreat of the Egyptian army through his lands, but the Mahdist overreaction is unbecoming. It gives one pause when considering further entangling ourselves in that corner of the globe."

"My current line of inquiry does not involve quite so imposing a pile of bodies, nor the accompanying sea of blood. Nevertheless, it remains a very serious matter of murder."

"Nonsense," said Mr. Mycroft, waving a dismissive hand.

"You do not share my impression of the sequence of events?"

"I do not. Though I expect that will not dissuade you from meddling."

I thought it might be a good time for one of those foolish questions Mr. Mycroft suggested I throw in to keep the exchange from getting too awkward.

"Who are we talking about?"

Wrong question. Both brothers fell silent, with neither of them willing to say names out loud. I tried again.

"Is this one of them delicate and personal state secrets Dr. Watson is always talking about not including in those stories he's working on?"

"Some of my cases require a certain degree of discretion, Wiggins," the younger Holmes explained to me patiently.

"Mum's the word then," I promised. "So which one is the delicate bit, and which one's the personal part?"

"The delicate element involves the volatile nature of Irish nationalism, which is precisely the debate our two members of the House of Commons have immersed themselves in below. The personal element comes from the fact that one of these men has been – *involved* – with the other man's wife for a decade now. It has been an open secret between the two for many years. Illegitimate children have resulted, and a challenge to fight a duel issued on at least one occasion. All water under the bridge now. But something has changed, and the *status quo* has been upset."

The elder Holmes continued where his brother left off.

"Captain O'Shea suffered the indignity for as long as he did because there was money in it for him. An inheritance was due to his wife, and from her to him by prior agreement. And so he waited, impatiently, for Katharine's wealthy aunt to die. Only, now that she has, the terms of succession have changed, and the money is being held in trust for Katharine's cousins instead."

The names meant nothing to me, but then I don't follow politics none too close, do I? I wasn't really the one they were talking to anyway. The conversation was between brothers, with me acting as the wire between two telegraph posts set many miles apart.

"O'Shea, as you can imagine, is rather put out," said Sherlock Holmes.

"Disappointed?" I prompted.

"Apoplectic," was the summary from Mycroft Holmes. "Despite the best efforts behind the scenes to talk him out of it, he's filing for divorce at last. Aside from being an affront to Irish Catholicism, the scandal, once it goes public, will be enormous. Careers will be ruined, and the House will be thrown into a state of turmoil when it can least afford to be. Worse, I will have to involve myself in putting out fires in Westminster, when my efforts are better spent elsewhere, containing far greater and longer-term threats than the ramifications of some foolish love triangle."

"Your current hornet's nest in Ethiopia, for one?" the younger brother said, like a poke in the ribs.

"For one of many."

The penny dropped once I'd had a few moments to think it through. Just one penny, but at least I made the connection.

"This man's wife, Katharine . . . . She's the Kitty in question."

"A name she has never used, but one whispered frequently behind her back, as a slight to her – shall we say – private conduct," said Sherlock Holmes.

"The principals involved in this scandal-in-the-making are not to be approached, spoken to, or communicated with in any fashion," insisted Mr. Mycroft. "I absolutely forbid it! This includes all family, close or extended. Do I make myself clear, Sherlock?"

Mycroft Holmes made a point of being excessively firm with his brother. There would be no misinterpretation.

"What about the cousins? One of them may very well be guilty of murder."

"Consider them equally off limits," said Mr. Mycroft, closing off all avenues of inquiry and making the detective's job impossible.

"How am I to conduct a proper investigation of a potential crime if I am prohibited from interviewing suspects?"

Mr. Mycroft was already rising to his feet and preparing to leave. He'd made himself clear and he wasn't about to stick around long enough to suggest there was room for debate.

"You love challenges, don't you?" he said. "Do they not excite your mind and keep you too entertained to stick needles in your arm? Embrace the challenge, Sherlock, and do not interfere in my affairs."

"Or, indeed, your attempts to cover up some else's affair," muttered the brother back at him.

"Come along, boy," Mr. Mycroft said to me, which caught me by surprise. I'd assumed we was all done.

"What? Me? Now?" I protested.

"I may have further use for you," was the only explanation.

"I was figuring on sticking with your brother," I said. "A murder case sounds like ever so much fun – unless you're the victim, of course. But still, there's an adventure to be had for certain!"

"I assure you, you will find it quite dull and unsatisfying. I have something for you that will be more to your liking, and suitable to you skills."

I looked back at Sherlock Holmes, who had risen to see his brother off. It felt like a betrayal to leave his side, even if it was for another Holmes. But then he gave me an approving nod.

"Rest assured, whatever errand Mycroft has for you may prove more fruitful on the adventure front. I expect my own inquiries to be slow and tedious now that I must go about them with both hands tied behind my back.

"Be sure you return him to me in good working order," he added to his senior sibling, pointedly.

"The boy can handle himself," Mr. Mycroft said. "He made short work of poor Henry and infiltrated the inner sanctum of the Diogenes Club in mere moments. There lies a messenger boy who won't let anything stand between him and his delivery. It is a useful talent, and a devotion to duty deserving of admiration. I can think of many uses for so promising a lump of clay."

"As you will," the detective agreed. "Wiggins is free to seek employment wherever he wishes.

"But a word of caution." This he said directly to me in a lower voice. "Be ever mindful of Mycroft's attempts to recruit you to his causes. Not all machinations of government are noble of intent or outcome."

The stairs back down were an easier go for the elder Holmes. Once we were descending together, I had to speak up.

"That won't put him off," I said. "Sherlock Holmes will find a way to see it through."

"Of course he will," said Mr. Mycroft, as though there were no other possibility. "All I have done is complicate things for him and cost him valuable time, which is well enough. What might have taken him a few days to wrap up may now consume a week or more. Only then will he discover that there is nothing to the case. A promising murder, seasoned with intriguing circumstantial evidence suggestive of complexity upon conundrum, will prove to be a disappointing death due to natural causes. I could tell him as much now, but he will insist on discovering this for himself."

"But why waste his time if the end result will be the same?"

"My brother is a creature of habit. Some of them are bad habits, self-destructive habits. You have, doubtless, observed for yourself the toll they take. Dr. Watson was instrumental in keeping such habits in check while they shared rooms in Baker Street. Now that he's married himself off, Watson is no longer there to stem to flow of stimulants into Sherlock's veins, and I fear for his good health. The longer a puzzle occupies his mind, the longer he will go without his favoured poison."

"So you do care," I said.

"Of course," said Mycroft Holmes, as though I had stumbled upon the most obvious deduction that could be made. "He is, after all, family."

Downstairs, the House of Commons had just let out. A steady flow of grand whiskers and fine suits flooded past us as the Members of Parliament went back to their lives outside the offices of government. More than a few nodded a respectful greeting to Mycroft Holmes, though none of them approached to distract him from whatever his current business might be. It was as if they all knew better.

"Look at them, boy," commented Mr. Mycroft. "Sealed chambers filled with men who think they can change the course of history with nothing but talk. How little they suspect that the important decisions –

the ones with the greatest impact – are arrived at by a different breed of men in another nearby chamber, who spend their time thinking rather than talking. Perhaps that is as it should be. The weight of the world should rest on shoulders that also bear great minds. Not with these glad-handers, whose loyalties are clouded by fickle mistresses and even more fickle voters."

Nearing the exit, I reminded him, "You said you had a job for me."

"Indeed!"

Mycroft Holmes stopped at the desk where we had first been directed upstairs.

"I need this," he said, plucking the pen from the clerk's hand.

"And this," he added, tearing the next blank page from the ledger. The clerk looked taken aback, but raised no objection.

He scribbled something quickly onto the page in handwriting that was either difficult to decipher or outright coded.

"I have a message most urgent that must be delivered," Mr. Mycroft told me, as we left the building. "Not to the master of the house, but to a seemingly minor party amongst the cooking detail in the basement. There is sensitive information to be acquired at a state dinner this coming Tuesday, and there is no one better positioned to overhear a private conversation during dessert than a well-placed member of the wait staff. The address is quite close, but the way will be barred. Guards are ever on duty to prevent unauthorized infiltration, and the building is filled with suspicious eyes who will question any perceived intruder."

"Makes no matter, Mr. Holmes, sir," I said. "I'll find a means to wiggle my way in."

"Good lad, that's the spirit!"

He gave me a description of who I was looking for, and how I would know him when I found him, as he folded over his note a few times and handed it to me.

"Where I am to get this to?" was all I needed to know.

"The address is Number 10 Downing Street. Know it?"

How could I not?

"It's only the second most famous address in all of London," I said.

"The second?" asked Mr. Mycroft, looking genuinely perplexed. "What address could possibly be more celebrated?"

"221b Baker Street, of course."

There was a funny look on Mycroft Holmes's face as I ran off down the road to deliver his message. I wondered about it the whole way to my destination until I was able to place it. My parting words had had an unexpected effect on the great man. I think I might have actually made him feel a bit stupid.

208

The Case of the
Golden Trail
by James Moffett

As I leaf through the vast notes accumulated over the first few months of 1890, I am struck by the tenacity of criminal minds intending to do harm to others and cause mischief in this great city. Truly, over the course of several weeks, my friend Sherlock Holmes was involved in no less than seven prominent cases. Some of these involved sensitive matters at a political or national level. Other were brought upon him by imploring officials from Scotland Yard. Inspectors Gregson and Lestrade visited the lodgings at 221b on a regular basis, seeking the assistance of the consulting detective.

Such notes as I now hold in my hands pertain strictly to those cases in which I have personally been involved – answering Holmes's summons as I temporarily postponed my medical practice and my duties as a husband. Without a doubt, numerous other cases must surely have come along and occupied the ever-active mind of Sherlock Holmes during my absence.

While leaving aside the more influential and delicate cases, I shall divulge a little problem which was brought to the attention of my friend towards the end of January of that year, during a bout of uninterrupted work.

It was the start of a hectic week, and having accompanied my wife to the train station on her annual visit to relatives outside the city, I settled down for another busy day overseeing patients who flooded into my consulting-rooms.

That Monday morning I felt somewhat analogous to Sherlock Holmes's typically active days, being presented with my own set of cases of a medical nature. Patients came to see me, while I listened to what ailments afflicted them, before assessing their physical condition and prescribing an appropriate treatment to resolve their problem.

By the time it was noon, I seemed to have finished my work for the day as I looked at the empty chairs in the outer room where my patients usually waited their turn.

At that moment, a young man walked in.

"Doctor John Watson?" he asked, peering at me with some trepidation.

Thinking it was another patient, I invited him to come in and returned to my desk. He timidly came forward and handed me a telegram, before nodding and taking his leave.

I took the paper and opened it up, to find the following note:

Little case in hand. Join me at 221b.

– S.H.

It was rather impossible to comprehend what perception the term "little" had in Sherlock Holmes's brain, but at the same time it was not easy to refuse any summons from London's greatest consulting detective. Surely, no matter what kind of case he had in hand, it would no doubt lead to a series of intriguing exploits and fascinating deductions which, on less drastic occasions, relaxed the mind and invigorated the senses.

Therefore, with the prospect of a fruitful afternoon, I left my lodgings and took a cab to Baker Street.

The short journey was a pleasant one. As ever, London's streets were bustling with its inhabitants attending to errands and other duties, or simply enjoying the comforting sun which now filtered through a few clouds drifting along, high in the sky. Looking out of the cab window, I beheld the familiar atmosphere of Baker Street, which seemed to welcome me every time I trod on its roughened cobblestones. There were many memories of my stay there to which I still clung, together with the numerous adventures I had shared with Sherlock Holmes. Although I had been whisked away by the duties of a married life, I always relished the opportunity to visit my old abode and reminisce on past times.

It was in such a state of emotion that I alighted from the cab and made my way inside 221b.

Ascending the stairs, I felt embraced by the comforting atmosphere of those lodgings: The hint of a musty scent from shelved books in the passageway, the creaking floorboards, and the familiar murmur coming from within the closed sitting room, where I had been privy to many a story of desperate individuals seeking the assistance of Sherlock Holmes.

I approached the sitting-room door and opened it, only to be greeted by the sound of voices. Going inside, it appeared I had stepped into the midst of a gathering.

Sherlock Holmes was sitting on his favourite armchair beside the fireplace. His eyes were closed and each of his elbows rested on an armrest. He was surrounded by four familiar faces and, as he spoke to them in turn, he raised his right hand to the individual he was addressing, all the while keeping his eyes shut.

"Lestrade, I shall send you a telegram upon the discovery of that missing finger. Inspector Gregson, do take the precaution of having a few additional constables assist you with the investigation of that warehouse in Regent Street. Inspector Jones, I shall accompany you to the trial of Mrs. Edwards and impart any evidence which may be deemed useful."

He paused a moment and opened his eyes, reaching out for a cup and saucer from the side table next to the armchair.

"Mrs. Hudson, more tea if you please." He glanced behind Lestrade's shoulder as he gave the order to the landlady who, having emphasised her discontent by a low wail, stormed out of the room, swiftly followed by the others.

"Ah, Watson! How good to see you," he exclaimed, noticing my presence. "What can I do for you, Doctor?"

I looked at him and laughed. He reciprocated with a subtle frown, thinking my response inappropriate amid the hectic business he had just been conducting that morning.

"Well?" he pressed – his tone of voice somewhat more serious.

"Holmes, you asked me to come here," I replied, presenting the telegram as evidence.

"Did I? Oh yes, capital!" He rose to his feet and beckoned me further inside. "Apologies, my good man. It has been such an enthralling day." He headed over to the sofa, picking up several papers strewn over its covers as he consulted each one in turn.

"More cases then?" I enquired, looking around the room and recalling memories I had forged there.

Holmes mumbled something inaudible, as he intensified his search amid the papers. He shuffled through torn envelopes, stained letters, and old telegrams, before exclaiming triumphantly upon producing a soiled note.

"A curious little thing," he said, handing me the piece of paper as he walked over to the Persian slipper which lay upon the side table. As was his custom, he extracted some tobacco concealed inside it and proceeded to light his briar pipe before sitting back down.

I opened the note, which ran thus:

sir holms ned yor help. ill bee baker street, after noon hour.

– will allen

I glanced at my companion for some guidance, receiving in return only a smile amid a plume of white smoke. Besides its ragged appearance, the paper was rather worn round the edges. The writing was more of a rough scribble, and barely legible.

"Our client is almost upon us if I read the note aright," broke out Holmes's voice. "But before that, allow me to make some trifling observations." He rose from his chair and snatched the note from my hands.

"Let us see what we can make of Mr. Allen's plight," he said, grasping his magnifying lens and running it along the edges of the note. "I received this from one of the members of the Baker Street Irregulars, that modest army of young informers, scurrying around London's streets, and every now and then assisting me in my cases." He raised his head from his inspection and smiled, before proceeding with his examination.

"So what can this piece of paper tells us about Will Allen? Primarily, based on the type of pencil and paper used, along with the grammatical inconsistencies of sentence structure, it is rather transparent that our writer is of a lesser educated disposition."

"Could he have just been in a hurry and missed a few words?" I proposed, moving beside Holmes to glance once more at the note.

"Doubtful. Look at how the inclinations of the 'y' and the 'b' have been produced, and the pressure in some of the strokes where the graphite from the pencil has brushed against the brittle paper. Both are an indication of a hesitant writer, as if he was uncertain how to proceed. The pencil has been held at an odd angle, as evidenced by the careless scratches at the bottom of each letter, giving the whole message its crooked appearance."

Upon closer inspection, and with the assistance of the lens, it was evident how the letters flowed unevenly across the surface of the paper.

"In addition, there is also the matter of the brick dust. It infests the whole note and has clearly become ingrained in the minute crevices of the paper," continued Holmes.

Indeed, the lens magnified the tiny reddish specks which would have gone unnoticed by the naked eye. Holmes sniffed the note and frowned.

"There's a stale smell to it, indicative of a damp and cold site. Whether our client comes from such a place, or merely acquired this paper from there when seeking to write his note, cannot be determined at present. And yet, I see no reason why this shouldn't be so. Surely our client has not been graced by fate and is in the same trials of life which beset the less fortunate inhabitants of London."

Holmes paused once more and gazed intently at the scribbling. At that moment, a noise was heard from downstairs, followed by furtive footsteps ascending towards Holmes's lodgings. I could not be certain whether a life away from Baker Street had altered my sense of hearing, but each footfall sounded strange – significantly peculiar and distinct from any footstep of man or woman who had ever walked into 221b.

"But there is something else," Sherlock Holmes suddenly added, ignoring the approach of the visitor as he took a second look at the intricacies of the writing. "Our client seems to be an adventurous individual with a stouthearted sense of determination, mixed with a sliver of frailty to him, which bears to the conclusion of our client being merely a child."

The door to our lodgings was slowly pushed back and there stood the unmistakable characteristics of a young boy.

It was a most unexpected turn. Of the numerous adventures and clients seeking my friend's assistance, never could I have thought the possibility of witnessing such an odd circumstance. That my companion's client could have been a child never occurred to me. And yet, I now recalled the scribbled letters and syntactical disparities to which Holmes had pointed just then.

The boy stood in the doorway, gazing at each of us in turn. His face was grimy and his clothes were tattered and stained, as if they had seen their fair share of hard life in the city, even though he could not have been more than eight years of age. Holmes's analysis on the poor state of the note's author had been correct.

"Master Allen, it would appear," said my companion with a gentle smile. "I am Sherlock Holmes." He walked forward and invited the boy inside. Clearly, Holmes was not as surprised as I was at our visitor. He treated every one of his clients the same, no matter their age or situation.

The boy said nothing, and although he put on a stern expression, his eyes faltered as the towering figure of my companion ushered him towards the sofa.

As he sat down, with his legs dangling high above the floor, my friend gave him the note, which he in turn held timidly in his hands. At that moment, Mrs. Hudson came barging in, holding a cup of tea, with a most horrified look on her face.

"Out boy! Out!" she cried, as she rushed towards the frightened lad.

"Mrs. Hudson! Do not agitate yourself," intervened Holmes. "This young man is here by my consent. He is a client and should be treated as such. Now run along to your duties, my good woman, and let us have some peace and quiet."

Sherlock Holmes gave her one of his impish smiles as he took the cup of tea from her hand and gave it to the boy. Mrs. Hudson gave a snort and walked out of the room. My friend directed his attention back to the child, who was taking a cautious sip from the cup.

"Now Master Allen, can you tell us why you are here?" he asked.

"To find the spinning top," murmured the boy, lowering his head. His voice was affected by a congested nose.

I leaned closer to my companion, who pressed him for clarification.

"What spinning top?" he asked once more. But the boy remained silent.

At that moment, we heard a loud thud and what sounded like a muffled altercation between two individuals, followed by a woman's voice coming from the staircase.

"Will! Where the devil are you?" she shouted.

I went to the door and opened it. A woman stumbled forward as she caught sight of the boy. Dashing inside, holding a wicker basket in the crook of her arm, she lunged towards him and fell on her knees before taking the boy in her arms.

"Never again! You ain't runnin' away like that, never again!" Her remonstrance was harsh, but a slight quiver was perceptible in her voice. The tone she spoke in was tinged with an abundance of concern and love.

"Mrs. Allen, I presume?" said Holmes.

"And who be you?" said the woman, standing back up and holding the boy close to her.

"I am Sherlock Holmes, ma'am. Your son requested my help and came to me seeking assistance."

"Sir, I ain't lookin' for trouble. My boy ran from the market and I only followed in fear, as a mother would. I came to this place after someone saw 'im run in 'ere." The woman stepped backward, her voice full of agitation. She must have been no more than thirty and, like the boy, presented herself in worn clothes and a shabby appearance.

"I mean no disrespect sirs," she continued, looking at both of us. "We shall leave you both to your daily business."

"But the top, ma! And the golden scraps!" broke in the boy. He looked at his mother and pulled her forward.

"Half-a-moment madam," said Holmes, raising his right hand. "Pray, sit yourself down and let us see what your son is asking for."

"It ain't nothing, sir. Honest. Nothing to burden your good selves with."

Despite her somewhat less than charming appearance, and clearly being a part of that unfortunate section of society from which the destitute are found suffering every day, Mrs. Allen spoke with as much

214

politeness as she could muster. She seemed most embarrassed, and troubled at having to drag her son away from the lodgings of someone she considered as being far superior to her, rather than as an equal human being.

"Madam, please," reciprocated Holmes with a smile, offering her a seat on the sofa.

The woman seemed to calm herself and took the offer. Her son sat beside her, his head bowed once again. Holmes and I settled in the armchairs opposite our visitors and waited.

"Now, Mrs. Allen," said Holmes after a few moments of silence, "would you be so kind as to shine some light on this situation so that I can offer my services to you and your son?"

"Beggin' your pardon, sir. The truth is, I ain't got any money for your help." Her voice broke with emotion as she stifled a whine.

"None of that, Mrs. Allen," said Holmes in a calming voice. "What I do, I do for the sake of the mind, and the pleasure of the art. Now please, do let us know what your son is seeking."

I cannot claim to have ever witnessed my companion opening up to the more fragile part of human nature. He was still the implacable, unrelenting machine. Yet he understood the behaviour of others and, while he kept to himself whatever emotion he felt, he treated the situation and the client before him with respect.

Mrs. Allen shifted with unease. She looked at her son and then at Holmes.

"I would think this all started but two days ago," she said. "You see, I peddle some fruit and local produce in the old market at Church Street in Lisson Grove. I help out a penny-pinching shopkeeper in Frampton Street for the odd shilling every now and then. 'Twas but 'alf an hour ago when I saw Will here runnin' away. So I followed him. I came straight 'ere from the market, with the basket and all." She lifted the basket from the side to demonstrate her point.

I hope the reader will forgive me at this stage. Mrs. Allen told us this, and much more. But I fear the account would go amiss if I were to continue presenting it entirely in her own words. I am therefore providing a brief summary of what more she told us, along with a few interjections of her own.

As Mrs. Allen explained, two days prior to bringing her agitated disposition to 221b, she had taken some items from the shop in Frampton Street, placed them in the basket, and headed to the market, hoping to assist her employer in selling the produce. She took young Will with her, as she always did, in order to keep an eye on him.

Throughout her account, no word was spoken about a husband, and Sherlock Holmes did not inquire any further. He remained seated in his armchair, motionless, yet aware of every detail – mundane or otherwise – that the woman recalled.

She had found her usual corner against the building which lined the north side of the street, and along which the market stalls were set up. Having emptied the contents of her basket onto a rag on the ground, her voice competed with the rest of the other costermongers in order to attract the attention of passersby.

"My boy 'ere, he went up and down the street with that . . . plaything – " Mrs. Allen faltered. "This spinning top made o' wood. Always in his hands, 'twas. He must 'ave pulled at it too strong, Will did, for it hit a honey jar I 'ad placed on the ground. It was batty-fanged, with glass all over the place and the honey too!"

Mrs. Allen bemoaned the fact that she had lost such a costly item without earning any money for it. She scolded young Will for his carelessness, while he in vain sought the missing toy amid the bustle of the market. The son's distress at the loss of his spinning top had gone unnoticed by the mother. She feared her employer's wrath and dismissal from work when he eventually found out that she had lost him a good shilling.

"I 'aven't 'ad the courage to tell 'im yet. When I do, I ain't got nothing left to 'elp me and my son no more," concluded the woman, with a perceptible sob. "Will 'as been scouring the entire street for the spinning top, even after the market's no more at the end of the day. He says to me he found naught but broken glass and golden specks on the ground where the jar lay shattered."

"What are these specks of which your son speaks?" I asked, leaning forward while glancing at the boy.

"Tripe!" she cried. "Pardon me sir. He keeps repeatin' things like that as make no sense." Mrs. Allen glanced at her son with an admonishing look, before directing her damp eyes back to my companion.

"So you see sir, my Will should 'ave 'ad no business disturbing you. The matter is no concern for so distinguished a gentleman."

Sherlock Holmes remained seated, immovable.

I thought the whole affair rather superfluous and unimportant in the vast web of criminality and human distress which sought solace in my friend's abilities. The broken honey jar and the missing top were a trivial situation, were it not for the clear distress exhibited by the woman for the wellbeing of her child. At the same time, I feared that London's greatest

216

consulting detective, consumed by more pressing matters, would react in an insensitive manner.

As these thoughts came to my mind, Holmes inhaled deeply. A discernible frown appeared across his forehead. He leaned forward, placing the tips of his hands against each other, while gazing vacantly before him.

"The problem presented is thus twofold," he began, his voice deep and calm as if in profound thought. "A child's toy vanishes, and a mother is in distress over the future of her employment. Superb! And all the while the boy refers to the strange presence of golden particles in the street. Say no more! We must settle the riddle of the spinning top, whilst safeguarding your reputation as a good woman, Mrs. Allen," he concluded with a smile.

Holmes rose from his chair and took down his coat from the hanger by the door. The woman gently placed her arms around her son, looking up at the consulting detective in earnest.

"You offer your time to help us, sir?" she enquired.

"Absolutely, ma'am. A pleasant distraction. Come, let us head to Church Street Market this instant and see to your troubles. Watson!" he cried, as he left the room and headed downstairs to call a cab.

I was still pondering the odd and unexpected behaviour of my companion when we finally arrived at our destination. It was early afternoon and the market had almost dissolved into nothing, leaving the street in a tranquil murmur. A few hawkers remained scattered along the way as an occasional voice rose above the serene atmosphere. The street itself was littered with puddles of water, remnants of trampled vegetables, and the odd wooden crate left behind in haste. Muddy newspaper scraps flew past us in the cold breeze which swept from the southwest.

We followed the woman and the boy as they led us to the spot where their troubles had begun.

"This 'ere is the place where I stood that day." She pointed at a shabby corner flanked by two mouldy brick walls that emerged from a decrepit building stretching all along Church Street. There were fragments of broken glass scattered on the cobblestones where the jar must have shattered, along with drops of honey now turned dark and dry.

"Are these the golden specks you spoke about, Will?" I crouched down beside him, pointing at the honey stains on the ground. He shook his head and pointed a yard or two further away. Holmes was soon bending over to where Master Allen had indicated. He extracted his magnifying lens and got down on his knees, bringing his head in close proximity to the rough cobblestones.

"Halloa! What is this?" he uttered moments later. He bent even closer to the ground, adjusting the distance of the lens to get a clearer view of what had caught his attention. Whatever it was, it was surely miniscule.

"Watson, come! Behold the mystery of the golden specks." He tugged at my trouser leg, with his gaze still fixed on the object of interest. I got down and crouched beside him.

"What is it?" I asked, still unable to discern what had caught my companion's eye.

"A most curious species. Fascinating, and yet a scourge to the city inhabitant. Look here!" He gave me the lens and pointed at a few particles with an unusual yellow hue to them. As I leaned closer, the crooked outline of a body, from which protruded several distinct legs and antennae, appeared.

"Ants!" I cried, unable to contain the sense of amusement that swelled within me.

"Perfectly sound analysis Watson," said Holmes, "and judging by the size and shape of the thorax and abdomen, the placement of the two nodes, and the overall colour, I would say we have a fine specimen of Pharaoh ants. Your son has keen observation, Mrs. Allen," he said, turning towards the woman.

"But what has this got to do with the boy's spinning top?" I asked.

"Everything, my good Doctor." Holmes took back his lens and glanced again at the dead insects, some of which lay scattered in several groups. "Look at the pattern formations of the ants as they are surrounding the hardened honey stains. They came out to feed."

Holmes rose to his feet and inspected the surrounding area until he had walked several yards away to the northwest from the initial spot, clearly having found a clue of sorts.

"There are several more such ants lying dead at certain intervals in this direction, and they all seem to point back towards the broken jar. No doubt they came out, foraging for food, before being attracted by the fragrant scent of the honey. Alas! The cold proved too much for some of them, it seems." He paused for a moment, putting his lens back in his coat pocket and looking at the shattered glass, before turning towards the woman.

"Mrs. Allen, would you happen to have another jar of honey in that basket?" he asked. She looked at him in a somewhat confused manner, before giving a slow nod.

"Excellent! May I kindly purchase such a jar?" Holmes fumbled in his trouser pockets before extracting a few coins and placing them in the bewildered woman's hand. She handed over the honey, before exclaiming in surprise.

"'Tis too much, sir. There's twice the shillings for one jar," protested Mrs. Allen, extending the palm of her right hand where the coins had been laid.

"I'm sure I counted correctly," said Holmes, with a slight grin.

"Thank'ee, sir!" replied the woman after a moment's hesitation. "Most generous of you," she added, with some emotion.

"Now, onto the mystery itself." Holmes patted the boy on the shoulder as he stood staring at the broken glass with a disheartened expression. My friend leaned down and whispered something in his ear, before handing him the honey jar. Will Allen ran off in the direction Holmes had surveyed a few minutes earlier, leaving a trail of honey droplets as he went along almost halfway up the street.

"What is the meaning of all this," I asked Holmes, as the boy returned.

"Hush, Watson. Let us allow Nature to take its course and show us the way."

Sherlock Holmes advised us to leave the place and meet again at that spot later in the afternoon. I confess that I failed to grasp how all this could lead to any fruitful resolution. This sentiment seemed also expressed by Mrs. Allen and her son. Yet my friend was adamant about revealing everything at the appropriate moment and, given the circumstances, we followed his instructions.

I returned to Baker Street with Holmes, somewhat disenchanted by the whole affair. What followed were the longest two hours I could have experienced. I sat listening to my friend ruminating on a few other pending cases, while he concluded one or two more in the comfort of the sitting-room. Eager as I was to learn more about his thoughts behind Mrs. Allen's honey jar, not once did he delve into the subject.

I have often remarked how fervent and dedicated he could become on a case, and yet he was equally able to completely disengage himself from it when the time arose. Such was his behaviour in this instance.

Finally, when the clock hands had crawled past four o'clock, we left our lodgings and headed back to Church Street.

When we arrived, the sun had started to dip behind the rooftops, and an even cooler breeze swept through the streets. The marketplace had turned desolate and the whole atmosphere presented itself as grey and dreary. Other than ourselves, no one else seemed to be around, as if the nearby inhabitants had long shunned that dismal place once evening began to settle.

We were soon joined by a concerned Mrs. Allen, while young Will followed in her trail, downcast and altogether forlorn.

"Excellent. We can now proceed with our investigation," said Holmes, with the slightest flicker of excitement.

Once again, he took out the magnifying lens from his coat and walked back towards the glass fragments. From there, he worked his way along the honey droplets which led outwards along the street. With his back bent, guiding his lens with purpose along the cobblestones and crooked pavement, we followed him as he furnished us with his process of investigation.

"It was rather superficial, but the combination of spilt honey, Pharaoh ants, and a missing plaything was too alluring not to even attempt a little experiment. Halloa!" he exclaimed, halting after a few strides. "The golden trail reveals itself to us at last," he added, bending down.

"With the force of the spinning top having shattered the glass jar, it was conceivable that traces of honey must have landed on the toy. The presence of the insect specimen was an obvious indication that they had emerged from some nest to forage, following the scent of the honey. That was but two days ago." He rose to his feet and pointed towards the ground. Even in the dim light and lacking the aid of a lens, a movement like the slow trickle of a stream was perceptible. Upon closer inspection, it was evident that hundreds of ants were passing to and fro in a long procession to hunt for the fresh supply of honey that had been placed there earlier. Their light yellowish bodies truly gave the impression of an unbroken golden ribbon or chain that emerged from somewhere nearby.

"Having lured the rest of the colony workers, it was indisputable to the simplest of hypotheses, that their trail would lead us to the spinning top itself. Ah!" Holmes stopped short and knelt to the ground. We were several yards away from Mrs. Allen's hawker spot and a small rusted iron grate, serving as a drain gutter, was tucked in between the pavement and the cobblestones marking the edge of the street. From that direction, the majority of the ants seemed to emerge for the hunt and return with replenished supplies.

Holmes reached out his hand to the grate and tugged hard.

He pulled out a grimy spinning top which had been lodged between two of the grate bars, concealed from anyone attempting to look for it. My friend handed it over to young Will, whose face lit up in delight at the sight of it. He took it in his hands and wiped off the muck on his tattered shirt.

"Thank'ee sir," he said. He looked up in glee at his mother who, in turn, repeatedly expressed her gratitude, much to the irritation of my friend. It was a rare sight to see Holmes somewhat uncomfortable, believing he had hardly earned the praise.

Having returned to 221b, the thrill of watching Holmes solve the case began to subside. I settled down on the sofa, while my companion's voice travelled downstairs to ask Mrs. Hudson for some tea and some sliced bread. Having made his request, he turned round to face me, while holding the jar of honey he had bought from Mrs. Allen and used successfully in his investigation.

"Before you leave, Doctor, what say you we try this produce for ourselves?" he asked, accompanied by his typical impish smile.

"What a splendid idea!" I remarked.

He sat down opposite me and there was silence for a few minutes.

"A rather fascinating art, is it not? Bee-keeping," said Holmes, inspecting the jar while sipping from his teacup, which had just been brought up by the disgruntled landlady. "Perhaps one day," he mumbled, as he trailed off his discourse onto some other matter.

That brought to a conclusion the whole affair of the Golden Trail. If this account has seemed to the reader to be lacking in additional details, it is merely a reflection of the truth as it occurred. Holmes's nimble thinking skills and reasonings brought this case to a successful conclusion within a brief, yet intriguing, afternoon.

What happened to Master Allen and his mother after this event, I have no record. However, some weeks later, when Holmes summoned me to another one of his cases, I fancied seeing young Will among the Baker Street Irregulars. I spoke nothing of it to my companion, but it seemed certain that Sherlock Holmes had invited him to join the gang after perceiving his steadfast behaviour and skill at observation. This position allowed the boy to earn the precious shilling that my friend often gave out for their services.

Truly, though Holmes was ever the calculating machine, he could prove himself to be both a superb mind as well as a decent human being.

The Detective Who
Cried Wolf
by C.H. Dye

Watson waited until we were in the cab to reach up and lay his hand across my forehead, but when he brought it down, and looked at the residue of the chalk I had employed to make my features paler, his frown deepened. "I thought as much. Another trick."

The awkward part of being correct, nine times out of ten, is that upon the rare occasions when you are in error you have had little chance to become inured to the condition. And by the disapproval on my friend's face, I was most certainly in error. "Watson, I . . . ." I began, but he had already rapped on the roof of the cab with his cane to attract the attention of the driver.

"Drop me off at the Underground Station, please," he ordered sharply.

He had come so quickly in response to word of my distress, had behaved with every appearance of concern at my condition, and had so effortlessly extracted me from the hands of my unscrupulous client that I had expected to be sharing the joke with him by now, but the deepening lines upon his features allowed for no explanations.

"It may come as a surprise to you, Holmes," he growled, "that I have patients. Real ones."

"I assure you, my dear fellow," I said, as graciously as I could, "I did need you. I may not have actually ingested the poison which Camberwell put into my food, but . . . ."

"I can't always be chasing across London to keep you from dying when . . . ." His hand tightened around the top of his cane and his nostrils flared as he fought to bring his voice back down to a reasonable level. "There are people who are dying. If in future you require a dupe . . . ." He broke off a second time, but didn't have time to formulate what he wished to say before the cab drew to a halt alongside the Underground Station at Notting Hill Gate.

"Of course, Doctor," I said quickly, diving for the door before he could disembark. "I never meant to inconvenience you. Take the cab, please. The Underground will do me very well." I tossed a half-crown up to the driver. "That should cover the fare." If I expected a protest from Watson, I was disappointed. He merely called up an address – not his own – to the cabbie and leaned back against the cushions, his eyes and jaw shut tight against his own anger. The driver snapped the whip and the cab drew away, and I was left on the pavement, contemplating my fall from grace.

I have never suffered the least difficulty in reading the tenor of Watson's thoughts upon his countenance, or so I had thought up until that moment. If he is annoyed, or concerned, or puzzled, the slant of his eyebrows alone semaphores the condition. But clearly, I had misread the cause of the furrows upon his forehead that morning. Certainly, they suggested that he had been unusually pre-occupied with his practice during the week since we had returned from Scotland and my investigation of the Grice-Paterson matter. But his anger implied a more immediate concern. Upon receipt of the message I had sent from Camberwell's, he must have abandoned or postponed a visit to a patient in precarious circumstances. He could not yet have realized that I would not dare trust another physician to maintain the pretense were the falsity of my ailment to be discovered while I was still at the Camberwell house. Still, he would forgive me. He had done so quickly enough over the Culverton Smith matter, although it might be best to solace his pride with an apology and a good dinner.

But first there was the problem of Camberwell to be dealt with. My midnight experiment with his dead uncle's watch had provided sufficient data to convince Scotland Yard of the need for an official investigation, so I walked to the nearest post office and sent off the requisite telegrams, adding one to Bradley's of Oxford Street as an afterthought, for the delivery of a box of Havana cigars to my rooms, and another to Mrs. Hudson, asking her to obtain a good cut of beef for the supper I hoped to share with my friend. The last wire I sent was to Watson, requesting his presence at Baker Street at his earliest convenience. I even added the word "please", although doing so depleted my pocketbook to the point where transport via the Underground became a necessity and not merely an excuse.

When I am traversing London in my own persona, I prefer to use hansom cabs. The Underground, for all its convenience, is crowded, contaminated, and cacophonous. It reeks of coal smoke, and worse, despite the best efforts of the engineers to bring fresh air down to the lowest levels, and the trains are awash in a near-indelible olfactory assault. But with the station at my elbow, convenience won out.

In retrospect, I might have done better to walk. Some trouble down the line delayed the train. After a few minutes, I dipped into my pocket for my cigarette case and joined the other men at the end of the platform who were attempting to disguise the noisome fug of the station with the more aromatic scents of tobacco. I had nearly finished my cigarette before the train arrived. Naturally, the delay meant that there were dozens more people on the platform needing to be accommodated in the carriages, and I was unable to obtain a seat.

It was not the first time I had been so discommoded, and I took hold of the overhead strap, my thoughts still upon my case. But I was soon distracted by a distinctly unpleasant sensation emanating from my stomach and throat. At the time, I ascribed my increasing nausea to the presence of particularly odoriferous fellow-traveller, a gin-soaked relic being escorted to his destination by an anxious and apologetic grand-daughter. He had already befouled himself with vomit, and the heat of the railway car rendered the effluvia of the drying stains on his coat and trousers more potent. I was not the only passenger to decide that it was preferable to leave the train early.

The walk from Edgware Road to Baker Street is not an unpleasant one, and I have made it thousands of times, but on that occasion I found it interminable. My discomfort, far from abating, was increasing, and I could feel a black mood coming upon me. The September sun was near its apex, and hot with the last of summer, summoning all of London to crowd the pavements and throw obstacles into my path. I stopped in at my chemist's, to obtain some cocaine upon account. Despite my best intentions, I knew that I would never manage to play a proper host to Watson without fortifying myself with stimulants. Not when I wished nothing more than to fling myself into my bed and not emerge from under the covers for several days.

Despite that, I felt cruelly disappointed when I was met at the door by Mrs. Hudson, bearing a telegram, sent in her name, advising her that Watson would be unlikely to be attending dinner at Baker Street for any occasion in the near future. "You shall share that cut of beef with your friends, then," I told her, imperiously. "No sense in it going to waste."

"Are you certain, Mr. Holmes?" said she, peering up at me. "You look as if you could use a good meal. Have you had your breakfast?"

"No, not yet." I would no sooner have breakfasted at Camberwell's table than I would have juggled scorpions, even if I hadn't need to play the invalid to escape his attentions. "But I'm not hungry."

"Are you certain?" she asked, long acquaintance having inured her to my whimsical appetite. "You've not a spot of color on your face."

"It's only chalk," I told her, swiping my cheek with my glove and showing her the evidence. "I needed to convince someone that I was unwell."

She sniffed. "Oh," she said. "That trick again. I can see why the doctor is piqued, then. He's got far too much trouble with his missus to be having you heaping more on his head."

"Trouble?" I echoed, for Watson had mentioned nothing of the sort to me.

"She lost the babe she was carrying last week," Mrs. Hudson informed me. "That's twice their hopes have gone wrong. Did you not know?"

"No, I didn't," I said, pressing my fingers against the bridge of my nose to ease the ache that was increasing behind my eyes. This was Watson's brother all over again. Had he only mentioned the man's demise, I might never have been so tactless in my deductions over that wretched watch. Why did the man insist upon concealing his griefs from me! That Mrs. Hudson knew of his wife's condition and I did not I could ascribe to the efficiency of the servants' gossip, for the Watsons' scullery maid was sister to the boy-in-buttons presently peeping around the door at the end of the hall. But that Watson had not seen fit to mention anything to me was gall upon an old wound.

In a better state, I should have recognized immediately that my increasing indignation was a severe instance of the pot calling the kettle black. My own reserve concerning familial matters is so ingrained that I had not mentioned my brother Mycroft to Watson for near a decade, and I would have found a fellow lodger who babbled on about his antecedents incessantly so intolerable our association would not have lasted a month. But I can be as churlish as the next man when the black fit is on me. I managed to bid Mrs. Hudson good day with some courtesy, but as I trudged up the steps to my sitting room, I nursed a grievance against my old friend. It was with a certain satisfaction at the knowledge that Watson would disapprove that I prepared an injection of cocaine for myself. Let him grumble about my drug to his heart's content. It, at least, I could rely upon.

As soon as I had rolled down my sleeve and donned my dressing gown, I rang for the boy to bring me fresh water. I'd not dared trust anything in Camberwell's house, not even the pitcher, and my overnight vigil had been a dry one. I was feeling the lack more than usual, for within a half-an-hour I was ringing for water again.

This time, Mrs. Hudson herself came, bringing a tray of sandwiches and coffee for my luncheon. The sandwiches held no appeal for me, despite my lack of sustenance since the previous day. Instead, I poured myself some coffee and returned to my perusal of the newspapers which had accumulated in my absence. Mrs. Hudson bustled about, collecting my discarded attire for the laundry. "It's Billy's half-day," she reminded me. "And I've just had word from my niece that it's her time, so I'm away off. I'll take that cut of beef with me, and no need for you to pay for it, since you'll not even share in the broth. But there's some soup on

225

the back of the stove for your supper, if you'll be wanting it." She cast me a look of disapproval. My black moods were a trial to her, and a worse one since Watson was no longer there to take the brunt of them. "Although I suppose you'll prefer to stay up all night, scratching that fiddle of yours."

"Just as well there'll be no one in the house to listen to it," I answered testily. The coffee was inadequate, quite unlike Mrs. Hudson's usual quality of brew. It was water I wanted. I said as much, although I refrained from criticizing the coffee. She, with the reminder of Mrs. Watson's recent loss coloring her thoughts about her niece, would be less than tolerant of my foibles; and I, with the all-too fresh discovery that I could overstep even Watson's forbearance to no purpose, found myself disinclined to antagonize the woman who saw to my meals and comfort. She was a woman, after all, and plagued by the emotionality and frailties of her sex, particularly where infants were concerned.

She sniffed, but she took the pitcher, and went away, muttering that she couldn't see why I didn't just fill it at the washroom tap, like any sensible person. Still, when Billy turned up a few minutes later, the pitcher was full of water, cold from the kitchen, and there were slices of lemon floating in it for flavor. "Here you go, Mr. Holmes," he said, pouring me a glass before setting down the pitcher. He started to depart, pulling his cap out of his pocket to set on his curly head, but then paused to bite his lip and study me. "You feeling all right, sir? Want me to send for the Doctor?"

"The Doctor," I told him, "does not want to be sent for." But when his frown only deepened, I relented. "And I don't need him. A nap will no doubt put me to rights."

The child's brow cleared. "Oh, is that it? Didn't know being sleepy makes you thirsty." He shrugged, and raised a hand in farewell. "Anything else before I go, sir?" he asked, that much at least of his position's niceties he had absorbed, although it was clear he was aching to depart.

"No, thank you," I said, and leaned back in my chair, sipping at my water and listening as he clattered down the stairs and secured the front door before departing by way of the kitchen entrance.

The nap I had suggested would have been sensible, but I had forestalled it with the cocaine. I read for a while longer, until the chime of the bell below reminded me that I was expecting a delivery of cigars for Watson. The moment I moved from my chair, however, my headache returned, accompanied by disorientation. I stumbled to my desk on feet benumbed by sitting too long in one position, and fumbled open the locked drawer where I keep additional funds (and where, at one time,

Watson's checkbook had resided alongside my own). The thought of the stairs repelled me. I took the money to the window and threw up the sash.

A moment's negotiation with the delivery boy sent Watson's cigars in the direction of his practice, and I was left with a craving for tobacco of my own. The Persian slipper was empty, and too late for me to call the boy back and ask for a delivery of pipe tobacco. I turned for solace instead to my cigarette case.

But without the stench of the Underground to confuse my senses, I soon realized that the cigarette I lit tasted wrong. The first two draws weren't bad, but the third had an acrid aftertaste. Watson will tell you that I am no connoisseur of fine tobacco, and mean no injustice. I'll smoke whatever comes to hand. But these cigarettes were from Thompson, just down the end of the street, his strongest blend, and I had smoked thousands like them.

Obstinately, I took another puff. Had Thompson changed suppliers? Had the tobacco harvest been affected by less-than-ideal weather conditions? I couldn't decide, and stubbed the cigarette out before it was half-finished, thinking to examine the leaf under my microscope. But, try as I might, I could not find the ambition to remove myself from my chair and go fetch the instrument. The dizziness I had experienced when standing was in no small measure eased now that I was sitting still, but it had not vanished entirely.

Having no desire to faint from a lack of sustenance (which I had done, once, in Watson's presence, and had been chided for forever after), I reluctantly reached for one of Mrs. Hudson's sandwiches. The mustard tingled on my tongue and lips, and after a few bites I gave it up as a bad job. The coffee was already lukewarm, the newspapers dull. I felt dull myself, thickheaded and miserable.

But there was something niggling at the edges of my attention. Something I should be noticing despite the petty nuisances of my body. I floundered after it, wavering between frustration and apathy. And then my stomach began to protest even the few bits of food I had taken. Violently.

I scarcely made it to the hearth in time to save Mrs. Hudson's Turkish carpet. A second spasm followed the first, but by then I had secured the coal scuttle to use as a reservoir for the remaining contents of my stomach. I huddled over it, shivering, as I clung to consciousness. My feet were cold, my hands numb, my heartbeat fluttering weakly in my ears despite the panic in my head. Poison. It had to be poison. But how Camberwell had managed to poison me when I had not tasted a bite of food nor had a drop to drink during the entire time I had spent at his house I could not imagine.

How many hours until either Billy or Mrs. Hudson would return? Too many. I would have to send for Watson myself. But would he come? Or would he think yet another summons to a dying man was merely yet another ruse? I cursed myself for a fool. Watson would not come to me. I would have to go to him.

But when I tried to stand, a painful convulsion prevented me. Even when it passed I could barely find the strength to push myself back to the table and the water pitcher. The room seemed to dim, a phenomenon I attributed to constriction of the pupils, but I could not account for the way my hearing seemed to dim as well. Using the chair, I managed to get to my knees, to reach the water and bring it down where I could drink, but I was awkward, spilling as much as I drank. Somehow, I managed to bring the pitcher safely to the floor before I was forced to lie down by the increasing weakness of my limbs, but that accomplishment gave me little satisfaction. My stomach was roiling, warning me of more humiliation, and the water closet seemed a dozen miles away.

I might have done best to stay where I was and shout for help, but I did not think of that. While some of my thoughts were clear enough, the logic which would make sense of them was tangled, broken by the melancholy conviction that I deserved the misery of my present condition. I would have to leave evidence, if I could, clear enough even for Scotland Yard to avenge me. But first, were I to preserve any dignity whatsoever, I would have to reach the water closet.

Tangled logic, indeed, that had me dragging along the water pitcher as well as myself. Long past the point when my body had obviated any possibility of dignity, I kept on going, a few feet here before huddling against another convulsion. A few feet there, before resting my face against the smooth cool glass of the pitcher, in vague hope of penetrating the numbness which was obliterating my senses.

I had achieved the desired door, but had not yet managed to open it, when the vibration of footsteps through the floorboards under my cheek advised me that I was not alone. Distantly I heard Watson's cry of "Holmes! Good God!" and distantly I felt his hands upon me. But it was not until the pinprick against my arm and the warm sting of cocaine in my veins spread apart the veil of dismay that I could truly see him, crouched over me and gently tapping at my face. "Symptoms, Holmes. Tell me the symptoms."

He wished to know with what I'd been poisoned, of course. "Aconite," I told him, for the answer was sitting already in my head. "Or something like it."

"Numbness? Tingling? I can see that you're weak and purging."

I nodded confirmation.

"All right then," he said, stripping off his coat and rolling back his sleeves. "You're not going to enjoy this."

According to Squires, [1] the antidotes for aconite poisoning are emetics, as well as stimulants both internal and external. I knew that, intellectually, but I was not prepared for the reality of having that advice applied to my own person. Mustard, applied both within and without, creating an aversion to the stuff which promised to persist. Water until I could drink no more, and then syrup of *ipecacuanha* to bring it all back again, alongside whatever traces of the poison might remain. Capsicum liniment countering the tingle of the poison with a tingle of its own upon my hands and feet. And Watson, dumping me into the tub for a much needed bath and then wrapping me into nightshirt and dressing gown with a brisk medical efficiency before forcing me to walk back and forth between further assaults with various stimulants until I ached with exhaustion.

It was nearing midnight when he at last declared himself satisfied enough with my condition to prop me up on the settee and leave me alone for a few minutes. He returned with a mug of Mrs. Hudson's soup for me, and a mop and a bucket for himself.

"Can't you leave that for Billy?" I asked, when Watson began to clean up the mess by the hearth, for he was limping and I could see his hands shaking when he went to turn up the gas for light.

"It's part of the job," he answered absently. "Drink your soup, Holmes. You need some food inside you."

"Yes, if it will stay inside," I grumbled, but without heat. The fatigue of the day had left me with little ambition, but at least I no longer felt as if I were trapped in a morass, and I had Watson to thank for that. "Oh, do sit down and rest, my dear fellow. You look as tired as I feel."

He shook his head. "I'll finish this first. It will only smell worse if you leave it till morning."

I leaned back against the pillows he'd set around me and observed him at his work, knowing that further protest would be met with the same intransigence. Not since his marriage had I seen him in shirtsleeves, with patches of perspiration plain in the light and his hair rumpled from effort. It reminded me of summer nights, far too hot for comfort, when he and I had whiled away the sleepless hours with Bach and brandy and philosophical arguments of the most desultory sort. Watson had always grown cantankerous after two or three such nights in succession, and it was clear to me, now that I was truly looking at him, that he was suffering from a distinct deficit in the amount of sleep he required to thrive.

I could surmise the reason why.

"How is Mary?" I asked, and he startled like a fly-bitten horse, flinging up his head to stare at me.

"Mary?" he echoed, before taking himself in hand and returning to his task. "Why do you ask?"

"Mrs. Hudson told me."

"Ah." A glint of reflected light at the corner of his eye warned me to keep my silence while he assembled what he wanted to say. "That explains where the booties went, I expect. Mary must have sent them back, since Mrs. Hudson's niece is expecting a child any day now." He was mopping very carefully, although the hearth by now was as clean as it was going to be without a scrubbing brush.

"Today, actually," I said. "That's where she's gone."

"Ah." He gathered up the bucket and the mop. "I'd best go mop then."

"If you insist."

He vanished through the door and I closed my eyes, wondering how long it would be before he left Baker Street entirely. But when I opened them again he was still there, sleeping in the chair opposite with a book drooping from his fingers, although the clock on the mantelpiece was chiming three in the morning. The room had cooled and the fire was lit, as if to ward off the rumble of the thunder that had woken me. By its light, I could see threads of silver at Watson's temples that I had not taken note of before, and the curl of his arm, meant to ease an aching shoulder. I didn't wish to disturb him, but I was as stiff as if I'd taken a beating. The moment I tried to move, I couldn't help but make a noise. Instantly he was awake and on his feet, coming to bend over me.

His hand rested on my forehead. "No fever," he said. "And you're not too chilled. How do you feel?"

"I need to move," I told him.

He made no demur, but helped me disentangle myself from blanket and pillow, offering his support when I came to my feet. I needed it, indeed, for the first few minutes, but as my equilibrium returned I ventured a short distance on my own. When I caught the corner of the table for balance and turned to look, Watson was watching me with the tolerant amusement he might, were fate ever kind, bestow upon a tiny child taking a few first daring steps. "Not bad, Holmes," he said. "But you'd best avoid bending for a while longer."

Just the thought of changing the angle of my head made my gorge try to rise. "Yes, Doctor," I agreed, not even nodding. "How long, do you think?"

"A day or so." He came to offer me his arm. "Without a sample of the poison, or a clear notion of the dose, I can't be sure I've done everything I can to counteract it. Hence, I can't be certain of the length of your recovery."

"If you analyse the cigarettes in my case, you might find your answers," I replied. "I can't think of when Camberwell had opportunity to adulterate them, but neither can I think of any other way he might have managed to poison me."

"'When you have eliminated the impossible . . . .'" he quoted at me, a smile tugging at the corner of his mouth as he escorted me back to the settee. "I'll have someone from Scotland Yard do the analysis. I'd prefer not to risk accidentally destroying whatever evidence remains of the man's perfidy."

"Perfidy indeed," I grumbled as I took my place again. "The Persian slipper needs restocking, and if I can't smoke the cigarettes in my case, I shan't be able to smoke anything at all until morning."

"Food would be better for you," Watson said, mildly. "Or sleep. I should think you'd be off tobacco, after what's happened."

I extended a tremulous hand, as much to study for itself as to display the symptom. "It's tobacco I want, though. Or cocaine," I said, "And I know how much you disapprove of the latter."

"Not as much as I did," he admitted, tucking the blanket up around me. "The dose you took earlier today probably did much to counter the poison. But I'd as soon you didn't indulge in it at this time of night. Wait here a while and I'll see what I can do."

He may have stayed away longer than necessary, hoping I would slip back into sleep – I'm not entirely certain, as I spent the duration of his absence in aimless contemplation – but it seemed a long while. I cannot say that I was thinking to any purpose at all. And yet, when Watson returned with a tray that, thankfully, had a box of cigars upon it as well as food, I looked up to him and asked, "Why didn't you tell me?"

He didn't answer straight away, but made himself busy helping me sit up and resting the tray onto my knees. He uncovered my plate, revealing a coddled egg and a few slices of bread. "Eat that and I'll give you one of these," he said, reserving the cigars before retreating to the armchair with a plate of his own. We ate together, the silence broken by only the stuttering of our forks against our plates and the soft rataplan of rain against the windowpanes.

At last he set aside his repast. "I haven't told anyone. Well, Anstruther knows. He helped . . . he helped Mary, when it happened. I was away. With you, as it happens; it was the day we were sailing back from Uffa." He didn't look at me, but took up the box of cigars into his hands, tracing the design upon the cover.

"Shouldn't you be with her now?" I asked, gently.

"She's not at home. The specialist recommended that she make a complete change and rest until she's properly recovered, so he's sent her off to a convalescent hospital in Devon. The air's better there than in London." Watson shrugged, still not meeting my eyes. "The servants have been told that she's gone to visit a relation for a few weeks."

As Mary Morstan Watson had no relations in the world other than the man sitting opposite me, I could see that the lie chafed him. What kind of hospital was it, I wondered, that required such discretion? Had Watson's absence at the crisis precipitated a break in her mind as well as her health? It did not seem likely, given the lady's strength of character, but even an admirable fortitude can crack under tremendous strain. Still, that was neither here nor there when it came to my obligations to my friend. "I'm very sorry to hear it, old fellow. Please, accept my hospitality here at Baker Street until she returns. Your old room is always at your command, and it would be churlish of me to send you out into the storm."

He made a sound that was neither laugh nor sob. "Holmes . . . ." He ran a hand through his hair in exasperation and then held up the box of cigars, glaring at me with a smile quirking up the corner of his mustache. "Did you know that when I came here to return these to you, it was with the intention of never darkening your door again?"

I raised an eyebrow at the melodramatic phrasing. "I knew you were angry with me," I temporized.

"Furious," he said, a spark of that anger rising again to color his cheeks. "And I've come to a realization. I can either be your friend, or your physician, but not both. You'll have to choose."

He was utterly serious, despite the smile, and I realized just how grievous had been my transgression. Never in my life had I more needed a clear head, and seldom had I felt so muddled. "Considering that as my physician you just saved my life," I said, carefully, "the decision is not a light one. I don't suppose you would allow exceptions in cases of emergency."

"It's the cases of emergency that are the problem," he said and got to his feet, going to look out the window. "I know you think I have no gift for acting. The Culverton Smith business proved that."

"You haven't." I had to agree. Watson's honest face is one of his most admirable assets.

He turned to one side, watching me from across the room, so that that face was more in shadow than light. "Then why on earth did you send for me this morning?" he asked. "You can't have expected that I should carry on a deception in front of Camberwell if I can't act. And yet, the moment I took your pulse you knew that I would be able to tell that you hadn't been poisoned."

"Yet." I amended ruefully, and earned a chuckle from him. I was grateful for it. It seemed I had not damaged our fellow feeling beyond all hope. But he had asked a valid question. "This morning I wasn't hoping for a deception so much as any excuse at all to leave Camberwell's house. Whether or not you could play the physician retrieving the patient or the friend rescuing a comrade-in-arms was immaterial. I needed you to hustle me out the door before Camberwell could work up enough nerve to fetch out his pistol and put paid to any future interference in his plans."

"Couldn't you have told me as much?" Watson asked. "When young Simpson turned up on my patient's doorstep, all out of breath from running, and told me that you'd been poisoned, I nearly broke my neck trying to reach you in time. And I abandoned my patient – a dying man, Holmes, who was in great pain – even if I did have Simpson go to fetch Anstruther for him." Now he was angry again, and not only at me.

"You gave him morphine before you left," I said, when he fell silent. His shoulders fell, ever so slightly and told me the rest. "But he died, didn't he? Before you returned."

"Yes." Watson began to pace. "It was inevitable. Anstruther knew it as well as I, but still, neither of us was there. He died alone."

I let him pace as I thought. I couldn't honestly regret having sent for Watson. His presence truly had saved my life, and preserved the case against Camberwell into the bargain. But I regretted the concern I had caused him as he rushed across London to be at my side. Given his recent loss, and the impending loss of his patient, the fear of having me imperilled as well must have been bitter indeed.

It occurred to me that Watson was not the only compatriot I had affrighted. "You did tell Simpson that I was all right?" I inquired.

Watson nodded. "Yes. Not that you were, as it turned out."

"Yes, well, it's no more than I deserve, given the circumstances," I said. "I did not think my investigation would require quite so much improvisation. In any case, I apologize for summoning you unnecessarily. It shan't happen again."

"No?"

"No." I saw the thread of a compromise laid out before me. "If you will consider continuing to take care of such small matters concerning my health as happen to fall under your eye – I can hardly ask you to ignore them – then I shall impose upon another practitioner for any ailments which strike me in your absence."

"You won't send for me if you're ill?" he asked, and I heard uncertainty, and perhaps a bit of indignation in his voice. It seemed that he had not yet forgotten the way I had denigrated his skills during the Culverton Smith affair.

"If I send for you directly, you may be certain that it is a ruse," I said. "If a fellow physician sends for you, you may be certain that my condition is real. And I will have them send for you, my friend. I'd far rather trust your medical opinion than that of any dozen Harley Street quacksalvers."

He huffed his disbelief as he came over to collect my plate and set it aside. "That's laying it on a bit thick, old chap," he said, but I could see that he was pleased. He set his hand briefly against my forehead once again. "Still, I suppose, I could stay a few days at Baker Street to oversee your recovery. As a friend."

I patted his arm and lay back among the pillows, glad that his anger was dissipating once more. "Well, doctors are two-a-penny in London, you know. Besides, as my physician, you might feel it incumbent upon you to dissuade me from taking a cigar, but as my friend I think you might be willing to share."

He laughed and set about preparing a cigar for each of us. By the time we were settled and the soothing smoke was drifting about our ears, the lines had eased upon his face and his hands were no longer trembling. Cigars were more to Watson's taste than mine, but I drew another puff into my grateful lungs. "Thank you, Watson," I said. "These are excellent."

"You ought to know," he said. "You purchased them."

"At least I've managed to do one thing right in all of this," I said, thinking back over the past two days with dissatisfaction. Despite the comfort of the tobacco, my body ached as if I'd been trampled by angry horses. Camberwell had managed to poison me, despite my precautions. And I had come as close as I ever wished to driving an intractable wedge of misunderstanding between myself and my biographer. "Whatever reputation I might have for omniscience you may consider scattered to the winds, Watson. Remind me to never again take on a case for a man I suspect of being a murderer."

"Or a woman!" Watson agreed heartily. He leaned forward, resting his elbows on his knees, his eyes alight with curiosity. "Is that what happened? Camberwell hired you? Why on earth, if he had committed murder?"

"Because the murder would do him no good without his Uncle Joseph's last Will and Testament, and Camberwell hired me to locate it. Uncle Joseph had hidden the document somewhere in the house, leaving only a string of elaborate clues and ciphers. And I took the case, having underestimated both Camberwell's cleverness and his ruthlessness." Were it not that our positions were reversed, Watson in my chair and I upon the settee, we might be having the same sort of conversation we'd had a hundred times. Disastrous as the day had been, we had survived it with our friendship intact. Already I could see Watson's free hand creeping toward the pocket where he kept his writing tools. "Would you like me to tell you about it? With the benefit of hindsight we might, the two of us, see where I went wrong."

"Were I your physician," Watson said, glancing to the clock, "I would waste the next hour insisting that you ignore the case and try to get some sleep. But as I am your friend," he set aside his cigar and took out his pencil and notebook, "I know better. Go on, Holmes. And start at the beginning."

NOTE

1 – *Squire's Companion to the Latest Edition of the British Pharmacopoeia,* various editions.

The Lambeth Poisoner Case
by Stephen Gaspar

The first days of spring in the year 1892 found me very alone. Not only had I lost my close friend Sherlock Holmes the previous year, but this past winter had deprived me of beloved wife Mary. I will not go into the details of her passing, as they are very difficult for me to relate. Suffice it to say, that spring I had never felt so alone in my entire life.

Each day felt much like the one previous, and so the days, weeks, and months strung together like one long day of simply existing. I had taken a sabbatical from my practice, as I did not believe I was in the best frame of mind to make important medical judgements. I tried the best I could to carry on a normal existence. I saw regularly to my toilet and was dressed by breakfast. The only activity that gave me any satisfaction during that time was to take up my pen to record the adventures I had shared with my friend Sherlock Holmes.

One day toward the middle of April I sat at the table drinking my coffee and reading *The Times* when an article in the paper caught my attention. The article ran thus:

LAMBETH POISONER STRIKES AGAIN!

Mrs. Vogt, who runs a rooming house on 118 Stamford Street, was awakened the other night by a ghastly shriek that had issued from one of her lodgers, Alice Marsh. Mrs. Vogt found Miss Marsh writhing in agony upon the hallway floor.

In a room upstairs, Mr. Vogt found another female lodger, Emma Shrivell, was also suffering from which appeared to be the exact affliction. Though food poisoning was first suspected, the police have now attributed the deaths to strychnine poisoning.

Both Marsh and Shrivell are young women residing in South London and are known to be members of the legion of the lost.

Readers will remember that in October of last year, another women of dubious distinction, also living in South London, died of strychnine poisoning.

It is clearly evident that a killer is loose, poisoning the unfortunate nymphs of the pavement *in Lambeth.*

No one in London is soon to forget the tragic and horrific killing of several women in 1888 by the killer Jack the Ripper, who was never apprehended. So far police have not admitted any connection between those killings and these latest poisonings.

As I sat there reading my article, I shook my head, and I could have sworn I heard my wife's voice say, *That sounds like a story that would interest your friend, Mr. Sherlock Holmes.*

So certain that I had heard her say it, I found myself replying, "Yes, indeed it would."

With a start I looked across the table, but, of course, she was not there. A deep melancholia came over me. I knew the best medicine for my condition was some kind of work, something to occupy my mind, but I did nothing.

I thought little more about the newspaper article until several days later, when I received an unexpected visitor. Answering a knock upon my door, I was surprised to see a gentleman of my own profession, Dr. Joseph Harper. I had not seen Dr. Harper since my training days at St. Bartholomew's Hospital almost twenty years ago. The last I heard of him was that he had a good practice in Devonshire. He was an elderly gentleman, distinguished-looking, but whose face displayed deep concern.

"Dr. Watson, is it not?" he asked, hopefully.

"Dr. Harper, I am Dr. Watson. Won't you come in?" I said, holding the door open wide and ushering him inside.

He removed his hat and gave the interior a cursory glance, quickly assessing his surroundings.

"Pardon me for intruding," he said, "but I find I am in need of advice over a very delicate and personal matter."

I gave him a curious look, wondering why he would come to me, an almost perfect stranger, over a something of such importance. He glanced about uncomfortably.

"Please, come in and have a seat," I said, bringing him into the small sitting room off the front hall.

237

Joseph Harper sat with a heavy sigh. "Thank you for seeing me. I was not certain where else to turn. I thought of the police . . . ."

"I am most curious how you ended up on my doorstep," I said with a grin, hoping to put him mind to ease.

"After receiving the letter, I thought I would consult a detective, and I was given the name of one, Mr. Sherlock Holmes, and his Baker Street address, but upon arriving there, I was informed by the woman of the house . . . ."

"Mrs. Hudson."

"Yes, that is the name. Mrs. Hudson informed me the Mr. Sherlock Holmes was out of the country and she had no idea when he would return."

I had not the inclination to give Dr. Harper the details of Holmes's death. It occurred to me that Mrs. Hudson also did not want to stir up such a painful memory.

"The woman mentioned your name and that you had worked closely with Mr. Holmes. She gave me your address, so I decided to carry through," he said. "As a fellow medical man, I was hoping you might advise me."

"Advise you as to what?" I asked. "What is this letter of which you spoke?"

From inside his jacket, he removed an envelope, and after a slight hesitation, he handed it to me. The envelope was addressed to Dr. Joseph Harper in a thick, bold hand. London postmark. No return address. From inside the envelope, I removed several newspaper cuttings and a handwritten letter. I read the letter aloud.

Dr. Harper, Barnstaple

Dear Sir,

I am writing to inform you that one of my operators has indisputable evidence that your son, W.J. Harper, a medical student at St. Thomas's Hospital, poisoned two girls named Alice Marsh and Emma Shrivell on the 12th inst., and that I am willing to give you the said evidence (so that you can suppress it) for the sum of £1,500 sterling. The evidence in my hands is strong enough to convict and hang your son, but I shall give it to you for £1,500 sterling, or sell it to the police for the same amount. The publication of the evidence will ruin you and your family forever, and you know that as well as I do. To show you that what I am writing is true, I am

238

willing to send you a copy of the evidence against your son, so that when you read it, you will need no one to tell you that it will convict your son. Answer my letter at once through the columns of the London Daily Chronicle as follows:

– W. H. M. – Will pay you for your services. Dr. H.

After I see this in the paper, I will communicate with you again. As I said before, I am perfectly willing to satisfy you that I have strong evidence against your son by giving you a copy of it before you pay me a penny. If you do not answer it at once, I am going to give the evidence to the Coroner at once.

Yours respectively,
W. H. Murray

I briefly scanned the newspaper cuttings. They were cut from several different London newspapers, but they all dealt with the deaths Alice Marsh and Emma Shrivell, who died of strychnine poisoning a few weeks ago, and another woman named Ellen Donworth, who was also poisoned last October. I vaguely remembered reading about these terrible murders.

"Well, Watson, what do you think?" Harper asked anxiously.

"I assume your son is not associated with these deaths," I said.

Harper stifled a cry of indignation against my comment.

"He most certainly is not!" the older man proclaimed. "I do not have to ask my son about this to know he is in no way involved."

"And you do not know anyone named Murray?"

"No, I do not."

"It is obviously an alias," I said, absentmindedly. I was studying the letter. "Strange," I uttered.

"The entire matter is strange," Harper said.

"I was alluding to the letter," I said raising it to eye level. "It was written by a man, but this man is peculiar. He is not uneducated, but his repetitiveness and wording caused me to consider he is not worldly or cultivated, but may suffer from a type of fixation or perhaps a mania."

"Do you think he may be dangerous?"

"It is difficult to say."

Harper rose and paced nervously while gripping the back of his neck. "I can't have it. I simply cannot have it," he said. "This man could

239

ruin not only my life and my practice, but with these allegations, he could also destroy my son's future as a doctor."

"So part of what Murray writes about your son is true? Your son *is* a medical student at St. Thomas's Hospital?"

"Yes, that part is true, though how this man knows that is a mystery."

"He may know your son."

"It does not rest easy in my mind that my son would know such a person." Joseph Harper sat down again, a bit more composed. "What do you think I should do, Watson?"

"You have several options," I said. "You can ignore it and see what happens next. You can respond and see what follows."

"What do you suggest?"

"I suggest you go to the police. Let them handle it."

The man bit his lower lip and turned staring at the floor. "I am not sanguine about asking the London police to get involved. Can't you do something?"

"Me? What can I do?"

"According to the woman on Baker Street, you have worked quite closely with Holmes, the detective. Can you not look into it for me? Perhaps you can find this man and see what his game truly is."

The pleading desperation in his voice was reflected in his tired eyes and quivering chin. I assured him that I would do what I could.

After bidding goodbye to Joseph Harper, I went out. I took a cab from Kensington and travelled east past Victoria Station, Westminster Cathedral, and across the Thames to Lambeth. I had the address where Dr. Harper's son, Walter, was staying, a modest rooming house on Lambeth Palace Road. It was a nice, neat house close to the river, and not far from St. Thomas's Hospital where young Harper was training.

I walked up to No. 103, and my knock was answered by a pleasant-looking middle-aged woman. I introduced myself and she said she was Miss Sleaper, the landlady. I told her I was a friend of Dr. Joseph Harper and was here to see his son, Walter.

Miss Sleaper raised her hand to the side of her mouth as if she had just heard a minor tragedy. "Young Mr. Harper is not in at the present moment, but I do expect him presently. Would you care to come in and wait for him?"

I kindly accepted and stepped inside the house. It appeared as nice and neat on the inside as the outside. Miss Sleaper led me into a sitting room on the main floor. Aside from the comfortable-looking chairs and a settee were the usual bric-a-brac on shelves and a vases holding fresh spring flowers.

Miss Sleaper made tea, and through polite conversation, I endeavoured to learn what I could about Walter Harper.

He had lodged at the Lambert Palace house for over two years while he trained at St. Thomas's, and probably would be leaving soon, once he qualified. He was a quiet, amiable young man who had his own latchkey and came and went sometimes without notice.

Did he entertain young ladies? No, not in Miss Sleaper's house.

Did he go out much in the evenings? It was difficult to say, since he had his own latchkey.

Did he go out much for meals? Not very often, for Miss Sleaper provided breakfast and dinner if her lodgers so desired it.

Do you happen to know his father, Dr. Joseph Harper? No, she never met the gentleman.

"I do believe I have seen a photograph of young Mr. Harper and his father," she said smiling. "I, of course, clean Mr. Harper's room and have noticed a very nice photograph of his family that he keeps on the mantelpiece. I have a picture of young Mr. Harper here in my album."

She went over to a small table and picked up the album off a beaded velvet mat.

"I like to have photographs of all my lodgers," Miss Sleaper said as she flipped through to the end and showed me a picture of Walter Harper. It was taken at the seaside. Harper was dressed in a tweed jacket and a straw boater hat.

It seemed like a long wait for Harper, as Miss Sleaper talked constantly. Finally the young man arrived.

Walter J. Harper was an average-looking man, slight and pale. His brown mustache lent him a mature countenance, but I saw little resemblance between Walter and his father.

I introduced myself and offered my card, which was met with a bit of confusion. I told Walter how I had known his father during my training days, and when I heard the name Harper from another doctor just by chance, I decided to pay Joseph Harper's son a courtesy visit.

"I am just about to put dinner on," Miss Sleaper said. "Would you care to stay, Dr. Watson?"

"That does sound delightful, Miss Sleaper, but I would like to pass on your hospitality and take Walter out for dinner, it he is agreeable."

"Thank you, Doctor. I would like that very much," he said. "I need to go to my room for a few minutes, and then I will be right down."

Wishing to remain in the general vicinity, I decided not to take Harper across the river, but enquired of him if he had a favorite restaurant nearby. He suggested the Dominion House.

During dinner, I gave Harper some background on how I knew his father, but mentioned nothing about his visiting me that very day.

"Strange that you have not seen my father in so long, but decided to look me up," Walter Harper said quite innocently. His comment did not betray any suspicion.

"To be truthful," I said, knowing that it was only partly truthful, "I was speaking with someone just recently, and the poisoning of some women in the area came into the conversation. I was speaking with a medical man and somehow your name came up."

"Truly? In what context?"

"Only that you lived in the area and are attending St. Thomas."

"Who was this medical man?" he asked.

"A man named Murray. W.H. Murray. Do you know him?"

Harper cocked his head. "No, I do not believe so."

"What do you think about these awful poisonings? You must be familiar with the story, since they occurred around Lambeth," I said.

He nodded thoughtfully. "It is a horrendous act, made even more so, so close to home."

"Did you know any of the women who were poisoned?"

He shook his head. "The bodies ended up at St. Thomas's. Dr. Wyman, the house physician, received the last two. One arrived at the hospital dead, and the other died soon after arrival."

"Do you know if the police have any leads?"

"Not as far as I know. The only thing that seems to link these women is that they were all wandering beauties of the night," he said with a knowing look.

"I am certain that you are not familiar with that sort of element, but if you had to guess, where would you say these types of women can be found?"

Walter Harper looked across the table at me and smiled slyly.

"Come with me. I will show you."

The Canterbury Music Hall sits at 143 Westminster Bridge Road. It is a large three-thousand seat building that features a variety of entertainment from comedians to classical singers. A perpetual gaiety exudes from the place. Mirrors and polished brass reflect the glittering globes of the gas lamps. Thick Persians carpets line the floors, and large oil paintings decorate the walls. The place is the epitome of gaudy excess. Even when there is no one on the stage, the entire place is noisy with laughter and deafening chatter. That day, despite the tall ceilings the air felt damp and hot, and smoke hung heavy throughout.

Harper and I found a small table and ordered drinks. We watched men dressed in ties and top hats, and women in tight jackets, flowing skirts, and hats with feathers. There was much carousing with blatant womanizing, amid excessive eating and drinking. Here was a modern-day Gomorrah where every carnal pleasure could be realized. It was a veritable hunting ground for the Lambeth Poisoner.

"If you were looking for wayward women, Dr. Watson, then there they are," Harper said.

"Which ones?"

"All of them, I would wager. They were either brought in here by men who found them on the street, or they came in looking for men."

"Do you think the women who were murdered frequented The Canterbury?"

"They may have."

We sat drinking for several minutes without saying anything. Finally Harper asked, "What type of man are you looking for, Doctor?"

"Who said I was looking for a man?"

"Aren't you?"

The main reason I wished to meet Walter Harper was to determine if he were indeed the Lambeth poisoner, as the letter suggested. I did not believe he was, but I could be mistaken.

"I must admit that I am more than curious about the identity of this man," I said.

"So are the police, but they have not made an arrest."

"Maybe the police are looking in the wrong places," I said, gesturing about the room.

"Are you saying he could be here? What sort of man are we looking for?"

I had given it some thought. "I believe he is a man with some medical training. It would take a medical man to know about strychnine and be able to have access to it."

"That could fit over a hundred men, including you and me," Harper said.

"That is true, but this man, I believe, is mentally disturbed. He has a hatred toward women. Not all women, mind you. Look at his victims. All of them are unfortunate young women. He has little or no regard for them, and may not even see them as human. The man might appear quite ordinary, and can function in society despite his mental problems."

"That still does not narrow the field very much," Harper said.

I shrugged.

We stayed at The Canterbury longer than we should have, before leaving the warm moist stale vapours of the music hall and stepping into the cool fresh air of the evening. Harper had hold of my arm and we looked for a cab.

243

The streets were busy with people. A man called out Harper's name and approached us. He was dressed in a top hat and black coat, and was accompanied by a young woman on his arm.

"Good evening, Harper. Good to see you," the man said jovially, thrusting out his right hand. He gripped Harper's hand and pumped it vigorously. Then he turned to me.

Harper introduced the man as Dr. Neill. He shook my hand while staring at me with a foolish grin half-hidden by a thick dark mustache. Behind his wire-rimmed glasses, his eyes glared at me slightly askew. I could not help but think that either the man had too much to drink that night, or I had.

After a few more words, the man and his escort walked down the street.

The cab dropped Harper off at his Lambeth Palace Street room and took me home. I had fallen asleep and the cab driver had to rouse me when we reached my residence.

I barely remember going to bed that night, and I arose late the next morning. I returned to South London to continue the investigation. After some inquiries, I found that the victim of the first poisoning from last October had been staying at 8 Duke Street, off of Westminster Bridge Road. I found Duke Street to be dark and dirty and No. 8 was a rooming house, but not as well-kept as the Miss Sleaper's on Lambert Palace Road. The woman who owned the house, Mrs. Collins, came to the door, and when I said I was inquiring into the death of one of her past lodgers she gave a shudder. She wore a faded and worn housedress, partly covered by a faded and worn apron. Upon her greying hair was tied a headkerchief. She spoke to me through the partly opened doorway.

"Ooh, that was horrible, that was," she said with a grim expression on an already careworn face. "I'm not likely to forget that night. Poor Ellen . . . . Ellen Donworth for that was her name. A good girl. Young, only nineteen. It was horrible sir, horrible. Two men carried her in from the street. They say she collapsed near Waterloo Road, and she was able to tell them where she lived. She was in awful pain, sir, awful pain. We had her on her bed upstairs. The whole house was roused. She was in agony. Ooh, I'll never forget how she cried out and writhed in agony. We sent for a doctor and they took her to hospital, but she died. Poisoned they say. I'll never forget it."

"No way of knowing who poisoned her?" I asked, not expecting an answer.

"No, sir. She was never able to say."

"Did you know with whom Miss Donworth went out? Who her friends were?"

Mrs. Collins brought a finger to her chin in thought. "You know who might know more about Ellen is Annie Clements."

"Annie Clements? Who is she?"

"Annie and Ellen were good friends."

"Where might I find her?"

"Right upstairs. She's one of my lodgers. Wait here. I'll get her for you."

I was left standing on the stoop for several minutes. Then the door opened, and standing in the aperture was a sleepy young woman in her nightdress.

"Annie Clements?" I said. She nodded. "Miss Clements, my name is Dr. John Watson, and I am interested in the death of Ellen Donworth. Mrs. Collins told me you and Ellen were good friends. Could you tell me anything about the men who called on her?"

"They didn't exactly call on her," Miss Clements said. "What I mean to say, her men did not come to the house."

"Did you ever meet any of the men with whom Miss Donworth went out?"

"There was Ernest Linnell. Ellen took up with him for a while. She sometimes went by the name Ellen Linnell, but they were on the outs for weeks before . . . before Ellen . . . died."

"Do you think Ernest Linnell could have poisoned Miss Donworth?"

"I don't know. I don't think so."

"Did you and Ellen ever . . . go out together?"

The young woman looked affronted. "Not the way you think. I don't do that sort of work. I have a day job. Sure, it's only as a cleaning woman, but it's good honest work."

"Of course it is. I meant no offence, Miss Clements," I said. "Do you remember anything about that last night that your friend went out?"

Annie Clements thought for a brief moment, and then spoke slowly as the memory passed before her mind.

"That morning, I was getting ready to go to work. Ellen showed me a letter that had arrived by the first post. She told me the letter was from a gentleman she had met. The letter told her to meet him outside the York Hotel, in the Waterloo Road. He added something strange."

"What was strange?"

"The man told Ellen to bring his letter with her to prove that she received it. Neither of us understood why he asked her to do that."

"The letter is evidence. He did not want it left behind."

"So you believe that this man who wrote the letter poisoned Ellen?"

"It is very likely."

The young woman released a soft gasp.

Annie Clements could not tell me the man's name, nor give me a description of him – only that Ellen Donworth described him as a gentleman.

I left Duke Street and headed for the scene of the most recent poisonings.

Stamford Street runs between Waterloo Road and Blackfriars Road. The street's past elegance is evident from its terraced houses, fluted columns out front, and round-headed windows. But many of the houses appear unkempt, unwashed, and have fallen into decay. The road surface is cracked or missing in places, and garbage clogs the gutters.

I knocked on the door of No. 118, and it was answered by a man whom I took to be Mr. Vogt. I remembered him from the newspaper article.

"Mr. Vogt," I began quite amiably, "My name is Dr. John Watson, and I am here to inquire into the deaths – "

"I don't care who you are!" Vogt said angrily. "I ain't got time to answer questions from every gadabout looking for gruesome gossip about those poor girls! Now you get yourself out of here, Mr. Busybody, before I set the dog on your heels!"

With that, Vogt slammed the door in my face.

I hadn't wanted to go to the police, but I had little choice if I wanted to gather any more information. After some discreet inquiry, I was directed to Inspector Harvey of the Lambeth Division.

He agreed to see me in his office. He was a burly man of medium height, with light brown hair and eyes. His face was wide, with wide features, and he wore a grim expression. He did not appear happy to see me, and he looked at my card and read it aloud: "'*Dr. John H. Watson, MD*'. What can I do for you, Dr. John H. Watson, MD?"

I was not certain why he had taken such a condescending tone toward me, but I was not going to let that dissuade me.

"Inspector Harvey, I was wondering if you might give me some information on the strychnine poisoning case involving the two women of Stamford Street."

"So, you would like me to discuss the Lambeth Poisoning case, would you, Dr. Watson? Plan on solving the case yourself, Doctor? Or are you here gathering information for Mr. Sherlock Holmes?"

"Inspector Harvey, let me assure you – "

Harvey held up a staying hand and, opening the top desk drawer he removed something, dropping it on his desk so that I could see it. It was the April edition of *The Strand Magazine*. I believed it carried the story of "The Noble Bachelor".

"You are *that* Dr. John H. Watson, aren't you?" Harvey asked.

"Yes, Inspector, I am."

He picked up the magazine and leafed through it.

"I never miss an issue. I particularly like your stories about your friend the . . . what did he call himself? 'The world's first consulting detective'. These stories make every policeman appear incompetent or foolish."

"If that is true, Inspector, then I apologize," I said sincerely. "Let me assure you, I am not here because of Sherlock Holmes, but I am interested in learning what I can about this bad business."

"You're not here related to the late Mr. Holmes?"

"No, I am not."

Harvey studied me briefly, then brought out a folder from the same top desk drawer and opened it. He scanned through some notes in the folder and read from them.

"Shortly before three o'clock on the morning of April 12th, Constable Eversfield was called to 118 Stamford Street by Mr. Vogt to see to one of his lodgers, Miss Alice Marsh, age twenty-one. Miss Marsh, in her bed-gown, was in considerable distress, screaming in pain, bathed in sweat, and shivering and shuddering uncontrollably. Just then another lodger, Emma Shrivell, age eighteen, cried out from the floor above and was found in the exact same condition.

"Constable Eversfield had brought a cab to the house, and both young women were rushed to hospital. When they arrived at St. Thomas's, Alice Marsh was dead. The house physician, Dr. Wyman, treated the other woman, Emma Shrivell, but by eight o'clock that morning, the young woman died. Both deaths were attributed to strychnine poisoning.

"Constable Eversfield attempted to question the women, even in their death throes, hoping for a clue. Their responses were hard to understand. The young women were able to say that they had eaten tinned salmon and beer.

"I personally went to the house and confiscated the open can of salmon. It was tested, but there was no trace of strychnine."

I had listened intently to Harvey's report. "Were the women able to say anything else?"

The inspector scanned the report and shook his head. "They were both in terrible pain. Most of what they said was indecipherable. There was reference to someone named Fred and some long thin pills."

"Was this Fred clue looked at?"

"No. Fred is likely an alias."

"Probably. The question remains: Why has Fred killed these three women?"

Harvey gave a strange look. I asked him if there was something. Harvey hesitated thoughtfully before he spoke.

"What I tell you now, Dr. Watson, is in the strictest confidence. Very few people know this, and I am asking you not repeat it. We now believe the Lambeth Poisoner has murdered *four* women. In late October, Matilda Clover, who resided at 27 Lambeth Road, became ill. She had been warned about her excessive drinking, and even after her death, it was assumed she died of epileptic seizure, ending in heart failure brought on by alcoholic poisoning. Her body was recently exhumed, and after a close examination, the true reason for her death was discovered."

"Strychnine poisoning," I said.

Harvey nodded.

"So that is four women."

"And there will be more unless we stop him."

"I agree."

We sat there in silence, knowing we had not one clue on how to identify the Lambeth Poisoner.

"I am curious about something," I said. "It may be important, or it may mean nothing."

"What is it?"

"There were two poisonings in October, and two poisonings in April. What could that mean? Why wait? What did he do for almost six months?"

"It's a good question, Doctor, but I don't have the answer."

I left Inspector Harvey with the assurance that if I learned anything about the Lambeth Poisoner, I would let him know immediately.

I hadn't told Harvey about the letter Dr. Joseph Harper had shown me, nor did I tell him that the younger Harper could be a suspect. I wished to eliminate Walter Harper, but truthfully I could not. I began to think about the man who had written the letter to Joseph Harper and had signed his name Murray. Was he simply a blackmailer, or did he know something? Did he know who the killer was, or *was* he the killer?

I decided to speak with young Harper again.

It was late in the afternoon when I arrived at 103 Lambeth Palace Road. Miss Sleaper appeared pleased to see me again. She invited me in for tea and informed me that Walter Harper was not at home, but that I was welcome to wait for him.

Miss Sleaper joined me for tea and was very talkative about her lodgers. She held Walter Harper in the highest regard.

I asked her if she had any other medical students lodging with her. She told me she has had many students in the past, but presently Walter Harper was her only student.

"Of course, I do not count Dr. Neill," she said absently.

"Dr. Neill?"

As if on cue, a man appeared in the aperture of the sitting room. Both Miss Sleaper and I started slightly at his appearance. He was of average height, but that was the only thing average about him. His hair was thin, and he was noticeably balding on top of his tall domed skull. He wore small wire-rimmed spectacles, but the dark eyes behind them were askew. His eyes and the strange grin beneath his thick mustache gave him an odd, almost manic appearance. He was well-dressed, but his clothes looked out of place with the man himself, as if someone had dressed up a smiling hyena or a grinning baboon. It was not a very kind observation, but it was my personal impression.

"Dr. Neill," Miss Sleaper said, half embarrassed, as if she had been caught speaking out of turn. "This is Dr. Watson. Dr. Watson, this is one of my best lodgers, Dr. Thomas Neill.

I rose and took a step toward the man, and he approached me, his eyes on my face as if he were studying me intently.

We shook hands and I said, "But surely we have met before."

"Have we?" Neill said slowly, as if suspecting some deception.

"It was only last night," I said. "It was outside The Canterbury. I was with Walter Harper. I am afraid I'd had too much to drink. My apologies."

"Outside The Canterbury with Walter Harper," he repeated absently. "Yes, I do recall." Then he smiled, but it did not appear genuine.

"You were with a young woman," I added.

The smile fell from his mouth. Neill had been chewing gum, but his jaw stopped moving. The man still had a grip on my hand, and it tightened.

I pulled my hand away and he released his grip.

"Dr. Watson, would you care to come up to my room where we can talk?" he asked.

"That is very kind of you," I said. I turned to Miss Sleaper and thanked her for the tea.

I followed him up the stairs to his room. He led me to a small living room with an adjoining door that presumably led to his bedroom. Dr. Neill's living room contained two chairs on either side of a fireplace, with a small table between the chairs. In the corner sat two trunks. Standing in another corner was a narrow hall tree, upon which hung a top

249

hat and a black coat. Against the far wall was a narrow window with a partially obstructed view of the river.

"Please have seat Dr. Watson," Neill said. "Feel free to smoke."

We sat, and Neill regarded me with those strange eyes, his jaw moved repetitively.

"You are American, Dr. Neill?" I said.

"Now why would you say that?"

"The chewing gum . . . and your accent. They are both American."

He gave me a crooked grin.

"I am Canadian. My family immigrated to Canada from Scotland when I was a wee lad. I graduated McGill. Do you know it?"

"I am afraid not."

"A fine university. First rate."

"So, do you have a practice here in London?"

He stopped chewing his gum

"I was doing some postgraduate work at St. Thomas's, but on my last visit back to Canada I was offered a job as the London agent for the Harvey Company."

"When were you Canada?"

"This past winter. I only returned to London in April."

"The Harvey Company?" I asked.

"Yes. The G. F. Harvey Company is a large and prestigious drug company of Saratoga Springs, New York. Let me show you something."

Neill sprang from his chair and entered his bedroom. He returned with a wide grin, carrying a salesman's polished wooden sample case, which he placed on the floor in front of me. Like a boy unwrapping his gift at Christmas, Neill opened the case to reveal its contents. The inside was divided into three sections. Over fifty small bottles lined the three sections, held in place by leather straps.

"Isn't it elegant?" Neill said, kneeling by the case and running his hands over it lovingly.

"What do you have in there?" I asked.

"They are samples only, you understand . . . medicinal doses."

"Medicinal doses of what?"

"All types: Cocaine, opium, morphine . . . strychnine."

"It is a very nice case," I said.

Neill closed it up and took it back into his room.

He came back in and stood before me. "Wait here and I will get us some drinks." He rushed out of the room and I heard him descend the stairs.

I rose from my chair and looked about the room. I went over to the bedroom door, opened it quietly, and looked inside. There was a small brass bed. The brass had long tarnished. A lamp sat upon a small table next to the bed. A portmanteau stood partly open in one corner of the room. There was another trunk. I did not see the wooden sample case. It was probably kept under the bed. I stepped into the room. I thought I heard Dr. Neill returning. I quietly closed the door and gingerly stepped over to the mantel. Next to it was a waste basket filled with newspapers. I took them out to look at them. There was copies of the *Evening Monitor*, *Echo*, *Globe*, *News,* and *Star*. Just then, Neill returned with a small tray holding two glasses.

"You certainly like to keep up on the news," I told him, dropping the papers back into the basket.

"Yes," was all that he said. He put the tray on the table and stood facing me with a glass in each hand.

"Have you been reading about the poisonings?" I asked. "I hear three women have died."

"I heard it was four," he said, with a playful grin.

"Four!" I exclaimed. "Are you certain?"

"I am positive."

"Four women. Wherever did you hear that?"

"Oh, I have my sources, Dr. Watson." He handed me a glass.

I took the glass. He held his up. "Cheers," he said.

I raised the glass, but there was something in the man's face that made me stop. I was shaken with a sudden horror as if I were looking at evil. Things came together in my mind, and I believed I was onto the answer.

The man regarded me questioningly as if wondering why I was not taking a drink. The hand that held my glass began to tremble. I did not know what to do or say. In a clumsy attempt to look clumsy, I spilled my drink.

We were both startled and I repeatedly apologized as he attempted to mop us the spilled drink. As he did so, I fled the room, down the stairs, and out of the house. I ran down Lambeth Palace Road and was fortunate enough to get a cab. I could not help but keep glancing behind me, wondering if Dr. Neill was pursuing me. Even when I stood in Inspector Harvey's office, I did not feel totally safe.

I told Harvey how Dr. Joseph Harper had come to see me yesterday and showed me the blackmail letter which started my investigation into the matter.

"I think you should definitely keep your eye on Dr. Thomas Neill at 103 Lambeth Palace Road." I said, and gave the inspector a description of Neill.

"I hope you do not suspect this man because he is peculiar-looking," Harvey said.

"His strange appearance is only a small part of it," I said. "For one thing, he is a fellow lodger of the very man accused in the letter. For another, Neill has medical background and is in possession of a sample case containing strychnine. When you and I spoke earlier, we discussed that there were no poisonings between November and March. Neill informed me that he was not in London during much of that time. I found numerous different newspapers in his room. When Dr. Harper showed me the blackmail letter, also in the envelope were clippings from some of the same newspapers that Neill reads. Now this is the one that may be most damning. When I mentioned to Dr. Neill that three women had been poisoned, he told me he knew it was *four*. How could he know that?

"None of these things by themselves add up to much, but taken together, I believe that he presents a viable suspect."

Inspector Harvey looked grim and nodded slowly. "Thank you, Doctor. We will certainly follow up and keep an eye on this man."

After some fine police work, Dr. Neill was arrested, and it was discovered that his true name was Thomas Neill Cream. The mill of the gods and the British justice system grind slowly. When Thomas Cream finally came to trial, the man's horrid past was revealed. It was discovered that he was also responsible for the deaths of women in Canada and in the United States, where he served a ten-year prison sentence. Cream had not only written the blackmail letter to Dr. Harper, but he had written letters to several people. Some were blackmail letters, and some were letters accusing other individuals of the murders. Cream had also lied about working for the G. F. Harvey Company. He had purchased the wooden sample case on his own.

Dr. Cream was put on trial solely for the death of Matilda Clover, the woman originally thought to have died from alcohol poisoning. A London court found him guilty of her death, and he was executed on November 15, 1892.

For my part in the case, it had been a chilling experience, one where I felt I had looked the devil in the face. I hoped to soon forget it.

A week or so later, I found myself again alone at my breakfast table drinking my coffee. There was another article in *The Times* about murders and the trial of Dr. Thomas Neill Cream. I shook my head at the tragedy of it all.

I could have sworn I heard my friend Sherlock Holmes say, *"When a doctor goes wrong, he is the first of criminals."*

So certain was I that I'd heard him say it that I looked across the table with a start. But, of course, he was not there.

The Confession of
Anna Jarrow
by S. F. Bennett

It was on the morning of the 15th April, 1894, that I returned to Baker Street to find that Sherlock Holmes had had a visitor in my absence. Inspector Tobias Gregson, doughty, steely-eyed, and greying around the temples, nodded to acknowledge my presence, not daring to interrupt Holmes's discourse whilst he was in full flow. Beholding this familiar scene, it was as though the interruption of the last three years had never happened. We had simply picked up where we had left off, and much the better for it.

"The discrepancy between the height of the victim and the length of the ligature should give you evidence enough for a conviction," Holmes was concluding as I laid down my parcels. "And if old Fazakerley gives you any trouble, you would do well to remind him of that old idiom: *Man proposes, but God disposes*. That should satisfy his Biblical sense of justice."

"Well, I never. It seems as plain as a pikestaff when you put it like that, Mr. Holmes," said Gregson, stooping to up gather up his hat. "It's just as well you returned when you did, or this fellow might have got away with it."

Holmes offered him a faint smile. "We are none of us infallible."

"Even you?"

"I have my moments."

Gregson allowed himself a snort of laughter before a more sombre expression took shape on his features. "That reminds me," said he soberly. "Anna Jarrow was released a fortnight ago. I thought, under the circumstances, you'd want to know."

I fancied I perceived a slight stiffening of Holmes's back, as though the mere mention of the name had sent a shaft of bitter remembrance down his spine.

"Did she say anything?" said he, turning back to Gregson.

"Not she, Mr. Holmes. Wild horses wouldn't prise that information out of her. She kept her counsel during her time in prison and never a word from the fellow. I don't know whether to admire her loyalty or think her a fool. All the same," said he, "we're keeping a watch on her movements, in case he tries to make contact. There's a fish I'd like to see squirming on a hook."

"I take it your observations have thus far proved unsuccessful."

Gregson nodded thoughtfully. "She's never been out of our sight for a moment. And I've had good men on the case, I can't fault them. Her letters have been intercepted and I've had several of the lads going through the dustbins. But there's not been a word from him."

Holmes accepted this news with equanimity. "Has a direct appeal been made to the lady? It may be that she was waiting for word from him on her release. A slight, after all this time, may prove to be the necessary incentive."

The inspector looked unconvinced. "You're welcome to try, seeing as how you have some personal interest in the business. To tell you the truth, I can't justify keeping men on the case without something to show for it. Well, here's her address. It's a lodging house in Portsoken."

With the interview at an end, Gregson left. Holmes considered the piece of paper before thrusting it into his pocket and turning briskly to me.

"Watson, you are busy this morning?"

"Not at all."

"Then if you would be so good as to accompany me, my dear fellow, I would be much obliged. I can tell you about the case on the way."

Once we were installed in a hansom cab and heading eastwards, Holmes began to elucidate.

"As you may have deduced," he began, pulling on his gloves against the chill of the day, "the Jarrow case is something of a thorn in my flesh. One I class amongst my failures, certainly."

"The name does not sound familiar," I admitted.

"You were abroad at the time of the trial, Watson, so we may excuse your ignorance. Anna Jarrow was found guilty of being an accessory after the fact in the death of her husband. But for my intervention, she would have hanged for the crime of murder."

"That does not sound like a failure."

Holmes shook his head. "Mrs. Jarrow has spent fourteen years in prison because of her refusal to name her accomplice. The lady's silence has been absolute and, despite my best efforts, I have been unable to put a name to the man. Such results are not to be applauded. They are what might be expected of a second-rate detective, who has barely mastered the ability to tell one footprint from another."

"But if the lady would not tell, I can hardly see why you would blame yourself. That you saved her from the gallows must count for something."

My companion released a long, troubled breath. "I have had many years to construct a theory as to the lady's silence. If she were to at least confirm my suspicions, that would be sufficient. Mysteries are my natural enemies, Watson, and this has eluded me for too long. Well, well, we shall see."

No sooner had the words left his mouth than the cab came to a shuddering halt. We were almost at the end of Oxford Street, and up ahead I saw a thick cluster of horses and cabman. Impatient passengers poked their heads from cab windows to shout at the medley of men who were attempting to clear the road of broken barrels from a brewer's dray.

"It appears we have time enough for the telling of the tale," said Holmes with forced joviality. "If you wish to hear it, that is. I am aware dredging up one's past is an indulgence which others may find tedious."

On the one hand, I had little choice, captive audience as I was. On the other, I was full of curiosity. I knew little of Holmes's cases in the days before I had become his biographer, and the times when he had proved less than reticent on the subject were few and far between. His early life had been as a closed book, seemingly sealed forever after the events in Switzerland. To find myself in a cab with him, with little to do but to listen to the details of a case from years before, was something which only a few weeks ago I could have only imagined with the deepest of regret. I would have listened had he conversed on the most banal subject in the universe and counted myself fortunate for the experience.

"On the contrary, I would be most interested to learn more about the case."

A smile of deep satisfaction took shape on his features. "Capital!" said he above the shouts and growing dissatisfaction of the waiting throng. He settled back in the seat and let his eyelids droop as he called upon his memories.

"Well, then, the case began for me in somewhat irregular fashion. It was in the early hours of the 7th November, 1879 that I awoke in my Montague Street rooms with the distinct impression that I was not alone. I was confirmed in that suspicion when I perceived a man standing by the open window at the side of my bed. I was less conscious of my need for security in those days, so that my pistol was out of reach. As it transpired, my concerns were unfounded, for my visitor had come, not to harm, but seeking my help.

"'Mr. Holmes?' said the fellow as I put a match to the candle. 'Mr. Shelduck Holmes?'

"'Sherlock,' I corrected him. 'But close enough.'

"'My apologies,' said he. 'You'll have to forgive my calling on you unannounced, but I've been told you do right by the likes of us.'

"In the yellow glow of the candlelight, I perceived a bull-necked man of about fifty years of age, dark-eyed and grizzled haired with a vigorous physique. In any other setting, his rough familiarity might have been vaguely menacing. To my mind, however, he seemed troubled to the point of desperation, so much so, that his manner appeared overly ingratiating.

"'I assume you require my assistance,' I replied as I rose and donned my dressing gown. 'I dare say the contents of my purse would hardly be worth your time or effort.'

"My visitor started. 'Who told you?'

"'That you are a burglar by profession? No one. It was a logical deduction based on the facts at hand. You have lockpicks in your pocket – not the first thing a man thinks to take with him when leaving the house, unless he has a particular purpose in mind. If you wish to pass undetected in the future, I suggest you conceal your picks as something other than a moustache curling-iron. Most inappropriate for a clean-shaven man. Then there is your appearance here this evening. Most of my clients are content to use the door in the hours of daylight. The fact you have scaled the drainpipe when respectable citizens are in their beds speaks of a desire for anonymity. However, whilst I do not object to your method of entry, I do require a name.'

"'Smith,' he offered grudgingly. 'Bill Smith.'

"'Well, Mr. Smith, what can I do for you?'

"I offered him a drink, which he took with shaking hand and downed all at once. I refilled his glass and gave him a moment to compose himself whilst I charged my pipe and made myself comfortable for what promised to be an interesting affair. When a case begins in such a manner, it must have something to recommend it.

"'It's as you say, Mr. Holmes,' said he, wiping his mouth on his sleeve. 'I've cracked a few cribs in my time. I make no apology for that. I only steal from them what have got a few bob to spare.'

"'The poor, by virtue of their condition, being exempt from your interest.'

"'Well, Mr. Holmes, there's no point robbing an empty box,' said he. 'But, whatever you may think of me, I do have a conscience. I'd never take a child's toys or hurt anyone on purpose. I know there's some folk that do, but that's not my line. I take what I want and go.' He paused and hurriedly swallowed the last of his drink. 'That's what has brought me here, sir. You see, the other night, I was out near Richmond and I saw something that fair turned my stomach.'

"'Surrey?' said I. 'A little out of your way.'

"'I take the Metropolitan Railway out west, sir. It's only a few changes of train from where I live.'

"I could not stop myself from laughing. 'And they said railways were the wonder of the modern age! How true. As beneficial for the criminal as the average man, I dare say. But please, Mr. Smith, pray continue.'

"He wetted his lips and, in the eyes he raised to mine, I read his depth of emotion as he recounted his tale.

"'It was several days ago, Tuesday to be exact, the evening before Bonfire Night. I had information from a good friend of mine that there was to be a recital at the church hall in Manstone Green, and a few of the locals were attending, so their houses were empty. The train got in about a half-past-eight, and I took a turn about the streets to see what I could find. It didn't take me long. A house in Fluxton Avenue, a decent-looking place, the real stilton I can tell you.' He appeared flustered for a moment. 'That is to say – '

"'An establishment worthy of your attention,' I replied. 'I understand.'

"He nodded uneasily. 'Well, I could see a woman at home on the ground floor, but upstairs at the top of the house, someone had put their best lustres on the window sill. I thought to myself, having come all this way, it was worth a look, and so through the back gate and up the drainpipe I went.' He cleared his throat, for, as I correctly surmised, he was approaching the point in the story that gave him the most disquiet. 'As it happened, I needn't have wasted my time. All for show – they were, no gold, no jewellery, nothing worthwhile for me. I don't like leaving empty-handed, so I went to see if the people on the first floor had anything worth pinching. I had to be careful in case the woman downstairs heard me, but quiet as a church mouse I am. In I goes, and I'm having a poke about in the sideboard and . . . well, that's when I seen him, Mr. Holmes.'

"He had stopped abruptly. His face had drained of colour.

"'Who did you see, Mr. Smith?' I prompted.

"He swallowed heavily. 'A tall, clean-faced fellow, sir, stretched out on the floor in the sitting room, dead. He had a towel wrapped around his head, all stained with his blood. Well, that was enough for me, I tell you. I got out of there as fast as my legs could carry me.' He had the decency to look shamefaced. 'On the train home, when I had time to think about it, I had my doubts about just leaving him there. I couldn't go to the police. How would I explain my being there? And anyways, it might have been an accident. But why was he left there, all alone in the dark? It's been playing on my conscience, I don't mind telling you, sir. Then yesterday, "Mindful" Jackson mentioned your name to me as being a trustworthy sort who'd have a look into the business but not mention names as to how you got the information. He said he knew you.'

"As you are aware, Watson, I have always cultivated a degree of familiarity with the criminal classes, and, as with the matter at hand, it has proved fruitful, both in terms of cases and information. Jackson was a petty thief and swindler, known as 'Mindful' on account of his favourite phrase: 'Mind how you go'. Good advice, I dare say, given his profession. I had exonerated him some time ago when he was wrongly arrested for the murder of a peer who had once had him whipped for a minor act of larceny. To say he thought himself forever in my debt is something of an understatement. In return for his ongoing assistance as my guide to the nefarious doings of his fellow criminals, I had always been discreet about my sources.'

"'Jackson was correct,' I told Smith. 'On occasion, I have been known to keep a confidence for the benefit of the greater good.'

"'That's what I was hoping,' said Smith eagerly. 'I thought someone should know what had happened, especially as there's been no mention of a death in the papers. That's what made my mind up to tell you about it.'

"'You are sure he was dead? Under the circumstances, you could have been mistaken.'

"'His eyes were wide open, and he wasn't blinking. And what with all that blood, Mr. Holmes, he was dead all right or my name's not Bill Smith.'

"'I sincerely doubt it is, but in any case I take your point.'

"'I've seen a few dead 'uns in my time to know what they look like,' my visitor continued, seemingly unaware of my comment. 'But I've never come across one like this afore. Right upset me, it did.'

"'I shall look into this business, never fear,' said I, ushering him to his feet. 'Time you made your exit, Mr. Smith. If I need to clarify any point, Jackson will find you? Capital. Ah, no, I think the front door would be preferable. I do not doubt your "talents" in your chosen field, but as my landlady is accustomed to my irregular hours, she would think less of a momentary disturbance of her sleep than of having the local constabulary descend upon the premises if you happen to be discovered in the act of leaving over the back wall.'

"So it was that the next morning, I took the early train to Manstone Green. My first stop was a newsagent, where I purchased a local paper. Smith had been correct when he had told me there had been no reports of a death. My attention, however, was caught by a report of a man missing since the morning of the 5th November. Mr. Charles Winslade had left his home in Fluxton Avenue at eight o'clock, caught the train into London, and had seemingly vanished into thin air. No word had been heard from him since. Confirming the address with the one Smith had given me was a mere formality, for I was certain I had my man.

"It also served to dispel any doubts I had about Smith's story. He would not have been the first to report a crime he had committed in the hopes of turning attention away from himself. One should exercise caution before jumping to conclusions, however, and the question remained as to how a man allegedly found dead on the night of the 4th had been seen alive on the morning of the 5th.

"The local public house is always a good source of information and, on the basis that latitude is given to the newly-wedded, I posed as a prospective bridegroom, seeking information as to suitable lodgings after my nuptials. As expected, the regulars of the Red Lion were most forthcoming, at least until I touched on the question of crime in the area.

"There was a long pause before a lean man with a weather-beaten face at the bar spoke up. 'If you'd asked me that last week, I'd have said there was no place safer for a young family than Manstone Green. But now . . . .'

"He clenched his pipe between his stained and chipped teeth and glanced at the landlord. 'Now, I'd have to say there were some rum doings about these parts. A lot of strangers wandering about in the dead of night. Why, only a couple of nights ago, Mrs. Higgins saw a man in Fluxton Avenue, and we all knew what he were up to.'

"'Now, Jem,' said the landlord disapprovingly, 'we don't know nothing of the sort. By all accounts, he weren't no grey-beard. Stocky, Mrs. Higgins said, with a furtive look about him.'

"If, as I suspected, Mrs. Higgins had sighted Smith, it added strength to his story at the expense of casting doubt on his abilities as a burglar.

"'T'were a nice neighbourhood, once,' Jem continued. 'If you ask me, he's the reason Mr. Winslade took off.'

"Naturally, I pressed them on the subject and soon had details beyond which the press had divulged. The Winslades had taken lodgings in Fluxton Avenue several weeks before. Mr. Winslade was a commercial traveller, away from home a good deal, so that it had been Mrs. Winslade who had made their domestic arrangements. She kept to herself, seen only occasionally in the local shops, and once a week at the church service. That is, until the night of the 4th, when Mr. and Mrs. Winslade had attended the recital in the church hall. It was the first time many of the locals had seen Mr. Winslade, and he was described to me as dark, handsome man of about forty years of age, somewhat about six foot in height, with a fresh, clean-shaven appearance, although that night it was noted he had a rash upon his chin.

"Mrs. Winslade was younger than her husband by fifteen years and more, and was slim, fair, and petite in stature, with the trace of an accent. It was the general consensus of the Red Lion clientele that she had more than a few admirers in the neighbourhood. Most of these were from afar, but speculation centred around one man, tall, grey of hair and beard, whom the neighbours had noticed loitering outside the Winslades' lodgings before finally being given admittance a week or so previously. Mrs. Higgins, the Winslades' landlady, would later testify in court that Mrs. Winslade had introduced this man to her as her father. She said there was something unnerving about him, as though they had met before, and he had the eyes of a devil.

"Such fanciful notions did not interest me. I placed more value upon the reports that Mr. and Mrs. Winslade, undoubtedly a handsome couple, were ill-at-ease at the recital. Add that to Mrs. Higgins's testimony of how the father had been visiting on the night of the 4th when Mr. Winslade came home, how she had heard the muffled voices of two men engaged in an argument and the sound of a window slamming shut, and I began to see how an elaborate crime had taken place.

"At this point, Watson, I should make it clear that the father left at approximately a quarter-past-seven. Mrs. Higgins heard a thump outside her door and found this grey-bearded gentlemen in the act of picking up his cane, which he had dropped down the stairs. She was certain it was him; it was the eyes, so she said. At ten to eight, Mr. and Mrs. Winslade left for the recital. They returned at ten past ten, and that was the last Mrs. Higgins saw of them until the husband left for work the next morning.

"And that was how matters stood. Jem, the self-appointed opinionist of the Red Lion, was convinced Mrs. Winslade had been having an affair with the man she had claimed was her father, and the husband, having confronted the pair, packed his bags and left. As the landlord said, however, if that was the case, why did they bother to attend the recital? There was some argument for keeping up appearances, although surely there are easier ways to accomplish a separation than for the wronged party to go missing.

"I had the advantage of Smith's information. It seemed to me the argument that night had resulted in the death of one of the men involved. The bang heard by Mrs. Higgins was almost certainly a pistol shot. That would have left them the problem of the body.

"I put myself in their situation and took a turn about the town to see if I could locate a suitable place for the disposal of a body. Manstone

Green is a small town, with a High Street boasting the usual variety of shops, and residential areas surrounded by common land. At present, the open land between the town and neighbouring Richmond is a bar to the latter's expansion, but not a permanent one. In time, I dare say the larger shall subsume the smaller. For the present, however, the residents have attempted to retain their sense of community by the maintenance of their traditions. One is these is the construction of a large bonfire to be burned on Guy Fawkes' Night. My eye was caught by its charred remains, which had yet to be raked over. A grisly possibility suggested itself. Sure enough, prodding through the blackened embers with my cane, I discovered what was left of the dead man.

"The local constabulary, with a missing man on one hand and body on the other, came to the obvious conclusion. The skull revealed the man had been shot in the head, the trajectory suggesting that the gun had been held above. The local detective, a saturnine and unimaginative man by the name of Jarvis, theorised that Winslade had been waylaid by thieves on the morning of his death. A struggle had ensued and he had been shot in the process. His body had later been placed in the bonfire under cover of darkness and burned by the unsuspecting organisers.

"So might the case have remained had I not interfered"

At this point in his narrative, Holmes sighed deeply and with, so I thought, what sounded to me like a touch of frustration.

"I raised the question as to timing of the fellow's death," said he at length, his gaze diverted to the busy streets of Cheapside as we continued on our way. "I convinced Jarvis that the time between dusk and the burning of the bonfire at seven o'clock would not have afforded an opportunity for the thieves to conceal the body as they did, since the stacked wood had been attended, lest any children attempt to hide in it. Furthermore, with the deed done, why would the thieves have remained in the area with a body which would have incriminated them? I suggested to the inspector that he should speak to the neighbours about the grey-bearded man and pointed to the significance of the rash on Mr. Winslade's face that night.

"Despite his dislike of 'meddlers', as he called me, he took my advice and soon had formulated another theory, namely that the husband had died earlier in the evening at the hands of the father. To conceal the true nature of the crime, the father had shaved off his whiskers and applied boot polish to his hair to achieve the necessary look and had attended the recital in the guise of the husband. This was confirmed by my discovery of short grey hairs on the window sill of the Winslades' lodgings, where the wife had attempted to dispose of the evidence of her father's beard-shaving by shaking the cloth on which the hairs had fallen out of the window.

"Mrs. Winslade was challenged to produce her father. Instead, she chose to flee and was arrested at Southampton on suspicion of murder. More facts became known at the trial. Someone recognised her picture in the press and identified her, not as Mrs. Winslade, but as Anna Jarrow, the wife of Anthony Jarrow, sometimes Lord Jarrow, other times as Sir Anthony Jarrow, as the mood took him. Little about the man's personal history was known. He seems to have been a man of indeterminate private means, with something of a reputation as a libertine and a thoroughly bad lot. It was discovered the couple had lived the high life around Europe. Both had suddenly disappeared, leaving considerable debts, three years before the lady's appearance in England. All we ever got from Anna Jarrow was a confirmation as to her true identity; she would admit to nothing else.

"You will understand, Watson, this put a different complexion on the case. The police alleged the pair had fled to escape their debts, and after travelling extensively, had come to rest in Manstone Green, taking the name Winslade. Their past had caught up with them in the shape of the grey-bearded man, who perhaps had recognised the couple and was trying to extort money from them. They had conspired to kill him, and so Mr. Jarrow came home with a gun that night, intent on doing the blackmailer harm. At the operative moment, the two men had struggled and Mr. Jarrow had been killed. The blackmailer had then taken his place to prevent discovery of the crime until he had a chance to escape."

Holmes paused and glanced over at me. "You do see the problem, don't you?"

I nodded. "Why would Mrs. Jarrow assist a blackmailer who had killed her husband?"

"Quite so," said Holmes. "If we give the spokesman of the Red Lion his due and cast the grey-bearded man in the role of her ally, then the events of that night begin to make sense. Mrs. Jarrow has a lover. When Jarrow returns home that night, he minds the pair *in flagrante delicto*. A confrontation takes place and one or the other produces a gun, the husband most likely, given their circumstances. During the struggle, the lover kills the husband by shooting him through the head. The pair then concoct a means of providing them both with alibis. The lover leaves, making sure he has a witness. He returns moments later, possibly by the same route taken by Smith. He shaves off his beard, darkens his hair, and takes Jarrow's place at the recital – the only time the couple had been seen in public, mark you! – secure in the knowledge few in the neighbourhood have directly encountered the man. Even the landlady

Mrs. Higgins said she only caught a few glimpses of his face, although by her evidence, she claimed to be familiar with the shape of his back and shoulders. That night, the lover takes the body to the bonfire which has been built ready for the next evening. He returns to the house and, still in his disguise as Mr. Jarrow, leaves the next morning and disappears."

Holmes sat back in his seat, his features relaxing somewhat after the exertion of telling his tortuous tale. "I put this theory to the prosecution and that is the line they followed. Anna Jarrow pleaded not guilty, but offered no defence save that she was innocent of the death of the man who had been known as Charles Winslade. You can imagine the effect this had on the jury. The judge was obliged to give her the maximum sentence as an accessory after the fact, given her refusal to name her accomplice. I was able to dissuade them from a charge of murder, for the preceding argument suggested spontaneity. Nor could I support the theory that Mrs. Jarrow had executed the crime herself. The lady was scarcely five-feet-two, and would not have had the reach necessary to achieve the downward shot."

"Unless Jarrow was sitting down at the time," I ventured.

"I had considered that. The evidence of the landlady placed what was presumed to be the fatal shot at the time she heard the two men arguing. In addition, the wound was towards the front of the cranium; even a man comfortable in his wife's presence would have felt some alarm at seeing her coming towards him with a pistol. No, my dear fellow, there was no doubt as to her being an accessory. But . . . ."

Holmes thumped his fist on the side wall of the hansom in frustration.

"But what has always eluded me is the reason for her continued silence. Even now, after a lengthy incarceration, she refuses to give up his name. Hamlet may have considered a woman's love brief, but he never met Anna Jarrow. I confess, my dear fellow, I find her loyalty to the fellow admirable, if misplaced. The motives of women will ever be a mystery to me, Watson." His face took on a brighter aspect and a smile twitched at the sides of his mouth. "Or perhaps not. Well, we can but try, my dear fellow."

The rest of the journey passed in silence. The time-stained walls of The Tower of London slid by, brooding over the soldiers in the barracks and visitors to its gloomy dungeons, a silent witness now to the jousts of kings and the deaths of queens in days of yore. Turning northwards, we wended our way through the busy streets, passing the shops of booksellers and clockmakers, into the area of Portsoken, bounded by Spitalfields to the east and Bishopsgate to the north. Our destination was a small court off the Minories, where red-bricked terraced houses slumped against each other like drunken men and sagged from every parapet and window ledge. Our cabman stopped in the main road, and we made our way on foot, passing lounging men and idle women outside a tavern on the corner, their faces mingling both curiosity and hostility.

The address proved to be a lodging house for destitute women recently released from prison, run by a charitable organisation for discharged prisoners. A painted board by the door listed the rules of the establishment: No gambling, no drunkenness, and no male visitors, to name but a few. This last I considered might be our stumbling block, but the matron in charge of the establishment was so suitably impressed by having a famous detective on the doorstep that she was inclined to wave the rule on this occasion.

Anna Jarrow had a room on the second floor, sparsely furnished with the bare essentials and embroidered religious quotations in frames on the walls. We found her seated by a table at the window, with a basket of clothes beside her chair and several garments spread out before her. She rose at our entrance, her expression registering recognition. She was thin, sallow, and hollow-eyed, the long years in prison ageing her before her time, but still there remained the shadow of the handsome woman she had once been.

"Mrs. Jarrow," said Holmes severely. "Do you remember me?"

"How could I forget the man who had me sent to prison?" said she, the slight trace of the accent Holmes had described in her speech still detectable after all these years.

"Your actions, madam, did that."

"As you say." She gestured to the other chair in the room. "Won't you sit?"

"This will not take long."

She smiled. "It may take longer than even you can imagine, Mr. Holmes. I can guess why you are here."

"Then perhaps you could save us all time by telling me what I want to know, Mrs. Jarrow. I see you are a busy woman."

She glanced over at the basket of clothes. "It is meagre employment, but I am grateful for the work." She took her own seat again. "Very well, let me hear what you have to say."

"I erred at your trial," Holmes asserted.

I confess I was taken aback to hear him admit such a thing. Mrs. Jarrow, however, maintained an admirable calm.

"I thought, as did many, that the man you were protecting was your lover," he continued. "That you should protect him then, as you protect him still, made little sense. Had you provided the court with a name, leniency might have been granted."

"Had I provided a name, he might have hanged. The crime was mine and mine alone."

"Ah, Mrs. Jarrow," said Holmes, shaking his head, "you did not fire the fatal shot that killed your husband."

She nodded. "But it was my fault he was there. Allow me some portion of blame. To have named him would have been to condemn him. I was not innocent. If someone had to answer for the crime, better than it was me. As your Lord Byron once said: '*They never fail who die in a great cause*'."

"It is your concept of the 'noble sacrifice', madam, and your enduring silence, which has led me to one inescapable conclusion as to the real identity of the grey-bearded man." Holmes paused for effect. "He was your brother, was he not?"

Anna Jarrow stared at him for a long time. "I have no brother," said she evenly.

"Not one I have been able to trace, admittedly," agreed Holmes.

"That is because he does not exist. I grew up an only child in Antwerp." She lowered her gaze and plucked listlessly at the pieces of cloth on the table. "I will concede, however, that he was not my lover."

"Then who?"

"After all, this time, what does it matter? I have paid for my crime, Mr. Holmes."

"It matters, Mrs. Jarrow, because a man died."

"A worthless man!" she cried, with sudden emotion. She stared at us, her eyes blazing, and then, as if making up her mind, she nodded and looked away. "I should hate you, sir, but in truth, I pity you for your ignorance. Leave now. I have nothing more to say."

And so we had no choice but to do as the lady said. No entreaty would sway her, and Holmes was forced to admit to Gregson that he had failed to extract the truth from Mrs. Jarrow. Over the next few months, other cases came to occupy us, and life at Baker Street settled back into our old routine. But still, as one after another came to a successful conclusion, I would see that faraway look come into his eye and he would fall to brooding on the Jarrow case. The reports from the Irregulars he had instructed to follow the lady petered out, and the case file was closed and consigned to the depths of his tin box.

Then, one morning at the end of November, Mrs. Hudson brought up an envelope, bearing a Dover postmark. I thought nothing of it until Holmes let out a cry and threw several sheets of paper across the kippers to me.

"See what you make of that, Watson!" he declared. "I did not fall so far from my mark. Read it aloud, if you will."

It was a woman's handwriting, flowing and elegant. The letter ran thus:

My dear Mr. Sherlock Holmes:

By the time you receive this letter, I shall have left England for good. I will not return. When last I saw you, you asked me for a name. You will never know that name. But that no one should be in any doubt, I thought someone should know the events which transpired that night, and the nature of the evil man who met his end.

I was a dancer in Amsterdam when I met my husband. I was young and thought myself in love. He was charming and handsome. He was also a thief. I did not know this when I married him, but even though I became aware of the source of his income, still I was content to live in grand style from the proceeds of his crimes. Then one day he received a letter, claiming to be from his father. He had told me he had been born in England, in Jarrow, which he had taken for his surname. His mother had died a few days after his birth, not before leaving a letter in which she claimed that he was the natural son of a well-born roué. That same man had known of his existence, and on his death, had bequeathed to my husband, as his eldest son, a diary, listing the dates and times of his many liaisons and the children who had resulted from his affairs.

I cannot speculate as to his intentions, unless to supply another living soul with evidence that his life had not been entirely without purpose, even one so base. For my husband, however, it was an opportunity. He began contacting the people named in the diary, demanding payment for his silence. They paid, fearing that even a breath of scandal would threaten their good names and inheritances.

Again, I said nothing. I enjoyed the money. Then one day, a payment did not arrive. We learned a few days later the young man concerned had killed himself. From then on, the money was poison to me. The food it bought turned to dust and ashes in my mouth. For all my silks and velvet, sackcloth was my preference. I saw my husband for what he was, and told him I would leave. He said he would not let me

266

leave, and if I tried, he would find me and kill me rather than let me be with another. Despite his threats, I did escape him, taking the diary with me, so that he could blackmail no one else with its secrets. For three years, I ran from him, always moving on whenever I thought he was close to finding me.

Then, when my money was exhausted, I came to England and, to my shame, I used the diary, not for blackmail, you must understand, but for assistance so that this foul document might never fall into my husband's hands. The man I chose agreed to help me, though he had the most to lose: His wife, his children, his home, his reputation. In exchange, I swore on the Bible that I would never betray his secret. This man was not wealthy, but he said he would find me the money for passage to Australia. Until such time, he provided me with enough to find lodgings to live comfortably. I chose Manstone Green, believing it to be insignificant enough to escape the attention of my husband. My knight errant, as I shall call him, visited me occasionally in the guise of my husband, so as not to attract the suspicion of the neighbours.

All was well until one evening a letter arrived. It was from my husband. He said he meant me no harm for he loved another and wished to start a new life in Canada. He said too that he would leave me in peace forever if I gave him £500, enough to pay for his ticket and a comfortable life abroad. I was cautious, but agreed to meet him at the house. He was older and greyer, but I recognised him. I told the landlady he was my father to allay her curiosity, although in truth he was but five years older than my knight. I told him I had limited funds, but I would see what I could raise. He agreed to return.

He was contrite that evening and seemed a changed man. But I was not convinced. I told my knight of his visit and we agreed that the sum must be found. My knight was the trustee of several funds, and he took the money from those accounts, with every intention of paying it back. I also advised him that we should take precautions, as I did not trust my husband. My knight said he would come armed. I did not know he meant a gun, but I thank Providence that he did, for surely I would not be here today.

On the evening of the 4ᵗʰ November, my husband returned earlier than expected. He was belligerent and had been drinking. By the time my knight arrived, he was angry, demanding not only the money, but the diary too. I refused to give it to him. He raised his fist to strike me and that is when my knight produced the gun. My husband leapt at him and they struggled. Somehow the gun went off. My husband was killed instantaneously.

You may ask why we did not both leave. My knight feared discovery if his description was given to the police and I was tired of running. After three years, I was finally free of Anthony Jarrow. And so we devised a plan whereby it would appear that my knight, the man believed to be my husband, had been killed the next day. I will never know how you discovered the truth, Mr. Holmes. We took such care.

As half-brothers, my knight shared a close enough resemblance to pass as my husband. My knight shaved my husband's beard where he lay and stuck the whiskers to his own face. Then he powdered his own hair and left, making sure he alerted Mrs. Higgins on the way out. He returned only to find that the glue had stuck fast and I had to pull the hair from his face, leaving red marks upon his skin. We went out together so that the people would see us. At midnight, he dropped my husband's body from the back window and carried him in a wheelbarrow to the bonfire. If anyone had stopped him, he would have said the body was a Guy for the fire. The next morning, he left and I later alerted the police that he had disappeared.

You were not too far wrong when you mentioned a brother, Mr. Holmes. Your only mistake was that it was my husband's relation and not mine. You will never find him. The diary was the only evidence of his blood-tie to my husband and that was burned in that bonfire alongside an accursed man, who was surely his father's son. I do not regret my actions. My knight killed in self-defence. Without him, I would be dead. Because of him, I would rather have died than had his death on my conscience. I kept my promise to him and all the others that wretched diary had damned.

I have paid for my sins, for the anguish I helped him cause to others and the lives he thought nothing of ruining. Now I must exorcise the ghost of the Jarrow name and begin my life anew, trusting that through my deeds, I may seek the forgiveness of a higher power.

Yours respectfully,

Anna Jansen (formerly Jarrow)

A silence fell over the table as I finished reading. Holmes had been listening with his chin sunk upon his chest and his gaze fixed on the fire. Slowly, he lifted his head and listlessly reached for the letter.

"I fear I have been like the dull, tiresome fellow of whom Dr. Johnson said 'he seems to me to possess *but one* idea, and that is a *wrong one*'." Holmes sighed. "Ah, the folly of youth, Watson. On the one hand, I had too much information; on the other, not enough. Had I known of Jarrow's history, had Smith seen the hair colour of the dead man, then my conclusion would have been different. As it was, I placed too much importance on Mrs. Higgins's evidence about the eyes."

"The eyes?" I queried. "I'm not sure I understand."

"The landlady said she knew it was the father because she recognised the eyes. She also said that the eyes had unnerved her, as though they were familiar. Of course they were. She had seen those same eyes in the brief glimpses she had had of the face of Mrs. Jarrow's 'knight'." He gave a rueful laugh. "Well, Watson, *potius sero quam nunquam*, as Livy has it."

"'*Better late than never*' indeed," I agreed. "But perhaps not too late, Holmes. Now you have the full facts, you could discover the name of her accomplice."

Holmes stared at the sheet and nodded slowly. Then suddenly, he screwed the pages into a ball and threw it into the fire. The flames caught and the paper shrivelled, glowing at the edges until nothing was left but a few blackened fragments.

"Yes, I could," said Holmes, rising briskly to his feet and brushing the crumbs from his trousers. "But I will not. The lady has furnished me with the facts because she knows I will not use them. Besides, without the diary, what other proof of this man's lineage exists? No, my dear fellow. Time enough has been wasted on this venture and we have other cases more pressing. The other letters in my morning post included a missive from Mycroft, demanding my presence at his club on a matter of some urgency. One should never appear too eager, especially where one's relations are concerned, but I feel I should make the effort to put in an appearance. Well, Watson, have you breakfasted sufficiently? Then come. The Diogenes awaits!"

The Adventure of the
Disappearing Dictionary
by Sonia Fetherston

"But the manuscript . . . is intimately connected with the affair."
– *The Hound of the Baskervilles*

"Someday, Watson, I should like it very much if one of those regrettable stories you spin for *The Strand* would dispense with terror and evil. The time has come for you to write about the lighter amusements that arrive on our doorstep." Sherlock Holmes stood gazing from the bow window of our sitting room, his eleven o'clock cigarette in one hand and a book in the other. He glanced over his shoulder at me, gray eyes sparkling merrily.

"'Regrettable stories?' Really, Holmes!" I admonished. I hope it will not sound immodest when I say that readers seem to enjoy my accounts of Holmes's exploits. Naturally they involve terror and evil. Sherlock Holmes is the world's foremost consulting detective, a man to whom desperate or frightened people turn when they need justice.

It was a fine spring morning, a little more than a month after my friend returned to London following his hiatus connected to the death of Professor Moriarty. I had joined Holmes again at our familiar Baker Street address, heeding his advice that work – at his side, of course – would be the best antidote to sorrow. After taking an early breakfast, Holmes and I busied ourselves, he making a few notes in his commonplace books, while I composed a letter to Captain Mumphries, a fellow officer I met while convalescing at the base hospital in Peshawar some years before. Holmes and I both were considering the next thing to do when he made his disparaging remark on my published works.

I expected he would let this subject drop, but my friend suddenly gestured toward the street below our window. "Here is just the sort light amusement I mean, Watson," he prompted. "There is Lestrade trying to free himself from the clutches of a couple of ancient fiends." I rose and quickly went to his side, where I beheld the wiry little Scotland Yard Inspector struggling on the pavement, his ferret-like features flushed with anger and exertion. To my astonishment, two old men were grasping Lestrade's elbows and pulling him toward our doorstep. I lifted the latch and raised the window. We could hear the strangers gibbering insensibly

270

while our policeman friend cried out, "Stop! Stop! You're mad!" and then "Stop!" again.

Holmes spun around and thundered down the seventeen steps. A moment later, he led Lestrade and his captors – their hands still clutching at him – into our sitting room. The settee in front of the fire was hastily cleared of yesterday's newspapers, and the three of them were made more-or-less comfortable while I rang for coffee. Our visitors sat like a pair of bookends, propping up the exhausted Lestrade in their midst. "Well, Inspector," Holmes commenced, rubbing his hands in anticipation, "you appear to be in custody. After you're convicted of whatever it is you've done this time, perhaps Watson and I will visit you in your prison cell."

The Scotland Yard detective recovered with a snort, gave Holmes a withering look, then brushed his captors' handprints from his jacket sleeves. "This is the pair who belong behind bars, Mr. Holmes," Lestrade said in his high, strident voice. "I should have known better than to try and help such obvious hooligans." As he spoke, I examined the hooligans in question. The one on Lestrade's right appeared to be a whirlwind contained in a small, stout body, his white curls protruding at odd angles from under an incongruous flat velvet cap. To the other side of Lestrade sat the antithesis of the first one, a tall, cadaverous man with a bleak, unhurried manner. He balanced a high black hat on his knee, revealing a close-cut steel-gray tonsure.

"We're not hooligans, we're scholars!" the one under the velvet cap replied with a flourish of his hands. "Mr. Holmes, I am the despairing William Bourne Forster."

"And I am the inconsolable Robert Dyvelstone," his companion added. "Doubtless you know our names. After all, we are preeminent in our chosen field."

"Which is?" I politely queried.

Holmes himself answered. "Why, the Northumbrian dialect, Watson. Obviously." He dipped a long finger into the toe end of the Persian slipper hanging beside the fireplace and extracted some tobacco, which he gently tamped into the bowl of his briar. I, being accustomed to what my friend called his "Method", made a rapid inventory. There were ink stains on the right middle fingers of both men, indicating that they engaged in a great deal of writing. I perceived a slight indentation for five inches along their sleeves just above the cuffs, the result of prolonged resting their wrists on a desk or table. Deep creases between their eyes suggested intellectual contemplation. Scholarly types, I granted, but how Holmes arrived at the Northumbrian dialect as their specialism utterly mystified me.

271

"I saw a bit of fanfare in *The Advisor* last week about a new volume on the Northumbrian tongue. Then, in yesterday's *Record*, there was a brief advertisement," he explained as he struck a match. "'*Apply to Bourne Forster and Dyvelstone with information about a missing manuscript. Reward upon return of said.*'" He viewed them through a blue haze of pipe-smoke. "And unless I am badly mistaken, those were Geordie blasphemies you were directing at friend Lestrade when I saw you through my window just now." So that was the nonsensical chatter I'd overheard. Holmes settled into the basket chair, winked at the inspector, and crossed his long legs. "Illuminate me, if you please, gentlemen. Tell me why you've disturbed my pleasant morning in the company of my friend and colleague Dr. Watson, to say nothing of disordering Scotland Yard's most eminent investigator."

"Our life's work!" Bourne Forster suddenly wailed. "It's gone missing."

"We went to the police, of course," Dyvelstone added, and he jabbed at Lestrade. "This feeble excuse for an inspector laughed at us, so we came to consult with you."

"And you brought the feeble excuse with you? Good."

Lestrade glowered wordlessly at Holmes, as Mrs. Hudson's stately tread was heard on the stair. She appeared in our doorway bearing coffee and rolls, and placed the tray on the table in front of the settee before subsiding into a corner so as to save us the trouble of ringing should we need anything further. Bourne Forster spoke again.

"Northumbrian vocabulary is the most distinct and difficult of all the provincial dialects. A great many words and expressions are so peculiar, one forgets that the local people really are speaking English. Why, from one valley to the next words change so that inhabitants of one rural settlement may have trouble understanding their neighbors just over the burn."

"It's more than the odd diphthong, or singular '*r*' overheard in the marketplace," Dyvelstone added. "The uniqueness is so pronounced that, left to its own devices, Northumbrian would soon evolve into a distinct language all its own. Over the years, we've managed to isolate some twelve-hundred unique words and quaint phrases."

"Very impressive," Holmes murmured, sending a blue smoke ring toward the ceiling. "Far more than Brockett collected for his 1829 glossary, which is still, I believe, considered authoritative." His unexpected acquaintance with an unusual subject surprised me. I made a mental note to add "*Northumbrian babble – functional*" to my list of Holmes's acquired knowledge. "Pray continue," he said.

272

"We've spent years traveling across Northumbria, for the most part on foot, listening to the speech of dairymen, servants, drovers, and fishing families," Bourne Forster explained. "The collier's speech is different from that of the shepherd not ten miles distant. The words a shopkeeper from Morpeth uses are very unlike those of his brother shopkeeper from Wooler. Everywhere we go, we interview the folk and catalog local derivations."

"Derivations, distortions, and distinctions," Dyvelstone interjected. "And the complex twists! Where you and I eat turnips, a Hexham man calls them '*neeps*', while his cousin in Berwick knows them as '*baggies*'. An apple core is a '*gowk*', not to be confused with the village idiot, who is also a '*gowk*'. And the animals! Kittens are '*kitlings*', owls are '*howletts*', a hen is a '*clocker*', and a donkey, of course, is a '*cuddy*'."

"Of course," Lestrade repeated under his breath. He helped himself to an empty cup. As I watched, he measured five spoons full of sugar into the bottom of it, and added coffee.

"Some men accumulate stamps, Mr. Holmes, and others hang Dutch masters on their walls," Dyvelstone concluded. "We are collectors of *words*."

"We are gatherers in the green meadows of expression," his colleague Bourne Forster corrected. "We endeavour to find out the everyday authorities – those who use the words beside their own hearths – and instruct others as to the philological state of things."

"You mentioned a manuscript." Holmes steepled his fingers and hooded his eyes. The pipe stuck out at a perilous tilt from between his clenched teeth as he awaited their response.

"To be sure." Bourne Forster replied. "The English Dialect Society is desperate to publish our findings; their Professor Skeat is jealous of us. He wants to use our work as a capstone for his group's series on British languages. Were we to associate with him, the Society would insist on sharing our triumph."

"Most unfair!" his companion said. "It marks the pinnacle of *our* careers. Why, I can easily imagine our names appearing on next year's Honours List. We can't be expected to combine forces with other people. Professor Skeat was furious, but we held firm."

"We decided instead we might publish our own findings," Bourne Forster continued. "Our dictionary is – or it was – promised to be the most comprehensive lexicon of the Northumbrian language ever produced. It is to be the crown jewel of obscure English variants, the zenith of etymological accomplishment in this half of the century. Three days ago, I put my own finishing touches on it and sent it over to

Dyvelstone for his final comments. He made his corrections and sent it back to me. But it never arrived!"

"How was it sent? Trusted courier?"

"No, sir. I tucked it in the seat of a hired hansom."

Dyvelstone nodded. "And I sent it back to him by hansom yesterday."

Bourne Forster assumed a woeful look. "It never arrived."

"How many copies did you make of your manuscript?"

"It was the only one, Mr. Holmes." Dyvelstone admitted. "Handwritten. Seventy-three pages."

"I see. The only extant copy of the dictionary made one trip to you and one trip to oblivion. Did you use the same cabbie, or were there two?"

Dyvelstone answered. "The same one. Tom Hedley is his name. We met him several weeks ago, when he drove us from the British Museum. A young Northumbrian fellow who came to the capital to seek his fortune. Naturally, we were attracted to his morphemes! He has recently performed a couple of small errands for us. We believe him to be trustworthy." Bourne Forster nodded his head in vigourous agreement. "Certainly, you'll want to speak with him, Mr. Holmes. Between ten-thirty and eleven o'clock each morning, when trains come in from Waterloo or Richmond, one might reliably find Tom waiting at the Addison Road Station. When he brought me the manuscript on Tuesday, I directed him to come back for it on Thursday, at the same time."

"Which was?"

"Five o'clock in the afternoon."

Holmes turned to Bourne Forster. "How was it prepared? Wrapped in paper and tied with string?"

"No, sir. I placed it in a document box with two hinges on the side and a clasp to hold the lid down."

"And you, Mr. Dyvelstone? How did you return the dictionary to your colleague?"

"In the same box. I placed the box on the seat and closed the hansom's door. Tom took it away."

"The box came back to me," Bourne Forster explained, "but it was empty. Perhaps we erred in relying on Tom. Perhaps he wanted the dictionary for himself?" The poor man looked near to tears.

"What was the route taken?"

They gave Holmes their respective addresses, one in Earls Court, the other in Bayswater. A few moments later, I showed them out with Sherlock Holmes's promise to investigate.

"A waste of your time," Lestrade predicted. "I can't think of anybody who would write such a ridiculous book, let alone want it back."

"Which is precisely why it should be easy to trace," Holmes replied. "Say it was the manuscript of the next nautical romance by Russell – like the ones Watson here is always reading. Why, every Watson in the world would attempt to get his hands on the thing." He turned to me. "What was the name of that new book of his you were reading last night?"

"*List, ye Landsmen*," I replied, stoutly.

"Observe how Watson nearly salutes when he says its name, then multiply him by countless other Watsons across the land, and at sea. We would confront a field of thousands of potential suspects. But a manuscript concerning an abstruse subject understood by experts exclusively . . . only a few will even be aware of the thing, let alone covet it. Therefore, it stands to reason that the more narrow the field of interest, the smaller our assortment of those who might be accused."

"Is not the most obvious suspect Tom Hedley, the driver?" I suggested.

"The most obvious suspect is ditch work along the Holland Road," Lestrade countered. "Likely the hansom drove over a hole, jarred the cab, and made the dictionary fly out of the box. Seek its pages in the gutter."

"Did you look for it there?" Holmes inquired sweetly.

"I did not, Mr. Nosy Parker. I have *real* crimes to solve and *real* criminals to catch. I am not inclined to squander my faculties on two old men and their absurd word list. I told them as much."

"And they dragged you here."

"When a professional would have nothing to do with them, they insisted on consulting an amateur instead," the inspector explained.

"Yet again I am indebted to you, Lestrade, for your fiery spirit of indifference." Holmes sniffed like a hound at the outset of the chase. "Ah, Watson! This case presents several points of interest. How did such a singular dictionary happen to vanish on a short trip, with a trusty driver, in the daytime? I shall begin my investigation at once. And so," he made several tight sweeping gestures with the back of his hand toward Lestrade, as if brushing away a crumb, "you are released from custody and are free to go."

The inspector gulped the last of his coffee and left us.

As our door closed, Sherlock Holmes strode purposefully into his bedroom. Immediately, I could hear him humming a cheerful tune. Mrs. Hudson emerged from the corner and came to retrieve her tray. She paused, dipped her chin shyly, and an uncharacteristic blush spread over her cheek.

"I'm very glad Mr. Holmes is back, Doctor," she said with a gentle smile. "I can tell you're happy, too, for the chance to renew your friendship and your partnership. Still I wonder," she took a step nearer to me, "if you'll soon prefer to be in your own home again, and, in time, have another Mrs. Watson to brighten your life?"

"In time, perhaps," I replied, with a sad smile.

"I mention it only because a dear young woman will be joining us at teatime to-day. She'll stop here for two nights, on a little holiday. She's my late cousin's girl, Jane – Jane Nugent is her name. She is intelligent and charming, and quite pretty. She is employed as companion to a widowed lady in the country outside of Newcastle. Naturally I hoped you might show her a bit of London, seeing as Mr. Holmes will be busy with this new case." We could hear Holmes, still humming in the other room. "Anyway," Mrs. Hudson sniffed and nodded toward Holmes's door, "I wouldn't want him to give her a fright." Her voice lowered to a whisper. "You know – the cocaine, those volatile chemicals, and his habit of shooting bullets at my walls. Jane is a gentle girl, and I'll not have her upset."

"I'd be delighted to meet Miss Nugent," I told her. "Perhaps she'd care to see the Serpentine, or stroll the Embankment?"

At this moment Holmes emerged: Brushed, shined, and neatly attired for a day in town. As he reached for his favourite walking stick, he trumpeted, "Not yet ready, Watson? Hurry into your hat and coat. Our game begins." I scampered after my things as he turned toward Mrs. Hudson. "We're off for the English Dialect Society, dear lady. Expect me for dinner the day after tomorrow."

Professor Walter Skeat adjusted his *pince-nez* and cleared his throat with a resonant rumble. A magnificent white beard cascaded down the front of his dark suit. The man's thick eyebrows plunged to form the letter "*V*" on his forehead as he glowered across his desk at us. His card, which he'd lately flipped toward Holmes, lay on the gleaming surface between them. It identified Skeat as a philologist, English linguist, phoneticist, and authority on authenticating dialectic texts, *etc. etc. etc.* Formerly of Cambridge, he now served as chairman of the Society that was desirous of publishing the new Northumbrian wordbook.

"Bourne Forster and Dyvelstone?" he queried. "They corresponded with me for years, tantalizing the Society with hints of the words and phrases they were collecting. I've followed their progress with keen interest. They promise to leave Brockett's work gathering dust. Naturally, the Society wants to collaborate with them on bringing their dictionary to the public. I have met with them twice in the past three weeks, and I offered to personally place their findings before our committee.

"I don't mind telling you, Mr. Holmes, and you, too, Dr. Watson," he continued, "that I am particularly anxious – even desperate – to get my hands on their manuscript. The Society most urgently desires to add it to the county-by-county survey of the native British tongue that we are preparing. Their Northumbrian dictionary will be not just a new landmark in language, but it can finally complete our shelf. Once that is done, I can pack up my laurels, dismantle the Society, and retire to the peace of my study."

"Are you aware that their book is missing?"

"One hears rumours," Skeat replied darkly, shaking his head. "Dear me, I've been so hopeful that the Northumbrian word book will be a triumph. Aside from my professional curiosity, I take a most particular interest in their work. My mother came from a village within sight of the Tyne, and I learnt a fair number of Geordie words at her knee. Ha! Our two scholar friends were thunderstruck to hear a few local phrases roll from my tongue when they were here! I've made it plain to Dyvelstone and Bourne Forster that I will be their staunchest ally before the committee." A sigh escaped him, and he shook his head. "It was a black day when they turned down the Society and told me they would seek to publish without us."

"Precisely what is the role of your committee?"

"To evaluate the book, to approve it, or to reject it. If the committee found fault with the dictionary, you might be investigating its demise rather than its disappearance."

"Perhaps, then, the authors did not wish to relinquish control over their own work?" Holmes said.

"There was never a question of control," Skeat countered, weaving his fingers together and placing his hands on the desk. "It was a question of whether they were going to associate with the preeminent philologists in the land. Like yourself, sir, Bourne Forster and Dyvelstone are amateurs – gifted, but amateurs nonetheless – whereas the gentlemen of the committee are long-credentialed experts in our field. Cataloging words is our mission. Our two friends are undoubtedly tenacious and hardworking, though as yet untested."

"Exactly how does a researcher pass the test?"

"Publish! And best to publish *here*. When one publishes with the Society, his work will forevermore be linked to the Pantheon of the profession. We are enlighteners of the language; to publish with us is to ascend the mountain."

277

The left side of Sherlock Holmes's mouth crooked in a sort of smile. "I see. They declined your offer of a rope and a pick ax?"

"They thanked me and firmly turned me down. I haven't seen them since. I was dismayed, and of course angry."

"How well would you say you know them, and their work, Professor Skeat?"

"I know them best courtesy of the Post Office," he admitted. "You understand, as researchers their work takes place in villages and towns, on farms, in factories, and even in mines. These are located hundreds of miles away. They are correspondents who keep me – and the Society – abreast of their findings in letterform." He pulled open a drawer and extracted a bundle of letters. "These I've received from them with the postal marks of Haltwhistle and Corbridge, of Newbiggin and Redburn, of Ashington and Prudhoe, and other towns located there." Holmes examined the envelopes, and then returned them to the professor.

"And as to the quality of their endeavour? Surely you, who also take an interest in Northumbrian words, will offer an opinion."

"Dialects should be learnt, like any other subject, by honest hard work," Skeat told us. Something of the professor stirred in him as he spoke, and he addressed his remarks to an area just beyond my right ear. "Old words ought to be lured from the lips of each individual and diligently catalogued. Such is the higher calling of men like Bourne Forster and Dyvelstone . . . . and me. Old words cannot be permitted to exist in isolation. They must be collected, considered, tested, proven, and then preserved by means of publication. It is only in this way that we can get nearer to the truth and beauty of our mother tongue."

I closed the door softly as we left, so as not to disturb his reverie.

Jane Nugent was just as Mrs. Hudson had described her: Charming, and lovely to behold. While her aspect was calm and intelligent, I found her wide hazel eyes to be beguiling. She wore a springtime suit of buff piqué. Her smooth skirt was caught in a neat row of box pleats at the back, peeking from beneath the hem of her jacket. She'd arrived from the station while Holmes and I were out. He deposited me on our Baker Street doorstep, saying he had some business to attend to. I climbed the familiar steps alone. So it was that Miss Nugent and I had our tea together in the sitting room. Despite my several entreaties, Mrs. Hudson would not join us; I suspected she wanted to give us time to become acquainted. Our visitor told me of her placid life in the country, serving as companion to an undemanding elderly woman. In turn, I shared with her a selection of my personal exploits in the Afghan campaign. I described how I came to be wounded by the murderous Ghazis, and told her that I yet carried inside one of my limbs a deadly Jezail bullet. She blanched most becomingly. I confess that I liked her very much.

Holmes came in late that night, and was away before the sun rose the next morning. As I'd promised our landlady, I accompanied Miss Nugent on a drive though some of London's neighborhoods. The mare clip-clopped along Oxford and Bond Streets, to Mayfair and St. James. It promised to be a delightful day, bright and pleasantly warm. Our route took us to the Mall, where I amused her with my story of a past visit to the Diogenes Club. As we passed the Palace, I described for her a couple of the small favours Holmes and I had performed on behalf of the Crown Prince. We went along Constitution Hill, when, to my astonishment, the cab did not double back to Park Lane and so on north and home, but very deliberately headed west in the Brompton Road. "Hey there," I called, knocking on the roof of our hansom, "you missed the turn! We're bound back to Marylebone!" I twisted round to look through the small opening behind us, where, to my astonishment, on the sprung I beheld my friend and associate Sherlock Holmes, grinning down at me.

I scarcely recognized him at these close quarters, so it's not surprising I hadn't known it was he who helped us into the cab back in Baker Street and had served as our driver for the past thirty minutes. He was dressed in a long close-fitting black coat, with leather boots and knitted gloves. Side-whiskers, along with a thick moustache, were newly applied to his face. His nose was reddened, giving him a look of a man who liked his gin. A black bowler was rammed onto his head, completing the disguise. Holmes waved a long whip in the air with a flourish, touching the mare on her point. She instantly responded by stepping into a rapid trot.

"Dr. Watson, what is happening?" Miss Nugent placed her small, trusting hand upon my sleeve, but I could see that she was troubled.

"Never worry, my dear," I responded warmly. I scarcely knew whether to chuckle or weep. Unbeknownst to her, Jane Nugent had been swept into an undertaking only Sherlock Holmes could devise. I had served alongside him on many a criminal campaign, while she was but a fresh recruit. "We're having a bit of an adventure, that's all," I reassured her. Still, I worried about keeping her out of harm's way.

And so we progressed, turning at the Natural History Museum, then again at Kensington Road. West, ever west, skirting the gardens and flying across High Street. By the time we'd achieved Holland Park, I was certain as to our destination: The Addison Road Station. There, Holmes pulled into the line with a half-dozen other hansom cabs, and released the lever so that our door opened. I leapt out and assisted Miss Nugent in alighting. Holmes climbed down and surveyed the other drivers waiting in twos and threes beside the hansoms.

"Really, Holmes, this is too much, even for you," I whispered. "Miss Nugent is with me . . . ."

"Silence," he hissed, never taking his eyes from the other cabbies. "We're just in time to make the acquaintance of Tom Hedley, he of Northumbrian manuscript fame."

I turned to make my apologies to Miss Nugent, but was stopped by a sudden expression of exhilaration on her face.

"Dr. Watson, tell me," she asked. "I heard you call him 'Holmes'. Is that really *Sherlock* Holmes?"

"I'm afraid so," I replied.

"But this is wonderful!" she said. "Cousin Martha's letters tell so little. She did write recently that she knelt under a window and turned his bust while somebody shot at it. Is that true?" I nodded wordlessly. "May I meet him?" she asked.

"We find ourselves in the middle of one of his investigations," I told her. "In my own experience of these things, it's best to remain composed and observe everything you can, for it may be helpful to him later."

She tucked her hand under my arm and we walked slowly along the pavement. We approached, and then passed, Hedley's cab. At the one in front of it Miss Nugent stopped and petted the nose of its tired brown horse. I remained beside her, shielding her from any danger.

Holmes assumed a rolling swagger. He rubbed his chin and grinned at Hedley. 'Say, now, you're the driver wot lost that dictionary!" he exclaimed. The man was nearly as tall as Holmes, rail-thin, with a shock of dark hair. Like Holmes, his attire was the sombre black of a London cabbie. But where Holmes affected a grin, Hedley scowled. "I backed my opinion with sixpence," Holmes continued. "Davy, over there, says you're not, but I say you *are*: You are Tom, the cabbie wot drives books." He added with a wink, "And loses 'em!"

In reply, Hedley swung himself up and onto the seat of his cab. He turned the vehicle and touched the horse with his whip. "*Gib nowt . . . gan on*," he called and the animal drew the hansom out into the lane and rapidly away from us.

Miss Nugent and I turned and made our way back to Holmes's hansom. I helped her into her seat just as Holmes came back.

"Surely you noticed his use of Northumbrian words, Mr. Holmes," Miss Nugent said, quietly. "I've lived and worked in Northumberland for the past four years, and I'm fairly certain that man is a native speaker. He told his horse not to be shy of the traffic, but go straight into it."

280

"I noted his use of the language," Holmes replied. "But I hadn't understood it." Ordinarily he maintained a doubtful opinion of women in general, but this one he regarded with something approaching approval. "There are possibilities about you, my dear Miss Nugent. I'm in your debt." Holmes, closed the door and climbed back on the sprung, then turned the hansom toward Baker Street. Only once did we slow, as we crossed the Holland Road. Looking along it, I could see Lestrade with four or five of his men. They appeared to be inspecting ditches. I heard Sherlock Holmes chortle.

I never learned where Holmes had obtained the hansom and the driver's clothes, or to whom he returned them. Forty minutes after he dropped us off at 221b Baker Street, he came back on foot. Miss Nugent was by this time resting in Mrs. Hudson's rooms downstairs, so I seized the opportunity to speak with my friend privately. "Where does the investigation go from here?" I asked him. "And please do not say 'to Northumberland'. I've no desire to travel any more to-day."

"I've no desire to go there either," he replied with a smile. Holmes settled himself before the test tubes and retorts that lay neglected on the deal table. It was his habit to dabble in chemical experiments in order to concentrate not just compounds, but his thoughts, as well. "I haven't been further than Yorkshire in this matter, and I don't care a plug about Northumberland. Still, it's curious, isn't it? Two amateurs produce a remarkable expansion to previous dictionaries of Northumbrian words. The man to whom they offer it admits he is 'desperate' to have their manuscript and 'angry' when they withhold it. The fellow they engage to drive the manuscript through London's streets seemingly originates from that same remote district – or at least speaks the Northumbrian language. And a young woman under our very roof is recently arrived from the area, where she's acquired at least some familiarity with the native tongue."

"Surely you aren't suggesting that Miss Nugent – ?"

"Of course not," he cut in. "She is one of the most delightful young ladies I ever met. And she's proven herself useful. Witness her prompt assistance at the station."

"Quick intelligence is one of her several attractions," I admitted. I saw him regarding me over a beaker half-full of some dark, noxious fluid. "It's too soon for me to form another attachment," I replied to his unspoken question.

"It's been almost a year since Mary died."

"As I said, it's too soon." I sought to steer the conversation back to the missing book. "What will you do next? Pay a visit to our elderly clients? Talk with Lestrade?" It was at this moment that his experiment produced a muffled report, followed by a cloud of thick gray smoke that filled the corner of our sitting room.

"Next?" his voice emerged from the hazy fumes. "Next I suppose I must clean this table, before Mrs. Hudson sees it."

An hour later he was out the door. I joined Mrs. Hudson and Miss Nugent for a late luncheon, then left on a few errands of my own. Outside a tobacconist in Portland Street, I was greeted by an old patient who invited me to come round for dinner the next week. Near the telegraph office in Plymouth Road, I bought an afternoon newspaper. On attaining the Marylebone Road, I looked in at a bakery, where I arranged for a box of small cakes to be sent round to Mrs. Hudson. I had just stepped into a break in the traffic to cross the street and go home when a hansom cab, hurtling past, nearly knocked me down! I could not swear to it, but the cabbie bore more than a passing resemblance to Hedley, the driver of the manuscript! Had I not been so shaken by this encounter, I might have had the wits to hire a second cab and follow him. As it was, he took advantage of my unsettled state and disappeared around a corner.

Holmes came back in the late afternoon, and I could see by his set features that the mission he'd undertaken was not fruitful. "I called at Earls Court, and then in Bayswater," he told me. "Neither Bourne Forster nor Dyvelstone was at home. Their landladies report they are in and out of London with some regularity, which supports the notion that their work requires travel." Bourne Forster's landlady provided dates when her lodger was away, and she gave Holmes the document box, which he brought to show me. It was polished mahogany, with a simple swing-hook clasp that appeared to fit snugly. He opened it to reveal a plain lining of purple cloth. To our regret, there was no false bottom, nor any other secret compartment where the manuscript might have lain overlooked.

I told Holmes of my experience with the hansom, and my suspicions that it was Hedley who'd held the reins. My friend settled into his chair with a whisky in hand and gazed long into our cheerful little fire. "What a very singular case this is, Watson," he commented. "It has attributes in common with other criminal adventures, notably that of Baron Tischler's distinctive traveling trunk some five or six years past. There are some crucial distinctions, naturally. Yet it's instructive to recall that misdeeds sometimes have a family resemblance." He stretched his long legs toward the dancing flames. "I expect to have a solution for you and your eager readers after breakfast tomorrow."

"After breakfast?"

"Anyway, I've left word for our distinguished 'dictionareers' to call on us then."

At precisely 9:55 the next morning, Holmes and I awaited our guests. Presently we heard the bell downstairs. Mrs. Hudson brought Dyvelstone and Bourne Forster into our sitting room. As we exchanged greetings with the two aggrieved scholars, the bell sounded again. Our friend Lestrade joined the little party, still holding Holmes's telegram summoning him to Baker Street. "I have better things to do," the inspector objected, "without sitting in your audience applauding on command."

"I'm glad you've arrived," Holmes told him. "Perhaps you'll entertain us with a report of the state of ditches along the Holland Road, hmm?" The little inspector reddened. A moment later, Miss Nugent slipped in and I offered her my chair. We heard the bell again, and Professor Skeat was shown in. The last to enter was Hedley, his hat in his hands and a look of unease on his face. Sherlock Holmes assumed a position in the center of the room.

"The facts of the case are simple, though sprightly," he began. "A manuscript box travels from Earls Court to Bayswater by hansom. Two days later, it is returned by means of the same hansom from Bayswater to Earls Court. When opened in Earls Court, the box is empty. A valuable, handwritten dictionary – coveted by an admittedly 'desperate' expert in philology – an authority who had beleaguered the book's compilers to the point of their severing ties with him – is missing. The English Dialect Society's national dictionary project is idled.

"Attention next centers on the hansom driver, Tom Hedley. In all London, how many cabbies do you suppose are Geordies who command their horses in the Northumbrian dialect? For her assistance, I owe thanks to Miss Jane Nugent." The lady smiled in acknowledgement.

"Yet desperation and dialect do not criminals make," Holmes continued. "Isn't that right, Lestrade?"

"I know that," the little inspector agreed, testily. "I represent the professional police force. That's why these men consulted me in the first place."

"Yes, they gave you the benefit of the doubt," Holmes replied with a bow. "Then they came to see me." Lestrade bristled at this, but said nothing.

"Professor Skeat was exceedingly anxious to obtain the manuscript," Holmes continued, turning to the venerable old man. "You described for Watson and me your determination to complete your Society's county-by-county survey of British languages, a series that lacks only the Northumbrian word book. You spoke of your own ties to Northumberland, and of your 'black' desperation when Dyvelstone and Bourne Forster would not agree to terms. You were quite angry. While their book would certainly reflect well on the Society, in truth its publication would be the final diamond in the crown of your own career. You have a motive."

"What are you insinuating?" Skeat's face was flushed with irritation. "I am a gentleman and a scholar, not a thief!"

Holmes exchanged a long stare with the professor while I held my breath. I freely admit I was very much in the dark. Abruptly, Holmes swung to face another man.

"You, Tom Hedley!" he ejaculated, and Hedley jumped in his seat. "There is this fact: No one had more opportunity than you to make off with the manuscript. You were alone with the thing on two occasions."

Hedley stood uncertainly and faced Holmes. He responded in English, but with an accent that was at times impenetrable, often slipping into the fulsome Northumbrian vernacular. Fortunately, there were decipherers in our midst. Miss Nugent translated, and we were able to understand the cabbie's statement. "I only did as I was told," he informed us. "I took the box to Mr. Dyvelstone, and two days later I brought it back to Mr. Bourne Forster. I never touched it; these gentlemen did that themselves." He maintained he'd never seen a manuscript, and even if he had, he could never understand it. "I don't know how to read, sir," he told Holmes with simple dignity.

Holmes patted Hedley's shoulder. "Despite your having a chance to take the thing, you were never really a suspect. Other cabbies have vouched for your honesty, and Bourne Forster and Dyvelstone both told me, the first time they were here, that you were to be trusted."

"Just a minute!" Indignation overpowered any civility I could lay claim to. I pointed at Hedley. "He tried to run me down in the street!"

"No, Dr. Watson," Hedley said, this time courtesy of Professor Skeat's translation. "It may have appeared so, but I only moved my hansom between you and a thug who was about to lob a cobblestone at your head."

"At *my* head?" This was unexpected.

"That's right," said Holmes. "Thrown by someone who worried I was getting uncomfortably close to unmasking him. He sought to warn me off the problem by attacking my biographer."

"Then I can only apologize," I mumbled, "and thank you very sincerely, Tom."

"Had they hurt you, Watson, they would have got out of London only after a long stay in jail," Holmes said quietly. Most people know him for his great brain; I have the privilege of also being acquainted with Holmes's great heart. I'd have risked any injury to live up to the words – and the esteem – of my friend.

"We play with the last pieces of the puzzle." Holmes continued. "For if Tom Hedley didn't steal it . . . if Professor Skeat remains very eager to have it . . . if Lestrade couldn't find it . . . where is the manuscript? And who would attack Watson to warn me to step down from the case?"

He stood and slowly walked to his desk, where the mahogany box lay. "Consider the manuscript, that rare and irreplaceable book which would greatly expand our knowledge of Northumberland's distinctive dialect," he said. "The dictionary represented the fruit of many years' labour for Mr. Dyvelstone and Mr. Bourne Forster. As Professor Skeat told me, such effort is urgent and sorely needed. How did the dictionary disappear from the hansom?"

"Well, how?" the impatient Lestrade wondered aloud.

"Elementary, my dear inspector. It never was in the hansom in the first place."

"But Mr. Holmes," Hedley protested, with the assistance of Miss Nugent. "That is the box I took back and forth between these two men. I recognize it."

Holmes shrugged. "This box was your passenger, yes, but I'm certain you neither saw, nor conveyed, a dictionary. The box was empty. Dyvelstone and Bourne Forster effected a hoax."

Disbelief rippled through the room. Dyvelstone struggled to his feet, then, to our astonishment, he fainted. Bourne Forster, pale and shaken, looked as though he might slump beside his friend. Miss Nugent and I looked after them. When they were sensible once more, Holmes went on.

"I can say with some degree of certainty that my clients did not intend malice," he began. "I don't doubt they traveled to Northumberland on some dozen or more occasions. Their landladies confirm they were away for extended periods with some regularity. Those trips coincided with letters they sent to Professor Skeat. I examined the envelopes, noted the postmarked dates, and saw for myself they were mailed from villages throughout Northumberland. Dyvelstone and Bourne Forster maintained a correspondence with the professor for several years as they collected local words. They have a demonstrable familiarity with the Northumbrian dialect. Watson and I heard them scolding Lestrade with Northumbrian words a few days ago. Furthermore, when Professor Skeat tried out some of his childhood Northumbrian on them, he reported they were 'thunderstruck'. In order for that to be so, they must first comprehend what he's said.

"The figure of twelve-hundred words that were overlooked by everyone else – including the eminent Brockett – strikes me as being overly hopeful . . . . one might even say far-fetched," Holmes continued "As I said at the outset, I am quite certain my clients didn't plan any harm. It is my belief they were swept along by their own enthusiasm for their hobby. It was only when they began to brag and boast that they found themselves dangerously exposed. Shame and ridicule lay ahead. While they no doubt collected some words, the total fell short of the figure they gave Skeat. No one has actually seen their dictionary, though the new words will likely be found scribbled in a notebook in one of their rooms."

"I fear it's true," a now downcast Dyvelstone said. "We hoped to add to Brockett's work, and we did, in one sense. We found some words he missed. But we never approached anything to match our claims. When Professor Skeat pressed us for the dictionary, we panicked. I dreamt up hiring Tom to carry the empty box."

"If we could convince the Society that our dictionary was lost or stolen, we would be sympathetic figures, never connected to fraud," Bourne Forster admitted, sadly.

"When you engaged Lestrade, he hesitated. You decided to consult a second detective, one who, like yourselves, is an amateur. And so you came to me," Holmes said. "Then you did something really wrong. Lestrade will determine whether it is actionable or not, though I suspect it must be. You implicated two innocent men, suggesting that Professor Skeat, or Tom Hedley, was behind the dictionary's disappearance."

"I am sorry," Dyvelstone said.

"Which one of you tried to throw the cobblestone at Watson?"

Bourne Forster half-raised his hand. "I'm sorry, too, Mr. Holmes, and I am very sorry, Dr. Watson."

"Well . . . I knew it all along," Lestrade assured us in a bored tone.

"Of course you did," Holmes said with an indulgent smile. "After all, you represent the official force."

That evening, Jane Nugent returned by train to her elderly employer near Newcastle. She was happy there, she told me, and couldn't imagine any other life for herself. She assured me, however, that she very much enjoyed the excitement she found in London, and she thanked Holmes and me for including her in this latest case. I wished her well. Once we'd said our good-byes, I decided that Mrs. Hudson was right. I'm nearly ready to contemplate my future.

Lestrade arrested the hoaxers, then released them the next day. He informed us that Dyvelstone and Bourne Forster ought to have seen a few weeks' hard labour for the trouble to which they'd put everyone, but for the intervention of Professor Skeat. The old linguist was finally allowed to look over the notes our clients had compiled on their trips to the North. Though not nearly the twelve hundred they'd bragged about, there were still almost three hundred previously uncollected words and phrases. If this seemingly fell short, it was still deemed an accomplishment. The would-be wordsmen quickly agreed to terms with the English Dialect Society, whose committee published their dictionary in the form of a supplement to Brockett's earlier work. Publication of this volume concluded its mission, and the Society disbanded. A week later, Skeat announced his retirement.

The bit of brainwork completed, Sherlock Holmes fell into his timeworn pattern, vacillating between the violin and the threat of the hypodermic syringe. "Bring me problems, bring me work, bring me mental exaltation," was his cry. "I'm through with lighter amusements." His pleas would soon be answered. I am always ready to help him and to bring his exploits – amusing or otherwise – before the public, no matter how "regrettable" my friend considers these "stories" to be.

The Fairy Hills Horror
by Geri Schear

Of all the cases my friend Mr. Sherlock Holmes handled, the one that caused me the greatest distress was the Addleton tragedy. For many years, I could not write about it, and I find my notes on those events singularly sparse. However, I think it will continue to haunt me until I set it down.

It was an unseasonably cold and damp August morning a few months after my friend had returned to London after his long absence. I had moved back into our Baker Street apartments and we two old campaigners had once again settled into the comfort of our former friendship. I came down to breakfast that morning to see my friend scouring the newspapers. An assortment of broadsheets lay strewn around the room with Sherlock Holmes sitting in their midst.

"You have a case, I see," said I, recognising the symptoms.

"Just so, my dear Watson. The matter of the missing Addleton family. You have been following the account in the newspapers?"

"Yes, indeed. I think all England is fascinated by the 'Fairy Hills Mystery', as the press are calling it. They make much of the fact that the barrow mounds near the village are called 'fairy hills' by some locals." He snorted and I added, "That a woman and four children should simply vanish in the middle of the day seems utterly bewildering. You have been consulted on the case then?"

"Yes." He handed me a telegram.

"'*Will call upon you at eleven o'clock Re: the missing Addletons. Lestrade,*'" I read. "Well, that's to the point. It is almost that hour now."

"Tell me what you know of the case, Watson," Holmes said. "It will help me clarify the details in my mind."

Like the entire country, I had been following the matter with great interest. As I sat at the table and poured a cup of coffee, I recounted the facts as they had been reported.

"On Monday last," I said, "that is to say the 30th of July, Dr. Winston Addleton said goodbye to his wife and four children at their home on the Essex side of the village of Bartlow and took the train to the university where he is a professor of archaeology. When he returned around six o'clock that evening, the breakfast things were still on the table. The house was otherwise in perfect order, but his wife and children had vanished.

"The professor searched the area and sent telegrams to his wife's family in Bristol, but no one had seen or heard from her. That was a week ago, and as far as I can tell, neither Mrs. Addleton nor her children have been seen since."

No sooner had I said this than there was a knock at the door below and, moments later, Lestrade entered our chambers.

"A rum business this, Mr. Holmes," said he. "A family doesn't simply vanish in the middle of a summer day."

"You have my full attention, Inspector," my friend said. He sat in his chair with his eyes closed. Lestrade gave me a long-suffering glance and then read the details from his notebook.

"Precisely a week ago today, that is, Monday, 30th July, Dr. Winston Addleton ate breakfast with his wife of eight years, Jenny, and his four children, Michael aged six, Elizabeth aged five, Rose aged four, and Charles aged two. He kissed them goodbye a little after seven o'clock and walked the two miles to Bartlow Railway Station. The Addletons do not live in the village proper, but about two miles beyond on the Essex side of the border in a cottage called Barrow House."

"He walked? They do not have transport?" Holmes asked.

"They own a trap, but Dr. Addleton leaves it for his wife. About an hour after the professor left, a neighbour, a retired farmer called Fairchild, saw the missing woman walking near the river – that's the River Granta."

"She was some distance from him, according to the newspapers," I said.

"Not close enough to speak to, but he recognised her all right. Mrs. Addleton waved to him, but continued her walk without stopping."

"Was she alone or were her children with her?"

"She was alone."

"Forgive the interruption, Lestrade. Pray continue."

"Dr. Addleton returned home a little after six o'clock that evening. He was surprised to find Barrow House empty and the breakfast things still on the table."

"Does the family employ a servant?" Holmes said.

"A woman comes in on Tuesdays and Fridays, so she was not due on that day, it being Monday."

"Do you know what precisely was on the table?"

Lestrade flicked through his notes. "There were a couple of glasses of milk and a half-empty cup of tea, as well as a full large pot of tea, and a loaf of bread."

"Butter?"

"It's not in my notes. I suppose not. Does it matter?"

"If your notes are accurate, Lestrade, it suggests, does it not, that the family had only just sat down to their meal?"

"I suppose the full pot of tea and loaf of bread do seem to indicate it," Lestrade agreed. "But how does that help us?"

"We cannot say at present, but we would do well to remember it. The information may prove useful when we can add to the picture of that morning. Do we know when Dr. Addleton arrived at the university?"

"His usual hour, which is a little before nine, I believe. He worked in his office for some time and then he began his first class at eleven o'clock."

Holmes sat up suddenly. "Bah!" he cried. "Why did you wait a week before consulting me? By now all the evidence will be washed away, particularly in light of this wretched summer we have not been enjoying."

"The husband kept insisting his family would show up. He persuaded himself that his wife and children had gone to visit relatives and forgotten to mention it, or that he himself had forgotten that they had told him. He is a rather scatter-brained gentleman, more interested in his books than in people, so it did seem perfectly possible."

"And you thought it likely that five people would suddenly rush away from the breakfast table to call upon distant relatives?" Holmes scoffed.

"Is there any suggestion Mrs. Addleton might have a paramour?" I asked, quickly changing the subject.

"There is no evidence of it, Doctor," Lestrade replied. "Given the isolation of the house, I cannot imagine where she would encounter any gentlemen other than her husband. She was, by all accounts, a devoted wife and mother. Still, I could understand why she would be tempted to look elsewhere. Dr. Addleton is not what you might call an ideal spouse."

"How so?"

"Well, he is obsessed with his work, by all accounts. One of those academics who assumes everyone must be as fascinated by his subject as he is. He is a professor of archaeology at one of the smaller Cambridge universities. I gather he is respected, if not particularly admired, by his colleagues. I suppose it's a difficult subject, and not many people share his passion for it, if passion is the word. Frankly, Mr. Holmes, I'm surprised Dr. Addleton even noticed that his wife and children were missing."

"Is there any indication that he has formed a dalliance with another woman?"

"I think it highly unlikely. This is a very self-absorbed gentleman – small, shabby, and hardly speaks above a whisper. He seems to have no conversation beyond his work. Why do you ask?"

"If a man is a professor, it is reasonable to suppose he is earning a decent salary, is it not? He lives in an area not known for a high cost of living, and yet he cannot afford a servant more than twice a week. Where is his money going?"

"Probably to his archaeology," Lestrade replied. "He certainly has a lot of books and instruments related to his profession. Still, it's a good point and I'll be sure to look into it. I need to go back to Bartlow this afternoon. Will you and the Doctor join me?"

"I think we had better," Holmes said.

On the train a couple of hours later, I asked Lestrade his own theory. "What do you think happened to the missing Addletons?"

"Now I've had a chance to think about it, I believe Mr. Holmes must be right. The woman must have a fancy man and ran off with him."

"And took the children?" my friend said. "And left the breakfast things on the table? Is the wife a poor housekeeper?"

"I think not," Lestrade said. "Everything was very neat, if rather plain and poor. Her husband seemed surprised that she would have gone out without putting the breakfast things away. He seemed quite cross about the waste."

We were met at Bartlow Station by the local constable, a tow-haired man called Lewis. He shook our hands and greeted Holmes with awe, much to Lestrade's irritation.

"Enough of that now," the inspector said. "Let us head to Barrow House."

"Take us by the river, if you please, Constable," said my friend. "I should like to speak to Mr. Fairchild first."

The weather was dry but overcast and unseasonably chilly as the carriage rumbled through the delightful country lanes. In the distance, I beheld the woods that surround the ancient barrows and I hoped we might have an opportunity to visit those strange ancient structures. We passed the so-called River Granta. This was little more than a swift moving stream. The banks on either side were steep, covered with long grasses and brambles. An odd place for a woman to take a stroll, I thought.

Mr. Fairchild's cottage sat back from the river. Tall beech trees surrounded the building, and it presented an appealing picture. The occupant was, I thought, in his mid-seventies, but still mentally alert. His eyes were intensely blue, and only the clouds in their depths revealed his age.

He welcomed us into his home and offered us tea. We sat in the front parlour which faced the river. It was from this window that Fairchild had seen Mrs. Addleton.

"A charming lady," he said. "I see her from time to time with the children. Such a devoted mother. They pass by on their way to the village and she always waves. Sometimes she stops and asks if there's anything I need. A very kind lady."

"Do you live alone here, Mr. Fairchild?" I asked.

"Hmm? What's that? Live alone? No, indeed. My son lives with me. He's a good boy, is Leonard. I think we both enjoy the company."

"Is he friendly with Mrs. Addleton?"

"He knows her slightly, but he'd be at work most of the day. He tends farm, like. Still, he'd know her by sight. We all know her by her hair."

"Was your son here that day when you saw her by the river?"

"Nay, he were out yonder in field," he said, nodding towards the land behind the house.

"Do you often see Mrs. Addleton without the children?" I continued.

"Not as a rule, no. They're too little to be left on their own, see, though on days when housekeeper is there, Mrs. Addleton goes into the village on her own from time to time. Not much of a life, being stuck in a house all day with four little ones. That husband of hers isn't my idea of a man. He works in town, you know, and he leaves that woman home for days at a time with no one but children to talk to, not even a servant. Ruddy disgrace."

I glanced at Holmes. He stirred himself from his reverie and said, "You are a good hundred yards from the river, Mr. Fairchild. I wonder how clearly did you see Mrs. Addleton last Monday?"

"Well, she was a distance away, but I knew it was her right enough."

"How so? How were you able to see her features from such a distance, and with your glaucoma?"

"Glaucoma's not so bad, not yet. But, no, I didn't see her features. I saw her hair, her bright red hair, for it hung loose down her back, as it always did. She wore her pretty yellow bonnet, and her blue dress. She waved at me."

"What time was this?"

"Around eight, I'd say. Yes, perhaps a minute or two after eight."

"Well, Mr. Holmes?" the constable said as we climbed back in the carriage. "That confirms it, does it not, that Mrs. Addleton was still in Bartlow on Monday morning?"

"It raises more questions than it answers. Why would a woman known to be tidy in her habits suddenly leave the breakfast table and take a walk? And where did she leave her children?" For a moment Holmes was silent. Then he looked up and said, "Tell me, Constable Lewis, how was the weather here last Monday?"

"It was quite dreadful. It poured rain all day."

"And yet we are to believe that a woman wore a yellow bonnet and a blue dress – no overcoat, mind – and took a stroll beside the stream. And with her hair loose, too. Does that not strike you as highly improbable?"

"But those are the facts, Mr. Holmes," Lestrade exclaimed. "You cannot argue away the facts."

"I am sure you are right, Lestrade. Well, let us see what the Addleton house can tell us."

We were very surprised to find that the professor was not at home. "Where can he have gone?" Lestrade cried in consternation. "Don't tell me he's gone missing, too!"

"I am sure there is some reasonable explanation," I said. "Perhaps he has gone out searching for his missing family."

"That must be it, of course," Lestrade conceded.

We looked around the grounds. The area was spacious enough and the view picturesque, but I found the isolation oppressive. If Mrs. Addleton had simply bundled her children up and left, I could hardly blame her.

"Constable Lewis," Holmes said. "You were the first officer on the scene when Dr. Addleton reported his wife missing, I believe."

"That's right, sir. The local minister, Reverend Bullard, called me over from the village of Linton to investigate. I cover both villages, you see. It was dark when I came into the house. Dr. Addleton was sitting by the fire, huddled into himself. I asked the minister to initiate a search, though there was little enough we could do in the dark, and it was still raining."

"And did the professor participate in the search?"

"He was grievously distressed, Mr. Holmes. I told him to stay put in case the woman and the children should return. I inquired at the railway station, but the missing people had not been seen there."

"And the trap? I believe Mrs. Addleton had use of it?"

"Yes. She does the family shopping, very difficult with four little ones in tow, I should think, and uses the trap for that and to take the oldest child to school. It was still in the barn out yonder. The mud on the wheels was dry, so I did not think it had been used for at least a couple of days."

"Well done, Constable. That was an astute observation. Let us take a look at this trap."

The young policeman led us to an outbuilding. "Barn" was really too elaborate a word for it. A run-down shed seemed a more accurate description. Lestrade, the constable, and I stood in silence as Holmes examined the vehicle. He began by scraping some of the dried earth from the wheel, which he then studied it under a glass. Next, he turned his attention to the trap itself. Something at the footrest made him chuckle.

"What have you found?" Lestrade asked.

"A footprint," Holmes said. "See here."

We gathered and looked at the clear outline of a boot.

"A man's footprint," Lestrade said, "What of it?"

"We are told that Mrs. Addleton is the only one to use this trap. Why, then, should we find a man's print here? It suggests, does it not, that a man was the last to drive this vehicle?"

"Holmes . . . ." I said, my mouth dry with fear, "Are you suggesting . . . ?"

"What?" Lestrade demanded. "What are you suggesting, Mr. Holmes?"

"We do not have enough evidence yet," my friend replied. "All I can say with any certainty at this stage is a man was the last to drive this carriage."

"Hullo?" a voice called from outside the barn.

We went out into the courtyard and were greeted by a small, shrivelled-looking fellow, aged, I suppose, about forty, but who could easily pass for a man some twenty years older. His coat looked ancient and very well worn. His hair was thinning. He was, as Lestrade said, an exceedingly unlikely candidate for a paramour.

"Dr. Addleton, I presume?" Holmes said.

Lestrade made the introductions. The little man's eyes burned when he heard Holmes's name. "Oh, I cannot tell you how glad I am that you are here, Mr. Holmes," he cried. "I am so worried about my family. If only you can find them, I would be very much in your debt."

"I will do my best, though you should not raise your hopes too high. So many days have passed since their mysterious disappearance, even Sherlock Holmes may have difficulty reading the traces."

"Anything you can do, Mr. Holmes. My neighbours and the constable have taken pains to find them. I was out just now, searching

294

the fields and the river. My wife was last seen walking by the Granta, you know."

"I see you brought your archaeological implements with you."

"Did I?" He looked in surprise at the kitbag on his shoulder. "Force of habit, I fear. I take them everywhere I go."

The professor led us into the house and we sat in a cramped and dark parlour.

"Can you tell us what happened the last time you saw your family, Dr. Addleton?" Holmes said.

"I will do my best, but it has been a week, and memory fades."

"Anything you recall may be of use. I am sure as a man of science you have better powers of observation than most."

"Thank you. It is a compliment, but I believe it is justified. The difficulty lies in the ordinariness of it all. I have played it in my mind so many times, but it was such a usual day. I was running a little late because I had overslept. The youngest boy had a restless night, and my wife let him come into our bed to try to settle him. My wife was always so indulgent with the children. In any event, my sleep was disturbed and I ended by coming down here to the settee, and so overslept. I was in such a rush to get the train on time that I really wasn't paying close attention to what was happening in the house."

"But you had breakfast together?"

"Yes. That is to say, the rest of the family did. I had a mouthful of tea and my wife made me a hard-boiled egg, which I put in my pocket to eat on the train. I left the house and cut through the fields to try to get to the station on time."

"And were you?" Holmes said. "On time, I mean."

"Yes. I just made it. The rush made me poorly, however, and I was still feeling exhausted from my broken night's sleep."

"Could you not have taken a later train? I understand your first class was not until eleven o'clock."

"That is true, and I might have done so, but I had a meeting with one of my students, a bright lad called Lexington. As it happened, the boy never turned up."

"Did he offer an explanation?"

"He said our meeting was for five o'clock that evening, not nine a.m. as I had written in my diary. I cannot imagine why I would have agreed to a meeting so late in the day. It would have meant rushing for my train. I can only assume I misheard the five for a nine."

"And the boy's integrity is in no doubt?" Holmes asked.

"No, not at all. He is a very sound student. I must confess, sir, I am a bit scatter-brained. I have my own ideas and they dominate my thoughts to the point where I completely forget everything else. That is why I was not initially too alarmed to find my family were not at home. I was unsettled, of course, but I convinced myself I had made another of my foolish blunders. I'm afraid my wife was always scolding me for my forgetfulness."

"Yes," Holmes said. "A common problem for brilliant academics, I believe." The professor bowed slightly. "I wonder, Dr. Addleton, if you can talk me through the events of Monday evening. Start with your meeting with Lexington, if you would."

"Very well, I shall do my best. Lexington arrived in my office at five o'clock, perhaps a few minutes before. He realised I needed to catch the train and I suppose he felt guilty about our earlier misunderstanding. The examinations were due to start, well, today, in fact, and there were a number of issues upon which he needed clarification. We talked for some time and in the end he walked with me to the train station. We continued our conversation as we went. I only just reached the station in time to catch my train.

"The weather was quite dreadful and I faced a long walk home. Ordinarily, I do not mind. I find a long walk helps me clear my thoughts. On that evening, however, the weather was so wretched I longed for my supper and the warmth of my hearth. You can imagine my surprise when I arrived at my home to find it utterly deserted. No one came to greet me as I came in. I called for my wife and children, but no one answered my call. I searched the whole house. I was alarmed to find the table still set for breakfast. There was the teapot and the bread. I confess I rather panicked and rushed to the minister's house to see if he had heard of any incident that might have stolen my family away from me."

"Very distressing, I'm sure," Holmes said in a calm voice. "Can you tell me what your wife and children were wearing the last time you saw them?"

The man frowned, trying to remember. "Uh, I'm afraid I am not very observant about clothing. Let me see, my wife was wearing a black gown with a woollen shawl around her shoulders. The children were still in their nightclothes. Yes, I am sure they were. I was concerned about them catching cold."

"You are doing splendidly," I said. "It is a very difficult situation, to be sure."

The man nodded and hugged himself with thin hands.

Holmes said, "Doctor Watson is correct, you really are doing very well. Now, I wonder if I could ask you to go back a step and describe as accurately as you can the contents of the table."

Addleton stopped and thought. "It was just the breakfast things. There was the pot of tea, stone cold. The remnants of tea in one cup. Uh . . . the bread."

"A whole loaf?"

"Yes, that's right. It might help my recollection if I could follow your reasoning, Mr. Holmes," the professor said.

"I am trying to determine when your wife and children left the table. From what you say, it appears it must have been very shortly after you left for the train station."

"Yes, I suppose so, but where could they have gone? They certainly were not on the train. I would have seen them at the platform."

"And you only just caught your train, so it does seem very unlikely that they would have been able to get there so quickly."

"They could have taken the trap," Lestrade said. "That would have enabled them to get to the station before the professor."

"Then how did the vehicle get back here, Inspector?" Holmes said. "Besides, Mrs. Addleton was observed by the river some hours later."

"If they had been on the train, surely they would have found me," Addleton said.

"It is reasonable to assume so. I suppose relations between you and your wife were cordial?"

"Of course. Never a cross word between us."

"And what of the neighbours? Has your wife ever spoken about anyone who alarmed her or caused her anxiety?"

The professor considered. "She spoke of Mr. Fairchild as a kind gentleman, and I think she knew his son to say hello to. There were some people in the village, mostly tradesmen, and the minister. She mentioned all of them from time to time, but no one in particular. Well, there was the schoolteacher."

"The schoolteacher?"

"Mr. Nithercott. Only our oldest boy was in school, but Mr. Nithercott spoke highly about him. My wife seemed to like the teacher very much."

"Is he a married man?" I asked.

Addleton said, "No, he is single. Of course, he's only in his twenties, I think. You understand, I don't really know him myself, but my wife always spoke of him as 'young Mr. Nithercott', so that was the impression I formed."

"Thank you, Dr. Addleton," Holmes said. "You have been exceedingly helpful. I wonder if I might look at the rest of the house? I doubt there is anything left to find after so long a delay – " He gave Lestrade a disapproving look. "But I would be negligent in my duty if I did not try. No, please do not disturb yourself. I can manage perfectly well on my own."

Lestrade, the constable, and I sat together with the professor. We could hear Holmes painstakingly making his way through the cramped and ancient cottage. The professor entertained us with tales of the barrow mounds that stood just outside the village. "My particular interest is the Neolithic period," he said, "So you can imagine how fascinated I am by these strange mounds. Of course, some of them are Bronze Age or even Roman, but they are all worthy of study. Amazing to think of primitive man walking these very fields thousands of years ago, is it not? These mounds close at hand are called by some the Bartlow Pyramids. Of course, these ones are fairly modern, comparatively speaking, being from the first or second century of the Common Era. These ones are conical, which is why they are compared with pyramids. A misnomer, of course, but such things intrigue the uneducated. Even less useful is the term 'fairy hills', which I have heard some use."

"I suppose anything that attracts people to archaeology is of use," I said, seeing both policemen looking exceedingly bored.

The professor continued to discourse on the 'tumuli', as he called the barrow mounds. "Yes," he said, "We have a Roman tumuli right here in Bartlow. There were seven at one time but, alas, only three remain. They were gravesites, originally."

"Have you been inside them?" I asked.

"Oh, no, not I. They were excavated about fifty years ago. Wooden chests, glass, and pottery were discovered inside, I believe. Even an iron folding chair, can you imagine?" He became quite animated as he spoke.

"Were they built by the Romans?" Lewis asked, trying to take an interest.

"During the Roman period, certainly, but they were built by Celtic chiefs. There are any number of mounds dotted around these islands. A man could spend his life investigating all of them. The highest is around forty feet. Very impressive. Of course, there are tumuli scattered around the rest of the world, too, but the ones here in the British Isles are among the finest. The Hill of Tara in Ireland seems especially promising, as is *Brú na Bóinne* in County Meath. Some Irish sites are older than the pyramids. Extraordinary. I should dearly love to conduct a dig there. It would be the opportunity of a lifetime, but my wife would not hear of it. She reminded me of my parental duties. 'Children before science, Winston,' she said. I am sure she was right."

For an hour, the professor droned on and in the background we could hear the creaking of floorboards and the occasional "A-ha!" as Holmes continued his investigation of the house.

298

At last he reappeared. "Yes," he said, chuckling. "Not quite as useless as I had feared. Someone made a very careless error. Very careless indeed. Thank you for your time, Dr. Addleton. I think I know where to find your wife Jenny and your four little ones."

"What – ?" the professor began but Holmes refused to reply.

"It is too soon to say more just yet, but I believe I know where they are. Yes, indeed. Inspector, I think we should return to London tonight, and in the morning we will make an early start. Good afternoon, Professor. Courage! All is not lost."

We rode away in the constable's carriage, but before we were too far along, Holmes said, "Tell me, Constable, is there an inn close at hand?"

"Yes, sir. The Three Hills is not far from here."

"Excellent. Let us go and have supper. We have a long night ahead of us."

"I thought we were going back to London," Lestrade asked.

"No, indeed, Inspector."

Over a splendid supper, the constable said, "Please, Mr. Holmes, you have obviously seen far more than we. What was it you found during your search of Barrow House?"

"Porridge oats."

"Porridge?" I exclaimed. "You speak in riddles, Holmes."

He chuckled. "Consider the facts, gentlemen," he said. "A man returns home on a Monday evening to find his family missing. The table is laid out with tea and bread. Monday last was a cold, wet day. Mrs. Addleton, who is widely acknowledged as a devoted mother, serves breakfast to her children. Tea and bread, though there is a half-full bag of porridge oats in the cupboard. Surely a far more likely meal for children on a cold morning?"

"And who would serve bread without butter?" I added.

"And there were only two glasses of milk, though there were four children," the constable added. "So the breakfast table was staged for the professor's benefit? But why?"

"Could Mrs. Addleton have staged it herself?" Lestrade asked. "After all, she was seen on her own . . . . Oh, dear heavens, could she have gone mad and murdered her children?"

"Drowned them and then herself like Ophelia?" I said. "It was odd that she went walking along the riverbank wearing such inappropriate clothing. Madness would explain it."

"Oh, really," Holmes scoffed. "What nonsense. Mrs. Addleton did not go mad and she did not harm her children."

"Wait," I said, "So someone dressed as Mrs. Addleton to make it look like she was still in Bartlow. A family member? Her hair was very distinctive. It is how Mr. Fairchild recognised her, that and her outfit."

"That is significant. He did not see her face, only her familiar clothing and that red hair."

"But what does it mean, Mr. Holmes?" Constable Lewis asked.

"Something unspeakable."

After we had eaten, my friend said, "We must return to Barrow House, gentlemen. Lestrade, you and the constable take the north side of the house. Keep watch on the back door. Doctor Watson and I shall remain to the south and watch the front. Be careful, gentlemen. This fellow has no scruples nor does he value human life. Follow him, but keep a very careful distance. We must not let him know he is being watched. I implore you, be as still as statues and silent as those barrows yonder. We have an ugly business ahead of us."

The sky was cloudy and the moon, such as it was, failed to appear. Around eleven o'clock, the light went off in Barrow House and a few minutes later, a figure emerged. He headed east towards the barrows. Holmes and I followed at some distance. On the edge of the wooded area, Lestrade and Lewis caught up with us. Silently, we followed our prey towards the mounds.

Once he was under the cover of the trees, the man lit a lantern which helped us to follow him. After some minutes, the light stopped moving.

"Softly, softly," Holmes said.

We crept forward and found the professor with a shovel at the base of the mound. He had dug an opening. That is to say, he had opened a doorway that had already existed. The man screamed when he saw us.

"Hold him!" Holmes cried as the man swung the shovel at us.

The young policeman leaped upon the villain and brought him to his knees with a sound right hook. He placed cuffs on him, though Addleton was hardly moving.

"Nicely done, Constable. Now, let us see what our friend is hiding." He paused and turned to us. "I fear this will be distressing, gentlemen."

Just a few feet inside the maw of the barrow we saw them. Even now, my gorge rises at the memory. There, side by side upon the heartless earth, lay the woman and her four babies, stone dead, already foul with decay.

"How could he do such a thing?" the constable asked. His face was red with fury and tears filled his anguished eyes.

The distasteful task of examining the dead fell to me. The bodies of the children were too decayed for me to say with certainty, but I suspected they had been suffocated. Mrs. Addleton had been strangled –

the ligature was still around her neck. Further, the woman's hair, her bright red hair, had been hacked off close to the scalp.

Much later, back at the police station in the nearby village of Linton, Holmes explained.

"It was a matter of a man trying to be clever, but having insufficient wits to carry it off. Each of the clues seemed compelling on their own, and yet they did not form a coherent picture. Therefore, it was reasonable to assume that some or all of the clues had been manufactured."

"The breakfast table," Lestrade said. "You kept asking about that, but even now I do not see the significance."

"The professor wanted to us to believe his family had vanished sometime in the middle of Monday morning. He set the breakfast things in place, but he did a poor job. There was a full pot of tea, a large pot such as one would make for a family, but only one teacup. There was a loaf of bread, but no butter or marmalade. What mother would serve dry bread to her children when there was porridge in the cupboard? The professor's indifference to his family told against him when he tried to present the image of a normal morning."

"That seems plain enough," the constable said. "And I wondered about the egg, too."

"The egg?" Lestrade asked.

"You remember," Lewis said. "The professor said he didn't have time to eat breakfast, and yet his wife was able to make a hard-boiled egg for him. That's a good six or seven minutes. Would a man in a rush have waited so long when there was bread right there?"

"Well done, Constable. You are perfectly correct. There was also Fairchild's report of seeing Mrs. Addleton by the river. This was to make sure the professor had an alibi for when she supposedly vanished."

"Who did Fairchild see, Holmes?" I asked.

"Addleton himself. He dressed in his wife's garb and cut off her hair to fashion a make-shift wig, so the old man would identify the dead woman for a time when the professor was apparently at the university. Addleton caught the train at the usual time, but got off at the next stop and doubled back."

"How dreadful," I said. Something about the hacking off of his wife's hair seemed chilling.

"The professor made an error when I asked what his wife had been wearing the last time he saw her. The question took him by surprise and he told the truth. She was wearing a black dress. That is what she was wearing when we found her. But why would she have changed into a different gown to go walking by the river?"

"And she wouldn't have gone walking without her children in any case," Lewis added. "Yes, he made a hash of it, all right, but we still wouldn't have found the bodies without your help, Mr. Holmes."

"I had to let Addleton believe he had made some mistake or other so he would go back to check on the bodies. He saved us an infinite number of pains by leading us right to them."

"What of Lexington?" Lestrade asked. "The student who made the mistake about the meeting. Was that a genuine mistake, do you think?"

"I spoke with Lexington myself last week," the constable said. "He confirmed that the appointment had been scheduled weeks ago."

"It was part of the professor's plan," Holmes said, "Furthermore, it proves the murders were premeditated.

"I believe the professor murdered his family on Friday night. There is evidence of a struggle in the couple's bedroom and in the children's beds. He then had a whole weekend to haul away the bodies, which left dried mud on the wheels of the trap. You did very well to spot that, Constable. I congratulate you. The fact that the mud had dried suggested some time had passed between the moving of the bodies and when you were called to the scene."

"But I don't understand why, Holmes," I said. "What sort of a man murders his wife and children?"

"Since Addleton continues to assert his innocence, we can only surmise. However, I suspect he already gave us the motive. He wanted to go to Ireland to study the mounds there. His wife reminded him of his obligations as a father. The fact that the murders coincided with the end of term suggests he had hoped to have the whole summer to indulge his passion for archaeology without any family obligations to trouble him. Once you look into his background, Lestrade, I believe you will find his money has been saved to pay for that expedition."

So it proved. Dr. Addleton protested his innocence to the last, but the jury found Sherlock Holmes's testimony compelling and he was hanged.

There. I have set down the tragedy. Perhaps now I will forget.

A Loathsome and Remarkable Adventure
by Marcia Wilson

"It would seem," said my friend Sherlock Holmes, "crime's capacity for dullness is infinite."

It was the latest evening in a fortnight short of clients, so his words were concerning if not surprising. Holmes feared for his mental powers, and only visiting cases or news could alleviate the pressure placed upon his brain.

I have noticed the Yard has an occasional genius for disturbing Holmes's boredom at the proper moment. By whatever mysterious lines of communication they follow, word had emerged concerning Holmes's restlessness. If there were no clients, there were at least a string of puzzled policemen with "wee matters" that could be solved within the hour, and their happy payment was in form of news, so fresh it had not yet reached the newspapers.

To my relief, this was providing a wonderful distraction. One is not likely to forget the sight of Inspector Hopkins pantomiming his way through a misfortunate raid of a den full of foreign animals. Holmes's examination of the man's "most genuine longfin bite wounds" led to a greater study at the photographer's, and now I believe Sherlock Holmes is the only person in all of England who may brag about the study of Australian eel attacks in his repertoire.

Today it was Inspector Lestrade who had come calling, and as they had a plethora of past cases with differences of option, the conversation was getting droll.

"As you often say to me when I comment on your writings, Watson," Holmes continued, "'*A problem without a solution may interest the student, but can hardly fail to annoy the casual reader.*' So! The reading of my own life is currently in wont."

Lestrade regarded him with a quizzical air. "I for one appreciate stupidity when it makes it easier to solve a crime."

"In a city of millions, you are also guaranteed smarter criminals part of the time."

"I'll tell you what's worse! When you have a problem and you can't understand a blessed thing about it because it might as well be from the earth to the moon!"

303

Holmes's brow shot up and he tipped his fingers under his chin with a particular sort of smile that, in my experience, foretold that he was prepared to have some fun. "Have you been reading Verne again?"

"I don't see what that has to do with our conversation."

"Perhaps nothing, but normally you are a better conversationalist, not the fellow I see who has been playing a bad form of chopsticks on his knee since he took the chair. Your latest tale over proper wages for police informants is amusing, but not important. You could have regaled us with the details in your sleep. On the other coin, you read Verne for his use of science – an inspector is daily wearied with superstition and nonsense among the public and his own constables, so you find his use of science appealing. Your absent quotation of his novel is revealing, Lestrade. The heroes need help for their dangerous quest but England does not give a farthing. So, in the tradition of Verne, I must imagine that you have some trouble that is not supported by your allies. Are you expecting an assassin?"

"No – and yes, come to think of it." Lestrade puffed upon his cigar before elaborating: "A character assassin."

"This is very grave. Who might this be?"

"Isadora Persano."

Our light atmosphere was transformed into astonishment.

"The duelist? The impersonator? The journalist?" I cried.

"I can't think of anyone else with that name and those qualifications." Lestrade said gloomily. "Perhaps it is all just folderol or I'm seeing things that aren't there, but tomorrow will tell everything and I am not looking forward to it."

"What, did he demand pistols at dawn?" I laughed.

"Yes!"

Holmes leaned forward and leveled his glass as a baton. "Tell us everything."

"Your reputation may suffer if you get involved."

"Kindly allow me the right to decide in my own house."

Lestrade took a deep breath to steady his composure.

"Persano is a cocklebur! I think Italy lets him be our problem, because it is always nicer for a country if another puts their popular troublemakers away."

Holmes sniffed. "Anyone who makes a career in journalism cannot be sedentary. He backs up his words with weapons and his weapons with words, but the gossips have had very little to show of either since he arrived on our shores."

"Now that isn't for the lack of trying! He's got a hot head and a quick pistol when he isn't going for his sword. If you knew how many incidents we've dealt with, even you would be surprised. But that's all backstride the point."

"And what *is* the point, Lestrade?"

"Persano still writes for his Italian audience and that annoys the Embassies. The man's pen cuts to the bone. Contradictors to his speeches on society's ills or the importance of the Persano Horse become his enemy. I think he cares more about that horse than his own bed and board. He has sunk his own fortune and others' into returning the breed to its glory, but with only two mares in his possession he's desperate for more. This has made him reckless. I don't pretend to know the manners of the Court, Mr. Holmes, but I know they exist and I respect how men in authority have their own way of doing things."

"Made enemies where there were none, eh?"

"That is my opinion."

"You are our expert in low emotion. Pray tell how you managed to raise his considerable ire."

"It started because Signor Persano has been sharing his luxurious opinions with his luckless neighbors."

"And they would be . . . ?"

"A club of Corsican and Pisan ex-patriates, mostly old bachelors and widowers. They have some means, and Persano hoped they would add their funds and names to the Persano Horse revival. Too bad for his hopes! They live quietly in the Etruscan Hotel, playing cards and trading exaggerated hunting stories of the glory days and a few bone-chilling fairytales about people who have the ability to murder in dreams." Lestrade shuddered. "I can't imagine how it must be for the police over there."

"How did you arrive on this case?"

"It started with Jones. It had nothing to do with the fight-to-be, just one of those cases where you have the bad luck to be present. Poor man was simply getting information on the hotel's guest list when the sounds of a quarrel came out of the meeting-room and into the lobby. As he explained it, Persano demanded more support than the old men could give, even if it promised preservation of their beloved horse.

"Persano is *a femminiello*, what they call a man who wears women's clothing, and they are traditionally allowed liberties." Lestrade shrugged. "They think his sort are lucky to have around. I suppose he thought they would indulge his request. When he was disappointed, his words dynamited. Jones called it a real Punch-and-Judy before he took a crystal bowl to the head – by accident, at least! I was sent to smooth things over."

"I should not envy you," I made bold to say.

305

"Thankfully, those old men didn't mind me. They're all really a calm, steady sort. It was Persano that kept angry, and demanded I meet him tomorrow to hammer out the 'details of our satisfaction', as he calls it, in the park of my choosing."

It was ludicrous enough that Holmes and I stared at him before we realised he had finished.

"Did you try telling him that a policeman in service to the Crown is expressly forbidden the satisfaction of duels?" Holmes murmured.

"Yes, I did. I also assured him I could arrest him for obstructing an officer in service to the Crown. He said if I wished to pursue this topic, I could plea my case in writing. So, again, I am to return to the Etruscan Hotel no later than eight o'clock on the morrow, and meet him at his rooms."

"You should bring your seconds." Holmes lifted his glass. "I nominate myself. Watson, there is nothing so rude as a dueling team without their personal physician."

"I shall have my bag ready."

"I'm not dueling him!" Lestrade shouted. "Dear me! Even if I could – this is Isadora Persano! The man has won nine out of ten duels since he was thirteen!"

"Luck." Holmes sniffed.

"Luck? You call his record luck?"

"Not I. *You*, Lestrade."

"*Me?*"

"You said the *femminiello* is lucky."

Lestrade sputtered for some time before he calmed enough to peer at Holmes with a sudden shrewd glare.

"I've seen that look in your eye before."

"I'm sure I don't know what you mean."

Lestrade threw up his hands. "I shan't be able to stop you, shall I?"

"Whyever would you? For all of his vitriolic ink, Persano is intelligent. He has often begged my acquaintance. Perhaps I might be able to offer some perspective into this trouble."

"How can you possibly offer a solution?"

"How can I if I do not come with you?"

Lestrade was still muttering feeble complaints as he left for the night, but not before Holmes wrung an oath upon his warrant card to pick us up on the way to the Etruscan.

"Well, well, well!" Holmes turned from the door after closing it, and rubbed his hands. "To-morrow may not be so humdrum after all!

306

Lestrade is amazingly over his head. A bored journalist is a deadly journalist!"

"That bored journalist is also a duelist whom, I daresay, possesses a full card for the season, all seasons of the year! Boredom should be an extinct disease against his campaign of vaccination."

"Your humour stings with satire's salt, Watson. A bored man creates or exposes injustice."

"But fighting with Lestrade! He is a policeman. A workman."

"Precisely."

Holmes went to the window, where the lamps were just beginning to peep out of the encroaching fogs.

"It is my business to know persons of interest, and Persano has been exactly that since he stepped foot on our shore. Have you seen him perform on the stage? Such a master of expression and silent language! His ability to mimic the foibles of both sexes simultaneously is astounding, and as a Scaramouche he is without peer. I admire his uncanny ability to notice the smallest nuances of human emotion. Alas for his purse, it will forever be the British-born Vesta Tilley whom the public adores and empties their pockets to see. Not that I have any complaints for her abilities, but I find them both unique!"

"I do not often have the pleasure of music halls, Holmes."

"Make the time! It is most informative in the nature of man. Persano's birth-name was replaced by the village of his origin, Persano, for his forefathers served the famous stables. He named himself Isadora in admiration for our Vesta Tilley, who chose the goddess Vesta as her stage name. Vesta is the patroness of hearth and home, reminding the audience of her respectability. In contrast, Isadora compels to the Goddess Isis, legendary for her willingness to listen to the slave and sinner as sympathetically as she would to Cesar. One of the latter was that rascally Caligula, who donned women's clothing in her name.

"The *femminiello* is no different from Vesta Tilley when she dons a tailcoat or bares her legs as a principal boy. The differences in appearance emphasizes attention, the same way the proper lens allows one to find the bacterium under the microscope. Mockery, japes, and scorn are their art, and their material is already written for them in the hypocrisy of mores.

"I have often wondered what brought Persano here if it was not political refuge. In his home lands, he would be far more lauded, and our solid sterling is worth twenty-five of their lire."

"And yet he does not seek the adulations of his own race."

"What keeps him here? Not knowing is a guarantee of my curiosity. Hum! I believe I shall request us an early breakfast. We may need it, and

Mrs. Hudson is better disposed to watch the wires and man the telephone when she is already awake."

My thoughts were against rest when I tried to sleep. Perhaps the lack of cases had affected my own mood. This was the most interesting event in weeks and my blood thrilled at the thought of a duel. Like Lestrade and Holmes, I believed there was more to this challenge than met the eye. But what?

My affections for the equine allowed me some familiarity with the duelist's passion. The Persano was a Salernitano breed founded by the Bourbon Charles III. It was not a frequent winner in our races, but it was reliably clever and capable. The strength for their size was astounding, and even the Russians praised their ability to endure the winters. From a military eye, there was no reason to permit its extinction, yet in 1872 the government chose to dismiss the bloodline and sold all its horses in public auction. The devastated equestrians responded with private attempts to keep the blood going in small stables, but the wide dispersal of the stock worked against its swift success. Was Persano's reckless act a mark of desperation for some unknown troubles?

When I rose on the morning, Holmes was already at the breakfast table, balancing his toast over a collection of wires, newspaper-clippings, and mysterious books sprawled over the tablecloth.

"Mind your fork, Watson. I must return these portentous tomes tomorrow."

"Did you sleep at all?"

"I don't believe so. I was prodding a few soft spots in my brain-attic. Persano's presence in England really cannot be adequately explained unless he was escaping the Mafia or pursuing a specific goal."

I shared my thoughts of the previous night about the horse.

"Hmm! I am constantly surprised at how often a horse becomes a supporting character in my cases. They were not generally part of my upbringing, save as a means to my ends. There is military value to the breed, so I am also puzzled at the erasure of a tactical tool. But this is all a distraction until we determine why Lestrade, of all people, would be the subject of Persano's ferment. Until now, no-one of unimportance has ever faced his challenge, save for a few incidents in the public houses where a red-headed, red-bearded man might expect to have his tastes, not to mention his colour-vision, questioned for wearing emerald chiffon with champagne lace. But, ah, that would be Lestrade! Five minutes early, which for him is just barely on the edge of polite as to be on time is unforgivably late. Impatient in all things, even his own potential funeral."

Despite Holmes's japes, I could see his interest was fully within this odd affair, and no-one would be spilling blood if he could help it. I made short work of breakfast and found my coat and bag. Our professional friend was stamping and pacing with his fists thrust deep inside his pockets on the kerb. Inside the cab, two uniformed policemen waited for whatever orders that may come.

"Good morning." Lestrade spoke absently without looking at us as he signaled the cab to start. His thoughts were far away. "We'll make good time. Thank you for being prepared."

"We do our best. Have you learnt anything else?"

"Not much." Lestrade was markedly paler than yesterday. "I was reminded that it would be a good idea to avoid scandal with Persano's kind. It wasn't anything I didn't already know." When I expressed puzzlement, he elaborated.

"I suppose you wouldn't know, Doctor, but the Yard keeps cordial with the sort that fills the Music Halls and performance stadiums. They're generally trusty informers, even if you daren't let some of them get too close to your purse-strings or a wager. Illusion may be the key to their success, but they treasure honesty amongst their own kind.

"They have personal friendships with us, these impersonators, burlesquers, principal boys, and stage beauties . . . Inspector Froest has especially good lines with them, and to be honest, if anyone will promote to Chief Inspector or Superintendent in a few years it will be he."

"And Froest is not a man to challenge," Holmes said dryly, "if the rumours about what he can do to a pack of cards are true." And he mimed ripping a brick-sized object in half.

"Those aren't rumours, Mr. Holmes." Lestrade said with heavy gloom. "You should see what he can do with a farthing between his fingertips!" To our amusement, the silent constables nodded vigorously in unison with Lestrade's words. [1]

"I am still curious about Jones. Why was he investigating the hotel?"

"J. Wigton Crosby, missing financial officer for the recently dissolved Trusteed Bank. The man upped sticks with three-thousand un-accounted-for pounds sterling. He spends time at the hotel, but the staff says he hasn't been by in a Welsh fortnight." [2]

"Jones was hoping to find proof of his presence in the attendance?" Holmes asked skeptically.

Lestrade scoffed. "That would be a bit too obvious, wouldn't it? We're trained to look at appearances, Mr. Holmes, not believe in a name.

Jones checked the signatures without much hope, but his real questions were based on Crosby's description, which is of a middle-aged man, grizzled tow with a terrier crop and a short box beard to hide his chinless jaw. His eyes are green, small, and close-set, with his face florid and pitted with smallpox scars. There's a missing left earlobe. On bright days he wears tinted spectacles, even indoors. Clothing is always formal black or dark blue, and soft neckties with low collars. But that is still Jones's case and I am to concentrate on the row that cracked his head open."

Holmes tutted in a sympathetic manner, and we fell silent until we arrived at the Etruscan.

Perhaps my modern readers will find reference to the Etruscan unfamiliar, for it was closed after the Queen's Diamond Jubilee. In its heyday, it was patronised by minor nobles as easily as wealthy merchants and robber barons. It was a fine old example of the Regency's ancient blue clay, fired and set into granite-hard black armour, impervious to age and veiled in ivy tresses like some time-forgotten castle of yore. The windows were more arrow-loops, narrow and high to catch light, even in the grey hours, and the roof was barrel-vaulted for the acoustics of music. Fine taste was the order of its realm, and many patrons made their seasonal homes at the Etruscan, for it never failed to live up to its reputation for comfort and convenience.

Indoors, the antique décor was a fitting statement for the aged patrons of money and name. Lestrade ignored the walls of art in favour of the front desk, where he announced us by name and reminded the clerk that Signor Persano was expecting him. He paced up and down in the lobby as Holmes smoked and I examined several of the hotel's fine marbles, but as the minutes grew long even Holmes began to share Lestrade's impatience.

"I don't care how rude I look, I'm going to ask again." Lestrade muttered. "I could be back at real work instead of whittling here."

"Ah, here comes the page." I said quickly. "But look!"

The boy was running across the carpet to urgently whisper in the ear of the clerk and his concierges, which in the miraculous ways of all hotels, spontaneously generate at the first show of trouble. Lestrade was at the desk in a trice and we were close at his heels.

"I beg your inconvenience, gentlemen," the clerk stammered. "Signor Persano was expecting you, yes, but he is not answering our attempts to calls. The page looked through the keyhole and he appears to be sitting at his desk, but he is not moving and he does not seem to hear."

"Here, now." Lestrade barked. "Take us there at once! Who among you carries the authority for the hotel?"

An olive-skinned man with improbably black hair against his advanced years stepped up. "I am Vezzani, Master Butler." He announced with trembling dignity. "It is my discretion to decide if the police may be called."

"That is good to know! The police are already here. Is there a way of opening Mr. Persano's door without damaging hotel property?"

So addressed, the old man blanched and produced a ring of keys. "Allow me." He led us up the lift and to the first guest-door across from it upon the third floor. Painfully he knelt, his fleshless knee upon the carpet and fumbled arthritically at the ornate lock. "Your pardon, gentlemen," he begged at last. "But I am old and cannot see the proper key. I shall use the skeleton." In a moment, the heavy door creaked open and sunlight blinded our faces.

My desert-scalded eyes were slow to see around the glare, but Lestrade and Holmes called to me and I moved forward. They were clustered around the duelist and trying to rouse him without success.

"Good Lord!" I heard Lestrade shout.

"Do not touch that, Lestrade! If you value your life, do not touch it! Draw the blinds so Watson may see!"

The burning brightness eased and I blinked until I could see. Persano had contrived some illusion of his home's hot lands. The lamps were unclouded glass and the curtains light blue. Plants twined back and forth from pots and even up the walls. Flowers posed in various stages of bloom, and large glass tanks held argentine fish and terrariums stocked with still more plants.

Persano had not moved. Before him on the table was a scatter of loose papers in Italian, English, Spanish, and French. He had been working on his daily assignments with his pipe. That pipe now lay in a scatter of tobacco on the carpet at his slippers, and a stained pipe-cleaner, a pouch of rum-soaked leaf, and a silver-chased pipe case was against a half-open gigantic Baroque silver matchbox.

This was my first chance to see the impersonator. He was taller than Holmes, and lean within his dressing-gown. His dark red hair was oiled and neatly combed back from his large, domed forehead, and traces of kohl flecked his eyelashes. Despite the cosmetics, he did not hide his masculinity, a confusing contrast to his feminine clothing. Holmes had not exaggerated his effect upon the public.

He did not see us. His large, round, black eyes were wide open, fixed unblinkingly upon his table. This close, I could see his fine-boned face drawn like taut rice-paper about his skull. Both hands were at rest upon his blotting-paper, finely manicured and the nails trimmed to a quarter-inch in length.

311

He did not react to my attempts to jar his mind back to his surroundings. I applied the smelling salts, shook him, examined his ears for blockage and his skull for signs of a blow. A deep cut ran across the palm of his right hand, so I thrust a needle into his left index finger. It might have been a sandbag for all the reaction I received.

"This man is cataleptic. Is there a physician of the hotel?"

"I will bring him!" Vezzani tottered out.

Lestrade had found a mechanical crayon and was tapping the matchbox shut at arm's-length. Even as I opened my mouth to ask why, I saw something quiver within its shadow, something dark and soft, and it gleamed wet in the dull light, as would light striking a clot of congealing blood. A chill of utter revulsion swept me.

"What is that, Holmes?"

"A pleasant little fellow, whose acquaintance I should still make. Lestrade, do be careful."

"I've handled my share of vermin, Holmes." Lestrade snapped. "If I don't know what it is, you can bet I won't touch it!" He kept his gloves on as he used the crayon and a ruler to pincher up the box and drop it into a bag held open by Holmes. "I don't want this thing anywhere near my men! They don't have training for this!"

Lestrade's uniformed police returned with Vezzani and the hotel doctor, the Pisan Fiora. Together we re-examined the patient as Vezzani hovered and wrung his hands, and a new discovery was made: Persano's reflexes responded to the needle test on his left hand.

"He has lost all dexterous sensation. How could it be from this cut? I treated it myself after the fight yesterday!" Fiora held up the afflicted hand. "It was but a gash from the broken crystal. Oh, but what is that?" He pointed to a dry excrescence upon the tips. Unless the angle of the light was exact one could barely see it. "Why, it appears . . . the slime of a slug?"

"It goes across the cut." I agreed. "Now that I see, the slime wraps around the fingers as though he had picked it up."

"There are slugs in the tanks." Lestrade frowned. "Perhaps he was using the slime to heal the wound." From his troubled expression I could tell he worried that an educated man would fall to folk-cures.

"Persano always keeps slugs for healing. There is truth to the old remedy," Fiora assured him, and suddenly gasped. "My fingers!" He held up his trembling hand. "I merely touched the slug-tracks but they are tingling, and now numb!"

The day was exhaustive. I took scrapings off Persano's hand for analysis. Fiora regained some sensation in his hand after many hours and a thorough alcohol wash. The duelist was not so fortunate. He had begun to drool and whimper, but was still not responsive when we bundled him up for the hospital.

While I focussed on my patients, Holmes and Lestrade buzzed like bees within a hive, and vanished to parts unknown only to re-emerge again. Before long, Jones showed up with two constables of his own. His head was bandaged and his demeanor irritable. I was busy with calls to suitable hospitals, so I only noted the timbre of Jones's voice, rising and falling with his agitation, and his enormous hands opening and closing like a crab's pincers wanting prey. With Fiora's help it still took us half the day to find that rarity among British Medicine, a specialist in neurology. Dr. Emil Hogan of Harley Street assured us he had the facility to see the patient, as well as analyse the scrapings and the specimen. Fiora was by now excited by the change from his usual examinations for the guests and personally volunteered to supervise the delivery with Lestrade's men. When they left, the hotel felt quite larger and quieter. It was with relief Holmes returned from mysterious business in the hall and announced we could do no more for the moment and may as well go home for supper. I was quick to agree, for my friend had not touched the hotel's offer of excellent food and coffee.

Mrs. Hudson is familiar with her lodgers. We came home to a princely cold supper. Sadly, I could not look at her summer pudding without recalling that red thing in the matchbox and shivering.

"There are so many questions to this case, Holmes. It is a muddle."

"A ball of different threads is always messy. I assure you this fact is still scientifically proven, for I had the pleasure of interviewing each and every member of the dons."

"That cannot have been pleasant."

"Ah, better than pleasant! It was useful. Lestrade is generally correct about those old gentlemen – confirmed solitary retirees, elegant of manner, and sophisticated of taste. They all regret 'their' *femminiello*'s sudden affliction, and that made interrogations awkward."

"You said 'generally correct', Holmes. Were there exceptions?"

"Oh, one or two. But I cannot separate the ash from the cinder just yet. At least Jones left in a better mood! He believes he has a thread for his missing banker. What a game, Watson! The angler must occasionally discard his pole for the trawler's net and use what he catches, be it coarse fish or fine."

"I suppose Lestrade need not fear a duel now."

Holmes snorted. "Speaking of fish, Lestrade happily plays *Il pesce d'Aprile* when it allows him to perform his duties unhindered. No, he is not at all comforted. I share his unease. You were too dedicated to your patient to notice, Watson, but one of Persano's prize dueling pistols is missing from its case, and my expertise in the language of the writing-desk assures me that documents are missing. Even Lestrade and Jones – two more unimaginative brains in the same room will never again be seen! – could tell the *Signore* had been writing for some time on paper that no longer exists."

"I wish I had noticed, Holmes! My thoughts are suspended until I see the results from Dr. Hogan. He must determine if the thing's toxin led to Persano's state, as well as how it reached his possession. Could it be a pet from his tanks, only to be poisoned by carelessness?"

"You did not hear Jones presume that very thing. Lestrade was quick to correct him. Neither you nor Jones were as close to that thing, but we could smell it. There was a heavy brine to the fetor, and those were freshwater tanks against the wall." Holmes shuddered. "Bah! It is too snakish for me. Lestrade is going to Harley Street on the morrow and perhaps deliver us some light on this murk. But for now I suggest we do service to Mrs. Hudson's platter."

In the swift ways of London, the weather changed. Thunderdrums woke me from a heavy sleep and I came down for breakfast to find a drenched Lestrade before the grate as a squall hammered sheets of water against the glass.

Holmes was still in his dressing-gown with his pipe pinched between his teeth. His eyes shone with the brightness of a child before a party, and he chattered as he poured the little detective a cup of coffee and tried to dress all at the same time. I hastened to take the coffee-pot for him.

"Oh, cheers!" Lestrade breathed. He was not only soaking, but had the unmistakable stench of a man hapless enough to travel over the Crossrail by Paddington on a wet day. "I apologise for the smell, Doctor." His free hand pressed to his torso with a wince.

I asked him what happened.

"We were taking the *Signore* to Barts. Your mates got them to keep him as a teaching subject, and he'll be treated better there than anywhere else." Lestrade's admiration for my colleagues made me smile. "Our cob slid on the wood pavement and down we went. Got my ribs roasted good, but that was all. If anything would shake a man back to his senses, it'd be his cab sliding into a lamp-post! But no, he just sat and cried to himself. Dr. Hogan thought that was valuable information, so I suppose something good came out of it." He nodded to a waterproof envelope on the table. "That's yours. They did you up a tight report."

314

"You are fortunate the other delivery is also unharmed."

I looked up and recoiled backwards.

Holmes was dressed and holding a wet-specimen pint jar. It was a house for a terrible thing, squat-coiled and red as old blood, with a sheen of Australian opal and fatty segments lined with short, black bristles. It gaped a fanged mouth, and its head was crowned with fleshy tentacles.

"I am glad it is no larger!"

"Hah! Quite! Dr. Hogan swears it a marine leech related to the venomous fireworm of Pallas' discourse in 1766. At the very least, it is a remarkable worm unknown to science. I suspect its natural environment is secretive, for it is designed to lunge. No harmless feeder of algae with this equipment!"

"There is nothing harmless about that thing! He writes it was fiendishly difficult to examine, even if it was already dead. A simple chemical test confirmed a touch will numb the nerve, perhaps permanently. Fiora will eventually recover full sensation, they believe, for his contact to the creature was secondary and belated. Both feel Persano's catatonic state is a reaction of the brain upon exposure to the toxin."

"However, Mr. Holmes, how he and that . . . thing . . . met – " Lestrade jabbed his fingers at the jar. "*This* looks very bad, and not just for me."

"Of course you would be concerned with your reputation, Lestrade."

"I was already worried before this! But I can't prove Signor Persano was the only target! What if there are others?"

Before Holmes could answer, the bell rang. Soon a panting constable was climbing up the stairs to tell us that Jones had found Crosby the Banker, dead, and in a most peculiar condition on Caledonian Street. He believed it concerned our own case with Persano.

The rain and thunder made misery of the trip, but it slackened by the time we reached the edge of the markets. Against the stolid Bruce Buildings were several police and the ever-present collection of those curious enough to brave sour weather in the hope of gossip. In the middle of it all we could see Jones, more gigantic than ever in the open, and bellowing back the crowd with considerably more success than poor Canute.

"I hoped you'd be with Holmes," he wheezed at Lestrade. "I suppose this means we'll both be writing different versions of the same report?"

"Wouldn't be the first time." Lestrade grumbled.

315

"Best keep your gloves on, gennulmen," Jones warned and led us down a tiny side-street, once a small alley but now a running brook. At the bottom of it rested a deep-set door over a perch of stone and a drenched constable guarding both sides of it.

"Normally we keep to our own territories, but in this case . . . ." Jones shook his head. "Lestrade, I wasn't joking. I'm glad you're here."

The building was the dark and cheerless architecture of those too poor to pay for proper heat and light outside of their wage days. It was quite cold, and the start of webs silvered the rickety rails up crooked flights of stairs smelling of dust and mildew. At long last we reached the top, where an inspector stood at attention, for a body stretched in the room he guarded. A single clenched fist peeped out from the edge of the sheet draped over the form.

Lestrade knelt and gently lifted the sheet. He whistled in surprise. "Signor Vezzani! What's he doing all the way over here? Doctor, isn't this the sign of a heart attack?" He pointed to the old man's face, which was quite black with congestion and still twisted in an expression of pain.

"Of course a more thorough examination is recommended, but this has all the marks of cardiac arrest."

"Oh, this sad show has only just started. Come, meet Mr. J.W. Crosby, absconder of funds and suddenly no longer missing." Jones nodded at the small room behind, where a bed and wardrobe rested against a cheap desk. In the middle of this room a second corpse sprawled on a cheap drugget, a few feet from an elaborate single-shot pistol. A pool of blood had spread and dried on the carpet. "Doctor, I'd be grateful if you could confirm my suspicion on his cause of death. It looks like a lung shot."

I could oblige. The bullet had angled, disintegrating the pulmonary vessels before lodging into the spine. Crosby was paralysed where he fell, unable to move or call for help as his lungs slowly filled up with blood, drowning him. Despite my campaigner's experience, I was horrified at the man's death.

"I can't imagine a worse way to die," said Jones. "The shot must have sounded like just another one of those blasted thunderclaps. Why, hallo, Mr. Holmes. Whatever is the matter?"

For my friend was wandering back and forth across the small rooms with a black scowl upon his brow and a fistful of papers tight in his clutch.

"It should be here . . . ." we heard him mutter. "Confound it! And so close!"

316

I saw all of the policemen were staring at me in hopes of some illumination, but I had none to give.

"We've already found the missing money," Jones said importantly. "Hidden under the floor, neat as you please."

"Notes? Bah." Holmes slapped the papers on a small end-table. "His other rooms. This is a bolt-hole, a hideaway! Where is his proper address?"

"I can take you, Mr. Holmes," Jones protested. "But there's nothing important there. We've searched everything, down to the smallest nib on the quill pen!"

"Nevertheless, I may find some answers you have missed – for I have questions you have not asked."

"Jones," Lestrade said quietly. "I would never take a case from you, and we have both learnt the value of listening to Mr. Holmes. I can stay here with your man – " He nodded to the other inspector. " – and you can take him to Crosby's other lodgings."

Jones thought hard, and nodded. "As you say, Lestrade."

There was no room in the cab, so I stayed behind with Lestrade and made a thorough examination of the dead men. It was in the perusal that we discovered the papers Holmes had discarded. It was a confession from Persano, admitting he had provoked a fight with Lestrade to gain a private audience. There was a spy at the hotel, acting against the interests of England and Italy, and his name was J. W. Crosby.

It took weeks for the combined discretion of the police and the Embassies to properly address this complexity of crime, but ultimately, an international scandal was averted. I could not finish my notes until the beginning of a cool autumn.

"Your notes may be finished, but it is an unfinished case, Watson," Holmes said at last.

"Nevertheless, I would value your summary."

"Well, that is small enough! Persano's letters were as illuminating as Crosby's. One of the dons at the hotel, an unimportant relative of what we would call a country baronet, had ties with insurgents. In the persuasion of money for his beloved horse, Persano realised this man was funneling money into these unsavoury practices.

"The don, whom we shall call 'Cervini', was funneling money through Crosby. Persano had his own business with the Trusteed Bank, and must have been surprised when Cervini revealed business with Crosby. Persano had just lost a small fortune to the dissolution of the Trusteed Bank and did not wish for any scandal to burn his nose, so in order to avoid discovery, he instigated a fight amongst the dons. In the time-honoured tradition of obfuscating details, this managed to distract everyone. Only the fight went too far, and Jones was injured. Persano was still trying to think of what he could do to pass the information without betraying his hand to Cervini and any possible allies, and when Lestrade was brought in to soothe everyone's feathers. Persano saw a better chance, and there was more strategy to his temper this time. He challenged Lestrade to a duel, solely in the hopes of a private audience where he hoped to reveal everything. His reputation for a temper worked in his favour, for who would imagine he was colluding with the very man he had challenged? He spent the night writing down what details he could give, and those were the missing papers that I sought.

"For his part, Crosby had an innocent informant in Vezzani. The old fellow was trusting of his masters, and Crosby had always been kind to him – servants are useful sources of information. The butler didn't completely understand our English politics, but he knew that the banker, who had so many fine friends at the hotel, was needing to avoid some 'troubles' and planned to go to Australia for a fresh start. For a little extra money, Vezzani delivered him food, supplies, and messages in his secret bolthole. It was in these communications that Crosby learned of Persano's odd behavior, and he must have realised Persano planned to expose him.

"Crosby made a dupe of poor old Vezzani and lived to regret it. He had already learned that Persano had a deep cut across his fingertips from the initial skirmish, and it was common knowledge he kept slugs to heal his wounds of honour. Somehow he arranged for his poisonous little house-guest to get to Vezzani, and then deliver it to his friend Persano on the faith that the worm was a miraculous method of healing. Vezzani's key to Persano's rooms was stolen at about this time.

"Persano probably didn't care about the negligible cuts before the duel, but he did have to keep up the appearances of a real duel and he trusted the old fellow. He accepted Vezzani's gift. Crosby took a risk, slithered his way to the hotel with Vezzani's key, and waited. The poison did its work and Crosby simply took the papers from the insensible duelist, but something must have startled him, some common error in judgment or an escape in haste, for he left the matchbox behind.

"Crosby misjudged Vezzani's honour. The old man was shaken to the core, but despite his very real grief, it did not take him long to realize how cruelly he was tricked. His key to the room was missing. Who else could have stolen it?"

"That poor old man," I said with feeling.

"He would not have appreciated our pity. I did some investigation into his life. In his youth, he was a personal guard for Napoleon III in exile! He dyed his hair black not out of vanity, Watson, but because he did not want his enemies to go soft on him. He stole that dueling pistol right under our very noses! As soon as he could, he found Crosby in his bolthole and confronted him, and I believe the lung-shot was a mark of his anger to the fugitive. The thunder did, as Jones suspect, hide the sound of the shot. A healthier man would have escaped, but the strain was too much and he died before he could return the papers and key to the hotel, his honour clean.

"This is all quite wonderful, but why did you insist on seeing Crosby's official address?"

"His bolthole was devoid of anything that permitted insight as to his personality, and that in itself was revealing. He was a man in hiding and determined to leave his past behind him. With Jones's escort, I went to his ostensive rooms on Marylebone Road.

"As soon as I went there, I knew I had my answers. Like Persano, Crosby had tanks of specimens, only he had the talent for keeping marine life. Most of them were ordinary fish that you or I would see in a tidal pool, but one exceptionally large tank was most interesting. It had a massive bed comprised of a lump of coral, and not a thing else.

"Well! Considering the pleasant demeanor and habits of our sinister little red leech, I suspected this solitary tank was the cell for the beast. Examining it from the outside was not illuminating, but Jones finally understood what I needed to find, and before long he and his constables opened up Crosby's personal safe a second time. In it I found what I was looking for."

Holmes chuckled, long and low around his pipe, and I asked him what he found so amusing.

"Why, the expression on poor Jones and his men. I fear I was overly delighted at the papers, and they simply couldn't understand why my happiness was so dependent on months of bills paid to local fishermen. Meticulous as any banker, Crosby kept his purchases on record – I doubt it would ever occur to him not to – and every week a boy was paid to deliver a pail of fresh water and live fish no larger than a child's longest finger. It was, of course, food for this thing."

"But can you prove it?"

"Ah, I suppose I could if a court wanted to bother. You see, Crosby had many healthy fish in his tanks, but the bill was revealingly vague. It only required the payee to bring him any species of fish, so long as it was a certain size. This voracious creature needed a week to clean out its offerings, and then another pail would be delivered. Even if I had any doubts at this point, Jones was convinced and, in his sanguine temperament, he had his constables lift that chunk of coral out of the tank for my examination. I admitted my surprise at his willingness to help, and his reasoning was that he would not knowingly expose the public to a possible threat like more of those bloodsuckers.

"What I found was a long tunnel in the underside of the coral. It matched perfectly the dimensions of our little guest, as did a rather chilling collection of tooth-marks where, we may presume, this marine leech or worm struck at its prey and missed. The dimensions were exact."

"That is completely chilling, Holmes."

"Crosby managed his bolthole below the Bruce Buildings and planned to wait it out until he could flee to Australia. French is the language of accounting and diplomacy, and Crosby was fluent enough that he could retire comfortably as some fashionable foreigner. It was a dirty case, but a worthwhile test of my energies, even if it will forever remain incomplete."

"But, Holmes . . . How do you mean by that?"

"Why, we cannot find this remarkable worm's true origin, Watson. Without such data, a perfectly valid and existing beast is but halfway to a yeti, or the fantastical flying turtles taken so seriously by our ancestors' cartographers. Add to this uneven mixture the scandal of an old guard of Napoleon's conducting his own vendetta, righteous though it may be, and the vindictive murder of a man who would stoop at nothing in his cowardice . . . . No, Watson, this is unfinished for many reasons. It shall never see print, for even your remarkable way with facts cannot create a tapestry with nonexistent thread."

"It may be unfinished, but it is still a useful exercise of your powers, Holmes."

"You are too kind, old friend." Holmes answered quietly. "But I shall risk insulting you with the low tactic of using your own words against you. '*A problem without a solution may interest the student, but can hardly fail to annoy the casual reader.*'"

NOTES

ACD had a lot of cross-pollination in his stories. This is only to be expected, as this was one of the world's erudite observers. We see multiple references to secondary characters in the Canon, and in "The Adventure of the Golden Pince-Nez" *and* "The Problem of Thor Bridge", *Watson mentions oh-so-casually two cases that are weirdly similar: A remarkable worm unknown to science, and a loathsome red leech. Both cases have a stricken male character attached to their existence. One is dated to 1894; the other properly vague – as*

320

proper as a dowager deflecting the rudeness of direct queries to her age – as to the timeline but we know it was not after 1900.

Leeches and worms are of the Annelid phylum, *Class* Clitellata. *They share almost as many differences as they do similarities, but ultimately (as far as science goes) the similarities rule out. Conan Doyle was not a bad jackleg naturalist, and his curiosity about the natural world inspired many of his works of fiction. He may, in the tradition of Watson, call them "poor writings" but we may respectfully disagree. That wonderful fascination with the Cosmos and the Master's skill in telling a story without divulging sensitive details lets us extrapolate a tale that involves both – and as anyone who has dealt with (even briefly) the snake-knots of politics knows, it is more credible to add detail than it is to subtract. I am thankful that this gave me the chance to explore two under-appreciated aspects of Victoriana: The Italian culture of homosexual males, and the proper respectability of British society that allowed a woman to wear men's clothing as a profession.*

1 – Physically imposing and incredibly strong, Froest did become Superintendent. His friendship with John Nash and his wife Lil Hawthorn, the cross-dressing performer, led to the arrest of Dr. Crippen. His physical appearance is everything the parodist would wish for in a fumbling policeman, but his mind was as sharp as razors.

2 – Fifteen days or eight nights.

The Adventure of the
Multiple Moriartys
by David Friend

Since first I picked up my pen to describe the peculiar methods – and, it could even be said, the peculiar character – of my friend, Mr. Sherlock Holmes, some readers have written to me in appreciation for doing so. Although most correspondents have been generous, there are those who attempt to mimic Holmes by noting a small number of trifling inconsistencies and fixating upon them. How, for example, could my bullet wound move? Additionally, have I been married more than once?

Such questions can readily be explained: I suffered two wounds, though it was only the one which caused my discharge from the Army, while I married again after the death of my second wife, Mary. Holmes's landlady, incidentally, was always Mrs. Hudson. Yet there was a time during the case of the cabinet card in which she was joined by Mrs. Turner, whose own husband we would later meet in the affair at Boscombe Valley.

I have never been the most observant – indeed, Holmes has complained as much himself on numerous occasions – and there will, therefore, be moments when a lapse of focus occasions a negligible error. On some points, however, I remain correct. The brother of Professor Moriarty, for one, does indeed share his forename. This may seem irregular – even, perhaps, unlikely – but, since so many of my readers are apparently interested, I will explain how it is perfectly sound. To do so, I must relate how Holmes and I uncovered such a secret. It should not be unexpected, considering the man involved, just how dark and deviant this was.

During the second week of April 1895, London was reeling from the arrest of Oscar Wilde at the Cadogan Hotel. I had been following the case through the papers, fully expecting Queensbury to recant his outrageous accusation. Holmes, who had recently solved the matter of the examination forgery, preferred to focus his attention on his chemical pursuits, and I heard him say little which did not concern either hydrochloric acid or olefiant gas. He had worked without pause since the end of his travels, and I had been worrying for his health and wanted him to rest. As his doctor, therefore, I forbade him from admitting any clients without my express permission.

"If you so wish it, Watson," he told me solemnly.

Holmes, however, may have enjoyed the lull between cases, but I certainly did not. On the second day, working as a *locum* at my old practice, I was disrupted by the unwelcome appearance of a rat, and I spent a good deal of time attempting to settle frightened patients and convince them that it was not an ordinary feature of my old consulting rooms.

"You would not believe what happened today!" I complained loudly upon my return to Baker Street. Holmes was in his bedroom, but I continued, loud and wretchedly, pacing the sitting room floor. "A rat in my old surgery! Calm as you please, sitting there as though it were waiting to be examined. Patients could be lost because of this!" I dropped heavily into an armchair and unshipped a resigned sigh. "The way Mrs. Clutterbuck gossips, the rest of London will know soon. I shall probably be reading about it in the evening papers."

In an effort to distract myself, I picked up *The Illustrated London News*. I had hidden it from Holmes, lest a potential case catch his eye, but I need not have worried. The pages were almost bare of interest, as though every figure who could have filled them had not wanted to compete with the Wilde scandal.

I was studying the crossword, trying to remember what a female mallard is called, when I suddenly sensed a movement in my peripheral vision, somewhere towards the mantelpiece. It was a sort of intermittent scurrying. I lifted my head and, to my utmost horror and outrage, saw another rat. It was smoothly brown, its back hunched in a parody of an Arabian camel, with pink ears and a worm of a tail. I stared distastefully as it scuttled past the clock.

With cold anger, I moved to the desk, opened the drawer and groped inside. I kept an eye on the vermin as my fingers fumbled through a pile of letters and curled gratefully around the metal handle of my Webley Bulldog revolver.

The rat was scratching softly towards the end of the mantelpiece. I levelled the gun and squinted. Suddenly, somehow, it froze. Maybe it wanted mercy from an old soldier. Even in war, however, I had never wavered, despite the grip on my heart and the roar in my head. Without a pause, I squeezed the trigger and the gun gave a loud and resolute retort.

I missed it cleanly and the damn thing scurried out of sight. As it did so, I heard a movement and the door to his bedroom was yanked open. Holmes stood there in his purple dressing gown, a cigarette dangling from his lips and a quizzical frown upon his face.

"Whenever I do that," he said wryly, "you tell me off!"

I returned the revolver to the drawer. "That wasn't shooting practice," I told him. "I saw a rat." I pointed to where the rodent had been running only moments before. Holmes did not seem at all alarmed. "I already had to deal with one at my old surgery," I said. "It is as though the damned things have been following me arou – "

I paused.

My friend continued puffing innocently on his cigarette.

I turned on him. "Did the rat at my surgery come from here?" I asked him harshly, realising how easily one could smuggle itself in my consultancy bag. "Are they something to do with you? It's not possible!"

Holmes gave a careless shrug. "Not at all, my dear Watson. It is perfectly possible to purchase a mischief of rats and examine their behaviour. It is not as though I am experimenting on them." He gestured limply to the room. "There are a few others running around and you would do well not to shoot at them." He had reached the end of his cigarette and was looking about for an ashtray. "There are pleasanter ways to be awoken."

Quite carelessly, he folded himself into the chair I had vacated and crunched his cigarette out on my newspaper. He seemed buoyant, untroubled, and it was a mood I could not match.

"You do realise that people will be avoiding the practice for weeks now!" I said in outrage. "It is supposed to be a place of cleanliness."

Infuriatingly, Holmes did not seem in the least sympathetic. "If you will prohibit me from accepting cases," he said airily, "I must lend my time to something else. The psychology of vermin is as interesting a topic as any."

I recoiled in disbelief. "You are saying this is *my* fault?"

Fortunately for Holmes, we were interrupted at this point by a knock at the door.

"That had better not be the arrival of a client!" I warned, pointing an officious finger towards him.

Holmes shook his head blandly. "It isn't," he said and, with an unexpected dignity, added, "That will be my tuba."

"Your . . . *tuba*?" I repeated, off-guard. "You no longer enjoy the Stradivarius?"

"A change is as good as a rest, and you do so insist on the latter. Admit Mr. Heppenstall, Watson. And carry it up, won't you? He isn't as young as he was."

I made to protest. I had been working, after all, and despite his convalescence, Holmes had the energy of ten men. He was, however, already picking up my paper and splitting it open.

Downstairs, I found Mr. Heppenstall on the doorstep. He was a short, lean old man with a frogged jacket, leathery skin, and wrinkles that curved towards a small, bland smile. I was surprised a man of his years and build had managed to carry such an unwieldy instrument, but he did so well and without any visible effort.

I took it from him and – to my surprise – felt my whole body sink with the weight.

"Good of you," Mr. Heppenstall nodded and, his assignment completed, turned around and strolled merrily away.

I spluttered something in response – a plea for help, perhaps, followed swiftly by an oath – but no assistance was forthcoming and I had little choice but to tackle the stairs alone. I could not see anything below my chest and tapped an exploratory foot about for the stair. Somehow, I managed to place it correctly and began my weary ascent.

By some miracle, I made it to the top without incident and ambled across the landing and into the sitting room. Holmes remained in the armchair, drumming his fingers together impatiently. I deposited the tuba on the table and dropped into the sofa with sweet relief.

Delight spread across my friend's thin, Grecian features, and he approached the table in wonder. "Certainly an exquisite piece of craftsmanship," he declared, patting the instrument affectionately.

He lifted it – quite easily, I am loathe to add – and carried it to the chair by the hearth. Then, to my incredulity, he began playing. His cheeks balled as the low, robust sound boomed across the room. Without accompaniment, it was a most unattractive noise and I could not fathom his enthusiasm. I proceeded to watch the performance with a sort of blank incomprehension.

"What has inspired you to purchase this . . . *this*?" I said, pointing bewilderedly at the golden beast of an object.

Holmes had taken a breath and was about to deploy it in another full-throated warble when he decided to answer me instead. "My mind, Watson," he told me tolerantly, "is like a racing engine, tearing itself to pieces because it is not connected up with the work for which it was built. The work which *you* told me not to involve myself during convalescence. Doctor's orders, you said."

It was typical of him to use my own words as a weapon against me. He pressed his fingers against the bell with satisfaction.

I could hardly protest, but I endeavoured to do so anyway. "Surely, you require silence in which to recover. You cannot have it while tootling away on this dreaded thing."

Holmes's mouth pursed petulantly, like an aesthete with a delicate temperament. "Without such sounds to distract my mind, I feel restive and empty. And since you will not even let me read the agony column, I can do little else."

He returned his attention to the tuba. I shall not describe what he did as playing, nor shall I grace it with any other term usually associated with musical performance. Instead, the burly brass instrument produced low, discordant rumbles of the kind I had only heard in an underground train station.

How such a great mind could, when searching for a suitable distraction, settle upon this noise instead of anything else, I failed to comprehend. Holmes, I had long since realised, was a man of impulse. His mood changed fast and often and his plans were altered accordingly. It was often the case, when in the company of my friend, to suffer a sudden sense of disorientation. Plans were abandoned as though they were never conceived and new ideas were hungrily seized upon. Often, I found myself going places and doing things of which, barely a minute earlier, I had no conception. In an abstract fashion, it was as though I were living the day out of its natural order and I was suddenly in another hour and another situation.

Many was a time in which I had made preparations for my colleague, Jackson, to oversee my surgery while Holmes and I were to leave London, only to discover at the last moment that my friend was in bed and refusing to stir. He would remain there for days, sometimes, and our rooms would become my own. I would take advantage of his absence and tidy the place anew, though he would inevitably arise and return it to its customary chaos.

Such were Holmes's contradictions, of course, that his slovenliness was only matched by the neatness of his dress. Likewise, those long and languorous days of pipes and papers could, at any point, be replaced with days of urgency and adventure. There were moments, too, in which he could appear conceited, while at others – such as when he spoke admiringly of his brother, which came easily and sincerely and with no apparent envy – he was humility itself.

Minutes later, Holmes drew away from the mouthpiece and gave a thin, triumphant smile. I recognized it from the countless other moments in which my friend had been proven correct.

"Indeed," he murmured, "exquisite."

I could not bear it much longer.

"I surrender!" I said, standing up and raising my hands. "You have infested my home with rats. You have imperilled my job. You have driven me to distraction with this intolerable music. As your doctor, I am ordering you: Go back to work!"

This outburst seemed to take my friend by surprise. He stared at me serenely for a long moment and then smiled again – this time, with a strange sort of pride.

"Excellent, Watson!" he enthused. He rose from the chair and discarded his gown, like so many things, with an impatient contempt. It was as though he felt such inanimate objects should have guessed he was done with them and act accordingly instead of leaving it to him. "We must begin immediately."

"You have a case?" I frowned.

"Of a sort," he said. "However, when you gave me the strictest instructions not to work, I had to take the most elaborate means to ensure that you would swiftly rescind them."

A smile slowly spread across my face. "Of course!" I said with delighted relief. "Learning the tuba and examining rats? Ludicrous ideas! Even, if I may say so, for you. So what is it?"

His plan was a success. I did not mind in the slightest that he was to work again.

"Professor Moriarty has returned to London," he declared.

I creased in confusion. "But . . . Moriarty has been dead for nearly four years. What are you talking about?"

The bulky instrument now on the floor, Holmes leaned forward in his armchair, his eyes bright with excitement.

"Since his death, Moriarty has been become a figure of folklore. Throughout London, there are men who claim to have worked for him, sitting in the smoke of taverns and telling of his crimes and masterful manipulations. He is an idol to such wretches – a martyr! And I use this religious terminology advisedly, Watson. Like such disciples, they claim relics. One of which is for sale. Nobody quite knows what this grizzly thing is worth, and the matter can only be settled by an auction."

This surprised me. "How can they do that? These people can't walk into Christie's, surely?"

"We must never underestimate the criminal fraternity, Watson," he cautioned.

"What is for sale?" I asked with a strange mixture of both eagerness and trepidation.

"The head of Moriarty," said Holmes simply, as though such a thing were to be expected.

I felt my stomach tighten nauseously. "I can't . . . ." I tried, repulsed, but was unable to find a suitable response.

Stunned, I settled back in my chair and reflected on what all Holmes had told me. The notion that the professor was idolised in disreputable quarters was somewhat understandable. There will always be those who admire and aspire, in every place and profession. To be morbidly interested in acquiring something so intimate, however, was surely beyond the pale. Yet I could not help but consider the religions with

327

which Holmes had alluded, and the relics which were so prized among their followers. The practice was at least a thousand years old. Indeed, I knew of people myself who revered sporting champions and operatic tenors and kept tickets for posterity. Holmes, similarly, kept portraits of some of the finest criminals on his bedroom walls. A couple of years hence, the Bronze Head of Queen Idia was brought back from the Benin Expedition and itself sold at auction.

"How do you suppose they found it?" I asked, once I had sufficiently recovered from the shock.

Holmes poured himself a cup of tea and cocked an indifferent eyebrow. "Perhaps someone saw him fall into the water, or maybe a fisherman found him. Either way, his body must have been crushed, with only the head salvaged."

I swallowed dryly. "The auction is today?"

Holmes nodded. "I wish to discover just who will purchase it. For such a person, I am convinced, will do so in order to signal his own status among criminals. He shall fashion himself as Moriarty's successor, and we should be wise to keep a watch on him."

Outside, we boarded a hansom and Holmes settled somnolently into his seat. His head was rested back, his aquiline nose more prominent than ever, and his eyes were closed as he looked inward. I knew not to disturb my friend when he was so clearly focussed. For many minutes, I was lost in thoughts of my own – of Mary and our holiday on Hayling Island in '92 – when Holmes finally folded back his eyelids and surveyed me unfavourably.

"I may not be the only detective to be present at this auction, Watson. There are, I know, more of them in London since I took my sabbatical."

I knew this already, but had not wanted to speak of such others for fear of offending him.

"There's Mr. Barker, of course. And that other man Blake. He even tries to look like me, walking about the place in a dressing gown and pipe. He shall be taking rooms in Baker Street next. And what's the journalist called?"

"Martin Hewitt," I said, a little too readily. "A stout, clean-shaven man – and a lawyer, no less. He did a most remarkable job on the Quinton Jewel case, according to *Truth*."

Holmes tilted his head back. I do believe he was sulking. For a few moments, all I could hear was the clapping of hooves without. "There was once a time when I was the only consulting detective in London," he said wistfully. "I believe it is *you* who is responsible, Watson."

"Me?" said I in surprise.

He lowered his head a fraction in lazy confirmation. "You brought me so much attention with your sensational little scribbles in *The Strand*. Now others are trying to emulate my success." He seemed to cast such efforts away. "Of course, it is a fool's errand."

"You do enjoy the better cases," I pointed out in an effort to cheer him. Often, I could not care less if my friend chose to remain in a dark mood. At such times, however, I was not expected to share a cab with him.

Holmes paused. He seemed to be considering my argument, his brows corrugating thoughtfully.

"It depends how one would define 'better'," he said, the matter clearly intriguing him. He stared intensely without, his eyes no longer half-hooded and the mind behind it focussed and fertile. "In my own view, the cases which warrant my attention are those which are unusual, yet not wholly reliant upon spectacle. The Dr. Grimesby Roylott case, for example, certainly held such features of interest. There were questions which taxed the mind and it is these which compensated quite pleasingly for its more gothic grandiloquence. Or the death of Willoughby Smith, for another. That was quite the study in observation and deduction, of which I remain proud. No perplexing job advertisements, I grant you. No diamonds hidden in plain sight. The cases of which you would consider notable, Watson, no doubt, include something rather more melodramatic. The kidnapping of Silver Blaze, I dare say."

I cocked an indifferent brow. "One of your more famous successes," I reminded him.

"Pah!" said Holmes in disgust. "The public interest in that case was due exclusively to the horse in question being a champion, and their own desire to see themselves profiting from their wagers. The subtle intricacies of the matter were lost on them."

"What about the Grant Munro case?" I suggested. "I have always had a fondness for that one."

"Underrated," said Holmes at once. "Though you did overstate the sentiments of its ending. Despite that, a curious matter which did not rely upon the folly of government for its interest."

I stared at my friend questioningly. "You look unfavourably towards a case such as the Prime Minister's stolen document?"

"And the disappearance of the Naval Treaty," he said, warming to his theme. "These are simply trifles with which I would ordinarily not trouble myself. Politicians would do better to look after such important papers to begin with, instead of punishing me for their own foolish mistakes." He looked at me shrewdly. "I read your account of the forgery case, by the way. You left it by the hearth after finishing it last night."

"And what do you think of it?" I asked, and braced myself for the outcome.

"As I recall, you rather clumsily avoided disclosing the name of the university town. I hardly think it would have mattered, Watson, had you told your poor readers that it happened at Oxford."

"It would have caused embarrassment," I said with dignity.

Holmes gave a disdainful shake of the head. "You pay too much mind to such things. If you make mention of the place, no such incident will occur there again."

My reply was stern, for I was tiring of my friend's rather difficult mood. "I chose not to, Holmes," I said, "just as you have the choice to write such records yourself." I could feel my irritation beginning to grow. "Aside from seeking permission for which cases I should record, all decisions are mine."

"You make it sound as though I exercise some control over your literary endeavours." He said it with a smile, but it was one of defiance and not humour.

I have never been a man who enjoys confrontation – it was an irony, therefore, that I sought it on the battlefield – and I avoided it now by shifting my gaze uncomfortably to the window. I have sometimes found it easier to protest when refraining from eye contact.

"I try to do what you want," I said coolly. "And not only in my writing either, but in general life, too."

Holmes's surprise was too crudely theatrical to be genuine. "Which instances do you have in mind?"

I barely needed to pause. "I let you play the violin," I pointed out. "It is not as though you do it particularly well, after all."

I forced myself to look at him and saw his eyes flash with something like anger. I was not sure if he was truly stung by this indelicate jibe. Indeed, he seemed, perversely, as though he were enjoying the exchange. "And in return I end with a piece you enjoy," he said with satisfaction.

"After which, I don't enjoy it anymore."

His smile curved wider. He was, I now realised, pleased. "Your irritability is a virtue," he said, "and one I make continued efforts to encourage." It was true that Holmes had tried to influence my outlook. Indeed, barely a week went by without some attempt to poison me with his cynicism. "Of course," he went on, "my musical practice is only one matter. In all others, I attempt to compromise."

I could not tolerate this. "What of the mess? There's so much of it I can barely tolerate being indoors at all! And that is another thing, Holmes: You never go out, unless I pester you to do so."

330

My friend's face was so surprised, anyone would think I was speaking untruths.

"I accompany you for walks occasionally," he said.

This was true, but I did not wish to admit it. All too readily, he seemed to be winning this particular argument.

"What about the times in which I wish to visit the Alhambra Music Hall in Leicester Square? You steadfastly refuse to join me!"

Holmes shrugged. "Only because I don't care to mingle with prostitutes," he said wryly. "But perhaps some patrons consider that an attraction."

I recoiled in shock. "That is beneath you, Holmes!"

He didn't reply, and his reticence suggested he had regretted the remark.

I felt the need to explain myself. "I go because I enjoy George Robey's performances."

Holmes rolled his eyes. "It is infantile nonsense! Any self-respecting churchman would be aghast at the way he wears that clerical costume."

"It is supposed to be amusing," I responded. "I would have thought a deductive artisan such as yourself would have gathered as much from the song. It is about a pimple, after all."

He had barely heard me. "The man has brows like Dan Leno," he muttered. "I can't be any more damning than that."

"If we are discussing entertainment," I said, with sudden inspiration, "what about all the symphonies to which I accompany you?"

"It is quite a different matter entirely," he said. "You enjoy those."

I sneered incredulously. "I enjoy the naps it occasions me to have. I'm fit for nothing else after seeing patients all day."

Our hansom, at this point, jerked to a crawl. I had quite forgotten we were in it at all.

This curtailed our somewhat spirited discussion and the two of us settled on an unspoken amnesty. Indeed, it was in silence that we disembarked from the cab, and I supposed it would be a while before we spoke again. It was often as such – though, as is the way with such intimate associates, Holmes and I could begin conversing again without any mention of our previous squabbling and there was never any memory of it. It was, indeed, refreshingly civilised and a manner which recalled in me the relationship I enjoyed with my late brother.

With a not unpleasant surprise, I observed ourselves to be in Limehouse, one of the most insalubrious districts in all of London. The street was damp and dirty – a cemetery, in effect, with crumbling houses for tombstones – while a stubborn chill slipped beneath my Norfolk jacket and settled into the seams. The sky seemed lower here, with grey clouds sinking onto battered roofs and merging with the soot and smoke. I had seen such godless places before and even knew of gentlefolk who visited for thrills and curiosity. Part of me was glad to see what our celebrated city had hidden away, if only because it made me feel fortunate to possess whatever wealth I did. However, I was also sickened by the state with which such wretched people were forced to survive. It twisted my stomach and weakened my belief in the righteousness of our social order, which persistently proposed that every man has his place and is satisfied with it. I doubted that the people whom Dickens had described as "houseless rejected creatures" were anywhere near satisfied.

Holmes did not seen to share my dismay, but walked quite easily forward as though he were perambulating through Covent Garden itself. I followed him meekly, wondering where he was leading me. Ahead of us, there stood another dilapidated building, streaked jaggedly with dirt, its windows boarded and shut with shame.

"This may look particularly ramshackle to you, Watson," he said as we moved to a rickety door, "but it is one of the most important places in the capital. Here, out of view from our diligent Yardmen, is a venue fit for every purpose – poker tournaments, memorial services. It's even a place to plan crimes."

I stared about in mystification. Surely Holmes was not serious?

As we moved inside, however, I found myself believing him. The interior could well have been another building entirely. Indeed, we could even have entered a different city. I was quite astonished as I took in the large room with the clean, carpeted floor – even, remarkably, a chandelier hanging glitteringly above us. Sofas and armchairs were positioned at regular intervals, and a long rug of blue damask was unfurled down a wide and welcoming staircase. Men in pressed suits were standing handsomely in each corner, like footmen in some lavish hotel. I certainly felt as though I were in such a place. Even the smell was convincing me. A large hearth in the corner was distributing a sweet and bewitching aroma which, with its warmth, made one immediately forget the chill without. Like Alice before me, it seemed I had fallen through a rabbit hole and into another world.

Holmes stalked assuredly across the foyer and towards the far corner. He seemed to have been here before. I held grimly onto this impression, as it also meant he had managed to leave. Such an escape was not something I was taking for granted at this point. I followed him, my head swivelling awesomely from side-to-side, taking in the tall paintings adorning the walls. With a Brooking on my left and a Reynolds on my right, I wondered how such masterpieces had come to be here. We curled around a sharp corner and found another man standing militarily beside a set of double-doors. He noticed our approach and, as though recognizing us to be venerable members of the Junior Carlton Club on Pall Mall, pulled the door open and gestured welcomingly with a limp hand.

I hesitated awkwardly, gripped by a soldier's intuition. The more we advanced, the harder it would be to retreat. Holmes, for his part, had no such qualms and walked casually into the wide hall with a soft pine floor, long Navajo rug, and rows of mahogany balloon-back dining chairs. Such a scene surprised me, and all nerves were forgotten as I glanced curiously around. More than fifty people were sitting, briefcases and bags at their feet, before a thin-faced auctioneer. Holmes and I took our seats on the third row. I was suddenly feeling quite self-conscious. For the first time, it occurred to me that many in the room where followers of Moriarty and, as such, would not take kindly to seeing Holmes. In their mind, he was a murderer who had killed the man they most admired.

I had just recognized the curly black hair and athletic build of Arthur Raffles when my friend nudged me in the ribs.

"The auctioneer," he whispered, "is Mr. Thorley. He's a most observant fellow – as much as I am, probably."

I was quite surprised by this humble admission but, on witnessing how the esteemed Mr. Thorley had mastered the bidding process, I could hardly disagree. He was a man of perhaps five-and-forty years with black, receding hair combed flatly across an angular head. His small, sharp eyes flickered vigilantly from behind a pair of wire-rimmed spectacles – a hawk out hunting for prey. Presently, the bidding ended and an antique rifle was awarded to its new owner. It seemed we had arrived just in time, for the next lot was the most interesting of all.

It was hidden beneath a purple sheet and unveiled with considerable deference. At which point, most everyone recoiled in fascinated horror.

The head of Professor James Moriarty was bare but for the stringy hair which clutched to the side like a tangle of damp seaweed, his deep-seated eyes staring ghoulishly out from a lined and waxen face. The disgraced academic may have been dead but, as I noted nauseously, he looked much the same as he had in life. I turned to Holmes. He was exhibiting the same insensible stare as the head itself, and I knew not of what he felt.

It was explained that, much like the other items in the auction, this one would not be purchased with money but exchanged with an antique. Something, I imagined, which had not been purchased either. Without any more preamble, the bidding commenced.

I peered cautiously about me. I noticed, as the first row terminated, the broad chest and bushy brows of Professor Abraham Van Helsing, his dark blue eyes staring contemplatively ahead as though he were considering whether or not he should bid himself.

"You are braver than I thought, Mr. Holmes," said a female voice quietly beside us. "Entering a room in which most everyone wants you dead."

"I could say the same to you, Miss Henderson," Holmes replied, without the briefest glance to his right. "Wanted on three continents, with no less than eight bounties on your head."

"Nine," the lady corrected him with pride. "Though it isn't *my* head you're interested in, is it? It's the one over there."

Mr. Thorley had established a rhythm as bidders sought to outpace each other. A tall, high-shouldered Asian man in robes seemed particularly keen, his unblinking green stare never leaving the auctioneer's face.

Tilting forward, past my friend, I looked curiously at the lady who had spoken. She was a brunette of perhaps seven-and-twenty years in a wool tweed dress with puffed sleeves of silk crepe and a wide skirt. A round emerald glimmered attractively from her necklace. I had heard Holmes speak of the lady – sometimes, in terms which he had only previously reserved for Irene Adler. An international thief of much distinction, Emma Henderson was considered to be as wealthy as any aristocrat and, for this reason, was known as "The Countess".

"Will you be competing yourself, Miss Henderson?" Holmes asked with polite interest.

"I never bid for anything," she responded wryly.

Behind us, a slim dandy of a man with glossy black hair and olive skin was sitting languidly, a black cat perched on his shoulder. He raised a small hand to bid, and I noticed a gold ring on his little finger in the shape of a snake. Most bidders, by this point, had fallen away and it was now a duel with another man in front.

The excitement was reaching uncomfortable proportions. Perhaps I am particularly susceptible to such things, but I was watching the spectacle with shallow breath. I had never had the means to visit an auction house before, but I had certainly attended horse races and was experiencing much the same exhilarating charge.

Finally, with the cruel abruptness which often characterises such moments, all bidding ceased. "Commiserations to Dr. Nikola," said Mr. Thorley respectfully. "The bid goes to the man on the front row."

Voices babbled as the winner approached the auction block. He was a short, pale young man with curly red hair and the look of a peevish public schoolboy. I watched as he lifted a valise and produced from within it a grey ornate vase. A briefcase, containing the head of Moriarty, was handed back in exchange. With a satisfied nod, the young man stepped away and cut a path through the middle aisle. I noticed a bitter glare from Emma Henderson, but did not anticipate what was to happen next.

Her face set dourly, the lady lowered her hand to her waist and pulled out a Belgian Pocket Revolver.

Several startled cries went up. People around her stared – some annoyed, others surprised. A restless young man with floppy brown hair and a red bowtie seemed delighted by the drama.

"Stop!" she trilled.

The young man carrying Moriarty's head paused immediately, somehow knowing the order was directed at him alone.

"Either I take that head, or I shall have yours," said Miss Henderson, her voice cold and definite.

I could see past the lady's shoulder and braced as three separate guards took out their own pistols and aimed them fixedly upon her.

Miss Henderson's resolve, quite suddenly, softened. With irritated surprise, she loosed a finger from the folding trigger and lifted the gun in surrender.

The chatter was even louder now. The two guards flanking the young man twisted him around and hustled him out through the tall doors.

The lady had a look of fierce frustration as her gun was taken from her.

"It's all right," said Mr. Thorley, walking down the aisle towards her, his hands lifted in soothing reassurance. "There is no need to throw her out. I am sure this was Miss Henderson's idea of a jest. Am I correct?"

He smiled amusedly, she rather less so.

"Yes," said Miss Henderson stiffly. She seemed too despondent to utter anything else.

"I appreciate the humour," said Holmes and, throwing back his head theatrically, released a quick, full-throated laugh. He was trying to help but, I fancied, caused more alarm than the sight of the gun.

"That head should have been mine!" protested Miss Henderson. "I'm the only one who has come anywhere close to what Moriarty did."

The room was emptying, but I lowered my voice anyway. "Why worship him so?" I asked with genuine concern. "The man was a murderer and everything else besides."

"But his genius!" she countered. "The way he assembled his plans and executed them with such precision. He controlled everything because of his intellect."

"A spider in a web," agreed Holmes, with almost the same admiration.

I shook my head without comprehension. "To me, such evil dispels all else." I looked sternly upon Holmes. "This building is making me feel ill. May we leave?"

It was true. For all that I had been impressed with the place upon our arrival, I had now seen all the sickening depravity with which it contained. It was the opposite of a church, built in worship to all that was wrong in the world, with a golden calf at the altar.

"I pray your indulgence, Watson," said Holmes. "There is someone with whom I would like to speak."

He turned around and observed the tall auctioneer as he headed across to a side door.

"Wait!" called Holmes, raising a hand.

Mr. Thorley paused. He had already, of course, noticed my friend in the rows and did not bother to feign surprise upon seeing him now.

"There is a matter I wish to address with you," said Holmes politely. "Perhaps you have an office here?"

The other man looked at him for a long moment. He seemed to be wondering whether to make an excuse or accept the inauspicious offer. "Of course," he said finally. "It's at the end of the corridor."

Holmes smiled, apparently delighted at the organization of the building's proprietors. "Come, Watson."

I nodded farewell to Miss Emma Henderson and followed Holmes.

Mr. Thorley's office was almost indistinguishable from that of any provincial solicitor. A wide desk stretched across the middle of the room, a bookcase had been pushed against the far wall, and a grandfather clock was standing authoritatively in the corner. It was lit well, with a fire burning beneath a Gauguin. I had decided that such paintings must be fakes, though it was only the disreputable occupants of the place which had caused me to believe so, for each work was without any apparent fault of its own.

The auctioneer took a seat behind his desk and beckoned for Holmes to sit opposite, while I remained standing.

"This is my associate Dr. Watson."

The man nodded. By this point in his career, Holmes's fame was such that even I received a little of it.

"Now observe, Watson, one of the greatest antique experts in London," said Holmes grandly. "Norman Thorley worked in Sotheby's for six years, but had his time there end abruptly when he was caught ignoring bidders. He was thereby forbidden to work in every respectable auction house in the country."

"Must you, really?" the man said blandly. He seemed tired of Holmes already, but I got the impression he treated most people with a weary contempt.

"He now finds work authenticating stolen antiques so they can be auctioned off to other criminals."

"Impressive," Mr. Thorley said, though did not seem to mean it. "You know about me. So, I must ask, what do you need?"

His little demonstration over, Holmes turned to business. "I wonder," he said with friendly curiosity, "if you knew the winning bidder. I did not recognise him myself."

Mr. Thorley cocked an eyebrow, but that was all the effort he could give his surprise. "I do not know," he said evasively.

"Oh, I think you do," said Holmes, smiling at the man's gumption. "This sale has been a fraud."

The auctioneer's thin face split into a smile of its own. "You remember, Mr. Holmes, that the vase in question was closely examined and authenticated."

"I have no interest in the vase," said Holmes dismissively. "That was certainly real. It was the head which was fake."

I turned to Holmes with a perplexed frown. "How can you say that, Holmes? We saw it ourselves!"

"Come, come, Watson. The real head was already sold. After the auction was announced, Mr. Thorley was approached by a particularly determined buyer and one who did not wish to risk losing it at auction. The sale we have just witnessed was a charade put on for the benefit of all others who wanted it."

"So there are two heads? In effect, multiple Moriartys?" A problem occurred to me. "But why," I asked, "would the head be sold outright when it could have raised more money at auction?"

"Because Mr. Thorley was paid handsomely for a private sale."

I turned back to the auctioneer. "Is this true?" I asked with righteous indignation. Such were our respectable surroundings that I was somehow shocked by the revelation.

The auctioneer lifted his hands in a reasonable gesture. "You forget, Doctor, *I'm* a criminal now, too."

I felt rather foolish. "That just leaves us with the identity of the buyer," I realised. "Who do you suppose it was? I didn't recognise him either. And I knew at least some of them out there."

"I dare say the man was a courier," said Holmes, "paid to bid whatever it took. That vase, I noticed, was worth a great deal."

"I meant to ask," I said to the auctioneer, "why don't you accept money?"

"Our bidders are not necessarily the moneyed type," he answered patiently. "Exchanging stolen goods is the best they can offer."

"As we know, you sold the head yourself," said Holmes, returning to the more relevant topic. "Are you willing to tell us the name of the real buyer? We could, after all, inform the unsuccessful bidders of your little ruse. I know from personal experience just how angry they can be."

Mr. Thorley smiled condescendingly. He seemed to think he was one of the wealthy gentlemen who had attended his auctions at Sotheby's. "I cannot do that, Mr. Holmes," he said. "The buyer wishes to remain anonymous. We respect such sentiments here."

Holmes paused, as though pondering his next tact. "What if we paid you more?" he offered.

My friend surprised me. Usually, deduction was his only method, but now he was considering bribery. I could not help but feel disappointed.

"I would never be trusted again," Mr. Thorley pointed out. "Among criminals, I mean." He seemed to enjoy Holmes's problem.

Holmes, however, shook his head. "That's another lie. You are an avaricious man, Mr. Thorley, who is willing to sell his principles for practically nothing. If you knew something of value, you would be bargaining with me right now. As it is, I probably know more than you do. I know, for example, that the private buyer corresponded with you anonymously, that it was Miss Emma Henderson, and that she is listening to this very conversation from behind the door."

"I might have known you would realise that, Mr. Holmes," said a female voice at our backs.

Holmes did not even have to turn. "Miss Henderson," he said suavely.

The lady entered, beaming. "You realised the auction was a charade?"

"Another charade," he pursued, "was the business with the gun."

Emma Henderson's smile remained as she crossed towards the desk and stood behind a faintly bewildered Mr. Thorley. "How so?" she prompted, as though indulging a child.

"Someone could well have stopped the winning bidder from leaving," said Holmes. "There were enough thugs in the room to do so, after all. If anyone tried it, and acquired the head, they would discover that it was a fake which could easily fall apart. The sale would be

338

revealed as similarly false. To prevent that from happening, you had to demonstrate the ineffectiveness of such a heist, so you tried it yourself and had the guards disarm you." He looked at her levelly. "I knew it was an act the moment you pulled that gun. Someone of your intellect, Miss Henderson, would never resort to the petty intimidations of a highwayman."

I frowned, trying to understand all that was happening. "You mean to say, Holmes, that Miss Henderson is the person who has bought the head, but that she did so with such discretion that not even Thorley knew it was her?"

"She sent him a letter, suggesting a private sale and that the real head be substituted for one made of alabaster, so no one would discover the arrangement. I dare say that the winning bidder was in her employ, and that the vase he exchanged it for was already owned by Thorley. I do not, however, believe that you bought the head for yourself, Miss Henderson. Despite what you said outside, you are no admirer of Moriarty's. You admire only yourself."

Her coy smile betrayed the truth of his words.

"Therefore, someone hired you to buy it," Holmes went on. "I will, of course, uncover his identity. Any man who wishes to own such a macabre relic must undoubtedly be positioning himself as Moriarty's successor, and I mean to stop him."

Emma Henderson looked almost pleased. "You will *not* do that, Mr. Holmes."

Behind his eyes, I noticed my friend bristle at her confidence.

The lady turned to Mr. Thorley expectantly. "Shall I take possession of the item now?"

The auctioneer was looking less self-satisfied than he had been a few minutes earlier. With a meek nod, he stretched to his full six feet and made his way to the longcase clock in the corner. I watched with puzzlement as he adjusted the hands to half past eleven. To my surprise, the ticking stopped abruptly and all was silent in the room. He then pressed his fingers against the clock face. As though a key had been turned, it opened, revealing only deep blackness behind.

"I usually keep antiques in here," he explained casually and reached two hands inside.

His body shifted and I could not quite see what he lifted out. Turning back towards us, however, it caught the light from the fire and I stiffened in shock.

He was holding an angular, fully-fleshed skull. It looked much the same as the one which had been positioned on the auction block earlier, and I found myself staring into its sightless eyes again. Not surprisingly,

Mr. Thorley kept the ghastly object at arm's length as he passed across the room and to his desk.

Miss Henderson was lifting a bag open, and the auctioneer pushed it carefully inside.

"And, in return," she said, lifting her necklace. The emerald glimmered in the firelight as she unfastened it from the lace and handed it to him. Mr. Thorley clasped it with hungry hands. "I must meet my employer," she added breezily, turning to Holmes. "I do not wish you to follow me, Mr. Holmes. I'm sure you understand."

"Naturally, yes."

"So I will be locking you all in here."

Mr. Thorley frowned at this, discomforted.

"I will be back in a couple of hours," she assured him, like a nanny promising a treat.

The three of us remained in the office as the young lady returned to the hallway and pulled the door closed. It felt strange, being wilfully trapped like that. As the key turned, I looked resignedly for a chair. I needed a sit down after all that had happened.

"Do you suppose she will come back?" asked Mr. Thorley worriedly. "We have never had a raid here but, if we did, I'd be locked up before I'm even caught."

A minute or two later, staring out of the window, I saw the lady outside on the street below, waving down a dog-cart. She certainly looked determined and, I thought, quite exhilarated as she bounded on-board and onto her next adventure. It was no doubt such excitement, and not the wealth alone, which kept her crossing continents and committing crimes.

It was a long wait and one which was mostly spent in silence. The sun began to sink and I watched it from the window. Afterwards, I became so bored that I wished for Holmes's tuba, or even, perhaps, for a session of shooting rats.

Finally, two-and-a-quarter hours later, we heard the scratching of the lock.

I turned to the door with excited expectation. With a click, it swung wide, revealing Holmes in the hallway.

I leapt to my feet. "You're back!" I said delightedly and clapped his hand in mine. "Did it go well?"

Holmes looked tired, but he proceeded gamely on. "Just as Thorley said, that secret door led directly outside. I was out there before she was, just as a dog-cart trotted down the street. The driver gave up his seat the moment I told him my name. With his hat pulled over my head, and a jacket draped about my shoulders, she didn't notice a thing."

"And you took her to her employer?"

"She directed me there herself," said Holmes and folded into his seat with relief.

"Where is she now?" I asked.

Holmes tilted his head ruefully. "I don't know, but I'm not interested. I know who her employer is, and that is all that matters to me now."

"So who is he? Where did she lead you?"

Holmes slapped his thigh restlessly. "I shall tell you elsewhere, Watson. Mr. Thorley, good evening."

The auctioneer could only bob his head bemusedly.

At our rooms in Baker Street, the hearth blazing a beautiful orange, Holmes told me all of what he had seen and heard since he had left Limehouse late that afternoon. I sat back in my favourite armchair and listened intently to a story which I had not expected, but one I was most fascinated to hear.

Chewing on a briar, Holmes told me all: "Miss Henderson requested that I take her to Waterloo. I thought this was curious, as there was more than one train station nearer than that. I did as I was told, however, and upon our arrival she disembarked. I waited a few moments before following on foot. I suspected she would head out of London. As it was, she didn't take a train at all."

"Why is that?" I asked earnestly.

"That is what I asked myself, Watson, and I received my answer well enough. Staying a good few yards behind, I followed her inside the station house. There was a secretary there, almost guarding the door through which Miss Henderson had just disappeared. I was able to send the fellow away and pressed my ear against the door of the station master's office. There, she met her employer."

"Well?" I pressed impatiently. "Who was it?"

"He is, Watson, none other than James Moriarty."

I stared at him, astounded. "But that cannot be!" I protested. "You saw him die. We have even seen his disembodied skull!"

Holmes waved a hand to calm me. "The man I saw today was not the Professor, Watson, but his brother. A colonel, no less. I met him, briefly, but as he was engaged in his work, I asked him if he would consider agreeing to visit here this evening and discuss the matter with us. He kindly assented, and we may expect him to arrive at any moment."

Throughout my friend's monologue, I had remained rapt and rigid. The notion that we should meet the brother of Moriarty – the man to whom the whole of the country, nay even the Continent, had been a devil's playground – was an honour of the most dubious variety. It shames me now to consider such sentiments, particularly as it was the sort of idolatry which had so intoxicated the Professor's many followers. Perhaps I was simply intrigued. I had heard so much of Moriarty. To hear more of him, and from someone so close, was a tantalising opportunity, if not entirely an outright privilege.

Holmes and I waited in the silent gloom for almost an hour before the doorbell signalled the arrival of our visitor. I heard Mrs. Hudson softly padding through the hallway and, a few moments later, the creaking of the stairs. Holmes had once told me how he had heard the Professor himself ascend those same steps, while he played nonchalantly on his violin. Something similar was happening now. Pulling the door wide, I found a short, thin man waiting without.

He leant forward slightly in a stoop, his head was bare and domed and his face was almost skeletally thin. I was surprised, and a little disconcerted, of the resemblance to his brother's skull.

"Good evening, Colonel," said Holmes and gestured hospitably towards the sofa. "You have heard of Dr. Watson?"

"Yes," he said, nodding to me politely, and took his seat.

"It is good of you to join us, Colonel. We certainly appreciate your coming. Perhaps, then, in your own time, you may tell us everything you wish."

Colonel Moriarty took a breath and, after a pause which felt like forever, he began his story. "My father was a mathematician," he said. "He was also named James, and was a criminal of the white-collar variety. A tall, slim man with deep-set eyes and a hooked nose, he was a foreboding presence – a man who believed in discipline and effort, and one who did not tolerate weakness of any kind. He tolerated, in fact, rather little, and we were greatly in fear of him. He never drank, however, like so many other males. He was always lucid and logical, which was one of the ways he was so fearsome. Any time we misbehaved and began a story to excuse it, he could fault it laterally with astonishing ease.

"Our mother, Ennis, relied on him – probably more than the other mothers. She was not what you might describe as a particularly strong woman. She looked to him for guidance on everything, even the most trivial of matters. His word was law and his decisions final. I think now, as I look again across the years, how much power he wielded, both in the house and the wider community. People respected him. Perhaps, in

342

retrospect, they were even scared. I do not remember a great deal about him as, one morning, he died in a boating accident. As you can readily imagine, Mr. Holmes, our mother was heartbroken. Quite profoundly, in fact. That was when things started to become strange."

"How so?" I prompted, but Holmes was more patient than I and waited silently for our visitor to continue.

"Our mother was lost without him. I appreciate that it often the way with spouses who suddenly find themselves alone, but this was different. More . . . desperate. She cried out to him in the night, when she thought we were asleep and could not hear her. But we did, Mr. Holmes, the three of us heard her well and became quite disturbed."

"Did you know your father had died?" asked Holmes, "or did she endeavour to keep the news from you?"

"Oh, no, we knew immediately. The whole village did. At first, she spoke of Father in wistful terms. She would say how much she wished he were with us. She then began saying we must act as he did. That may sound innocent enough to your ears, Mr. Holmes, as it did to ours at first, but she meant it most seriously. After a short while, she became more earnest about it, more intense, and demanded we behave just as he had done. We were not to behave like children, she said, but like grown men who were mature of thought and temperament. And so we did not play, like the other children, and we did not laugh. Before it was truly time for it, our mother began to teach us mathematics. We proved to be precocious students, sharing our father's abilities, and we learned it well. There is no denying, however, there were particular standards we were expected to meet. She urged us, most aggressively, to be just as able as he.

"Even when we became the best of our age, our mother did not desist. She taught us, too, of thievery and blackmail. I was, by this point, almost eight years old, and our names had already been changed in tribute to our father. It is curious now how we could ever correctly refer to the other. Somehow, it seldom seemed to be a problem, and we were rarely apart to make it one. Something she could not replicate, however, was our father's personality. I was reticent and less eager to flourish than my brothers. It would have been fruitless, in any case, as my elder brother was truly the cleverest in all that we did. He was determined and hungry for praise. He was seven years older than I, and had known Father rather better, and had therefore been accustomed to his frequent foul moods. Perhaps this was why he had some himself.

"This brother, whom you knew, was twenty-one when he penned a treatise on the Binomial Theorem. It was a most impressive work, and one in which there is no equal. Indeed, it is said that there is no man in the country able to competently critique it. For this, he was awarded a Mathematical Chair at Durham University. I slowly began to lose touch with him. At this point, I do not think he wanted to be reminded of his father and someone such as I, with the same name and perhaps even resemblance, would have done just that. By the time he had written *The Dynamics of an Asteroid*, he was not a relative, but a relative stranger. I can only speculate on his subsequent thinking. It is my belief, however, that his ambition to prove to himself, as well as to others, that he was no mere imitator became an obsession. He was driven not only to excel himself but *exceed* our father."

Holmes nodded understandingly. "He became a far more formidable criminal than he or, indeed, any other before him."

"Quite," agreed the Colonel.

"Ironically," I added, "in his fall at Reichenbach, he died in much the same way."

The man's eyes clouded wistfully, as though he had not hitherto considered this tragic similarity.

"And what of yourself, Colonel?" asked Holmes.

He looked up at Holmes and half-shrugged. "Well, as my brother was much older, I was able to perceive the effects our childhood had wrought upon him. I recognized that our mother was quite insensible and turned my back on mathematics. Instead, I enrolled in the military and, as you know, I am currently enjoying an early retirement as a station master."

"Then why," I said, "do you wish to purchase your brother's skull as a semi-religious relic?"

The manner in which I had framed this sentence seemed to take the old man by surprise. "I wish no such thing."

"If you would permit me to answer for you, Colonel," said Holmes, interrupting with a raised hand, "I think I know the reason."

I looked at my friend expectantly.

"The Colonel, Watson, is saddened by the trajectory his brother's life had taken. He has seen the mania which has infused the Professor's followers and sees parallels in his own childhood. He knows what such adoration can inspire. He does not want the same to happen to somebody else."

I turned to Moriarty for confirmation of this curious analysis. With what I believed was relief, he bowed his head in approval.

"I heard that my brother's body was, in some semblance, being returned to London and initially believed it would be buried here. To my distaste, I learned that only the skull remained and that it would be sold to one of his many devotees. I had no way of knowing where it was, so I

344

decided to investigate. I quickly came upon Miss Henderson who, rarely for a criminal in London, did not wish to acquire the head herself."

"Miss Henderson has always preferred to carve her own path," said Holmes with open admiration.

"I enlisted the lady's help and, with her considerable knowledge of the underworld, she was able to establish just how the head was to be sold. To avoid it falling into the hands of zealots, I had no choice but to purchase it myself and did so in a private sale which she arranged. All else, such as designing a fake as a decoy, was her own idea."

"What shall you do with it?" I asked. It was indiscreet of me, but I was too intrigued not to ask.

The Colonel did not seem surprised at the question and answered. "I have already thrown it in the Thames," he said heavily. "Yet another watery grave."

A moment of silent calm passed between us, almost in respect for our fallen enemy. Then, slowly, the old man rose from his chair and Holmes did the same.

"It is a pleasure to meet you, Colonel," said my friend and gripped the man's hand.

"As it is for me, Mr. Holmes. It is reassuring to know there are men just as clever as my late brother, but without his . . . idiosyncrasies." He smiled weakly, and Holmes returned it.

After our visitor had left, I moved to the hearth and began poking the fire.

"Wait, Watson!" came Holmes's voice behind me.

I felt an unpleasant stir and, turning, found my fears had been realised.

Holmes was positioned in an armchair with the tuba perched portentously on his lap.

"I thought that was a ruse," I said quite desperately. "You never really had an interest in this monstrosity."

"That is correct, Watson," said Holmes happily. "But, in playing it this morning for the purpose of my prank, I decided the music was rather heartening."

Before I could stop him, he pressed his lips to the mouthpiece and fiddled his fingers along the buttons.

My protests were inaudible above the noise, but I was not about to give up. I looked about for something to cram into the bell. As I did so, my pained gaze settled on something I had forgotten entirely.

In the corner, stood a rat.

The Influence Machine
by Mark Mower

The early part of 1895 had already proved to be one of the busiest periods that Holmes and I had experienced in taking on the many cases and conundrums that presented themselves from week to week. And it was in June of that year that we were thrown unexpectedly into a short but ultimately unique affair which now deserves public attention.

I had returned to Baker Street that particular afternoon to present Holmes with a gift. Knowing his fondness for rare manuscripts on obscure topics, I had managed to purchase, at no great expense, a first-edition of Francis Hauksbee's 1715 lecture notes on *A Course of Mechanical, Optical, Hydrostatical, and Pneumatical Experiments*. My colleague was immediately enraptured by the tome, eagerly flicking through its delicate pages and taking in the exquisitely printed diagrams which accompanied the text. It was a good twenty minutes before he re-engaged me in conversation.

"A most curious feature, Watson!"

I looked up from *The Times* and cast him a glance. I could see by his intense concentration that something inside the leather covering of the front cover had caught his attention. Slipping his bony fingers under an exposed section of the binding, he had withdrawn a small folded letter which he then began to scrutinise.

"This is most unexpected. You might remember that Hauksbee was the son of a draper. He ran a business off Fleet Street specialising in air-pumps, hydrostatic devices, and reflecting telescopes. But as a scientist he is known principally for inventing an early electrostatic generator, which he demonstrated at meetings of the Royal Society."

I had to confess, that beyond the name, I had little knowledge of Hauksbee or his work. "So what did this electrostatic generator do?" I asked, placing the newspaper down on the arm of my chair.

"The contraption consisted of a sealed glass globe which could be rotated rapidly by a hand-cranked wheel. While spinning the wheel with one hand, Hauksbee would use his other hand to place a light cotton cloth on the top of the rotating glass. The electrical charge he created would produce a light which stunned everyone in his packed lecture theatres."

"Most fascinating. And was the note that you now hold in your hand written by Mr. Hauksbee?"

He smirked mischievously. "No. That is the curious feature!" He was in a state of some excitement and rose from his chair to retrieve a magnifying glass from the mantelpiece. He then sat at the table before the window and began to examine the document through the lens. "A short, personal note, written on cheap paper. The high concentration of cotton fibres suggests it was manufactured close to one of the Northern mill towns. The watermark is crude but reveals the words *'Lewden Mill'*. My supposition is thus confirmed – the paper mill is in Worsbrough, Yorkshire."

I was, as ever, stunned by his ability to retrieve such trivia from the depths of his memory. "What else can you discern, Holmes?"

"This is a non-standard paper size and the residue of gum along the top is most suggestive. It has been torn from a notepad. Possibly one used by a professional man. It is written in cheap black ink, which has faded considerably over the years since this was written. The hand is free-flowing, but lazy – undoubtable that of a person well-used to firing off short missives. It will not surprise you to learn that the author is a medical man."

I coughed unexpectedly at the disclosure. "Really! You gathered that from some black ink and the style of handwriting?"

My colleague grinned once more. "No, he's signed it *'Owen Douglas, MD'*."

We both laughed and Holmes went on to reveal more. "It's dated *'12th March 1884'*, and starts simply, *'To my dearest James'*. The address of the intended recipient is *'7 Crescent Grove, Clapham Common'*. As for the contents, you had better read that yourself."

I joined him at the table and was handed the note. It read:

Please accept this book (one that I remembered you had wanted for your collection) as a small token of my appreciation for what you have given me.

I used the Influence to re-start the heart of a local man, Wright Littlewood, who had suffered a heart attack. He has recovered admirably, but I will keep you informed of his progress.

I am loath to broadcast my success more widely, for fear that it may be deemed to have been a dubious professional act. However, I am now even more convinced that your invention has the power to save lives.

I am forever in your debt and remain,

Yours faithfully,

"Well, what are we to make of it, Watson? Is it not a most baffling, yet fascinating, memorandum?"

"It is," I replied. "I know that others have claimed success in using electricity to resuscitate patients. In 1774, a country doctor claimed to have applied an electric shock to the chest of a young girl to re-establish her pulse. Since then, many have carried out experiments on the power of defibrillation, albeit mainly on animals. Most recently, in the 1840's, the Italian physicist, Carlo Matteucci, published his studies into the electrical properties of animal tissue. So the idea that a doctor could successfully induce ventricular fibrillation using shock treatment is within the realms of possibility."

"Excellent!" exclaimed Holmes. "Then let us assume for the moment that the incident referred to is genuine. The note is a personal one, so we have the task of discovering who 'James' is or was."

"Well clearly he is also a medical man," I ventured.

"It would be tempting to think so, but the use of the word '*invention*' makes me wonder if our man might be a pioneer in a broader field. That he wanted to own a copy of the Hauksbee book further suggests that his interests may be more scientific and mechanical rather than medical." He pointed once more at the note before us. "And there is something about the use of this term '*Influence*' – I believe I am right in saying that some of the electrostatic generators that have been developed in recent years are sometimes referred to as *Influence Machines*."

"That may well be the case, but where does that leaves us? Without a surname, we may still be on a wild goose chase. In any case, Holmes, are you really intent on pursuing this, given all of the other demands on your time?"

I could already tell what his answer would be. When my colleague was fired up to this extent, he was hard to dissuade. "There is more to this matter than we have yet discovered. And you forget – we have an address!"

"But how do you know that this fellow has not died and his book collection has been sold or given to the dealer from whom I purchased it?"

"A good point, my friend. And one that is easily checked. Let us test your theory. What was the name of the book dealer?"

"It was Bumpus's on Oxford Street."

"Splendid. Then we will take in some fine London air and enjoy a stroll on this particularly pleasant afternoon."

It was less than a mile to the bookshop. The capital was bathed in warm summer sunshine and the temperature had soared. Walking at the pace dictated by Holmes, I found it uncomfortably clammy, clad as I was in a thick tweed jacket with matching waistcoat.

I took the opportunity to fire questions at Holmes in an attempt to slow him down, but the quest proved fruitless. "How do we know the book wasn't stolen?" said I, breathlessly.

"The Bumpus family are reputable dealers – their business is built upon that. They will keep records, or know from where all their stock comes," he shot back at me. "Now, come on, Watson, keep up!"

Once inside the large book shop, it took me just a few seconds to spot the assistant who had sold me the book earlier that day. He was most helpful, if not a little concerned at first that I wished to return the book. Having satisfied him on that score, Holmes explained the nature of our quest, saying that we had discovered a personal note within the cover of the book and now wished to return it to the book's original owner. *Could he therefore tell us anything about from where the book had come?*

The subterfuge worked perfectly. "The book was brought in the previous week by a well-dressed man of about sixty. He had only the one volume to sell. Naturally, before agreeing to buy the manuscript, I asked him why he wished to sell. In response, he said that he knew the book to be collectable, and of great value to those with a mind for science. As such, he was loath to dispose of it. But for very personal reasons, he could no longer bear to hold on to it."

"I see," said Holmes. "And did the man give any indication of where he lived?"

"Yes. I think I remember him saying something about travelling in from Clapham Common."

"Excellent! Then we will not trouble you further. For that is indeed our man!"

The assistant seemed slightly disconcerted by Holmes's exuberance, but, when thanked, bid us, "Good day then, gentlemen," as we headed for the door.

Out on the street, Holmes was elated. "Our man is still alive, Watson! It just remains for us to pay him a visit. Then, hopefully, all will become clearer."

"I wonder what these 'very personal reasons' were for wanting to sell the book after a decade or so."

"That we cannot know until we speak to him," replied Holmes. "Now, we will catch a cab back at Baker Street. Before we make the journey out to leafy Clapham, there is something I must just check."

Holmes insisted on leaving me out on the street when we made it back to 221b. He had only been gone for some six or seven minutes when he re-emerged from the door, a broad grin lining his face.

Seated within the interior of a hansom cab a short while later, he explained, "I am getting sloppy with age, Watson. Had I checked my trade directories earlier, we would have discovered that our man was indeed still alive. A quick search of the address revealed that the occupant of '7 Crescent Grove, Clapham Common' is none other than a 'James Wimshurst'. Interestingly, I could find no doctor by the name of 'Owen Douglas' registered in the county of Yorkshire. If necessary, I will check later whether there is a doctor of that name elsewhere in the country."

It was a six-mile cab journey out to Clapham. I was surprised by how much the area had changed since I had last ventured there. Alongside the grand mansions in Old Town and those that fronted the common, there were newer developments, including those of Crescent Grove and Grafton Square.

The cabbie set us down outside the large gates of 7 Crescent Grove. It was an impressive building set within a fair-sized plot. Holmes wasted no time in passing through the gates and heading up the gravel drive towards the grand doorway. At the door, he pulled on a bell cord and, some moments afterwards, we were greeted by a thin, wan-faced maid. Holmes presented his card and we were told to step inside while the master of the house was informed of our arrival.

The James Wimshurst who came to greet us was an affable fellow of medium build, with a full, greying beard and balding head. He instructed the maid to arrange for some tea to be brought to his study and invited us to follow him to the room, which sat across the entrance hallway to the left.

Inside the study, we could see that he had something of a passion for scientific and mechanical devices. On every surface stood telescopes, small steam engines, and strange globes containing wheels, cogs, and metal wiring. Framed around the walls were engineers' drawings and technical charts, and in the bay window was housed a large collection of reference books, all of a scientific or technical nature.

Wimshurst was the first to speak. "It is indeed a pleasure to meet you, Mr. Holmes. I enjoy reading of your exploits. And I am hoping that this is your chronicler, Dr. Watson?"

350

I nodded and, having shaken hands, Wimshurst invited us to take seats around a small oval table. At Holmes's request, he then explained the nature of his work. He had been born in Poplar and was apprenticed as a shipwright. Following a move to Liverpool, his career progressed rapidly, and he had eventually become the chief shipwright surveyor for the Board of Trade at Lloyds.

Encouraged to say something about the assortment of devices scattered around the room, Wimshurst beamed and explained that he devoted much of his free time to experimental works. He had invented a vacuum pump which enabled the stability of ships to be determined, and had experimented with ways of electrically connecting lighthouses to the mainland. But in the late 1870's he had begun to focus on his real interest – the creation of electrical influence machines for generating electrical sparks for scientific purposes. He went on to say that he had a well-equipped workshop in the garden containing all of the tools and instruments he treasured.

With these pleasantries completed and the arrival of the tea tray, Holmes then took the lead, keen to explain the nature of our visit. He withdrew from a pocket the note written by Dr. Douglas, opened it and placed it on the oval table in front of Wimshurst. The demeanour of our host changed immediately. He looked visibly shaken, his hands began to tremble, and tears began to well up in his eyes. As he looked up from the note towards Holmes, he could only whisper, "Where did you get this?"

Holmes apologised for his abruptness in revealing the document. He explained how he had been given the Hauksbee book as a gift and had discovered the note tucked within the leather binding of its cover. He then added, "I sincerely hope you will forgive us, sir, but we wished only to discover the story behind the note. If you would prefer us to leave, we will of course do so."

Wimshurst had begun to regain some of his composure. He smiled weakly and then replied. "Gentlemen, this has come as something of a shock. I had no idea that the note was still with the book. It must be a good ten years since I received both from my good friend Owen Douglas. It was only last week that I sold the manuscript, for I could no longer bear to have it in the house."

I did my best to ease the tension. "Yes, Mr. Wimshurst, we called in a Bumpus's and were told that you had sold the book for personal reasons."

"That is something of an understatement. I will do my best to outline the story for you. You may then understand why I felt it necessary."

351

He took a final sip of his tea and placed the cup down on the tray. "After the move to Liverpool, my wife and I became acquainted with a young country surgeon named Owen Douglas. He had a thriving medical practice in the town of Lepton on the outskirts of Huddersfield. Owen was something of a medical pioneer and shared my interest in all things mechanical. Like me, he collected rare scientific texts.

"For the three years from 1880, I began to work on a new type of electrostatic generator, capable of producing very high voltages. The influence machine was very different to some of the early generators upon which I had worked, relying on friction to produce an electrical charge. My machine was constructed with two large insulated contra-rotating discs mounted in a vertical plane, two crossed neutralising bars with wire brushes, and a spark gap which was formed by two metal spheres. In this way, an electrical charge is separated through electrostatic induction, or *influence*, rather than friction.

"The new generator proved popular with many other scientists and engineers. Douglas was particularly enamoured with the device and insisted on taking possession of one of my early working models. He also tried to get me to take out a patent for the machine, but I resisted this, fearing a legal challenge from others who were working in the same direction.

"Throughout 1883, Owen began to tinker with the machine, believing that he could use it for some of his pioneering medical treatments. He was convinced that small electrical charges could be used, for example, to stimulate damaged nerve tissue. He would write to me on his progress, but insisted that I keep quiet about his work, fearing that he might be struck off by the British Medical Association for unethical conduct.

"In March 1884, he believed that he had achieved some success while operating on a worker who had been injured in an accident at a local meat factory. Wright Charlesworth Littlewood was a thirty-six-year-old tripe dresser who had been badly wounded with a cutting machine. He was carried from the factory to Owen's surgery in a terribly weakened state, having lost a significant quantity of blood. On the operating table, he then suffered a heart attack and stopped breathing. Alone with his patient, Owen believed he had but one hope to save Littlewood. With his adapted electrostatic generator in full motion, he sent a sizeable electrical charge into the man's chest and was stunned to find that the heart had indeed restarted. The note you have before you, Mr. Holmes, was written that evening."

I was amazed to hear this and gripped by his narrative. I was both shocked and awed to hear of the surgeon's conduct, but recognised that I too had occasionally resorted to unorthodox practises in an effort to save men on the battlefield. I was therefore in no position to sit in judgement on the ethics or efficacy of the man's approach.

Holmes took the opportunity to ask a direct question. "I take it that this Wright Charlesworth Littlewood survived the ordeal?"

Wimshurst gave him a solemn look. "Sadly, yes."

It was not the response I had expected to hear, and our host had evidently noted my look of surprise. "You must forgive me, Dr. Watson, but there is much more to tell. Littlewood was patched up and confined to bed for many weeks. Slowly, with the support of his wife, Helen, the man recovered and eventually went back to work. In time, he opened up his own meat factory with some success.

"Owen was delighted to see Littlewood recover. He wrote to me frequently in the weeks and months that followed convinced that my influence machine had real potential for saving lives. But try as he might, he was never able to replicate the outcome he had achieved in the factory worker's case. With the passage of time, he shifted his attention to other ground-breaking surgical work."

"And how did you feel about the incident?" I asked.

"At that time, I was thrilled to think that the influence machine had saved a life and might have a medical application. And every time I leafed through the Francis Hauksbee manuscript, I was reminded of Owen's work and the close friendship we shared. That was all to change in December 1892 . . . ."

". . . when Wright Charlesworth Littlewood was found guilty of the murder his sixteen-year-old daughter, Emily."

It was Wimshurst's turn to look surprised. "Then you know of the case, Mr. Holmes?"

My colleague answered him directly without conceit. "I have made it my business to study the details of all major criminal cases in recent years. The man's name was so unusual that I felt it could not be a coincidence. As I recollect, the factory owner lived with his wife and daughter in the village of Honley. Emily was a sickly child of no great intellect and prone to epileptic fits. She was never allowed to leave the home on her own. Prone to bouts of depression and suffering from his addiction to alcohol, Littlewood slit her throat one night and was tried for the murder. He was found guilty by reason of insanity and is currently detained within the Broadmoor Criminal Lunatic Asylum in Berkshire."

The solemn look had returned to Wimshurst's face. "All true, I'm afraid. And the case was to have a devastating impact on poor Owen. It was talk of the villages around Huddersfield and one or two people remembered that the surgeon had once saved Littlewood's life. Sinking into depression, he began to blame himself for what had occurred, believing that he had committed an unnatural act in using the influence machine to revive Littlewood's heart. Twelve months ago he took his own life, convinced that he had been wrong to try and play God all those years before."

I could not hide my dismay. "That is a truly distressing story. I can understand now why you took the decision to sell the Hauksbee book."

"Thank you, Doctor. After Owen's death, I could not bear to see the book in my library. I just hope that it gives you more pleasure, Mr. Holmes."

Holmes rose from the table and extended his hand towards Wimshurst. As the two men shook hands my colleague made a final, telling comment. "Sir, you must not let this dreadful business dent your faith in science and technology and its potential to change the world for the better. We need men and women like you: The inventors, the pioneers, and the free-thinkers. Our progress as a species depends upon it."

For much of our journey back from Clapham, Holmes and I sat in silence, each mulling over private thoughts and reflecting on the heart-rending nature of what we had discovered. This had been a short interlude in a year which saw the two of us engaged in numerous assignments, travelling the length and breadth of the country in pursuit of the strange, the criminal, and the inexplicable. But it was an episode which Holmes was never to forget. A few days after our trip to Clapham, a boxed package arrived at Baker Street, addressed to my colleague. Inside was a perfect working model of the "Wimshurst Machine". Alongside the Hauksbee manuscript, it was a gift he has treasured for the rest of his life.

NOTE

Readers may like to know that between 1899 and 1900, Jean-Louis Prévost and Frederic Batelli – two physiologists from the University of Geneva - first demonstrated a device that used small electrical shocks to induce ventricular fibrillation in dogs. It was a forerunner of the modern defibrillator. I was fortunate enough to meet both men at a medical conference in 1902. I am not aware if James Wimshurst knew of their endeavours. Sadly, he passed away in the January of 1903. – JHW.

About the Contributors

The following contributors appear in this volume
The MX Book of New Sherlock Holmes Stories
Part IX – 2018 Annual (1879-1895)

Deanna Baran lives in a remote part of Texas where cowboys may still be seen in their natural habitat. A librarian and former museum curator, she writes in between cups of tea, playing *Go*, and trading postcards with people around the world. This is her latest venture into the foggy streets of gaslit London.

Brian Belanger is a publisher and editor, but is best known for his freelance illustration and cover design work. His distinctive style can be seen on several MX Publishing covers, including *Silent Meridian* by Elizabeth Crowen, *Sherlock Holmes and the Menacing Melbournian* by Allan Mitchell, *Sherlock Holmes and A Quantity of Debt* by David Marcum, *Welcome to Undershaw* by Luke Benjamen Kuhns, and many more. Brian is the co-founder of Belanger Books LLC, where he illustrates the popular *MacDougall Twins with Sherlock Holmes* young reader series (#1 bestsellers on Amazon.com UK). A prolific creator, he also designs t-shirts, mugs, stickers, and other merchandise on his personal art site: *www.redbubble.com/people/zhahadun*.

S.F. Bennett was born and raised in London, studying History at Queen Mary and Westfield College, and Journalism at City University at the Postgraduate level, before moving to Devon in 2013. The author lectures on Conan Doyle, Sherlock Holmes, and 19th century detective fiction, and has had articles on various aspects from The Canon published in *The Journal of the Sherlock Holmes Society of London* and *The Torr*, the journal of *The Poor Folk Upon The Moors*, the Sherlock Holmes Society of the South West of England. Her first published novel is *The Secret Diary of Mycroft Holmes: The Thoughts and Reminiscences of Sherlock Holmes's Elder Brother, 1880-1888* (2017).

Nick Cardillo has loved Sherlock Holmes ever since he was first introduced to the detective in *The Great Illustrated Classics* edition of *The Adventures of Sherlock Holmes* at the age of six. His devotion to the Baker Street detective duo has only increased over the years, and Nick is thrilled to be taking these proper steps into the Sherlock Holmes Community. His first published story, "The Adventure of the Traveling Corpse", appeared in *The MX Book of New Sherlock Holmes Stories – Part VI: 2017 Annual*, and his "The Haunting of Hamilton Gardens" was published in *PART VIII – Eliminate the Impossible: 1892-1905*. A devout fan of The Golden Age of Detective Fiction, Hammer Horror, and *Doctor Who*, Nick co-writes the Sherlockian blog, *Back on Baker Street*, which analyses over seventy years of Sherlock Holmes film and culture. He is a student at Susquehanna University.

Leslie Charteris was born in Singapore on May 12th, 1907. With his mother and brother, he moved to England in 1919 and attended Rossall School in Lancashire before moving on to Cambridge University to study law. His studies there came to a halt when a publisher accepted his first novel. His third one, entitled *Meet the Tiger*, was written when he was twenty years old and published in September 1928. It introduced the world to Simon Templar, *aka* The Saint. He continued to write about The Saint until 1983 when the last book, *Salvage for The Saint*, was published. The books, which have been translated into over thirty languages, number nearly a hundred and have sold over forty-million copies around the world. They've inspired, to date, fifteen feature films, three television series, ten radio series, and a comic strip that was written by Charteris and syndicated around the world for over a decade. He enjoyed travelling, but settled for long periods in Hollywood, Florida, and finally in Surrey, England. He was awarded the Cartier Diamond Dagger by the *Crime Writers' Association* in 1992, in recognition of a lifetime of achievement. He died the following year.

Ian Dickerson was just nine years old when he discovered The Saint. Shortly after that, he discovered Sherlock Holmes. The Saint won, for a while anyway. He struck up a friendship with The Saint's creator, Leslie Charteris and his family. With their permission, he spent six weeks studying the Leslie Charteris collection at Boston University and went on to write, direct, and produce documentaries on the making of *The Saint* and *Return of The Saint*, which have been released on DVD. He oversaw the recent reprints of almost fifty of the original Saint books in both the US and UK, and was a co-producer on the 2017 TV movie of *The Saint*. When he discovered that Charteris had written Sherlock Holmes stories as well – well, there was the excuse he needed to revisit The Canon. He's consequently written and edited three books on Holmes' radio adventures. For the sake of what little sanity he has, Ian has also written about a wide range of subjects, none of which come with a halo, including talking mashed potatoes, Lord Grade, and satellite links. Ian lives in Hampshire with his wife and two children. And an awful lot of books by Leslie Charteris. Not quite so many by Conan Doyle, though.

Sir Arthur Conan Doyle (1859-1930) *Holmes Chronicler Emeritus*. If not for him, this anthology would not exist. Author, physician, patriot, sportsman, spiritualist, husband and father, and advocate for the oppressed. He is remembered and honored for the purposes of this collection by being the man who introduced Sherlock Holmes to the world. Through fifty-six Holmes short stories, four novels, and additional Apocryphal entries, Doyle revolutionized mystery stories and also greatly influenced and improved police forensic methods and techniques for the betterment of all. *Steel True Blade Straight*.

C.H. Dye first discovered Sherlock Holmes when she was eleven, in a collection that ended at the Reichenbach Falls. It was another six months before she discovered *The Hound of the Baskervilles*, and two weeks after that before a librarian handed her *The Return*. She has loved the stories ever since. She has written fan-fiction, and her first published pastiche, "The Tale of the Forty Thieves", was included in *The MX Book of New Sherlock Holmes Stories – Part I: 1881-1889*. Her story "A Christmas Goose" was in *The MX Book of New Sherlock Holmes Stories – Part V: Christmas Adventures*, and "The Mysterious Mourner" in *The MX Book of New Sherlock Holmes Stories – Part VIII – Eliminate the Impossible: 1892-1905*

Steve Emecz's main field is technology, in which he has been working for about twenty years. Following multiple senior roles at Xerox, where he grew their European eCommerce from $6m to $200m, Steve joined platform provider Venda, and moved across to Powa in 2010. Today, Steve is CCO at collectAI in Hamburg, a German fintech company using Artificial Intelligence to help companies with their debt collection. Steve is a regular trade show speaker on the subject of eCommerce, and his tech career has taken him to more than fifty countries – so he's no stranger to planes and airports. He wrote two novels (one a bestseller) in the 1990's, and a screenplay in 2001. Shortly after, he set up MX Publishing, specialising in NLP books. In 2008, MX published its first Sherlock Holmes book, and MX has gone on to become the largest specialist Holmes publisher in the world. MX is a social enterprise and supports two main causes. The first is Happy Life, a children's rescue project in Nairobi, Kenya, where he and his wife, Sharon, spend every Christmas at the rescue centre in Kasarani. In 2014, they wrote a short book about the project, *The Happy Life Story*. The second is the Stepping Stones School, of which Steve is a patron. Stepping Stones is located at Undershaw, Sir Arthur Conan Doyle's former home.

Sonia Fetherston BSI is a member of the illustrious *Baker Street Irregulars*. For almost thirty years, she's been a frequent contributor to Sherlockian anthologies, including Calabash Press's acclaimed *Case Files* series, and Wildside Press's *About* series. Sonia's byline often appears in the pages of *The Baker Street Journal*, *The Journal* of the *Sherlock Holmes Society of London*, *Canadian Holmes*, and the Sydney Passengers' *Log*. Her work earned her the coveted Morley-Montgomery Award from the *Baker Street Irregulars*, and the Derek Murdoch Memorial Award from *The Bootmakers of Toronto*. Sonia is author of *Prince of the Realm: The Most Irregular James Bliss Austin* (BSI Press, 2014). She's at work on another biography for the BSI, this time about Julian Wolff.

David Friend lives in Wales, UK, where he divides his time between watching old detective films and thinking about old detective films. He's been scribbling out stories for twenty years and hopes, some day, to write something half-decent. Most of what he pens is set in a 1930's world of non-stop adventure with debonair sleuths, kick-ass damsels, criminal masterminds, and narrow escapes, and he wishes he could live there. He's currently working on a collection of Sherlock Holmes stories and a series based around *The Strange Investigators*, an eccentric team of private detectives out to solve the most peculiar and perplexing mysteries around. He thinks of it as P.G. Wodehouse crossed with Edgar Allen Poe, only not as good.

Mark A. Gagen BSI is co-founder of Wessex Press, sponsor of the popular *From Gillette to Brett* conferences, and publisher of *The Sherlock Holmes Reference Library* and many other fine Sherlockian titles. A life-long Holmes enthusiast, he is a member of *The Baker Street Irregulars* and *The Illustrious Clients of Indianapolis*. A graphic artist by profession, his work is often seen on the covers of *The Baker Street Journal* and various BSI books.

Stephen Gaspar is a writer of historical detective fiction. He has written two Sherlock Holmes books: *The Canadian Adventures of Sherlock Holmes* and *Cold-Hearted Murder*. Some of his detectives are a Roman Tribune, a medieval monk, and a Templar knight. He was born and lives in Windsor, Ontario, Canada.

Denis Green was born in London, England in April 1905. He grew up mostly in London's Savoy Theatre where his father, Richard Green, was a principal in many Gilbert and Sullivan productions, A Flying Officer with RAF until 1924, he then spent four years managing a tea estate in North India before making his stage debut in *Hamlet* with Leslie Howard in 1928. He made his first visit to America in 1931 and established a respectable stage career before appearing in films – including minor roles in the first two Rathbone and Bruce Holmes films – and developing a career in front of and behind the microphone during the golden age of radio. Green and Leslie Charteris met in 1938 and struck up a lifelong friendship. Always busy, be it on stage, radio, film or television, Green passed away at the age of fifty in New York.

Melissa Grigsby, Head Teacher of Stepping Stones School, is driven by a passion to open the doors to learners with complex and layered special needs that just make society feel two steps too far away. Based on the Surrey/Hampshire border in England, her time is spent between a great school at the prestigious home of Conan Doyle, and her two children, dogs, and horses, so there never a dull moment.

John Atkinson Grimshaw (1836-1893) was born in Leeds, England. His amazing paintings, usually featuring twilight or night scenes illuminated by gas-lamps or moonlight, are easily recognizable, and are often used on the covers of books about The Great Detective to set the mood, as shadowy figures move in the distance through misty mysterious settings and over rain-slicked streets.

Roger Johnson BSI, ASH is a retired librarian, now working as a volunteer assistant at the Essex Police Museum. In his spare time, he is commissioning editor of *The Sherlock Holmes Journal*, an occasional lecturer, and a frequent contributor to The Writings About the Writings. His sole work of Holmesian pastiche was published in 1997 in Mike Ashley's anthology *The Mammoth Book of New Sherlock Holmes Adventures*, and he has the greatest respect for the many authors who have contributed new tales to the present mighty trilogy. Like his wife, Jean Upton, he is a member of both *The Baker Street Irregulars* and *The Adventuresses of Sherlock Holmes.*

David Marcum plays The Game with deadly seriousness. He first discovered Sherlock Holmes in 1975, at the age of ten, when he received an abridged version of *The Adventures* during a trade. Since that time, David has collected literally thousands of traditional Holmes pastiches in the form of novels, short stories, radio and television episodes, movies and scripts, comics, fan-fiction, and unpublished manuscripts. He is the author of *The Papers of Sherlock Holmes Vol.'s I* and *II* (2011, 2013), *Sherlock Holmes and A Quantity of Debt* (2013, 2016), *Sherlock Holmes – Tangled Skeins* (2015, 2017), and *The Papers of Solar Pons* (2017). Additionally, he is the editor of the three-volume set *Sherlock Holmes in Montague Street* (2014, recasting Arthur Morrison's Martin Hewitt stories as early Holmes adventures,), the two-volume collection of Great Hiatus stories, *Holmes Away From Home* (2016), *Sherlock Holmes: Before Baker Street* (2017), *Imagination Theatre's Sherlock Holmes* (2017), a number of forthcoming volumes, and the ongoing collection, *The MX Book of New Sherlock Holmes Stories* (2015-), now at ten volumes, with two more in preparation as of this writing. He has contributed stories, essays, and scripts to *The Baker Street Journal, The Strand Magazine, The Watsonian, Beyond Watson, Sherlock Holmes Mystery Magazine, About Sixty, About Being a Sherlockian, The Solar Pons Gazette*, Imagination Theater, *The Proceedings of the Pondicherry Lodge*, and *The Gazette*, the journal of the Nero Wolfe *Wolfe Pack.* He began his adult work life as a Federal Investigator for an obscure U.S. Government agency, before the organization was eliminated. He returned to school for a second degree, and is now a licensed Civil Engineer, living in Tennessee with his wife and son. He is a member of *The Sherlock Holmes Society of London, The Nashville Scholars of the Three Pipe Problem* (The Engineer's Thumb"), *The Occupants of the Full House, The Diogenes Club of Washington, D.C.* (all Scions of *The Baker Street Irregulars*), *The Sherlock Holmes Society of India* (as a Patron), *The John H. Watson Society* ("Marker"), *The Praed Street Irregulars* ("The Obrisset Snuff Box"), *The Solar Pons Society of London*, and *The Diogenes Club West (East Tennessee Annex)*, a curious and unofficial

Scion of one. Since the age of nineteen, he has worn a deerstalker as his regular-and-only hat from autumn to spring. In 2013, he and his deerstalker were finally able make his first trip-of-a-lifetime Holmes Pilgrimage to England, with return Pilgrimages in 2015 and 2016, where you may have spotted him. If you ever run into him and his deerstalker out and about, feel free to say hello!

New Yorker **Nicholas Meyer** is the author of three Sherlock Holmes novels, *The Seven-Per-Cent Solution* (forty weeks on the New York Times bestseller list), *The West End Horror*, and *The Canary Trainer*. His screen adaptation of *The Seven-Per-Cent Solution* was nominated for an Oscar. In addition, Meyer has written and/or directed *Star Treks II, IV*, and *VI*, as well as several other films and novels. He also directed *The Day After*, the most watched film for television ever broadcast. *The Day After* garnered one-hundred-million viewers in a single night and changed Ronald Reagan's mind about a winnable nuclear war. He lives in Los Angeles and is currently working on *Star Trek: Discovery*.

James Moffett is a Masters graduate in Professional Writing, with a specialisation in novel and non-fiction writing. He also has an extensive background in media studies. James began developing a passion for writing when contributing to his University's student magazine. His interest in the literary character of Sherlock Holmes was deep-rooted in his youth. He released his first publication of eight interconnected short stories titled *The Trials of Sherlock Holmes* in 2017, along with a contribution to *The MX Book of New Sherlock Holmes Stories - Part VII: Eliminate The Impossible: 1880-1891*, with a short story entitled "The Blank Photograph".

Mark Mower is a member of the *Crime Writers' Association, The Sherlock Holmes Society of London* and *The Solar Pons Society of London*. He writes true crime stories and fictional mysteries. His first two volumes of Holmes pastiches were entitled *A Farewell to Baker Street* and *Sherlock Holmes: The Baker Street Case-Files* (both with MX Publishing) and, to date, he has contributed chapters to six parts of the ongoing *The MX Book of New Sherlock Holmes Stories*. He has also had stories in two anthologies by Belanger Books: *Holmes Away From Home: Adventures from the Great Hiatus – Volume II – 1893-1894* (2016) and *Sherlock Holmes: Before Baker Street* (2017). More are bound to follow. Mark's non-fiction works include *Bloody British History: Norwich* (The History Press, 2014), *Suffolk Murders* (The History Press, 2011) and *Zeppelin Over Suffolk* (Pen & Sword Books, 2008).

Sidney Paget (1860-1908), a few of whose illustrations are used within this anthology, was born in London, and like his two older brothers, became a famed illustrator and painter. He completed over three-hundred-and-fifty drawings for the Sherlock Holmes stories that were first published in *The Strand* magazine, defining Holmes's image forever after in the public mind.

Tracy J. Revels, a Sherlockian from the age of eleven, is a professor of history at Wofford College in Spartanburg, South Carolina. She is a member of *The Survivors of the Gloria Scott* and *The Studious Scarlets Society*, and is a past recipient of the Beacon Society Award. Almost every semester, she teaches a class that covers The Canon, either to college students or to senior citizens. She is also the author of three supernatural Sherlockian pastiches with MX (*Shadowfall, Shadowblood*, and *Shadowwraith*), and a regular contributor to her scion's newsletter. She also has some notoriety as an author of very silly skits: For proof, see "The Adventure of the Adversarial Adventuress" and "Occupy Baker Street" on YouTube. When not studying Sherlock Holmes, she can be found researching the history of her native state, and has written books on Florida in the Civil War and on the development of Florida's tourism industry.

Roger Riccard of Los Angeles, California, U.S.A., is a descendant of the Roses of Kilravock in Highland Scotland. He is the author of two previous Sherlock Holmes novels, *The Case of the Poisoned Lilly* and *The Case of the Twain Papers*, a series of short stories in two volumes, *Sherlock Holmes: Adventures for the Twelve Days of Christmas* and *Further Adventures for the Twelve Days of Christmas*, and the new series *A Sherlock Holmes Alphabet of Cases,* all of which are published by Baker Street Studios. He has another novel and a non-fiction Holmes reference work in various stages of completion. He became a Sherlock Holmes enthusiast as a teenager (many, many years ago), and, like all fans of The Great Detective, yearned for more stories after reading The Canon over and over. It was the Granada Television performances of Jeremy Brett and Edward Hardwicke, and the encouragement of his wife, Rosilyn, that at last inspired him to write his own Holmes adventures, using the Granada actor portrayals as his guide. He has been called "The best pastiche writer since Val Andrews" by the *Sherlockian E-Times.*

Geri Schear is a novelist and short story writer. Her work has been published in literary journals in the U.S. and Ireland. Her first novel, *A Biased Judgement: The Diaries of Sherlock Holmes 1897* was released to critical acclaim in 2014. The sequel, *Sherlock Holmes and the Other Woman* was published in 2015, and *Return to Reichenbach* in 2016. She lives in Kells, Ireland.

Shane Simmons is a multi-award-winning screenwriter and graphic novelist whose work has appeared in international film festivals, museums, and lectures about design and structure. His best-known piece of fiction, *The Long and Unlearned Life of Roland Gethers*, has been discussed in multiple books and academic journals about sequential art, and his short stories have been printed in critically praised anthologies of history, crime, and horror. He lives in Montreal with his wife and too many cats. Follow him at *eyestrainproductions.com* and *@Shane_Eyestrain*

Robert V. Stapleton was born and brought up in Leeds, Yorkshire, England, and studied at Durham University. After working in various parts of the country as an Anglican parish priest, he is now retired and lives with his wife in North Yorkshire. As a member of his local writing group, he now has time to develop his other life as a writer of adventure stories. He has recently had a number of short stories published, and he is hoping to have a couple of completed novels published at some time in the future.

Amy Thomas is a member of the *Baker Street Babes* Podcast, and the author of *The Detective and The Woman* mystery novels featuring Sherlock Holmes and Irene Adler. She blogs at *girlmeetssherlock.wordpress.com*, and she writes and edits professionally from her home in Fort Myers, Florida.

Kevin Thornton lives in Fort McMurray, Alberta, Canada. It is a place chiefly known for being cold. How cold? The type of cold where Fahrenheit and Celsius meet at minus forty and say to each other, "We have to stop doing this." Kevin writes poetry and short stories that are published and read by dozens of people, and books that are not. Nevertheless, he has been a finalist in the *Canadian Crime Writers* awards six times, and was honoured with the Literature "Buffy" award in his locale up there in the north (where we might have mentioned it is cold). Kevin is or has been a member of the *Crime Writers*

Association, the *Edmonton Poetry Festival*, the *International Thriller Writers*, the *Writers' Guild of Alberta*, the *Crime Writers of Canada*, and the *KEYS*, the Catholic Writers Guild founded by two chaps called Chesterton and Knox, albeit before his time. He studied at one of those universities that had two Nobel Laureates in Literature on the staff. It didn't seem to do much good. Kevin now works as a writer and editor, having been a contractor for the Canadian military, a member of the South African Air Force, and a worker of such peripatetic habits that he is now on his fourth continent and many-eth country.

Marcia Wilson is a freelance researcher and illustrator who likes to work in a style compatible for the color blind and visually impaired. She is Canon-centric, and her first MX offering, *You Buy Bones*, uses the point-of-view of Scotland Yard to show the unique talents of Dr. Watson. This continued with the publication of *Test of the Professionals: The Adventure of the Flying Blue Pidgeon* and *The Peaceful Night Poisonings*. She can be contacted at: *gravelgirty.deviantart.com*

**The MX Book of New Sherlock Holmes Stories
Part X – 2018 Annual (1896-1916)**

Hugh Ashton was born in the U.K., and moved to Japan in 1988, where he remained until 2016, living with his wife Yoshiko in the historic city of Kamakura, a little to the south of Yokohama. He and Yoshiko have now moved to Lichfield, a small cathedral city in the Midlands of the U.K., the birthplace of Samuel Johnson, and one-time home of Erasmus Darwin. In the past, he has worked in the technology and financial services industries, which have provided him with material for some of his books set in the 21st century. He currently works as a writer: Novelist, freelance editor, and copywriter, (his work for large Japanese corporations has appeared in international business journals), and journalist, as well as producing industry reports on various aspects of the financial services industry. Recently, however, his lifelong interest in Sherlock Holmes has developed into an acclaimed series of adventures featuring the world's most famous detective, written in the style of the originals, and published by Inknbeans Press. In addition to these, he has also published historical and alternate historical novels, short stories, and thrillers. Together with artist Andy Boerger, he has produced the *Sherlock Ferret* series of stories for children, featuring the world's cutest detective.

Derrick Belanger is and educator and also the author of the #1 bestselling book in its category, *Sherlock Holmes: The Adventure of the Peculiar Provenance*, which was in the top 200 bestselling books on Amazon. He also is the author of *The MacDougall Twins with Sherlock Holmes* books, and he edited the Sir Arthur Conan Doyle horror anthology *A Study in Terror: Sir Arthur Conan Doyle's Revolutionary Stories of Fear and the Supernatural*. Mr. Belanger co-owns the publishing company Belanger Books, which released the Sherlock Holmes anthologies *Beyond Watson, Holmes Away From Home: Adventures from the Great Hiatus* Volumes 1 and 2, *Sherlock Holmes: Before Baker Street*, and *Sherlock Holmes: Adventures in the Realms of H.G. Wells* Volumes I and 2. Derrick resides in Colorado and continues compiling unpublished works by Dr. John H. Watson.

Maurice Barkley lives with his wife Marie in a suburb of Rochester, New York. Retired from a career as a commercial artist and builder of tree houses, he is writing and busy reinforcing the stereotype of a pesky househusband. His other Sherlock Holmes stories can be found on Amazon. *https://www.amazon.com/author/mauricebarkleys*

Steven Ehrman is an American musician and author of the *Sherlock Holmes Uncovered* tales. These are traditional Sherlock Holmes stories with every effort to adhere to the canon. He is a lifelong admirer of Sir Arthur Conan Doyle and spent countless hours as a youth reading The Master's works.

Paul A. Freeman is the author of *Rumours of Ophir*, a novel which was taught in Zimbabwean high schools and has been translated into German. In addition to having two crime novels, a children's book, and an 18,000-word narrative poem commercially published, Paul is also the author over a hundred published short stories, articles, and poems. Paul currently works in Abu Dhabi, where he lives with his wife and three children

James R. "Jim" French became a morning Disc Jockey on KIRO (AM) in Seattle in 1959. He later founded *Imagination Theatre*, a syndicated program that broadcast to over one-hundred-and-twenty stations in the U.S. and Canada, and also on the XM Satellite Radio system all over North America. Actors in French's dramas included John Patrick Lowrie, Larry Albert, Patty Duke, Russell Johnson, Tom Smothers, Keenan Wynn, Roddy MacDowall, Ruta Lee, John Astin, Cynthia Lauren Tewes, and Richard Sanders. Mr. French stated, "To me, the characters of Sherlock Holmes and Doctor Watson always seemed to be figures Doyle created as a challenge to lesser writers. He gave us two interesting characters – different from each other in their histories, talents, and experience, but complimentary as a team – who have been applied to a variety of situations and plots far beyond the times and places in The Canon. In the hands of different writers, Holmes and Watson have lent their identities to different times, ages, and even genders. But I wanted to break no new ground. I feel Sir Arthur provided us with enough references to locations, landmarks, and the social conditions of his time, to give a pretty large canvas on which to paint our own images and actions to animate Holmes and Watson." Mr. French passed away at the age of eight-nine on December 20th, 2017, the day that his contribution to this book was being edited. He shall be missed.

Jayantika Ganguly BSI is the General Secretary and Editor of the *Sherlock Holmes Society of India*, a member of the *Sherlock Holmes Society of London*, and the *Czech Sherlock Holmes Society*. She is the author of *The Holmes Sutra* (MX 2014). She is a corporate lawyer working with one of the Big Six law firms.

Dick Gillman is an English writer and acrylic artist living in Brittany, France with his wife Alex, Truffle, their Black Labrador, and Jean-Claude, their Breton cat. During his retirement from teaching, he has written over twenty Sherlock Holmes short stories which are published as both e-books and paperbacks. His contribution to the superb MX Sherlock Holmes collection, published in October 2015, was entitled "The Man on Westminster Bridge" and had the privilege of being chosen as the anchor story in *The MX Book of New Sherlock Holmes Stories – Part II (1890-1895)*.

Arthur Hall was born in Aston, Birmingham, UK, in 1944. He discovered his interest in writing during his schooldays, along with a love of fictional adventure and suspense. His first novel, *Sole Contact,* was an espionage story about an ultra-secret government department known as "Sector Three", and was followed, to date, by three sequels. Other works include four Sherlock Holmes novels, *The Demon of the Dusk, The One Hundred Percent Society, The Secret Assassin,* and *The Phantom Killer,* as well as a collection of short stories, and a modern detective novel. He lives in the West Midlands, United Kingdom.

Greg Hatcher has been writing for one outlet or another since 1992. He was a contributing editor at *WITH* magazine for over a decade, and during that time he was a three-time winner of the Higher Goals Award for children's writing; once for fiction and twice for non-fiction. After that he wrote a weekly column for ten years and change at *Comic Book Resources,* as one of the rotating features on the *Comics Should Be Good!* blog. Currently he has a weekly column at *Atomic Junk Shop* (*www.atomicjunkshop.com*) He also teaches writing in the Young Authors classes offered as part of the Seattle YMCA's Afterschool Arts Program for students in the 6th through the 12th grade. A lifelong mystery fan, he has written Nero Wolfe pastiches for the Wolfe Pack *Gazette* and several Sherlock Holmes adventures for Airship 27's *Sherlock Holmes: Consulting*

Detective series. He lives in Burien, Washington, with his wife Julie, their cat Magdalene, and ten thousand books and comics.

Mike Hogan writes mostly historical novels and short stories, many set in Victorian London and featuring Sherlock Holmes and Doctor Watson. He read the Conan Doyle stories at school with great enjoyment, but hadn't thought much about Sherlock Holmes until, having missed the Granada/Jeremy Brett TV series when it was originally shown in the eighties, he came across a box set of videos in a street market and was hooked on Holmes again. He started writing Sherlock Holmes pastiches several years ago, having great fun re-imagining situations for the Conan Doyle characters to act in. The relationship between Holmes and Watson fascinates him as one of the great literary friendships. (He's also a huge admirer of Patrick O'Brian's Aubrey-Maturin novels). Like Captain Aubrey and Doctor Maturin, Holmes and Watson are an odd couple, differing in almost every facet of their characters, but sharing a common sense of decency and a common humanity. Living with Sherlock Holmes can't have been easy, and Mike enjoys adding a stronger vein of "pawky humour" into the Conan Doyle mix, even letting Watson have the second-to-last word on occasions. His books include *Sherlock Holmes and the Scottish Question*, the forthcoming *The Gory Season – Sherlock Holmes, Jack the Ripper and the Thames Torso Murders* and the Sherlock Holmes & Young Winston 1887 Trilogy (*The Deadwood Stage*; *The Jubilee Plot*; and *The Giant Moles*), He has also written the following short story collections: *Sherlock Holmes: Murder at the Savoy and Other Stories*, *Sherlock Holmes: The Skull of Kohada Koheiji and Other Stories*, and *Sherlock Holmes: Murder on the Brighton Line and Other Stories*. *www.mikehoganbooks.com*

Kelvin I. Jones is the author of six books about Sherlock Holmes and the definitive biography of Conan Doyle as a spiritualist, *Conan Doyle and The Spirits*. A member of *The Sherlock Holmes Society of London*, he has published numerous short occult and ghost stories in British anthologies over the last thirty years. His work has appeared on BBC Radio, and in 1984 he won the Mason Hall Literary Award for his poem cycle about the survivors of Hiroshima and Nagasaki, recently reprinted as "Omega". (Oakmagic Publications) A one-time teacher of creative writing at the University of East Anglia, he is also the author of four crime novels featuring his ex-met sleuth John Bottrell, who first appeared in *Stone Dead*. He has over fifty titles on Kindle, and is also the author of several novellas and short story collections featuring a Norwich based detective, DCI Ketch, an intrepid sleuth who invesitgates East Anglian murder cases. He also published a series of short stories about an Edwardian psychic detective, Dr. John Carter (*Carter's Occult Casebook*). Ramsey Campbell, the British horror writer, and Francis King, the renowned novelist, have both compared his supernatural stories to those of M. R. James. He has also published children's fiction, namely *Odin's Eye*, and, in collaboration with his wife Debbie, *The Dark Entry*. Since 1995, he has been the proprietor of Oakmagic Publications, publishers of British folklore and of his fiction titles. (See *www.oakmagicpublications.co.uk*)He lives in Norfolk.

Will Murray is the author of over seventy novels, including forty *Destroyer* novels and seven posthumous *Doc Savage* collaborations with Lester Dent, under the name Kenneth Robeson, for Bantam Books in the 1990's. Since 2011, he has written fourteen additional Doc Savage adventures for Altus Press, two of which co-starred The Shadow, as well as a solo Pat Savage novel. His 2015 Tarzan novel, *Return to Pal-Ul-Don*, was followed by *King Kong vs. Tarzan* in 2016. Murray has written short stories featuring such classic characters as Batman, Superman, Wonder Woman, Spider-Man, Ant-Man, the Hulk,

Honey West, the Spider, the Avenger, the Green Hornet, the Phantom, and Cthulhu. A previous Murray Sherlock Holmes story appeared in Moonstone's *Sherlock Holmes: The Crossovers Casebook*, and another is forthcoming in *Sherlock Holmes and Doctor Was Not*, involving H. P. Lovecraft's Dr. Herbert West. Additionally, his "The Adventure of the Glassy Ghost" appeared in *The MX Book of New Sherlock Holmes Stories Part VIII – Eliminate the Impossible: 1892-1905*.

Robert Perret is a writer, librarian, and devout Sherlockian living on the Palouse. His Sherlockian publications include "The Canaries of Clee Hills Mine" in *An Improbable Truth: The Paranormal Adventures of Sherlock Holmes*, "For King and Country" in *The Science of Deduction*, and "How Hope Learned the Trick" in *NonBinary Review*. He considers himself to be a pan-Sherlockian and a one-man Scion out on the lonely moors of Idaho. Robert has recently authored a yet-unpublished scholarly article tentatively entitled "A Study in Scholarship: The Case of the *Baker Street Journal*". More information is available at *www.robertperret.com*

Martin Rosenstock studied English, American, and German literature. In 2008, he received a Ph.D. from the University of California, Santa Barbara for looking into what happens when things go badly – as they do from time to time – for detectives in German-language literature. After job hopping around the colder latitudes of the U.S. for three years, he decided to return to warmer climes. In 2011, he took a job at Gulf University for Science and Technology in Kuwait, where he currently teaches. When not brooding over plot twists, he spends too much time and money traveling the Indian Ocean littoral. There is a novel somewhere there, he feels sure.

G. L. Schulze is a life-long resident of Michigan and a retired officer with the Michigan Department of Corrections. Gen enjoys gardening, walking, woodworking, wood burning, and beadwork, as well as reading and writing. She also enjoys spending time with her rescue dog, Java. She is the author of six books in her *Young Detectives' Mystery Series*, as well as her first Sherlock Holmes novel, *Gray Manor*. A second Holmes novel, *The Ring and The Box, A Sherlock Holmes Mystery of Ancient Egypt* is slated for release in early spring. For further information about Gen's books visit her Amazon link at *https://www.amazon.com/Gen-Schulze/e/B00KTH36LO*

Tim Symonds was born in London. He grew up in Somerset, Dorset, and Guernsey. After several years in East and Central Africa, he settled in California and graduated Phi Beta Kappa in Political Science from UCLA. He is a Fellow of the *Royal Geographical Society*. He writes his novels in the woods and hidden valleys surrounding his home in the High Weald of East Sussex. Dr. Watson knew the untamed region well. In "The Adventure of Black Peter", Watson wrote, *"the Weald was once part of that great forest which for so long held the Saxon invaders at bay."* Tim's novels are published by MX Publishing. His latest is titled *Sherlock Holmes and the Nine Dragon Sigil*. Previous novels include *Sherlock Holmes and The Sword of Osman*, *Sherlock Holmes and the Mystery of Einstein's Daughter*, *Sherlock Holmes and the Dead Boer at Scotney Castle*, and *Sherlock Holmes and the Case of The Bulgarian Codex*.

Thaddeus Tuffentsamer is the author of the young adult series, *F.A.R.T.S. The Federal Agency for Reconnaissance and Tactical Services*, and the satirical self-help book, *Are You SURE About That? Observations and Life Lessons from a High Functioning Sociopath*. He resides in Goodyear, AZ, with his wife and youngest daughter. He has always been a fan of Sherlock Holmes, but his passion was reignited when his daughter took an interest in reading those wonderful adventures, for which they together now share a deep appreciation. He is not on social media – doesn't know how – but loves to connect personally with his readers by email at *thaddeustuffentsamer@gmail.com* His books can be found on Amazon.

Peter Coe Verbica grew up on a commercial cattle ranch in Northern California, where he learned the value of a strong work ethic. He works for the Wealth Management Group of a global investment bank, and is an Adjunct Professor in the Economics Department at SJSU. He is the author of numerous books, including *Left at the Gate and Other Poems, Hard-Won Cowboy Wisdom (Not Necessarily in Order of Importance), A Key to the Grove and Other Poems,* and *The Missing Tales of Sherlock Holmes (as Compiled by Peter Coe Verbica, JD).* Mr. Verbica obtained a JD from Santa Clara University School of Law, an MS from Massachusetts Institute of Technology, and a BA in English from Santa Clara University. He is the co-inventor on a number of patents, has served as a Managing Member of three venture capital firms, and the CFO of one of the portfolio companies. He is an unabashed advocate of cowboy culture and enjoys creative writing, hiking, and tennis. He is married with four daughters. For more information, or to contact the author, please go to *www.hardwoncowboywisdom.com.*

Daniel D. Victor, a Ph.D. in American literature, is a retired high school English teacher who taught in the Los Angeles Unified School District for forty-six years. His doctoral dissertation on little-known American author, David Graham Phillips, led to the creation of Victor's first Sherlock Holmes pastiche, *The Seventh Bullet,* in which Holmes investigates Phillips' actual murder. Victor's second novel, *A Study in Synchronicity,* is a two-stranded murder mystery, which features a Sherlock Holmes-like private eye. He currently writes the ongoing series *Sherlock Holmes and the American Literati.* Each novel introduces Holmes to a different American author who actually passed through London at the turn of the century. In *The Final Page of Baker Street*, Holmes meets Raymond Chandler; in *The Baron of Brede Place,* Stephen Crane; in *Seventeen Minutes to Baker Street*, Mark Twain; and *The Outrage at the Diogenes Club,* Jack London. Victor, who is also writing a novel about his early years as a teacher, lives with his wife in Los Angeles, California. They have two adult sons.

The MX Book of New Sherlock Holmes Stories

Edited by David Marcum
(MX Publishing, 2015-   )

Part I: 1881-1889
Part II: 1890-1895
Part III: 1896-1929
Part IV: 2016 Annual
Part V: Christmas Adventures
Part VI: 2017 Annual
Part VII: Eliminate the Impossible – 1880-1891
Part VIII: Eliminate the Impossible – 1892-1905
Part IX: 2018 Annual (1879-1895)
Part X: 2018 Annual (1896-1916)

In Preparation
Part XI: Some Untold Cases
Part XII: 2019 Annual

. . . and more to come!

The MX Book of New Sherlock Holmes Stories

Edited by David Marcum

(MX Publishing, 2015-   )

"This is the finest volume of Sherlockian fiction I have
ever read, and I have read, literally, thousands."
– Philip K. Jones

"Beyond Impressive . . . This is a
splendid venture for a great cause!
– Roger Johnson, Editor, *The Sherlock Holmes Journal,*
The Sherlock Holmes Society of London

MX Publishing

MX Publishing is the world's largest specialist Sherlock Holmes publisher, with several hundred titles and authors creating the latest in Sherlock Holmes fiction and non-fiction.

From traditional short stories and novels to travel guides and quiz books, MX Publishing caters to all Holmes fans.

The collection includes leading titles such as *Benedict Cumberbatch In Transition* and *The Norwood Author*, which won the 2011 *Tony Howlett Award* (Sherlock Holmes Book of the Year).

MX Publishing also has one of the largest communities of Holmes fans on *Facebook*, with regular contributions from dozens of authors.

www.mxpublishing.co.uk (UK)
and
www.mxpublishing.com (USA)

Lightning Source UK Ltd.
Milton Keynes UK
UKHW01f0734130518
322449UK00001B/48/P